Of Time and Space

We Are Gods
Book Two

Lee Nash

DEDICATION

To my brother, for all the years he put up with me, his annoying little sister.

Other books by this author

We Are Gods

Of Earth and Sky
Of Might and Magic

For a more up to date list, please visit
www.bearbootbooks.com

ACKNOWLEDGMENTS

A big thank you goes to Erich, for help with editing, and his invaluable input. It simply wouldn't be as good without you. And thank you to all those who supported my first book, making this one a little easier. I appreciate you all.

PROLOGUE

He saw it coming even as the call came in. A red streaking flash in the sky that would be mistaken for a meteor by anyone else.

"Agent Estard," his CB radio blared. "We've got a live one coming in near your location. Projected coordinates will be forwarded momentarily."

He leaned against the kitchen door. It led onto a desert backyard, with a few stubborn patches of desert grass that refused to die. He didn't have neighbours, no one to be concerned about his loud music, or the fact that his dog was always digging holes near the fence line. Though the fence was now laying on its side, the slats coming loose and drying out in the desert heat.

Estard flicked back an errant strand of dark curls and turned to the radio. He picked up the hand mic. "On it," was all he said, and threw it down.

A few long strides took him to an inner door, which he knocked hard on, and yelled, "Come on, boys! Got one coming in!" He heard footsteps coming up the stairs, and that was enough for him.

He turned on his heel, grabbed up his faded brown leather jacket from the hook on the back of the kitchen door, then made for the truck.

If anyone were to pass this place, they would think that it was just an old house, barely maintained. There was junk all over the yard, potholes everywhere, dug by the Sniffer Dog, and tyre tracks in relentless circles.

Just hoons and hillbillies, he thought. *Nothing to see here.*

Julian Estard snapped up the keys from his pocket and got into the driver's seat of his brand-new Dodge D100. He counted three heart beats, tapped the accelerator and started the engine. She came to life with a roar that made him smile.

Three more agents came jogging out of the house. They were dressed just as he was; in jeans and plaid shirts, wearing comfortable boots, and baseball caps.

Estard made a note of who was last out. Once again, they'd not bothered to turn the lights off. He'd give Harris a slap upside the head.

The windows were down, and he yelled out. "Hurry it up will you, or we'll miss them. We're not the only team that's been called out, you know."

Claude and Paul Wagner — two burly twins, with close cropped blonde hair and intense blue eyes that bulged and made them look insane — jumped into the back and tapped the sides. Harris got in the front, then started loading his pistol.

Estard glanced at him with a frown — he should have done that in the house — and then took off, a cloud of dust trailing behind them.

He could still see the bright object in the sky, and he watched as it banked to land in a patch of desert not far from the Area 23 bunker.

"They've picked a strange place to land," Harris noted, his gun now loaded and held in a firm hand.

Estard didn't bother answering, he just tapped on the back windscreen to let the brothers know to get ready. It was always a challenge when they had to face down with those who trotted a smooth landing.

Better had they crashed. Diplomacy is not my area.

The truck slowed to a stop a hundred meters from the giant ovoid craft. It was different from any he'd seen or heard of during his time with ISAC — Investigative Service for Alien Contact — and he wondered what kind of monstrosity was going to climb its way down the gangplank.

He kicked open the driver's door, seconds after shutting off the engine. He grabbed up his shotgun from the rack on the B-pillar, and moved forward with it cocked, eyes following the sight line of the shaft.

He heard three sets of footsteps, equally as cautious, range out to either side of him.

There were no lights on the outer hull of the ship, just a jagged array of protrusions that Estard couldn't guess the use for.

They weren't waiting long before the hatch came open with a whining thud. It crashed into the ground with such force that it sprayed up a large cloud of dust, and Estard was forced to hold his breath and squint his eyes. But he kept them on the ship.

A few moments later, he heard footsteps on metal, and through the clearing dust he saw a figure stop just inside the ship. It was outlined by dim light, tall with two legs, and two arms, one head. As far as he could see, very human looking.

To his left he heard Claude snort, disbelieving, "It's a fucking coloured woman."

Estard could now see, in the clear afternoon sunlight, that Claude was right.

He took a few steps forward, the point of his shotgun aimed squarely at her chest. At his current range it wouldn't do more than severely wound, which was just fine, as his employers — the US Government — would prefer them alive.

"You just step down from there, nice and slow," he instructed the woman, who glanced over at him with raised brows.

"I'll be pleased to do so, if you'd lower your weapon," she answered in a Texan drawl.

Estard looked to each of his team members in turn, then lowered his weapon, nodding for the others to do the same. He'd never really understood the wisdom at coming in guns raised, as any race advanced enough to travel the stars could probably make short work of them. But he followed protocol.

Obviously satisfied, the woman strode down the ramp. Then Estard saw a few more follow behind her. They all wore navy blue coveralls, and, he saw on a few, flag patches.

He gestured to Harris without taking his eyes off the bunch. The man came over. Quietly, he told him, "Go back to the truck, and call in Area 23. Tell them to bring trucks. These ain't no aliens, but they sure as shit don't come from here."

The man nodded brusquely and ran off.

When the people from the ship had come within thirty paces, Estard said, "That there is far enough, if you don't mind." He gestured with his gun to the ground at their feet. They pulled up.

A blonde haired, hazel eyed man strode to the front. "Major John Harvey, USAF," he introduced himself.

Estard measured the man. He was about the same height as himself, five-ten or so. Not bulky, but certainly muscular, with a stance that bore a quiet confidence.

United States Air Force? Doubt it. He sucked on his teeth for a moment before answering. "Well, *Major*, I'm Julian Estard ISAC. Until we can verify your claim, you'll be staying in our custody."

A bald-headed man behind Harvey rolled his eyes and half turned back toward the ship, revealing eye tattoos on the back of his head, and muttering something under his breath. Estard raised the shot gun in his direction.

"What did you say, baldy?" he asked in a threatening tone.

The man swung back to face him. "Watch who you call baldy, mop-head." He thought the accent might be British.

Mop-head?

At that moment, Harris returned and whispered in his ear. "They've already sent out a couple of trucks. We've got some back up and the suits are comin' with 'em."

Estard nodded, and Harris took his position on Estard's right. Even as he did, Estard could make out dust trails in the distance behind the craft. They'd not be long in coming.

"Right," he told them. "Line up nice and straight, and co-operate and what not, and we'll see if we can't get you all sorted and out of here nice quick. Just be sure to note who's holding the guns, here."

He looked over at Claude, then Paul, and pointed at the ship. "You two! Go check that out. If there's anyone left inside, get them out here, got me?"

Estard settled back to wait for the soldier boys who'd take care of this lot. All in all, he considered, this was probably the strangest UFO case he'd ever come across. *Not a UFO. Some kind of test ship. Unless these ones are just faking at being human...* The thought gave him pause.

Either way, though, it was probably time to get out of the slum house and put his suit back on. It'd been years since the last incident, and they'd been waiting for him to come back to it. He'd ask the boss.

This one might get interesting.

Part Three

~ Time ~

Chapter One

She blinked at the man in front of her, struggling to remember his name. She knew he'd said it, back when they'd disembarked from the ship. Curly brown hair, dark hazel eyes, close to herself in height. He had large, strong hands, was lean, and possessed a self-assured posture that spoke to years of experience in his field.

He wore a black suit, now. Though why that was important, she wasn't sure. In fact, she wasn't sure about much of anything.

The metal table between them was bare of accoutrements, and there was a large mirror behind him. A singular door was the only way in or out, the walls, bare concrete. She frowned at the walls.

What was she doing here? How did she get here? The details were eluding her.

"What's my name?" She repeated the question the man before her had just asked.

"That's what I asked." He leaned back in his chair and sucked at his teeth.

She tested the cuffs on her wrist. Not in any desire to free herself from them, but in an effort to understand why they were there. *Why is everything so hazy? I feel like I should know what is happening.*

"Deidra," she said, finally. She'd had to dig for it, but she felt knowledge buried deep. "Deidra Ward."

The man leaned forward, elbows on the table. "Well, I know I mentioned it before, but my name's Julian Estard."

Deidra kept her eyes on the cuffs, fascinated by the chain going taught and then sagging again as she moved her hands together and apart.

He must have misunderstood her intentions, for he said, "I'd remove them if I could, but we're not there yet, you understand."

She nodded. She didn't understand, but nor did she care.

He stared at her, but she was oblivious to it. He turned toward the mirror and then stood to pace on the other side of the table.

"From your accent I'd guess you're Texan." It wasn't a question. She didn't answer. "Are you?" he finished finally.

"I think so." She put her hands palm down on the table and stared up at the man. "I can't remember."

She bit at her bottom lip. Brain racing, eyes peering into some distant space.

Whatever was happening to her, it came with a sense of familiarity, like it had happened before. There was loss, but there was no emotion attached to it. But if one were to forget, should they not mourn that loss? Struggle with every breath to retain what little they held? Should she not be concerned for her health? For the state of her mind? What had she already forgotten? How much of herself had she lost?

Everything before they'd landed, and not much of that.

She refocused on the man, realising that he had spoken again, but she hadn't heard him.

"I'm sorry," she told him. And meant it. "How long have we been here?"

He glanced down at her with something like sympathy. "Not

long," he said. "Few hours maybe. Just enough to get you washed and into some suitable clothes."

She looked down again at the cuffs on her hands. Stretched and released.

Estard tapped hard on the mirror, then faced her. "Should not have been questioning you before quarantine procedures anyway. But I was there at the landing, and I was curious." He shrugged and flashed a smile of perfectly straight white teeth. If it was meant to be comforting, it wasn't.

The door opened and Deidra turned her head toward it. Someone in a white coat stood in the dooryard, — *I was wearing a white coat. Wasn't I? But not now. Maybe not at all.* — and waited until Estard had removed the leg-irons so Deidra could walk herself over.

The man in the white coat did not speak, he just held her by the upper arm and directed her into the concrete hall beyond. Aside from large white stripes painted along one side, and a few blue-grey doors with mesh and glass portals, the halls were completely unadorned. And there was something strikingly familiar about that.

Estard didn't close the door as he came out and followed close behind. Presumably, in case she attempted escape. *Not that I'd know how to get out of here or where to go.*

"This is Doctor Freid," Estard said. "Since he hasn't the courtesy to introduce himself."

Freid snorted and glanced back at the agent. "To a coloured?" She vaguely remembered someone at the ship uttering that same sentiment. Though she understood it was intended to be derogatory, she had no idea what it was in regard to.

"Now, Doctor Freid, be nice. She may not be a woman of colour. She may be an alien, in which case courtesy pays. Or, you could consider how you might like to be treated under similar circumstances."

The Doctor harrumphed and muttered something inaudible as he turned them into an adjoining hall.

"Or you might consider that you are an American citizen, and not long ago we passed the Civil Rights Act."

"Hardly worth the paper it's printed on, Agent Estard." He pulled her roughly around as they came to a set of closed white double-doors. He keyed in a code on the numeric pad to the side of the door and it beeped open.

He pushed her inside ahead of him and she knocked the bone of her right eye socket against the edge of the wooden frame. It stung. Badly.

"You may leave us now, Agent. Continue your questioning. Or whatever it was you were doing." He waved a dismissive hand at the door behind him.

Estard scowled at the man's back, but then turned and left without further comment.

They were in some kind of lab. At least, that was what it appeared to be to Deidra. Long tables, full of instruments and vials of liquid. A refrigerated unit at the end of the large room housed many more vials.

There was a padded table with restraints placed up against the right hand wall, with a large lamp directly above it.

Unaccountably, the place gave her the creeps.

Will I remember this tomorrow? She didn't think so.

~

Kristin thumped her fists against the concrete wall of her cell. Then winced as they grazed on the uneven surface. She'd thought she was stronger than that.

She glanced back at the wooden pallet, suspended against the left wall with taught chains. No pillow, no blanket, no mattress. She imagined it would be uncomfortable to sleep on but given her options over the past couple of months, it actually appeared inviting.

Beyond that pallet, was a small metal toilet, a flush button in the wall, and a single roll of toilet paper. There was no window, and only three bars in the door.

Taking a deep breath, she prepared to yell out to the rest of the crew. "Harvey! Lance!"

There were a few heartbeats, where she waited. She was about to call out again when there was a sound in the hall. A rattling of keys, two sets of steps clacking on concrete.

Kristin moved over to her pallet and sat down. They were going to need to find a way out of this place, she could feel it. These people were not going to believe anything they told them, whatever Harvey thought.

The footsteps stopped; keys jangled in the lock. A click, then her door swung open.

It was the man from the landing, only now he was wearing a suit. He had his hands in his pockets and was staring at the back of the soldier who'd opened the door for him.

"Sorry about this," he told her. "But Wilson here has to cuff you."

Kristin put her hands out palm up and waited. The soldier came over, and without a word, he took the cuffs from his belt and put them on. He tested each before he stepped away with a nod for the suited man.

"In case you missed it earlier, I am Julian Estard. I'll be handling your verification process."

"Interrogation, you mean," she said as the soldier grabbed her arm, and escorted them into the hall.

Estard stayed close to her side, and they followed a white painted line along a concrete wall. "Well, call it what you like. But I have to call it a process."

"Like your job, do you?" The soldier pulled roughly as they turned a corner, and she was of a mind to break his nose but refrained.

"For the most part." Estard nodded. "Pays the bills. Keeps me out of trouble. And I get to do a lot of things that other people would never dream of."

They entered a hall with an extra white stripe on the wall, and the soldier shoved her into a room with a table, a chair to either side, and a mirror on the wall.

"Well, call it what you like," Kristin muttered as the soldier guided her to a chair where he attached the leg chains that had been bolted to the floor.

Estard gave the soldier a nod and the man moved out of the room, closing the door behind him. Only then did Estard come to sit himself across from her.

He removed his jacket and put it on the back of his chair. "I had a feeling you'd be difficult," he sighed.

Kristin frowned at him. "I'm not difficult. I'm charming."

He laughed. "I suppose you could be."

"So, what do you want to know? Let's streamline this process so I can get the fuck out of here."

"Sounds like a plan."

Silence. Kristin stared. Waited. "And... the question of the hour is..." she said finally.

"Well, what we'd love to know is; are you're *really* human," he told her. "But since you're unlikely to answer that with anything but yes, it's a pointless one, don't you think?"

"Of course not, since we're actually alien human hybrids. There is a parasite on my brain stem that occasionally takes control of my body and unleashes hell."

Estard sat forward, interest on his face. "Really?"

"No."

Disappointment. "So, who are you?"

"Lieutenant Annabelle Kristin, ATF Comms Officer, fed from

the Australian SAS."

"Explains your accent."

"It does, doesn't it?"

"Is that all you're giving me?"

"What else do you want?" This, she decided, was going to be a very long game. Harvey had told them all to be truthful, but she didn't think that was going to help them. This guy wanted aliens. Interesting aliens. And all she could give him were a few humans out for a jaunt who found themselves in the wrong time.

Finally home, almost five hundred years in the past. I could kill Deidra. Actually, what have they done with her? They never sent her back to my cell. When they'd first been incarcerated, she'd shared the cell with the Scientist.

Estard sucked on his teeth. A habit that would get very irritating she decided. "Where'd you get the ship?"

"You don't have the clearance to know that." Not true, of course, but it was how the game was played.

"Then why did you land it *here,* where you clearly knew there would be a military presence?"

"We had to land somewhere. Here seemed like a good spot." *This will be Earth Base in five hundred years. Hard to imagine, and yet it hasn't changed much.*

Estard leaned back and rubbed at his jaw. He patted his suit pockets, then pulled out a pack of something. He took a single white stick from it, placed it in his mouth, then rummaged his pockets again. This time he came back with a lighter and placed it in front of the stick.

"Mind if I smoke?"

Kristin shrugged. "If it makes you happy."

He grunted and lit the stick end. He inhaled deeply, and her eyebrows rose. Then he exhaled, the cloud of smoke slowly filling the room and giving off an unpleasant scent. *Interesting custom.*

"Are you going to give me any useful information?" he queried.

"Depends on what you classify as useful."

"Something other than your name, rank and country of origin."

"Then no. Probably not."

"Why not?" He flicked ash off the end of the stick and placed it back in his mouth.

Kristin's nose twitched. "Orders."

"Whose Orders?"

"Captain Harvey."

"Thought he was a Major?"

"That's his USAF rank. Captain is his ATF designation."

"Oh? What is this ATF? That is the second time you mentioned it."

Kristin coughed and waved her hands in front of her face to push the smoke away. Estard frowned at her and put the offending material out on a corner of the table.

"You don't have the clearance to know that," she breathed.

"You know," he sighed. "I might be able to help. If you tell me. I could get you out of here, no problem. Just walk you to the surface, see you on your way."

"You'll excuse me if I am a little less than convinced by that."

"Think on it." He got up, put on his suit jacket and moved to the door. "The only reason you're in the cells and not the guest wing is because we are trying to verify who you are."

"You can't."

"Why not?"

"Because we don't exist."

There was no further conversation as the door opened and the soldier came back in. He removed the leg irons and escorted her back to her cell.

Estard did not come with them.

CHAPTER TWO

Julian went straight to the mess after his meeting with Kristin. That woman made his head spin a little bit. But she had given him more information than Deidra had, and that was something.

Square tables, covered in blue paper tablecloth, each with sugar, salt and pepper in shakers placed in the centre. The chairs were the fold up kind, and not very comfortable.

It was empty of people, except those standing at the self-serve counter. He held his hand out, and a portly woman in a shower cap handed him a plate.

Beans, meatloaf, some kind of gelatinous stew. Ick, I won't have that. Looks like a dog threw up. Which, of course, reminded him that he should pick up his dog from the slum house.

"You gonna put something on that plate, boy? Or just stand there and stare at it?"

Estard smiled at the woman who'd handed him the plate. Boy. He was into his late thirties. He'd fought in the Second World War. He may not have had a shot of grey on his head, but there was plenty in his beard when he didn't bother to shave.

He scooped up some meatloaf, dumped it on his plate, and moved over to the vegetables, none of which looked any more appetising than the stew.

When he was done, he sat himself by the door and hoed in. It wasn't very good. He pretended it was.

Harris walked in, looking lost. It was the first time he'd worn a suit, and he didn't look comfortable in it. But the brass had decided that if Estard was coming back in, he'd need a partner, and Harris had put his application in over six months before.

Estard eyed him up and down, as he shovelled another mouthful of cardboard meatloaf into his gob. The suit fitted well enough, and was of standard cut, black with a white shirt. His dark blonde hair was slicked back in the current style, the sides closely cropped, and his brown eyes managed to dance in every direction without settling even once.

He swallowed. *It is a delicious steak,* he told himself. "What do you need, Harris?"

The young man looked at him. "Just got my suit." He pulled at the lapels, then took out a chair and sat across from Estard.

"That's nice."

"Ain't it though?"

This man can't even load his gun before we leave the slum house, and they want him in a suit? It didn't say much about the organisation that he worked for.

"So, you'll be conducting the interviews with me, then?" Another mouthful.

"Is that any good?"

"Best steak you'll ever have."

"Doesn't look like steak." He squinted at it in confusion.

"Astute observation." Estard pushed what was left to the side of his plate and abandoned the notion of a filling dinner. That would have to wait until he was allowed to leave Base.

Harris' long, feminine fingers tapped a rhythm on the table. "No music in this place."

"Only serious business here."

"And we're conducting interviews?"

Estard got up and moved toward the door, Harris followed, stumbling in his haste to get out of the chair.

"Yes, we're doing that," he confirmed. "But right now, we're going to the morgue."

"The morgue?"

This kid is going to get very irritating very quickly. "The place where we put dead people, Harris."

"I know what a morgue is, Julian. I'm not that stupid. I want to know *why* we're going to the morgue."

They trotted down a red lined corridor to a blue-grey lift where a silent sergeant in army greens stood at attention beside the lift doors.

"Then the more astute question would have been 'why?' as opposed to repeating my statement as a question." Estard breathed as they waited for the doors to open.

"Why are we going to the morgue?"

"Better." The doors clicked open, they got in. "Because they found three bodies on the ship."

They went down three levels. "Were they human?"

"By all appearances."

They exited the lift and made their way down a green lined hall to a set of double doors. Estard pushed through them without breaking stride.

There were four metal tables, upon each of which was a body. From the look of it, none of them were the ones he was looking for. So, he continued on through the door at the back of the room, into a completely white tiled area. There was another door on the other side of the room, which would lead to the freezer drawers, but he wouldn't need to go in there.

In a corner, reading a magazine and chewing on a length of candy while he sat on a stool, was a less than fit looking intern. He still had pimples on his face, and patches of stubble from poor shaving. There were six tables in this room, all occupied.

Estard glanced at the intern, then at the bodies. None of them had toe tags yet.

"Doctor Reigner will be down soon; he's just gone to the can," the intern said without looking away from his magazine.

Julian Estard sucked on his teeth and backed up against the wall, arms crossed to wait for the man. The place smelled of disinfectant and rubbing alcohol. There was a single trolley pushed to one wall, full of sterile equipment that the doctor would use to perform autopsies.

Harris drummed his fingers on the wall. "Got some tunes?" he asked the intern.

The boy glanced up, took a bite of the candy and spoke around it. "I feel you. But Reigner doesn't like it in the dungeon."

A few moments, and Doctor Reigner walked in. A short man, in a white lab coat, with jeans and a plaid shirt beneath. He wore horn rimmed glasses, and his hair was a mess of white curls. Estard had a sudden vision of himself at this man's age and shuddered slightly, brushing a hand over the top of his own hair.

"Guests," the doctor said as he stopped in front of them. "Come to see the others, I take it?"

Julian nodded and pushed himself off the wall. "That we have."

The Doctor spun on a heel and strode to one of the tables. He pointed at each as he listed them. "This one here was the first. A woman, as you can see, early to mid forties by the look, cause of death a deep wound in the femoral artery. Next, an older man, I'd say late sixties early seventies, cause of death a shot to the back of the head. And the other is probably about forty, I'd say. Cause of death a laceration of the carotid artery."

"So, two of them bled to death, but one was shot point blank?" Estard sucked on his teeth. He needed a smoke.

"That's what it looks like," Reigner confirmed. "But until I've done a complete autopsy, there is no way to tell for certain. I have these other three bodies to get through first, so don't expect a detailed report until sometime tomorrow."

The intern mimed something behind Reigner's back, and Harris chuckled. The Doctor looked back, but the intern expressed innocence.

"Let me know as soon as you're done."

"Of course."

Estard grabbed Harris by the sleeve of his suit jacket and dragged him out of the room. Once they were at the lift, he let go and smacked the button in the wall. "You want to do well in this job, Harris, you have to learn to keep your cool and not get distracted. You get me?"

The young man nodded. "I got you, Julian."

"And that's another thing." The doors opened, they got in. "From now on you have to start addressing me as Agent Estard."

~

Five hours later, six interviews down, and Julian Estard was no closer to working out what these people were doing in the Nevada Desert. All he could get out of any of them was their military rank and country of origin. None of them would explain what this ATF was, despite the fact that they all alluded to it.

He smacked a red button in the wall next to a blast door and waited, looking up at the camera. A moment and the door was opened.

The ramp beyond led upwards to the guard's barracks, through two more solid blast doors.

When he arrived, he was accosted by Lieutenant Adams and drawn off to his superior's office where he was informed the Colonel was waiting for him. Estard didn't bother telling him that the Military had no jurisdiction over ISAC agents or officers. It was a cooperative effort. He just waited in a padded chair until the door opened and he was ushered in.

Inside, cigar smoke hung thick in the air. The Colonel, his grey hair cropped short, gold rimmed glasses halfway down his nose, had his boots up on his desk and a cigar hanging out of his mouth.

"Shut the door," the man said in a strong Bostonian accent.

Estard obliged. "You wanted to see me?" He pulled a cigarette out of his pack and joined his fumes to those already pervading his nostrils.

The Colonel took a long hard drag on the cigar, then clenched it between his teeth. "You get to make use of this facility," he said. "And I don't mind. I mean, it's got to be used for something, right?"

"Yes, Colonel Everette."

"I'm curious about these ship dwellers."

"I can imagine."

"You're not going to tell me anything about them, are you?" The Colonel retrieved the spent cigar from his mouth and doused it in a well-used ashtray.

Estard flicked the ash off his smoke to land just short of the Colonel's fingers before he could remove them. "What's the brass said?"

"You haven't spoken to them?"

"Not about talking to you."

"So, you'll tell me then?" He looked hopeful.

"If it were up to me, I'd probably tell everyone. Not an answer most would want to hear, given how things work." He took a drag, then continued. "I do what I am told, however. So, in answer to your question — not unless the brass tells me I can. And you'll probably speak to them before I do. That all?"

The man grunted, a half-smile on his weathered face. "That'd be about it."

Estard leaned over and put his butt out in the ashtray. "Most exciting thing to happen on this base in a while, is it?"

"You have no idea."

"I can go?"

The Colonel waved at the door. "Go then."

"A pleasure, Colonel." He walked out the door, where waited the Lieutenant. He made to walk past the man, assuming that he was waiting for an audience with the Colonel, but instead he followed beside.

"You have a call in the guard station," Adams told him.

Julian swore. It was late. He wanted to go pick up his dog and get home to a real dinner before a good night's sleep.

They walked to the office, and a private handed him the phone. "Estard," he stated testily.

It was Doctor Reigner, and he sounded spooked. "You have to get down here, Agent Estard."

"What's happened?"

"You'll see. I'll explain when you get here."

Julian slammed the phone down. "Better let me back through, Adams."

The Lieutenant nodded, gestured to the private and escorted him back to the first blast door.

"I like you, Adams." The man didn't reply. "You want to know why? Cause you don't fill the space around you with unnecessary noise."

The blast door opened. Estard walked through.

~

In the morgue, Estard found the Doctor standing over the table where the woman had been earlier. His face was pasty white, his light grey eyes wide, and he wrung his hands a few times every couple of seconds. Probably a nervous twitch.

Estard examined the table and found nothing that would indicate a body had ever been on it. "Did you clean it?" he asked the doctor.

The man shook his head. "I haven't touched it!"

"So, you were going to explain this to me when I got down here. I'm here. Explain it."

Reigner shook his head throughout his explanation. "I was over there, cutting into that corpse," — and there was indeed a corpse open on the surgical table, ribs spread wide, coagulated blood spilled over onto the metal — "when I heard a noise. I looked up. I was the only one in here. Simon — the intern? — went home hours ago. There should not have been any noise. I like silence while I am working."

"Are you trying to tell me that she got up and walked away?" *Zombies. Could get* very *interesting indeed.*

"No!" the man replied emphatically. "No. No and no indeed."

No zombies. Damn. "So, what happened?"

"I looked. I couldn't work out what had made the sound. None of the bodies were moving — obviously, they are corpses and corpses don't move — but still I could hear this sound. Like something grating on metal. Then I see. The woman, her head had thrown back in a gasp, her body must have been expelling gases, I guessed, not uncommon for a corpse, it's all got to go somewhere, you know." He took a deep breath.

"And..." Estard rolled his wrist in a gesture to get the man's story moving along.

"She disappeared! Poof! Just like that." He clicked shaking fingers.

"Just like that?"

"Just like that." He clicked his fingers again.

Julian rubbed at his eyes. *I could have tracked a zombie. Couldn't have gone far. But no, she disappeared. Poof. Fuck me.* He was very tired, and he still had things to do before bed.

He glanced at the corners of the ceiling and saw no cameras. He mentioned the lack to the Doctor, who seemed to be calming.

"No. No camera's in here. Out in the hall. In the first room. Not in here. I don't like them watching me work."

Estard was starting to get the feeling this man was some kind of savant. Not unusual in the sciences, he'd found. They tended to do the best work, but they were very particular. And peculiar.

He turned on his heel and headed back to the lift.

"Where are you going?" Reigner asked behind him.

"I am going to get some answers," he told the man.

He raced to the elevator, cursed at it when it didn't go fast enough, jumped out when it stopped, and ran to the holding cells.

A single guard with a chain of keys stood at the entrance. Estard slowed, bouncing on the balls of his feet as the man opened the door. Then had to walk to the cell he needed. He gestured for the guard to open it.

Inside were two wooden pallets chained to the wall, and a small metal toilet in the far-left corner. Both occupants were awake.

"John Harvey?" He'd questioned the man earlier. The hazel eyes glared at him.

"What?" He didn't move from where he was sitting on his pallet, knees raised, arms dangling.

"There were bodies on your ship." How was he going to say this?

"Yes. I know."

"A woman and two men."

"Yes."

"The woman disappeared."

Harvey shot upright at that. And, though they were about the same height, the other man suddenly seemed a lot taller as he leaned toward Estard. "What?" he asked between clenched teeth.

"She disappeared." He glanced at Xavier, the other occupant. A silent question. *Should I be worried?* But Xavier looked pale.

Harvey held onto the chain of the pallet and spun to sit back down. His eyes stared out at nothing, and his face took on a sickly caste.

"Do you know what's happened to her?" Which was why he'd come running.

"Not for sure," Harvey breathed. Xavier stared at the man, pity in his eyes.

"But you have an idea?"

"Not one I'd care to share."

"Why are you here?" Estard roared in sudden fury. "Clearly you expected to be bought in. It's obvious that you knew we were here. And yet with every question you balk. 'You don't have the clearance to know that'. Bah!" He threw his hands up, turned to the door, settled himself, then faced the airman once more. "I'll have my answers. I'm not convinced yet that you're as human as you say. You all seem to know very little about the world. I'll find out why."

But he didn't think that Harvey was listening. His mouth moved in some kind of silent prayer, and his eyes continued to stare at nothing. Not even Xavier had moved during his tirade. Either they did not care, or the news he'd delivered was more devastating to them than was fitting, given the woman was already dead.

He stood there a moment longer, eyes flashing between the two in the cell. *There is something going on here. Something that they don't want to tell me. An Ace up the sleeve maybe? But no. They look like they're about to fall apart. Who was that woman?*

Realising that he wasn't going to get any more out of these two, he left. He paid no attention to the soldier who followed him, locking the doors.

Estard was going home. After he picked up his dog. In a few hours he'd have to be back.

This was his case, and he would get to the bottom of things.

~

Once the door had closed behind Estard, Harvey let out a long breath and looked to his Navigator. The man stared back at him, thoughtfulness painting his features.

"She disappeared," Harvey breathed.

"That's what the man said," Xavier replied.

"But what does it mean?"

"Could mean anything. Could mean nothing." The Navigator shrugged.

"Do you think she's still dead?" Harvey couldn't imagine she'd be alive, just because her body disappeared. But, even so, he found himself hoping.

"Who can say? Ever since that day..." Xavier let that hang there.

"But where did she go?" He found that pain gripped his chest in a tight embrace. His throat closed over, and tears welled in his eyes. His hands shook. She'd died in his arms little more than twenty-four hours ago, while he tried in vain to stem the bleeding from her thigh. And now... there would be no proper goodbye.

"Back to the planet, I think," Xavier said.

"Why do you say that?"

His voice was soft, sympathetic, as he answered, "It's just a feeling."

Harvey wept alone, with mixed feelings of hope and grief, while Xavier gave him what privacy he could.

Chapter Three

Lance scratched at the stubble on his pate, which was a challenge with the cuffs he had on. Agent Estard sat on the other side of the table, just watching. He'd yet to ask him any questions.

It had been four days now, since they were brought in. He'd known, when they landed, that they were probably making a mistake. That the Earth Base they knew was not what this place was. Not in this time. And it wouldn't be for almost four-hundred and fifty years.

He let his hands drop from his head and stared at the man in the suit. He looked tired. His hair was in curly disarray, something that Lance could sympathise with, as his own hair was curly when he let it grow. He had bags under his eyes, and his mouth was turned down in thought. Occasionally, he sucked at his teeth.

"Not going to ask me anything?" Lance said after a while.

Estard glanced at him, brown eyes glassy. "Should I bother?"

"Well, I am the pilot of that ship." *Probably shouldn't be saying these things, but I am bored as all fuck sitting in that cell. Get me back to the ship, turd-bucket, and I can get us out of here.*

"That pilot, is it?" Estard sat up and put his elbows on the table. He breathed a sigh. "So far all I have gotten out of any of you is your name, military rank and country of origin. Yet none of you seem to know anything about Earth. Which is strange, given your claims."

I don't know how Harvey expected them to help us if we can't tell them anything. Name, rank and country of origin. I don't recall Harvey giving me those orders. But was I paying attention? He thought back to the bridge of the ship just before they'd disembarked and recalled frowning at the burning console where Deidra had been sitting. The damned thing had burned out, and he sure as shit didn't know how to fix it. Harvey had said something, but he couldn't remember what.

Lance shrugged at his own memory. "I can answer that," he said.

Sudden interest in the man across the table. "You can?"

"Sure, why not. Shoot, ask your questions Agent Man."

"Let's start with your name, then, Pilot."

"Lance Viatri, Lieutenant in the Italian AM, ATF pilot. Next."

"Who built the ship?"

Uh-oh. Can't answer that one, buddy. "I don't know."

"But you were flying it."

"We butchered parts of our own ship to throw in it. We found that one lying around on the planet we'd landed on."

Estard leaned back in his chair. "So, you're from another planet?"

"Not originally. We just happened to get stuck there for a while."

There was a knock at the door, then it opened. A man popped his head in and gestured to Estard, who got up and left the room. The door remained partially opened as a quiet conversation was had outside.

A few moments later, Estard came back in, hands in pockets with an expression of annoyance on his tired face. The soldier who'd attached the leg irons came over and took them off, then dragged him out of the chair.

"It seems, that the scientists would like you to go down to the ship," the Agent told him.

Well, shit, that was quick. I was expecting that to take at least an hour. He didn't let those thoughts show. No surprise. No hopefulness. Just nonchalance. "Suppose they want to see how it works?"

"I imagine it's something like that."

They walked down semi-familiar corridors, coloured lines painted on the walls denoting sections of the base. He already knew the direction to the hangars, but he was held steady by the guard, and Estard lead them on, a white coat beside him. No one spoke.

When they reached the hangar, it was a virtual hive of activity. Voices, tools, music, all vying for the attention of his ears.

They stood on the grated catwalk above the ships in the hangar. And his was not the only one. He was surprised to see a few he recognised, including one that resembled the fighters from his last space battle a couple of months ago. *Has it only been that long?*

"I can see by the look on your face that you recognise more than your own ship." The white coat noted. "I'll be sure to ask you about them, soon enough."

Lance shrugged. "Can't tell you much about them, except that they're shifty little fuckers. Hard to kill. Like shooting at a floating feather with a twelve gauge."

Estard raised a brow in his direction. Perhaps he'd said too much.

"I am Doctor Elroy Brown. You can call me Elroy or Doctor as you like." He led them down to the ship.

They stopped at the hatch ramp, and the doctor yelled up at those inside. Three excited scientists came out. All young. All *men*.

"Got a distinct lack of women in this place," Lance mumbled.

"Something I had noted your forces are in no lack of," Estard returned. "Which I might note, is strange, given that women are not allowed in the front line of armed forces."

Must have missed that history lesson. "Front line or not, I haven't as yet seen a single one on your base."

"Base? Yes, I guess you could call it that." The Agent sucked at his teeth, stroked his chin. "We do have some, of course. But no more than two percent. That is law. And they're mostly nurses."

"So, when you're feeling sick..." Lance let the sentence hang. The others seemed to get it, as they all gave knowing smirks, but none of them joined in the joke.

The scientist on the left, an average-in-every-way kind of man, was introduced as Richard Moore. The fellow in the centre was tall, lean, and prematurely balding, with tufts of blonde hair above the ears. His name was Fredrick Peltzer. And the guy on the right, short, dark hair, lean, and small black eyes, was called Carson Li Cheng.

The introductions done, Elroy lead him onto the ship. The guard removed the cuffs at the Doctor's urging, but the man himself stayed, keeping a close eye on him.

They were on the bridge, and Lance stood behind the pilot chair, a slight smile on his face. If any place was home at this moment, it was this ship.

"You can start by telling us what everything is for," Elroy said.

With a shrug, Lance began pointing to things. "Pilot's chair, controls, Nav console, comms console, frequency generator and light speed propulsion controls." He spun in a circle. "If you want to know how they all work you'll have to ask Xavier, he's our Navigator. Kristin, our Comms Officer. Or for the Generator, Deidra, the Io Scientist."

When he stopped to face Elroy and the other scientists, they were scribbling furiously in their notebooks. Estard was staring blank faced, arms folded and looking like he didn't believe a word.

"Io scientist?" the Agent questioned.

Lance blinked at him a moment before he understood what he was asking. "Oh. Well. Deidra, she was a scientist on Io research station before everything went down and we got stuck."

"Io, as in the moon?"

"Yes." *He doesn't believe me.* It occurred to him belatedly that they would not have had an Io Research Station in this time. That tech was new in his time. These guys hadn't even been to the Moon yet.

Lance cocked his head to the side and scratched at his pate again. It was damn itchy.

Elroy didn't seem at all bothered by the Agent's sour look. "Can you show us how to turn it on?"

"I could," Lance replied. "But we're running low on fuel. One of the reasons we landed. We'd only planned on making the one trip, so it didn't seem imperative at the time. Need to recharge the fuel cells."

"Recharge. You can do that?"

"Need an electrical storm and some heavy water."

"What do you need heavy water for?"

"The plutonium engine core." They stared. "Don't look at me. We didn't design that part of the ship. But Deidra did explain some of it to me while we were landing."

"She's either a very good actress, or she's lost her memory," Estard said.

Lance looked straight at him. "Again?"

That was not the answer the man expected, Lance judged by the way his eyes widened. "This happen to her often then?"

"Just once." He wasn't sure he should tell the man about their powers. Best to leave that until they decided on breaking out. Then they'd see for themselves.

While Estard and he spoke, Elroy had been directing the other scientists, and now they ran out of the hatch. "They'll get us some heavy water. And I believe I know just the place for an electrical storm." The man rubbed his hands together in an anticipatory gesture. There was delight on his face.

Estard was still all business. "You going to need your Navigator?"

Lance thought about it. He didn't really need anyone else to fly the ship over land, he could see where he was going through the view screen. He wasn't going to veer accidentally and without knowing that he'd done so. But he shrugged. "Probably a good idea."

The Agent studied him for a moment before he ordered the guard to get Xavier from his cell. The guard did not look happy, but he followed the order.

"This is fantastic," Elroy was saying as he paced around the deck. "In all my years, we've never seen one operational before. We can't even get into half of them!"

When it came to the time thing, Lance wasn't sure what he was meant to tell them. Obviously if he said too much, they'd run ahead of the technology they were meant to produce and that could stuff things up. But they had it all here. And if memory served, they did manage to open up an alien ship in the late nineteen-fifties. *My ship? Possibly. When did Deidra say we were again?*

"What's the date?" he asked.

The scientists stopped pacing and his hands stilled. Estard stared at him as if he'd gone mad. "November second," the scientist told him.

"Year?" *Maybe should not have asked that.*

"Nineteen-fifty-seven," from Estard who was now looking more thoughtful than Lance would have liked.

Lance nodded. *Probably my ship.* He felt a kind of pride in that. They'd not understand half of what they were looking at, and not one of the airmen could have explained *how* anything worked. Deidra would need to do that, and if she'd lost her memory... *Just as well, I suppose.*

It didn't take too long before the other scientists came back in hazmat suits and trailing a pallet of barrels.

Elroy clapped his hands together. "So where do we put it?" he asked.

Lance glanced at the barrels, at Estard and then Elroy. At the ship in general. "Good question."

The Doctor's face dropped. "Where is the engine?"

He gave a flick of the hand. "Under the passenger section somewhere, I think. At least, they spent a lot of time working in there."

Elroy looked less than impressed with his answer, his lips pursed and brows drawing to a V above squinted green eyes. "Find it!" he ordered the other three scientists, then addressed Lance. "How much heavy water will it require?"

Lace thought back to what Deidra had told him. It felt like forever since he'd helped her with the ship, though it had only been a couple of weeks. "Four litres, I think. Or something close."

"Four litres? What's that in gallons?" He conferred with his companions before yelling, "One gallon! You can't be serious."

"Might have been less. But that sounds about right."

"Surely *forty* or *four hundred*," Elroy insisted.

"No." Lance gave the top of his head a cursory scratch. "No. I am pretty sure it was four. At any rate, a single digit number."

"Like oil in a motor," Estard offered.

Motor. Car. They run on oil in this time. And petrol. They haven't even had the fossil fuel debate yet. Well, they'll get there soon enough. "Exactly," was all he said.

After they discovered the engine grate, and worked out where to put the heavy water, Lance pointed to the burnt-out console.

Doctor Elroy took a long indrawn breath, then nodded slowly. "Can you fix it?"

Lance shook his head. "Deidra would be my main go to," he told them.

The look that Estard gave him spoke volumes about how he felt.

You think I am up to something, Agent? I think you might be right. Dare you to catch me, though.

~

They'd placed Lance at a desk in the corner, a silent soldier in khaki's watching over him, while they performed the necessary repairs to the ship. At some point they brought Xavier over to sit with him, but aside from brief greetings, they barely said a word to one another, somewhat concerned by what they might accidentally reveal.

Lance never even saw Deidra, but within an hour or two, Doctor Elroy was hovering over him with a frown. "I believe it's ready."

"You don't look happy about it."

The Doctor waved a dismissive hand. "Just trying to absorb the knowledge."

He led them to the ship, and it wasn't long before they were on their way. Lance's passengers included the four scientists and Estard, Xavier and the guard that had brought them from the cells.

"What have you told them?" Xavier asked him, disappointment and agitation a war of expressions.

"Not much." He pointed to the Nav console. "Going to need my wingman on this. Not sure where we're going, yet."

Xavier mumbled something inaudible as he pushed past Lance to take up station. "If we run out of fuel because of this, I will kill you myself, Sinatra." That was clear enough.

Lance took his seat in the pilot's chair and advised the scientists to find something to strap down in. "Relax, Superman, they just topped up the oil, and now we're going to find some gas."

The other man glanced askance, but Lance let it go.

Estard had decided to sit at the comms console, and he was watching the large view screen, which was currently blank.

"We got all the doors open, Elroy?" the Pilot wanted to know.

"We do, yes." The man had decided that he'd just hold onto a bar protruding from the wall, as if that would give him enough stability when they started climbing.

"And where are we headed?"

"Levelland Texas. Got some good electrical storms out that way."

Lance nodded and switched on the engines. The screen came to life, and they could see in detail, everything that lay before them. Lance flicked another button, and the screen had a row of other views along the bottom.

"Xavier, can you put us in a heading for Levelland?"

"Are none of you concerned that we might be seen?" Xavier asked even as he input the coordinates.

"A mild consideration," Elroy answered. "If we ascend to twenty thousand feet, it's unlikely anyone will notice our passing through. We can just go down once we reach our destination."

"If we get caught," Estard put in, "then we'll just say it was something else. Like we always do."

Lance grunted as he pulled up on the controls. He hadn't thought about the people who would be close to the ship, so when he started rising, he was amused to see fifty or so scientists run away from the hull. Odd, since there was no noise or exhaust.

He noted that the roof was open and had them climb straight up. "This is going to get uncomfortable for a while," Lance said, then pulled hard up. As they shot up, the air began to thin. He was not surprised to hear at least one of the scientists in the back throw up.

Can't stay up here too long or I'll pass out too.

"Heading, West, Southwest on twelve degrees," Xavier told him.

Lance adjusted the controls, and hoped it would not take too long.

~

He saw the lightning well before they reached it, and he dipped below the clouds. "How far to go?"

"We're just about there."

"We'll want to land to take advantage of this weather," Lance told Elroy.

The scientist cocked a brow and then shrugged. "It's late enough I suppose. Most sane people should be at home."

"We're just a few K's outside of the town," Xavier said.

Lance let them drop. Estard held on to the comms console with a white knuckled grip and looked like he might puke his guts up all over the screen. He made his tattooed eyes dance for the scientist behind him. Xavier sighed. The man was used to him doing things like this.

He bought the ship to a stand-still a metre above the ground and guided her the rest of the way down. It was harder in this ship than it was in the MM class ships he was used to piloting, but it still gave the same effect.

Lance looked down to the arm of his seat, where the fuel gauge was and was surprised to see it was already climbing. Whatever system Deidra had rigged up was very effective.

A flash, then all the systems died.

"Shit," Lance flicked switches and buttons. "Did any of you see that?"

"That would be lightning," Estard asserted through clenched teeth. "I believe that's what you were looking for."

A few seconds and all systems came back online. "Like getting hit with a mini-A," Xavier said.

Lance glanced down at the fuel gauge. It was full. *Jesus fuck, woman, what did you do to this ship?* Maybe it was simply a more effective storm than the one he'd created back on Eridu. He couldn't rule that out. They certainly hadn't had a flash like that. *Well, it was channelled through those devices Deidra made.* He wasn't sure how it worked, but it was enough for him that it did.

He lifted the ship off the ground and limped it a few kilometres before setting down again.

"What's going on?" Elroy demanded.

"We got what we came for, but she's not a happy ship." The instruments went off again. He slammed his hand down on the arm of the chair.

This time it took more than a few minutes for her to get back up and running. He limped a further few kilometres and landed again.

"Fuel cells are full," Lance informed them. "But there's something pushing down. Can't say what. We might have to wait this out." Though he wasn't sure why or what was going on exactly. They'd not had this problem when they'd taken off from Eridu.

"But the ship is fully fuelled?" from Estard.

"Fully fuelled," Lance agreed.

~

Being on a ship, Estard decided, was no better than being on a plane. Worse even. The altitudes they climbed to, and the way it plummeted out of the sky like a falling brick. His stomach twisted remembering it.

He strode down a green painted hall now, on his way to see the Colonel. Escorted on one side by Lieutenant Adams, Harris scuffing along on the other. He wanted to smack the boy over the head.

"Why didn't you tell me you were going up in the ship?" Harris whined. "I'd have wanted to go."

"It was a last-minute thing."

Adams stopped them in front of a door and entered without knocking. A few moments later and he came back out. "The General will see you now."

Estard raised a brow. "General? I thought we were to see the Colonel?"

Adams moved to one side of the doorway and took up a guard position. "General Hays decided this was worth his personal attention, Agent Estard."

Estard shrugged and pushed the door open.

Inside was a bare room, except for a very large table with maps spread all over it. There were three lights hanging over it, making the area one of the most well-lit he'd seen, but there were no chairs. The General was alone at the far end. He didn't look up from whatever he was studying when he raised his hand.

Estard stopped.

He waited.

Harris fidgeted, and Estard wanted to elbow him, but refrained.

In full dress uniform, General Hays was tall, lithe, and his hair was mostly grey. His face, clean shaven, and blue eyes piercing. He cut an imposing figure.

Technically, the man had no jurisdiction over Estard and Harris, but courtesy paid.

"Got a call in from the Brass." The General looked up from his examination and his eyes brooked no nonsense. "They told me to explain a little something that went down in Levelland Texas last night. Which, of course, I could not." He strode down the length of the table, hands behind his back, until he was inches from Estard's face.

Julian held his own and would not let his eyes drop. That little joy ride had not been his idea, and he was not going to take credit for it. It was the scientists. And they *were* in General Hay's jurisdiction.

"So, tell me, Agent," the General said quietly, head bowed over Estard, so their noses almost touched. "What happened?"

He didn't move. To move would be a sign of weakness. Instead, he used his own eyes, from under drawn brows, to intimidate. *Two can play at this game. I'll not be bowed again.* "The Pilot offered to take your scientists out in the ship. He needed heavy water and an electrical storm, apparently, to get it fuelled up. It was Doctor Elroy Brown who told them where to go. You want to know more; I suggest you ask him."

The General stood over him for a few seconds more, their eyes locked. Then, he spun on his heel and strode back to his end of the table.

"We intend to explain it off as ball lightning," he told them. "But at least four different people saw you all jaunting around out there."

"Not us," Estard said. "A ship."

"You imagine that makes it any better?"

"Not in the least. Worse in fact."

The General's eyes shifted to Harris. "And what are you? A wallflower?

"Junior Agent, Sir," Harris said. And once more Estard wanted to whack him. Generals were not addressed as 'sir' by agents.

"Are we done here, General?"

"Spirit of cooperation," Hays grunted. "I'd like to tell you exactly where to shove it, but you have your orders and I mine."

"So, we're done."

"We're done."

Estard grabbed Harris by the tail of his jacket and pulled him out the door. He gave Adams a nod as he walked by, and the man returned it. It was safe to say that the Lieutenant was the only one who showed them kind courtesy and not grudging. Everyone else in this place was a member of the USAF or were contractors under their direct command. ISAC Agents got their commands from the same place as the General, which put them on a level field and put them under no obligation to share anything they learned.

Once they'd rounded a corner, Estard pushed Harris up against the wall. The boy looked down on him with confusion in his eyes.

"Never take power away from yourself when speaking to the military," he told him.

"What do you mean?" he stammered.

"I mean, you don't call them 'sir'. We cooperate with them; they are not above us. None of them outrank us. You understand? None of them."

Harris gave a mute nod. Estard stared into his eyes for a while longer, then let him go.

"Go home. Get some sleep."

The boy straightened his suit, gave a nod, then walked away stiff-backed. Estard watched for a few moments before turning and moving in the opposite direction.

So much of what was happening made little sense to him, but he thought he may have an answer, as insane as it seemed. The ship was not a *spaceship*. It was a time machine. He had a thought to confront Harvey about it, get some answers — some *real* answers — but decided that he was going home instead. He'd been awake for almost twenty-four hours, and he was not thinking clearly.

Can't let this turn into another incident just because I am sleep deprived. Plenty of time to get this done tomorrow, Julian. Got to check on Bob, have a beer and catch some Z's.

CHAPTER FOUR

The place to which they had all been led reminded Harvey of Docker Rec Rooms. In the centre of the room were six small round tables, six chairs surrounding each, all made with white plastic. To either side of the room were cabinets filled with board games, puzzles, cards and craft supplies. At the far end were a pool table, a ping-pong table, and a serving area with paper cups, water and coffee.

Seated now at the table nearest the door, eyes on the two guards who watched over the room, Harvey thought about their current situation, and the fact that they needed to leave. Coming to this place had been a mistake. One that Harvey would have to swallow. They were getting nowhere telling half-truths, and what Harvey had expected had not come to pass.

The higher ups of this time don't bother with speaking to their prisoners face-to-face. Unfortunately, he'd been counting on them coming down to speak with them. He'd have told a General or a Senator. Having to speak to people whose rank he couldn't guess, was a risky business. How many people would they speak to on the way up the chain? Who would find out things they shouldn't know, and take advantage in a way that might endanger the future that Harvey was familiar with? Was it already too late?

Kristin sat across from him with her head in her hands, dark hair falling like a mop on the table. She'd not been feeling well. Lance sat to his right, head thrown back, eyes on the ceiling. And Deidra was to his left, biting at her bottom lip, cheek occasionally twitching, a permanent look of confusion on her ebon features. She'd be no help, but she was one of them.

"What is happening to us?" Kristin mumbled at the table.

He scowled at her, knowing that she couldn't see it. It may not have been rational, but the schism between himself and Weiz had grown because of this woman. He could not look at her and feel anything but resentment. *I spent time with you instead of her. So sure that that we'd have Earth to look forward to. But she died, and I am stuck with you.*

"We just need to get out of here," he said gruffly.

Lance rolled his head and eyed the Captain. "Just like that?"

"Just like that," Harvey asserted.

"If they have even half the security of Earth Base, we won't make it out." Kristin put her palms on the table and looked up.

"What's going on?" Deidra asked, looking between them all.

Harvey put what he hoped was a comforting hand on her shoulder. "Don't worry. We won't leave without you."

"You're too important to us," Lance agreed.

Kristin nodded. "We cannot leave anyone behind."

Deidra appeared soothed by their reassurances, but it was difficult to see her this way.

"So, we looking at bad weather?" said Lance as he cracked his knuckles with a stretch.

"I'm of a mind to just walk out. Though I could only take one of you with me."

"Have you tried, since we landed?" Kristin asked.

"I've had no reason to."

"It won't work."

"Why not?"

"'Cause we lost it all when we got here." Kristin let her head drop back into her hands.

Harvey glared at her. "How do you know that?"

"I just do."

"A vision?"

"No." She looked up at him again. "I haven't had one since we came back. Should tell you something."

Lance groaned. "Whatever is going on between you two, work it out later. Right now, home time. Suggestions?"

"There's nothing going on between us." *Except that I can hardly look at her.*

The Pilot snorted. "Whatever you say," he said, then immediately went back to his examination of the ceiling.

"I'll put some thought into it. There's what? Seventeen of us? With the exception of Deidra here, we're all trained. We could do this."

"Do what, exactly?" Kristin moaned at the floor. "Get out and then...? What? Live out the rest of our lives in the dark ages?"

"It's hardly the dark ages."

"Tell that to Deidra when we get outside."

Harvey grunted. She was not wrong about that. "We'll take the ship, make it do what it did before, only in reverse."

Deidra was shaking her head, and Lance gave him a sideways glance. "You make everything sound so simple," he droned.

"Well, I don't hear any of you coming up with anything."

"Given how closely monitored we are," Deidra discreetly pointed out a camera above the door, "I suggest not talking about it here."

Well. *A complete and coherent sentence. Are you still in there,*

Doctor? Harvey shook his head. He had noted the cameras, but didn't think they were an issue. He expected them, given where they were.

The Captain stared at her a moment, trying to gauge just how much of her was in there. "You..." He found he couldn't form the question.

She gave him a tight smile. "On and off. Like blackouts, I think. Can't tell you why or how."

He nodded. It made a kind of sense, he guessed. If her powers had disappeared as Kristin suggested. He was sure, she at least, would prefer they did not come back.

"If we can't talk about such things here, and we're separated everywhere else, this just got a lot harder."

"Do you think?" Kristin said sarcastically.

Lance waved a hand without looking away from the ceiling. "Whether they see us, or hear us, it doesn't matter. If we can get away."

Kristin gave off a low growl, almost a sigh. "What a brilliant plan. Be taken by the military. Yes, smart." The look she gave Harvey was death.

"Done is done," Lance glanced at her. "You can badger him about it later — I surely intend to — but, for now..." He waved his hands toward the ceiling. "Let's just get out of here. I don't fancy spending the rest of my life in this place. *Or* in this time. We know this place as well as any of them who work here. We'll take the ship."

Harvey shook his head. "Like you said, it wouldn't be that simple. And you're the only one who's seen it since we were locked in here."

Deidra seemed to have developed a twitch in her face, and Harvey kept an eye on her in his periphery. If she was lucid enough for just one helpful suggestion, he would take it. She was the one with the smarts, even without the powers in her head. A bona fide scientist, long before his teams' disastrous prior mission.

Lance looked down, swung his feet onto the floor. He was serious now. "Look, we're not going to be able to effectively plan anything. That's the truth of it. We have to keep an eye out for opportunity, though."

Kristin nodded. She wasn't looking so well.

"What kind of opportunity?" Harvey asked.

"Same as any. We need a way to get to the others. Drag them out of their cages, as it were." He glanced at the door, the camera, the guards, dismissed them all and continued. "Ships on the orange line. Prisoners on the white. The opportunity is getting our people out. If we have that, everything else will come on its own."

"We could be stuck here for months." Harvey was not objecting, only stating a fact. In his experience you had to create your own opportunities.

"Could be," he agreed. "But, no weapons, no superpowers, and only the barest communication between us and the rest of the townies limits us all somewhat, wouldn't you say?"

"So, we wait?"

"We wait." Kristin nodded.

"We wait." Lance threw his legs back up on the table and resumed his intense study of the ceiling.

~

Estard had wrestled with sleep, despite how tired he'd been. He'd tossed and turned, his brain coming up with all kinds of scenarios concerning the crew of that ship. A time machine. Shape-shifting aliens. A secret government experiment. They were spies sent to keep an eye on him. Maybe they were Russian spies, or British. Even friendly nations sometimes had a go at each other.

He knew they were all thin explanations — especially that last — but there was something in that first, he was sure. And today, after a scant four hours of fitful rest, he planned to find out.

Estard absently wound his way down into the familiar complex, passing the check station, nodding a greeting to those he past in the halls. He wasn't sure where he was going, who he was planning to speak to. He let his subconscious do all the work. He worked best on instinct.

When he found himself following a white line down to the cells, he thought he had an idea.

A uniformed guard strode beside him, though he wasn't sure when he'd picked the fellow up. He gave him an absent nod. If the man returned it, he didn't see.

It's the only thing that makes any sense, his mind kept telling him, like a record that kept skipping. *It's the only thing that makes any sense.*

When he stopped at a cell door, he was sure. He motioned for the guard to open up, and he strode in.

Harvey wasn't there. It was the other guy. Estard tried to remember his name while he raised an eyebrow at the guard. "Someone else questioning them?" he asked.

The guard shook his head. "Sending a few at a time to the rec. It's not daylight, but even top siders get to stretch now and then."

Estard nodded. "Wait outside."

With the door closed, Estard stared at the cells occupant and the man stared right back. He sucked at his teeth and squinted.

"Xavier," he said.

"That's me," the man replied.

"It's a time machine."

The man's eyes opened wide, and he looked as if he were about to laugh. He didn't though, he just bobbed his head in a way that looked as if he wasn't sure whether to nod or shake.

"It's a time machine," Estard repeated.

"Not exactly," Xavier said.

Estard took a step toward him. *Not exactly. It's the only thing that makes any sense.*

Xavier threw up his hands as if expecting to be attacked, showing that he was unarmed. "Not exactly," he said again. "What else would you have me say? I'm no tech."

"Which one do I speak to?" He felt his fists clenched at his sides and made them relax.

I'm close to the edge, he thought, *I need to relax. It's the only thing that makes any sense.*

"Deidra," Xavier's face sagged.

"The woman who can't remember her own name?" he said, disbelieving. He also had a vague recollection of Viatri saying something similar. If it was true, he may never find out for sure.

"She's the scientist," Xavier said, once again raising his hands.

Estard shook his head, not in denial. Just to clear it. Calm down a little. His rage could surface at the oddest times. He did not *feel* angry. He did not need another incident.

"Thank you," he managed.

Though he was not sure what it was yet, there was a plan forming in his head. Something daring. Something dangerous. And when it was done, he would have little time to make it happen.

What am I doing? he asked himself as the guard closed the cell behind him. *It's the only thing that makes any sense.* Maybe he was going insane.

He needed to know.

CHAPTER FIVE

Lance sat by himself in the cell. His roommate had been taken off when he was brought back in, and he supposed it was only fair.

There was nothing to do in the cell except sleep and think. He could have practiced making his tattooed eyes move, but without anyone there to watch, and no mirror, it seemed a pointless task. Besides, he was sure he'd already mastered the art.

It was the *how* he thought of now. They all knew what they wanted to do. None of them knew *how*. And it bugged him.

He'd gotten the ship fuelled up, and it had been easier than he'd thought. He'd gotten the console fixed, and the ship running. He'd managed to get Xavier along for the ride, if no one else. It was a great deal more than anyone else had managed.

Could he convince the scientists below that he needed everyone? No. Not after he'd already done it with only Xavier.

He made a pop with his lips and tapped his own head. "Think, man. Think. You got this."

Lance was the joker. The clown. The one who broke the tension with laughter and witty asides. He could be a moody beast just like the rest of them, but on the outside, he was always poking fun, no matter how much trouble it got him into.

Not today. He didn't have it in him today. This was serious business, and he was a serious man.

"Think, Lance Lawrence Adame Viatri. Just think."

His brain raced and the harder he tried to concentrate, the less focused he became. Sometimes it was like that for him. He remembered the way his mother used to get up from the couch and sigh, looking out the window toward the sea, and say '*Abbiamo finito per oggi, il mio cuore*', because he could no longer stay on task. He'd be frustrated, because he'd want to do what was asked, but just couldn't. He had to let everything come naturally. He couldn't force it.

"*Abbiamo finito, Mama,*" he whispered to himself.

Lance kicked his heels up and laid back on the uncomfortable bed, hands behind his head. He wasn't really looking at anything, just images in his mind. Mostly of his mother, who he missed. But the problem he worked at was a way out. *How? How do we get out?* There was a part of him screaming it was so simple if he'd just turn his head that way and take a look... but he couldn't turn his head. He didn't know what his mind was trying to tell him. Not yet.

He heard the footsteps before the keys, but even as the door opened, Lance did not move. He wanted to crack this nut if it took him all day. *Hell, if it takes the rest of my life. If I'm stuck in here, there'll be nothing better to do.*

"It's a time machine," Estard said, and Lance practically leapt off the bed.

"Say what, now?" Lances heart thumped a hard rhythm in his chest.

Estard looked back at the closed door, then leaned against it. "Your ship. It's not really a spaceship. It's a time machine." The look in his dark eyes, though tired, was incredibly serious.

Lance couldn't help himself. He laughed.

Estard pushed himself off the wall with a flash of anger, fists tightened. His nostrils flared and his teeth clenched. Despite the threatening posture, or perhaps because of it, Lance doubled over in his laughter, clenching at his sides. He tried to contain it, but it spluttered through his pursed lips.

"What is so damned funny!?" Estard demanded. A fist connected with the wall of his cell in a muted thump.

Temper, temper, Agent man. "Everything," Lance said, trying to straighten and swallow his mirth. "Nothing." He shrugged.

Estard did not look amused. He looked dangerous. Until this moment, it was not a word he'd associated with the suited man. But looking into his eyes now, he could see the rage that lurked beneath.

In a flash, that was gone, and Estard stood there casual as ever, hands in pockets, eyeing Lance up and down as he sucked at his teeth. "It gets away from me sometimes," he muttered. "I'm just tired."

Lance nodded as if he understood. He didn't.

"Look, that ship," the Agent continued, "it's a time machine."

The Pilot shook his head. "No, sir. No, sir, it is not."

"It's the only thing that makes any sense!" He threw up his hands, then let them drop. "Xavier told me to speak to Deidra, but that woman is as useless as tits on a bull! When she isn't gazing at me like a puzzle, her mind is god knows where, doing god knows what. I'm not entirely certain she's sane." He thumped down onto the edge of the hard pallet and put his head in his hands. "I don't know why you and your friends came here," he said, looking up, "but you, at least, seem mildly cooperative. So, I ask again, is that ship a time machine?"

All his hysteric mirth was gone now, and Lance Viatri gazed down into the brown eyes of a man who was struggling to understand something. That was a feeling he could empathise with.

He nodded slowly. Not in an affirmative, but as of a decision made.

"Look," he said, "it's not a time machine." The man looked crestfallen. "But, it did take us back in time. About five hundred years."

Estard's mouth opened and closed a few times before anything came out. "Five hundred years?"

"Believe me, it was an accident." He sighed and sat beside the Agent. "Deidra did all the calculations, and if the first trip had have been right the way we thought, then she'd have been dead on. But it wasn't and she wasn't and here we are. *Capisci*?"

Estard barked a laugh, and for a moment Lance thought he'd be taken by a fit of hysterics himself. Sometimes knowing a thing could do that to you. Maybe now he'd understand why Lance had laughed so hard. The Agent just shook his head, though.

"An accident," he said.

"An accident," Lance agreed.

"Can you reverse it?"

"Not me. I just fly the ship. But Deidra..."

Estard snorted. "How is that woman any help to anyone? But you all say her name, as if it's the only answer."

"Well, that's a tough one to explain, Agent Man," Lance breathed. He wasn't sure he honestly could.

Estard seemed to take a hold of himself and got up. He looked off into the distance, then down at Lance. "I don't know what I can do for you lot, given the givens," he told him. "But I will see what I can do to get you out of here."

Lance raised his brows. "You'll let us out?"

"Not into the general population. God knows what you might do out there." He gestured at nothing in particular. "Assuming you're telling the truth, do you even know how to blend into this time? No, don't answer. I don't want to know."

Lance hadn't been planning to, since the answer was 'no' and emphatically 'no fucking idea.' But he wanted out. A way out for all of them.

Didn't need to think for yourself this time, Viatri. Just wait and the answers come. He knew it was a cop out, a kind of deus ex machina. How likely was it, really, that the man questioning them would try to free them? But he wasn't going to question his good fortune out loud and have it disappear. Not until after they were on their way out. Then he would have plenty of questions.

"So, what would you have me do, then?" he asked instead.

"Just sit, and wait, and cooperate," the man told him. "As you have been thus far. You more than the rest, which is why I came to you after I tried to speak to Deidra."

"Ohhh," he said, "you actually tried to talk to her."

"Load of good it did me."

"But you got the answer you were looking for, now."

The Agent nodded and looked at the door. "For now." He tapped at the door and the guard opened it. "Just wait." And the door closed behind him.

Lance kicked up his heels once more. He couldn't believe that conversation. Short and blunt as it was, it was the kind that you only had in dreams. It was *too* easy somehow, and he found that a piece of him was waiting for the other shoe to drop. Harvey was going to be angry.

He grinned to himself, hand behind his head, staring up at the ceiling.

Don't think, Viatri. Never think. Just let things happen.

~

It wasn't simple. These things never were. Agent Estard thought of and discarded several ideas of how he might be able to get the crew of that ship out of the cells. If they were aliens, there was no way that that would happen. That they were out of their time... He thought that *might* sway some of the brass into letting them go. They were, after all, not only human, but some of them, at least, were American. Which meant a very great deal to some. And almost nothing, to others.

He was sitting in the mess, now, a coffee in front of him. His appetite had been less than enthusiastic lately, and the lunch menu didn't help. Harris was sitting across from him, trying and failing to be invisible. The kid knew that something was up, but he also understood that when Julian Estard got quiet, you got out of the way. They'd worked together at the slum house for more than six months, so it wasn't new to the man.

Julian raised his styrofoam cup and sipped at the bitter brew. He never liked how coffee tasted out of styrofoam. There was always a smell, as pervasive as spraying perfume directly up one's nose, that tinted the coffee with an acrid flavour. It made Estard feel like he was lapping it up off a factory floor. But, like most things in this place, he pretended it was the world's best.

"Julian," Harris began, but with a look from Estard, he started again. "Agent Estard. Do you want to give me something to do?"

"Do you have no initiative?" he asked the young man.

Harris looked abashed but went on. "You are supposed to be training me," he said, "but come down to it, all you've done so far is tell me not to do things. You questioned most of the prisoners without me. You went to the morgue without me when that woman disappeared. You went up in that ship without me. You've been trotting around this place all day, popping in here, going in there, saying a few words to this person or that person. All without me." He let out a breath. "If you don't want to train me, Julian, then I will request a transfer."

Julian nodded. The kid had a point. He didn't want to train him. He was stuck with him, because of the brass. They wouldn't *let* the kid transfer. But Harris didn't know that. He just thought he'd scored when they let him put on that suit.

"It's a tough nut," he said, "when you first put on the suit. You're all full of excitement. You get to work with aliens. You can ignore the military — to an extent. There are all sorts of things to explore, and stories to hear. Adventures to take part in." He took another sip of coffee and grimaced at the taste. "But no one ever tells you, just how dull all that really is."

Harris frowned at him. "What are you trying to say?"

Estard shook his head. "This job isn't everything you think it is, kid."

"How do you know what I think it is?"

"You think it's like being a detective, only you're chasing aliens instead of people." From the look on the kid's face, Estard had hit it dead on. "If that's the kind of work you're looking for, go be a cop in New York. You'll have more excitement than you can stand."

"That's not want I want," said Harris. "What I want is for someone to tell me what I am supposed to be doing here. Yes, I am a Junior Agent. I don't get to make the decisions, I'm on the training ropes. I get that. But the way you've been, *Agent Estard*, I might as well be twiddling my thumbs at home for all I'm learning."

True, Estard though, *and I truly wish you were. You grate on me.* But it wasn't fair, and he knew it. "You want something to do?"

"I really do."

"Go down to the hangar and speak to the scientists. See what they've learned about that ship." It would be helpful to Estard, and it wouldn't seem suspicious. A rookie learning his way around the place, how to talk to the people he was to work with. "Find out if it's operational."

Harris got up and turned, then quickly turned back. "You are serious? You're not just trying to get me out of your hair?"

Estard nodded. "Serious. I want to know what you find out, so come back when you're done and tell me all about it."

The kid gave a tight nod, then left.

This, right now, was his only case. It wasn't as if aliens landed or crashed too often in these parts. Or any parts, really. He'd been working with the organisation for almost ten years, and he'd seen but a handful of craft, and no aliens to speak of.

I thought this was the one, he thought, *when they came down off that ship. I thought for sure, aliens. Real aliens!* He crushed his styrofoam cup in a fist and the last dregs of coffee dribbled through the cracks onto the blue tablecloth. The way they darkened and spread made Estard think of the ink blot tests psychiatrists gave.

He had nowhere to go, in this moment. He'd gotten all the useful information he could out of the Pilot. And what he had — he could not give to the brass. He'd certainly considered it, but he knew it was a bad idea. They might not do experiments on them, but they may be tortured for the information they likely possessed about the future. He was not sure there was *anyone* he could tell. It was one thing to believe in aliens, but if he told them about time travel... well, it would be the psych ward for him, and plenty of ink blots to keep him entertained.

The argument circled over and over in his head. He could tell them, and maybe the brass would let them go. Or maybe they would just decide that Estard had finally cracked and send him off some place nobody would have to think of him again. He'd seen it happen to others. Agents who grew paranoid or delusional, seeing things that weren't there. Sure that everyone was out to get them, that the aliens were watching. They sounded like the first-rate whack jobs found in desert diners and country trailers that would tell you, in all seriousness, they had been abducted by aliens who performed invasive experiments.

Estard sighed and rubbed his face. He wasn't entirely sure he *wasn't* going insane.

With a flick of his wrist, he threw the cup into the trash by the wall and got up. He needed a smoke, and he felt like chaining it, so he thought it best to step outside.

He threaded his way through the complex just as absently as he had been all day. The check points, the nods, the greetings, all on autopilot.

Once he was topside, breathing the fresh desert air, he pulled his smokes from his top pocket and lit one up. Fresh air was overrated.

The other question that he had to keep asking himself was — why? Why did he want to help these people? He didn't know them. He didn't owe them anything. He had no cause to put his own skin on the line for them. So why was he even considering it? *Why do I care?*

Empathy and sympathy had never been high on his list of personal motivators. So why was he doing this?

What am I doing? he asked himself as he dragged heavily at his cigarette. *I'm not even sure yet. But I plan to get them out, don't I?* He frowned at his own thoughts.

An image came to his mind of Annabelle Kristin, sitting across the table from him, waving her hand to dispel the smoke from her face. The way she gazed at it with her brown eyes, the way her nose crinkled, and the look of confusion. He had known then, in that moment, that this lot he was questioning, were not from this neck of the woods.

So, what was he going to do about it?

"I'm gonna bust 'em out," he was surprised to hear himself say, in a mutter so low even someone standing next to him would have had trouble understanding his words.

"Yes, yes," he said in the same low mutter, "the question is *why?*"

The usually still desert had picked up a breeze that blew the smoke back in his face.

That image of Annabelle popped back into his head. And he knew. Deep down inside, he knew. But he shook his head anyway.

"It can't be that," he said, but before he could get any further into the argument with himself, Harris was by his side.

"Did like you said, Agent Estard," the man told him.

How long have I been out here? "And what did you find out?"

"Fully operational, near as they can tell. They want to get the Pilot back in there." He scrubbed a hand through his hair and gestured to Estard's smokes. "Bum one?"

Estard held out the pack and proffered the lighter. "What do they need the Pilot for?"

Harris shrugged as he lit his smoke. He took a deep inhale before answering. "They think it would help getting to know the how and why of everything. They wanted to question the scientist — Deidra? — but they can't get much out of her. Seems most of the time she's not even sure of her own name."

"I can attest to that."

"You've spoken to her, then?"

"She was the first one I spoke to, before you got here in your fancy new suit." He jabbed an elbow at the other man, trying to find some humour. He was getting too dark, lately.

"I got a question." Harris seemed hesitant at first, but then he let it out. "Why aren't we interrogating them? Why are they being left, for the main, to themselves? You did a few interviews, sure, but aside from the accommodations, they may as well be honoured guests."

Estard sucked at his teeth a moment. "It's been less than a week," he said. "They've been honest, if not forthcoming, about the things we want to know. At first, we were just trying to verify they were human."

"And now?"

"Now we want to know *why* and *how* they happen to be here."

"You got a theory on that?" The younger man flicked his butt to the ground and squashed it with the toe of his shoe.

"There's one forming. I'm sure. But, I'm not ready to share it. Wouldn't do to embarrass myself if I'm wrong."

"I can get behind that," Harris said. "Is there anything else you wanted me to do?"

Estard shook his head. "What do *you* want to do?"

"I want to talk to the people from the ship. Get some answers out of them."

"Do you think you can?"

"Won't know till I try."

Estard waved a hand toward the entrance of the facility. "Then be my guest. Take a lead. You don't need me following you about. You're a good kid, you know what you're looking for."

Harris made to leave, then paused, turning his head. "I got a feeling..."

"What?" Estard pulled another smoke from his pack.

"Something about this whole thing is fishy, you know?"

"You're not wrong."

"Do the brass know everything that's going on?" The young man ran a hand through his hair, eyes darting nervously.

Estard nodded. "They know what we know. Now, go. Do your thing."

Left to himself once more, Agent Julian Estard let himself wonder, why exactly he was going to help these people get out. Sure, there were a lot of questions he was hoping to get the answers to, but it was more than that. More than just some Australian brunette looking at him with those brown eyes.

Yeah, like what on earth happened to that body from the morgue? They know something about that, too, and you know it.

"If I do this," he told himself, "there'll be no coming back this time. Not like last time."

A vision formed in his head of a boy, about ten years old, clasping fearfully to his mother's hand as his old partner, Stevenson, tried to pull her away. He had a bright red truck clutched to his chest with the other hand.

Estard ruthlessly shook the vision away before it could more than form at the edges. He did not want to think about the last incident. What had happened after.

I'm really going to do this, aren't I? He couldn't give himself a good answer as to why. But he was sure, in time, he would work it out. He knew he would have to go with them, however he got them out. And there would be pursuit. Hot and heavy pursuit. *They'll let the military handle this one. They'll hunt us down and take us out. They're not so interested in the answers if it doesn't help them build bigger, better weapons.* It was an unfair assessment of the institution, he knew, he'd been a soldier once himself. But not altogether wrong, either.

Looking across at the sun, already well on its way toward the western horizon, Estard crumpled his empty pack of smokes and made his way back inside.

He needed to make a plan. One that would get them all out. One or two would be easy enough, but seventeen... that was going to be a lot tougher.

Chapter Six

It had been two days since that agent had come to his cell, and he hadn't seen hide nor hair of the man since. His previous optimism after their short conversation was beginning to wane.

Sitting now in the Rec Room with Harvey, Xavier, Kristin, and Deidra, Lance assumed his regular position of staring at the ceiling. He didn't like having so many people about, and eye contact be damned. He never knew where to look if his eyes weren't on a view screen.

Zim, Rich, Ellis and Fyord were all in their own tight little group, standing around the pool table. Each thump and clack he heard was followed by a smiling comment or jeer, but it all felt subdued.

Everyone knew Harvey had taken lead, even before Weiz had been killed, and they were all just waiting for him to make a move. Once he did, they would follow, but until then, the grunts laughed and smiled and pretended they were on an Earthside retreat. What he'd give to be one of those grunts.

Kristin still wasn't feeling too good. Her face had drained of colour, she kept holding her head, closing her eyes. None of them had been feeling well, but it showed most on her.

"...keys. That's the main thing here," Harvey was telling the others. Well, Lance too, he supposed, though he hadn't really been listening.

"How do you propose we do that?" Xavier asked. He kept darting glances at the other group, as if torn. But he stayed with his crew.

"We're not exactly exposed to a great many people, here," Kristin said. "Three places we've been allowed, all under guard. Here, our cells, and the showers — on the days that they bother to take us."

"We're coming on eight days now, Captain." Xavier again.

"If we don't do something soon, I'm not sure I'll be of much use." Kristin.

"The ship." Deidra.

Lance let his legs fall and sat upright so fast he got a little dizzy. He was more than a bit surprised that the woman had spoken. Her brief moment of lucidity the other day had been a brief spark in a deep well.

"The ship?" Lance asked before any of the rest could form a question.

"I can do it," the scientist said. "I have been thinking about it, when it's working." She tapped her head. "I think... my memory... I keep trying to hold on." The way she looked at Lance then, he understood. The rest of them had lost their powers. All of them.

"You're holding onto the knowledge!" he said.

Deidra nodded. "As much as I can. As soon as I knew."

Harvey and Kristin exchanged looks. Xavier nodded thoughtfully.

Lance stared directly into the Io Scientists big brown eyes. "Is there a way for you to write it down, get it out, while..." He gestured at his own head, unable to form the sentence.

He saw it then. Right there in her eyes. That moment when she got confused. And then there was a clearness to them again.

"If they'd let us take anything back to the cells," she managed.

"No pressure in the here and now, my dear," he told the woman. "If you can think of a way to use the ship, you do what you have to do. You take as long as you need to take, and never mind the rest of us. You hear me?"

For answer Deidra quirked a slight smile and darted her eyes around the room. He'd lost her.

"Nice job, Sinatra," Xavier said, and for once, didn't sound mocking.

Sit and think and talk, that's all we've done since we got here. I'm getting bored. He thought about his brief jaunt in the ship. *But that was days ago. Where's my agent man?*

As if he'd read his thoughts, Harvey turned to him. "What about Agent Estard?"

Lance rubbed a hand over his now smooth head. The soldier boys wouldn't let him have a razor, but they'd let the barber come down and take care of it. A small mercy he was grateful for.

"What about him?"

"He indicated that he was going to do something. Help us out," the Captain prompted.

Lance just shook his head. "I wouldn't hold my breath on it. That was two days ago, and I might add, he didn't exactly seem in his right mind. I wouldn't be surprised if he's on forced leave."

"What makes you say that?" Kristin asked.

"Have any of you seen him?"

There was silence around the table as they all thought about it. It was like going around in circles. How, oh how, were they going to get out of here? And if they managed that much, *how* were they going to get back to the time in which they belonged?

Among their challenges were guards — a handful, but enough — closed doors, blast doors, and scientists. It would be easier to get to the ship than out to the surface, but what would they do once they got to it? Fly it out into space and wait until they ran out of fuel and were forced to land again? That would leave them in a very similar predicament to the one they now faced.

If Deidra really had been working on it, though... The only problem there was the woman's lucidity. If she lost it at the wrong moment, it could be a disaster. If they got to the ship somehow, but she couldn't get them out, they'd all end up back in cells. Under heavier guard.

"We're the Giant Killers," he said. "We made ourselves untouchable legends. We became separate," he glanced at Xavier whose camaraderie he'd most keenly felt the loss of on that other planet. "and we took over."

Harvey shook his head. That man was holding on by the thinnest thread. Less than a week since the love of his life died, and for some reason, he had been taking it out mostly on Kristin.

"It's up to us," Lance said.

"We all know that," said Kristin.

"If Deidra can hold onto some of it, why can't we?" From Harvey.

"Would it make a difference if we could?" Kristin asked.

"You know it would," snapped the Captain, but the woman just grunted at him.

"Settle." Lance didn't know how he'd come to take the lead. He hadn't, really, and yet he had. By some unspoken rule inside his own mind. Because Kristin was sick, and Harvey was being stupid. Because Deidra was only half there, and Weiz was gone. He was like a reservist. Capable, but reluctant to commit.

"Look," he continued. "Who have we got and where is everyone?"

Xavier took another glance at the other group. "Rich, Zim, Ellis and Fyord." He nodded toward them, then looked back at Lance.

"Hadley, Constance, Bridges, Walt, Dames, East, Duntz and Gordon. The ones who died on the ship; Ainsley, Heinrich and..." He trailed off looking at Harvey.

"Weiz," the man finished for him.

"Weiz." Xavier nodded.

"How many did we leave behind?" He hadn't meant to ask that out loud, and he found it strange he'd not even thought of it until now. But, that list of those with them... it was too short. *Much too short.*

"More than twice the amount," Harvey said quietly.

"Have any of you seen the rest of them since we've been down here?" Lance hadn't.

"I hadn't even seen Rich until today," Xavier said.

Kristin and Harvey only shook their heads. Deidra was off in her own little world, and she bunked in with Kristin anyway. If Deidra had, Kristin would have too.

Thank you so much, Harvey, he thought, *for getting us into this mess.* It wasn't fair to blame him like that, he'd been the one to land the ship, after all. But he couldn't help it.

He opened his mouth — and shut it again, as the door opened. In strode the airmen; a few he immediately recognised, others he did not. They were slow, and looking a little dazed, but they took up seats around the room in their own little groups, one or two joining those by the pool table. Some glanced in their direction, but none came to join them. Though one of them, the last to walk in — Gordon, he thought — gave them a nod.

Before the door could close behind them, Estard walked through and took a look around. When he saw Lance, he walked over to him, grabbed a chair and turned it around, falling into it and leaning on its back. The way he studied Lance, the others may as well not have been there.

"It's not a pretty scenario," the man breathed in a whisper, "but I think I got us a way out, if you can keep up." His eyes darted to Kristin and Deidra.

"I'm all ears, Agent," Lance assured him, and saw the others were paying close attention.

"It's not ideal." The Agent shook his head and looked around the room. His eyes settled on the two guards by the door.

With the whole lot of them in here, Lance thought he knew where this was going.

"You got everyone out so we wouldn't have to look for them."

Estard sucked at his teeth and nodded. "That was the hard part," he said. "Getting you all together in one place. But, complain as the Colonel might, you lot are my prisoners, and under my jurisdiction."

"It's a rookie error," Kristin said slowly, raising her head to look around. "You should always keep your prisoners separate."

Harvey shook his head. "You helping us out, then, Agent Estard?" He said it loud enough that Estard quickly glanced at the guards before shooting him a glare that should have melted stone.

"Captain," Lance said in a warning tone.

Estard shook his head. "There are terms," he said. "Before we do anything, we need an agreement."

"Say the words, Agent man." Lance crossed his arms, breathed deep and prepared for the worst. It was not advisable to bargain if you weren't in a position of strength. And they certainly were in no position to argue.

The man glanced at Kristin and Deidra again. "I want answers," he said. "But that can wait. Until after. Because..." he hesitated a moment, then let it out in a rush. "I want to come with you. Wherever you're going, whatever it is you lot are up to... I want to come."

Lance looked into the Agents brown eyes, searched them. "You're sure about that?"

"No. But let's pretend I am."

"You got a few screws loose," Kristin breathed, barely audible.

"Well, if you're sure, then —"

"No!" Harvey cut him off.

"Hang on just —"

"No!" Harvey repeated, planting a fist on the table.

Kristin looked at the Captain with tired eyes. "Don't be like Greenway," was all she said.

The colour drained from Harvey's face, but he backed down without another word.

"So," Lance turned his attention back to Estard, and the Agent to him. "If it tickles your toenails, you can come with us."

Estard looked confused for a moment but then nodded. "Good." He glanced at Kristin and Deidra again. There was something going on there.

"So, what's your plan, Agent man?"

"I'm going to walk out of here," he said. "You're going to give it five minutes." He pointed to the clock on the wall. "A *full* five minutes. Then you lot in here can take care of these two easily enough. Do it as you like, though I prefer you didn't kill them."

"We're not murderers," Kristin said, indignant.

Estard shrugged. "You're in a tight spot, and you're military. I need to assume you'll kill for your objective."

Kristin grunted but said no more.

"And then what?" Harvey asked.

"Then I open that door, and I lead you to your ship." He looked apprehensive about that. "We can't plan it. There are no set guards inside, except for at the cells. We might get all the way there without seeing anyone, or we might have the entire complex down on our heads within seconds." He sucked at his teeth again. "That's why I need five minutes. To take care of the men in the monitoring station. It's not far from here, but if I get it wrong... I won't even be able to open that door."

You'll end up a prisoner, just like the rest of us. "You sure you want to do this, Agent man?"

"Sure enough, Pilot man," he replied.

"Then you do what you got to do, and we'll wait." He looked at the clock. "Five minutes to the second, after you walk out that door."

Estard got up. "If the door doesn't open..." he let that hang in the air, and turned before anyone could answer.

You're fucked. Lance finished in his own mind. *If the door doesn't open, you're fucked. And you're on your own.*

"It's too convenient by far," Harvey said after the Agent had gone.

"You don't think he'll come back?" Kristin asked.

"Whether he does or doesn't, I don't trust him," the Captain said.

"Should we...?" Xavier indicated the others in the room, who had been paying no attention to what was going on.

Lance shook his head. "We'll take care of that part ourselves. They'll know to follow as soon as that door opens again, and we walk out."

"And if the door doesn't open..." Kristin said.

"We're fucked."

~

Estard couldn't believe he was doing this. Truly could not believe it. The world around him had taken on a grainy surreality, like he was in a scene from a movie. Or a dream he couldn't wake up from. One where he couldn't make himself stop before he got himself killed.

The lyrics to *There was an Old Lady* popped into his head, and he found himself humming as he entered the monitoring station. There was only one man seated there, feet up on a desk, book in his lap, only occasionally gazing at the black and white screens before coming again to his book.

"Help you?" he asked without looking up.

"Just taking a look," Estard said.

He leaned down over the guard who didn't move, or even flinch. And why would he? He wasn't expecting any kind of danger form Estard. Which was his mistake.

Estard slipped a needle into to the man's neck and pushed until the syringe was empty, then stuffed it back into his pocket, placing the cap back on with a finger. It was only a fast-hitting tranquiliser. The kind they took with them when they went to search a crashed spacecraft. The guard was out before he even had time to notice what was happening.

He glanced at the screens, checking out the corridors they'd need to pass through to get to the hangar. Then he leaned back and shuffled out the door at an unhurried pace.

No going back now, he thought. But then, if he was truly honest with himself, he'd known there never was.

He felt more relaxed as he walked back toward the Rec Room. More himself than he had been since the end of the Second World War. More himself than even since that first incident... but he wouldn't go there.

Estard glanced at the watch on his left wrist. Less than a minute. He didn't pick up his pace. He was close enough that he wouldn't be late.

The corridors were empty. The guards were inside the room with the prisoners. And there were only two of them. It shouldn't be a problem. Still, as he placed his hand on the door and keyed in the entry sequence, he prepared himself to have to take care of it. There was no such thing as too prepared.

He opened the door.

One step and a quick glance to either side showed the guards propped up against the walls in chairs. It appeared they'd just fallen asleep on duty, though one had a drop of blood on his chin.

At the same time, he heard shuffled footsteps, and chairs being scraped back, accompanied by that dangerous silence that Estard associated with ambushes and cold anger.

He scanned the small crowd. Lance was at the forefront. He gave the man a nod and turned around.

Estard didn't need to check if they followed, he knew they would. There was nowhere else for them to go. And besides, he could hear their footsteps, quiet as they were in their prisoner's slippers.

My heart isn't racing, he thought. *This just doesn't feel real.*

He led them down corridors lined with a blue stripe. The blue line connected to a green line, and they followed that until they came to a junction of five coloured lines. They had yet to see a soul, for which Estard was grateful. Once they got to the ship, he was sure they'd find plenty of scientists. But he wasn't as worried about them. He led them down a red lined corridor that would lead to the orange line and became a little more alert.

Estard gestured to Lance, requesting that he come up close. The man obliged. "It's Friday, so most of the men here are up at the barracks. But we will run into some when we get down to the hangar. They won't have left them completely unsupervised."

Lance nodded at him and trailed back to the others.

There was a shouted whisper from the back of the line. "Guards!"

Estard spun, expecting to see uniformed men with guns drawn. But all he saw were a line of airmen looking down a side corridor, standing very, very still.

One of them gave a nod, and the tension visibly relaxed.

Estard led them on.

It felt like hours. It took minutes.

They were still in the red section, two corridors away from the orange line that would lead them straight to the hangar, when he saw them coming down an adjacent corridor.

Estard motioned to the men behind him to stay where they were and not move.

There were eight of them. Six in full uniform, their sidearms holstered but ready to be drawn. Two others, stripped down to undershirts, sweat evident on backs and underarms, were walking along beside, speaking to some of their number. They were laughing, relaxed. They weren't looking for trouble inside the complex. They were just on their way to some other duties. They didn't see Estard.

He was waiting to see if he would need to usher the airmen back down the corridor and into a safer passage when the alarm began to sound.

The soldiers were on alert now. The two in the lead pulled their firearms and motioned to the others without words. The group split up into twos at a run. They wouldn't know what they were looking for just yet. But twenty odd enemy combatants loitering in the halls might be a little obvious.

Lance took him from behind and pulled him around. "What now, Agent man?" he asked in a whisper.

Estard glanced about for inspiration, but he found none. These people weren't armed. They couldn't stand up to a fight against the soldiers. If it came down to that, it would be low odds they'd make it to the ship. There was only one word that came to his mind.

"Run!" he said and suited his own words.

He was glad they didn't scatter. He could hear them all behind him as he ran into the corridor where there were now only two soldiers. They looked up in surprise at the prisoners running toward them, Agent Estard in the lead.

One of the soldiers managed to raise his gun and get a shot off. Lance dove by on his left, Harvey on his right, and within moments, those two soldiers were subdued. The airmen stripped the outer gear with a proficiency that spoke of practice. But they didn't have time to get everything, as two more pairs of soldiers came hurtling around corners further up the corridor.

As soon as the soldiers saw them, they stopped and planted themselves, guns raised. Harvey took the gun from the unconscious man in front of him, and without warning, fired several shots off into the distance.

The bullets didn't take care of the soldiers, but it did make them dive for cover in the adjacent corridors.

Harvey continued stripping his man. Lance was already done, and now wearing army jacket and cap, as well as the boots. He was strapping on the thigh holster but held onto the pistol.

"They'll live," Lance assured him.

Harvey grunted as he got up. Garbed now as Lance was. Estard noticed a small trail of blood under the man's feet. "You get hit?"

"Just winged," Harvey said. "It'll heal itself, no worries."

Shots were fired into the corridor. Tiny chips of concrete fell to the floor.

"We going after them?" Lance indicated the direction with a nod, gun at the ready.

Estard shook his head. "Back up to that other corridor."

Harvey took the lead, while Lance stayed in the rear. Estard was only one step behind Harvey, and the airmen followed in silence. Not one word spoken between them.

Shots were fired from behind, answered by shots from Lance. But if any hit a target, it wasn't obvious to Estard, and he didn't look back to find out.

Up ahead, the red line became orange, and Estard indicated left. Harvey charged out in front, gun raised, looking first down the right of the corridor, then the left.

Estard took a step into the corridor, and nearly lost his head as a shot flew into the concrete next to him. He ducked. It was automatic. His hand felt for his own gun, which wasn't there. He had a syringe full of tranquiliser in his coat pocket, but that would be no good at a distance.

Harvey was his shield now, and the airmen had bunched up behind them. Estard tried to look around the man, to see who was shooting, but he couldn't get a good look.

There were two quick shots — *Bam! Bam!* — and Harvey moved forward.

"How many?" Estard asked as he got back on his feet.

"Two." Harvey kept moving forward.

He couldn't hear any shots from behind, but there were too many people between them for Estard to ask what was happening in the rear. He'd have to take it on faith.

With the alarm going, Estard knew that the complex would be on lockdown. All outside passages and doors heavily guarded. They'd need a special code to open any of the blast doors, or the hangar doors. This was going to be a problem. A big one. They needed to find someone with that code.

They were moving forward at a jog, now.

They passed by two soldiers, both taken down with a single gunshot to the head. *So, Harvey is a good marksman.* Oddly, he wasn't as upset by their deaths as he knew he should have been. Not because he knew them — he didn't — but because they were *people.*

His mind threatened to take him back to France in 1945, but he wouldn't let it. He had to stay in the here and now.

They came to a heavy metal door that would lead them out onto the catwalks of the hangar. Estard stopped, slapped the wall. Harvey pulled up to guard his back while he entered the access code. When it worked, he breathed a quiet sigh. They wouldn't need to find someone in a cooperative mood.

Estard strode through onto the grated catwalk and the first of the airmen held the door open for the others to come through.

Down on the hangar floor, scientists were working on the ship. He could see four of them, but it was possible there were more inside, or in the offices nearby. He saw no soldiers.

He heard running boots, and the airmen were hastening. Harvey was beside him. "I've only got a couple of bullets left," he said. His face was pale and waxy.

"You weren't just winged, were you?" he asked.

The Captain gave him a steady look. "Never you mind about that. Just lead the way down."

~

He'd already gone through his first clip. The soldiers were following at a respectable distance, dodging into cross corridors and doorways to give themselves cover. He was one man with a gun, and he'd never been a good marksman. But they were being cautious. Not wasting their bullets on pot-shots.

They'd stopped, and now Kristin was beside him. "Give me the gun," she said.

He didn't look at her, just kept his eyes on the corridor. On the men who were coming forward, now more confident. He took a single shot. The men moved into what cover they could find. But it wouldn't last long, he knew.

"Give me the gun," she said again.

"You've not been looking so well, Belle," he said.

"You couldn't hit a stationary target at fifteen feet!" she yelled in his ear. "Now, give me the gun Viatri!"

He gave her the gun.

She took a step back, and so did he. He took a moment to glance behind him and see that the others were already entering the hangar. The sound of running boots brought his head back around.

Down the corridor was at least a squad of soldiers, heading toward them in formation, those in front with their guns raised. So much for a skeleton crew, it seemed every available soldier had been called in.

They backed up all the way to the door. Kristin took aim. Five shots were fired in a steady stream, like the beat of kick drum. *Bam! Bam! Bam! Bam! Bam!* And then the gun clicked. Empty.

Kristin was about to throw the gun; he could see that. He knew that was what she was about to do. He couldn't see the corridor, as he'd backed into the Hangar at the first shot. He didn't know what was happening in there. But as she raised her arm, he heard shots, and a red bloom formed on her forehead.

Hands pulled on his shoulders from behind and the door was closed in front of him before his mind could register what had happened. Before her body had even hit the ground.

"Get to the ship!" The voice was a muted buzz in his head, but he recognised Xavier. "We need you to fly the damned thing, Sinatra. If there's anyone we need to stay alive here, it's you."

Lance found himself nodding as he was hauled around and pushed through the crowd of airmen. They were crossing the catwalks at speed and being led down the stairs to the ground floor.

There was thumping at the door behind him.

Estard was at his shoulder, Harvey a few steps in front. "They won't get through easily," the Agent said. "I busted out some of the wiring." He looked around. "But it's not the only way in."

Lance was moving mechanically, barely aware of his own body as he strode forward. They were already at the hatch of the ship, and though he could see the scientists eyeing them all, both curious and wary, they were like background noise in his mind. Not worthy of notice.

It was like the Day of the Giants all over again. It was nothing like it, but it was exactly the same. He couldn't put his finger on it.

His steps were slow, and Xavier still pushed him from behind. He could hear gunshots and shouts, footsteps and clangs, all echoing off the concrete walls of the hangar.

His foot hit the end of the ramp, and he was on the ship. The noise melted behind him. Xavier turned him toward the bridge, and a great rushing sound filled his ears. He took one step, and...

CHAPTER SEVEN

Xavier fell forward with a startled, "Shit!" Estard looked on, mouth agape.

"What the fuck just happened?" he asked.

"What is it?" Harvey shouldered past him into the main cabin, looking around. "Where's Viatri?"

Xavier turned. "He just..." He made a gesture with his hands and looked around.

"Disappeared," Estard said.

Harvey looked back out the hatch, cocked his head toward the bridge. Estard felt a slight nudge behind him, then Deidra was walking past on the other side.

"Keep an eye out from here," Harvey told him. "When the last one is on board, close her up."

What am I doing? He took two steps back down the ramp. *This is what you wanted, isn't it?*

To his right, airmen were trotting a pair of scientists away from the ship, biceps held in tight grips. A few paces further on, some grappled with soldiers who'd made it in, or who had already been there. He wasn't sure which. There weren't many.

There were no gunshots now. *How could I have left my gun?* Two airmen, a man and a woman, ran up the ramp beside him, and dodged inside.

At least some part of you had to expect this, he chided himself. *Did you think you could get them out without anyone noticing?*

The thing of it was, he really had. He honestly, truly had.

~

Inside the ship, Harvey leaned against the pilot's chair. His breathing was shallow, and he knew if he didn't get help soon, he was going to die.

Didn't think you'd get out of here that easily, did you? Nothing *is ever that easy, John Harvey. You know it.* He swallowed a dry chuckle.

He gritted his teeth against the pain in his side. The bullet was lodged somewhere in his gut, having entered at an angle. It was a slow way to die, and he didn't cherish the thought. He was starting to feel very cold, though the wound burned.

"You know what you're doing?" Harvey asked.

Deidra didn't look up from what she was doing, just shook her head. "Some of it is me, some of it that other thing. I am trying to hold to it..." Her small tablet device was in her hands, fingers dancing across it.

Harvey slid down the back of the chair to seat himself, legs splayed, on the deck. "Do you ever think," he wondered aloud, "maybe Greenway was right?" *Why did I say* that? If she responded, he didn't hear it.

His head drooped. His eyes fluttered. Everything was dimming out, and he knew he was coming to the end.

Weiz. I'll see you soon.

~

Deidra saw Harvey begin to fade from the corner of her eye, but when she looked right at him, it was the surroundings that faded.

There was a sort of curious fascination somewhere deep down inside her, something that should not be there without her memories, and her sense of self.

She reached out a hand toward him, knowing what she'd find. He'd taken his last gasp.

She was engulfed in light.

~

The fight didn't last long. There weren't many soldiers, and the scientists didn't put up a fight. The airmen trotted their prisoners to an office, where they were locked in, and then made their way to the ship.

After he'd counted them out and knew that the last of them were on board, Estard got inside. He nodded to Xavier, who pressed a button, and the hatch whined shut behind him.

"We have a serious problem," Xavier said.

"What's that?"

Xavier looked to the rear where airmen were strapping themselves in, giving each other congratulatory pats on the shoulder, and knowing smiles. They were going home. And if their behaviour was moderately subdued, it was because they knew — it wasn't over, until it was over.

"Well?" Estard asked, impatient.

Xavier looked at him again, then motioned with his head to the bridge.

Estard strode over. He looked around the empty room. He heard Xavier breathing beside him.

"Tell me they..." he couldn't finish.

"Disappeared."

Estard sucked at his teeth a moment, then laughed. A hearty, full bellied guffaw that bounced off the metal walls and struck his ears like a fold-back speaker.

The Navigator was looking down on him as if wondering

whether he was in his right mind. It only made Estard laugh harder, stretching out a hand to grab at the pilots chair and stop himself from falling.

No one else had come up from the back to see what was going on. He thought that was a small mercy.

"What the hell is going on!?" he asked once he'd managed to subdue his laughter.

Xavier looked him over. "They were the Giant Killers," he said, as if that should answer everything.

"Why I bother saying words sometimes," Estard addressed the heavens, "I do not know." He turned his attention back to Xavier. "What does that have to do with the price of tea china?"

"China?" Xavier mouthed, a perplexed look on his face. But he shook his head and let it slide. "They are... were — Gods, I guess."

"Gods."

"Gods."

"As in, smote thee from the heaven's, let my vengeance rain down on thee, here's my son for sacrifice — gods."

Just as Xavier was about to reply, a thump sounded on the hatch of the ship.

"Fuck me," Estard breathed.

"We do not have time for this." Xavier turned and yelled toward the passenger section. "Gordon! Zim!"

Another thump sounded on the hatch.

"I hope that holds," Estard said.

Two airmen came up from the back. One a Latino woman and the other a European man. They stood at ease before Xavier, waiting.

"Can one of you fly this ship?" he asked in a near whisper.

They looked at each other, then back at the Navigator. "All the controls are the same as the MM ships," the woman said. "So, I don't see why not."

"All right. Both of you stay in here. I don't want to panic the others."

"Where's Viatri?"

Thump. Bang!

Xavier shook his head, eyes on the hatch. "All who are here, are all who's coming. Start her up."

After a single look at each other that seemed to speak volumes, it was the man who jumped into the pilot's seat and strapped in.

Remembering his first jaunt in this spacecraft, Estard looked around quickly for a place to secure himself.

"What about the hangar doors?" The Pilot asked.

Shit! Shit, shit and shit! Fuck!

Xavier looked at him expectantly.

Estard looked at Xavier with wide-eyed horror.

"Don't you have any kind of futuristic, super fantastic weapon?" Estard asked, desperate.

"There aren't any weapons on this ship," Xavier said, his words almost drowned out by the sound of *Ping! Clang!* in a fast tattoo on the hull. "And those blast doors are built to withstand explosives."

His mind worked quickly. Thump. Clang! *Ping! Ping! Ping!*

How were they not inside already? By the racket they were making, they were doing their best to get inside without damaging any vital systems. His eyes lit up.

"They're not penetrating the hull," Estard said.

Xavier shook his head. "Small arms. Maybe a battering ram. It's not the same as twelve-inch blast doors."

"What about concrete?"

"It could seriously damage our space-worthiness," said the Latino woman.

"Gordon's right."

Estard looked toward the pilot in the chair. He had the forward view screen on, and at the bottom, several other smaller views were available. Like a security monitoring station.

He came up behind the man and leaned over the seat to get a better view. Zim looked at him with disapproval but said nothing as he studied the screens.

Still, the clatter from outside did not cease.

He could see them, their M1911A1's firing ineffectively against the metal, even at close range. If he were their commanding officer, he'd tell them to stop wasting bullets.

A pair of soldiers with a battering ram between them stood at the hatch taking steady swings from the ground. There was no way for them to get the kind of momentum required to do any real damage.

Up on the catwalks, one soldier held a bazooka and was speaking to his superior, while another soldier held a shell, ready to load.

"Would this tub hold up against that?" He pointed to the screen.

"Should," Xavier said with a shrug.

But Estard wasn't really worried. He was looking for something. The catwalks were lined with soldiers, and at least two squads were searching for a way to get onto the ship from the ground level, some shooting, some running a hand along the smooth surface. But they weren't getting in. In his gut, he felt that.

"Is there any way for you to move these cameras?" he asked.

"Where do you want to look?" the Pilot asked in a French accent.

"Other side of the ship, closer to the blast doors."

The Pilot tapped a few buttons and suddenly the exact view he wanted was up on the main screen.

"That," he said in triumph, pointing to a large lever a few feet away from the blast doors that would take three men to move. "Can you trip that lever?"

"With what?" Zim asked.

"With the ship."

Zim's eyes opened wide, and he breathed out slowly, what sounded a fervent curse passing his lips in a whisper. "I'm no Viatri," he said, "but if it's the way out.... I can try."

Gordon looked at the screen with a face turning green. But she didn't say anything.

Xavier moved over to a console on the left of the bridge. "Gordon, take care of Deidra's part."

The woman looked at him in surprise, but gave a wordless nod.

"Strap in, my friends," Zim told them as he started the engines.

Xavier looked back at Gordon. "I need you to man that console!" He pointed to the chair right beside the pilot's seat.

"I wouldn't have the first —"

"I'll tell you what to do, just go!"

There was no more argument.

The ship moved forward by the slightest increments at first, like a car being backed up by a cautious driver.

In the screens, which now had the forward view prominent, Estard could see the soldiers backing up hurriedly. The man up on the catwalk with the bazooka was taking aim.

I really hope that doesn't blast us to bits. He couldn't help himself — he made the sign of the cross and prayed as he watched.

The soldiers spread out to either side of the man, who had the bazooka propped on a shoulder. He followed the ship down the sightline.

It was less than a second between seeing the rocket launched in a line of thick smoke, and the thump and crash as it hit the roof. The ship shook, but nothing fell, nothing broke. Nothing obvious.

In the forward screen, Zim was coming up on that lever at a crawl. It disappeared from view, and there was a soft thump underneath them. There was a look of intense concentration on the Pilot's face.

Estard almost held his breath. *This is what you wanted, isn't it?* he asked himself.

There was a groaning, more felt than heard. And then they could see light beginning to filter down on them.

"Hold this position!" Estard told the Pilot, and he obliged.

Once they moved, that roof would begin to close again. Also, with them sitting right on top of it, those soldiers would not be able to close it.

"Hold it until they're fully open," he said, "and then take off as quick as you can."

It wasn't long. Two minutes at the most. But it felt like hours as they all watched through the cameras. The soldiers forming up around the craft again. They didn't shoot at it, this time, or try to batter at the hatch. There was a sense of helplessness about them.

Those on the catwalk didn't make another shot with the bazooka. Some turned and ran back into the corridors of the complex at a gesture from Colonel Everette. *That old man is just as curious as me. He's just better at holding it in.*

The roof was halfway open.

As he watched, one side of the roof shuddered — and stopped. "No," he whispered. "No, no, no." He was holding onto the back of the pilots chair in a white knuckled grip. "They're cutting the hydraulics."

"We'll have to risk getting through as is," Xavier said.

"Will it fit?" From Gordon.

Zim was shaking his head. "What happened to Viatri?" he asked, though he sounded as if he were talking to himself.

"That end will stay as it is with the hydraulics cut," Estard said. "Unless they start pushing it back manually." *Which is probably exactly what they'll do next.*

"So, we do not have much time," Zim said.

"No, we do not," Estard agreed.

"Hold on tight," said the Pilot.

Estard let go of the pilots chair and grabbed at the harness on the left wall. This was going to be a very uncomfortable ride. His previous experience made him clench his teeth and hold tight. Like a frightened child, he wanted to close his eyes, but he forced them to stay open. To watch what was going on.

They backed up from the switch, their position evident by the way the roof first slowed, then stopped. Then there was a short whining sound, and they were moving through the air so fast, that between the G's of pressure and the shaking, Estard thought he was going to vomit.

Estard closed his eyes and held onto the straps for life. His feet wanted to sink through the deck, his head was trying to force its way down his neck into his stomach, and his stomach was trying to get to his feet. A roaring sound erupted around him...

And then there was no pressure. The hands gripping the harness seemed to want to float away of their own accord. His entire body felt weightless. *We made it,* he thought.

He opened his eyes.

The interior of the ship was dim, almost like only a single candle burned. The backwash of screen light was so muted, even the moon would have been brighter.

Xavier held onto his console with one hand, while the other danced over the screens.

"Well, Agent," Zim said, "let's see if you like this view." And suddenly the forward screen showed Earth. Half in daylight, the rest shrouded in twilight and night. Clouds moved and twirled in slow motion over oceans of deep muted blues. The continents, America and Europe, visible in spectrums from the white of northern glaciers, to the green of southern grasses, and so many shades of brown and yellow, he couldn't pick them all out. In the darkened section, he could see lights. Not many, but he knew, that would be where the cities were.

"The first time is to be awestruck," Gordon told him. "But it never gets any less beautiful, the more often you see it."

He believed that. "So, what now?" he asked.

"It's a one-two-three-go, system," Xavier explained. "I'm keying in the coordinates and trajectory, that shouldn't take too much longer."

"Where are we headed?" Estard asked.

"Back to the planet we came from," Xavier said.

From their reactions, you could have thought the man had slapped the other two in the face. Hard.

"You can't be serious!" Gordon protested.

"You have got to be kidding!" said Zim.

Xavier didn't look up from what he was doing. "Look, I don't know how much time Deidra had to do what before... before she disappeared. We can't stay stationary."

"But do we have to go *back*?" Gordon asked, while Zim muttered what sounded fervent prayers under his breath.

"Unless you want to end up lost, somewhere else, then yes," Xavier said.

The woman grunted and looked down at the controls before her. "So how does this work? One-two-three-go, you said."

"Three levers, left to right. Then one, six, eight, three, seven, zero on the keypad. It's not numbered. I don't know what they mean. But think of it as alphanumeric, and I am not sure how much it matters."

Gordon repeated the numbers back to him to make sure she had them right, when he assured her she did, she said, "Tell me when."

Estard had yet to take his eyes off the view of Earth.

"Break orbit," Xavier commanded.

The view of Earth slowly retreated, and the view screen turned to stars as Zim pulled them away from the tug of Earth.

Estard watched on, fascinated.

Xavier turned from his console. "Heading locked. Now."

Gordon mumbled to herself as she pulled each lever — one, two, three — and keyed in the sequence.

There was no sense of movement. No bright lights in the view screen. Nothing happened. He hadn't realised he'd spoken out loud, until Zim responded.

"*Au contraire, mon ami.* Just wait a moment, if you please."

And sure enough, within moments, a planet became larger and larger in the view screen. At first Estard thought it was Earth, and a triumphant thought, *I was right*! flittered through his mind. But as it grew large enough to see the shapes of continents, the size of the oceans.... He knew.

"Where are we?"

"Roughly five hundred light years from Earth," Gordon told him. She did not sound happy.

"And we're..." He sucked on his teeth.

"Going down there," Xavier finished for him.

"All well and good, *Capitan*, but where are we landing?" Zim asked. "The mountain, it is no good. The landing site... I am not fond of the idea of running into Greenway."

"We don't have a lot of choices," Xavier rubbed a hand over his jaw. "It'll have to be somewhere very close to the old camp site. We need to be where they can find us."

"Where who can find us?" Gordon wanted to know.

"Deidra, mainly," Xavier said, "but Harvey and Lance, Kristin and Weiz. Any of the others who got left behind last time."

The two pilots looked at him like he'd gone mad. "Dead people," Gordon said flatly. "You want us to wait for dead people."

Xavier shook his head. "Just take us down, Zim. Either I am right, and you'll all see soon enough, or I am wrong, and we'll have to work out the way back ourselves. Either way, we need to land."

Zim gave a faux salute, and they were on their way toward the planet.

The grainy, movie-like unreality that Estard had felt all day, became even more prominent as they descended through the atmosphere and weight returned. He decided then, with a most adamant will, that he *never* wanted to be on this ship again.

~

It was the sound that woke him. Leaves rustling, wind roaring, birds cawing. The wind brushed at his face with a cold finger, and spores picked up in the air made him want to sneeze. He didn't sit up, he wasn't ready for that, but he opened his eyes.

Above him, an almost clear blue sky. A face appeared, so haloed by the light, that at first, he could not make it out. But the voice...

"It's about time," Weiz told him.

Well, he thought with a smile, *this is death.*

Part
Four

~ The Price ~

CHAPTER EIGHT

Her eyes opened on a morning sky. Clear except for a few wispy white clouds. The sounds of leaves rustling in a slight breeze, birds chirping and insects buzzing, greeted her. The ground beneath her was dew wet, and grass tickled her thighs. It was then she realised she was naked.

"So, this is death," she thought aloud, puzzled.

"No," replied a gruff man's voice behind her, "it isn't."

Weiz rolled over, hastily getting to her knees. Unclothed, and unarmed, she was ready to defend.

In front of her stood an old man, clothed in faded red canvas robes, leaning on a walking stick. His hair was grey, and sparkling blue eyes peered out of a stern leathery face marred with fine lines.

They stared at each other. The silence grew. Many questions ran through her head, but she asked none. Her nakedness made her feel vulnerable, and she wished that she knew where her clothes went.

As if he had read her mind, the old man nodded to her left. "Get dressed," he said, and turned.

Weiz kept her eyes on the man, not moving. Her mind raced, searching for a way out. *Out of what? Hell? Heaven? Where am I? What happened?*

The old man seemed amused, as he said, "Just put on the clothes, and we'll talk when you're done."

She stretched out an arm and grabbed at the clothes without taking her eyes off him. They were heavy canvas, much like his own, though brown, and instead of robes, they were pants and shirt. No socks or shoes, no undergarments. She got dressed.

"You can turn around, now," she told him.

He took a step toward her, and she took a step back. He stopped. "This is silly," he muttered and shook his head.

"That, there, is close enough for my liking," Weiz said. It was only a few paces away. They could not touch one another, but they could hear each other without raising voices, and that was good enough for her.

The old man bowed his head, then sat cross-legged on the ground, the walking stick across his knees. He watched her and she watched him, though he seemed on the brink of amusement, while Weiz was wary.

How was she here? Where was here? If she wasn't dead, then what was she? She certainly *remembered* dying. It was not a sensation she cared to repeat. And who was he? Where had *he* come from, if not some dark corner of her mind? Was this a hallucination? Was she still dying, on the ship in the mountain? Had she yet to finish bleeding out? Some kind of neurochemical response giving her a false sense of reality before she petered off into real death?

A short laugh escaped the man, and she glared at him. His lips quivered with the struggle to contain his mirth.

"What's so funny, old man?" she asked.

He sighed heavily and shook his head. "What isn't, *young woman?*"

She growled at him, but he just laughed again. "What do you want?"

The old man looked as if he were struggling to find the exact right words. "Waking up the way you did is... disorienting, the first time."

"That answers nothing."

"No," he said, "I suppose not. And answering questions *is* — partially, at least — why I'm here."

"I'm not dead?"

"No."

"I'm not nearly dead."

"No."

"Hallucinating?" She was reaching, she could feel it. But the amusement that seemed a permanent fixture in the man's eyes subsided somewhat.

"No. Not hallucinating." He shook his head. "You're very much alive. Very much *here*. As am I."

"And where is here? And who are you?"

The old man got to his feet, using the walking stick for leverage, and used his chin to point behind her. "You'll know when you see it," he told her, and began off in that direction. When she made no move to follow, he looked back at her. "Do you want answers?" was all he said before moving off again.

Weiz followed, hesitant but determined. She wanted to know what in God's name was going on.

I was on the ship. An airman attacked me. Someone saved me... Heinrich. The memory of the moments just before was a little hazy, but she brought them to the surface, searching. *Heinrich tried to get me. Someone shot him in the head. Harvey came...* And that was where it ended. There was nothing after that, except waking up here.

They didn't go too far. The old man stopped on a rise, near the edge of a stream and pointed to a mountain.

"It's a mountain, old man." She shook her head. "I don't recognise it."

"Look closer. At the foot of it."

She was sceptical. If you didn't recognise a mountain, why would you the foot of it? But she looked — and gasped. At the foot of the mountain, that appeared to be growing, were *ships*. MM ships. She couldn't tell how many, but more than a few.

"What happened?" Weiz breathed.

"One of yours got it into his head there should be a slow growing mountain here." He looked around, into the sky, at the tree line, at her. "These answers are going to take some time; would you care to join me at my hut? It's not far."

Weiz gave a sharp nod. What could it hurt? *I'm not dead*, she thought with wonder. *This must be what Viatri felt like.*

The old man moved back down the rise and across the grassland to a thicket. He pushed through trees, that upon close inspection, had been carefully trimmed, so as they moved inward, the small path widened, and a hut came into view.

It was small, from the outside. Perhaps two rooms, or three if there were a cellar. Made of wood with mud to fill the cracks and thatching for the roof. There were two windows, one in front and one on the side, both shuttered and without glass. It looked better than the ones she'd seen in the village. But not by much.

"We'll sit inside," the old man said, and opened the door for her. He indicated that she should go in first. She shook her head, he shrugged, and moved inside.

The space he ushered her into was sparsely furnished. Four wooden chairs around a small wooden table, upon which sat an empty wooden vase. There was a shelf against the wall, which held wooden crockery, and a few finely carved ornaments. At the far end, under another window that could not be seen from the front, was a bench, the centre of which held a metal tub.

The old man opened the shutter closest to the table, and daylight warmed up the space. He pulled a chair out for her, facing the door, and took his own on the other side.

"I can't keep thinking of you as *old man*," Weiz said as she took the proffered chair.

A broad smile stretched across his lips, and his eyes twinkled. "My name is Galsin."

"Just Galsin?"

"Just Galsin. And you?"

"Catherine Weiz. But I thought you knew already."

Galsin shook his head. "I don't know everything. I don't see everything. That was always the province of the Bearer of Knowledge."

"You make very little sense to me, old man," Weiz still felt wary, but a part of her was beginning to relax. She wasn't sure if she should let it.

"And so quickly we're back to that." Galsin put a hand to his heart, a smile in his eyes. "You wound me, so."

"Sure I do, grandpa, sure I do."

He laughed, short and sharp, but full of warmth. "She chose right with you, I think. You are embattled inside, but you will find your way clear of that, in time."

Weiz was tired. Weeks of helping Deidra put that ship together, ready to go home. The goal. Get home, get everyone home. And the weeks before that, spent trying to make sure no one else died after the Day of the Giants. Keep their spirits up, move them forward. *But that wasn't me,* she thought, *Kristin was right about that. It was Harvey and her. I haven't been in charge of anything since we landed on this damned planet.* That filled her with conflict, in who she was, and who she thought she should be.

"Don't get all melancholy on me," Galsin said, not unkindly.

"Who are you?" Her defences were suddenly up. She looked at

him with sharp, considering eyes.

His eyes looked inward, his mouth a sad smile. "I believe you would think of me as..." he hesitated briefly, "as, a Giant."

She was on her feet, the chair falling behind her, before she knew what she was doing. Her eyes never left the old man, and he didn't make a move. But the Giants... "You killed more than three quarters of my men," she said, her voice cold.

He shook his head. "Not me."

But she didn't hear him. She was back in that night when they'd first come. Watching that Captain be torn apart and thrown back at them.

"You took them, and you killed them." Her voice trembled with rage. "They were helpless against you, and you knew it. And you killed them."

Still, the old man didn't move.

"We were waiting for the scientists. One day, two at most, and then we were leaving. We never meant to come here! And you killed them!" She picked up the empty wooden vase and threw it at Galsin, who caught it one handed.

"Again," the old man said softly, "not me."

Her entire body was trembling. She felt light-headed. Rage suffused her and the images that flashed through her mind of tearing this man's head right from his shoulders.... *I am not like this*, a part of her said, *I don't give in to anger. Not like this. I am not a murderer.* That image in her head served to bring her back to herself.

I don't know who I am any more. Harvey...and that thought triggered a deeper sense of loss. She was never going to see him again. They'd left, she knew it. The ship was moving before...

"How did I get here?" That had not occurred to her before. "If I am not dead, should I not have risen where I fell?"

"You're welcome to sit back down, if you've expended your shock," Galsin said.

"Answer. You said that's what you were here for."

"True."

"So, tell me!" A piece of that rage still lingered, and she tried to force it down. To push it away from her like a poison viper.

"Will you sit?"

Obstinate old man, she thought. But she picked up the chair, and slamming it on its feet, sat down.

He gave a nod. "I have many answers, not all of them," he said. "You awoke in the field, because that is where we all awake. Beyond that, I cannot say."

"All?" Weiz arched an eyebrow, her clam returning in small dribbles. "How many of you are there?"

"Including your six? Thirteen." He shifted uncomfortably in his chair. "I suppose you'll want to know why what happened... happened."

"You'd guess right," she said.

"Very long ago, now. Many thousands of years, though I cannot recall exactly how many, there was a great civilisation here." Weiz nodded, it was clear from the cavernous city, though she kept that to herself and allowed him to continue. "We stretched the bounds of science, as far as we could. We searched the stars, we built great cities, great monuments, and we thought of ourselves as advanced in our knowledge." He gave a bark of a laugh. "Ego. Hubris. Men at the height of arrogance."

"What does that have to do with the Giants?"

"I'm getting to that."

"Get there faster."

The look he gave her was ice, but he went on. "There was an accident, of a kind. Though I couldn't tell you what exactly, as I just happened to be there, with no involvement. A bystander, caught up in the crossfire, as it were. We all were. Before all this..." His hand moved in a gesture that indicated everything, and nothing.

"Whoever it was, who did what they did, they perished, while we, those few close enough to suffer effect, and not devastation, ended as we are."

"I am not sure I follow you," Weiz admitted.

The corner of his mouth quirked up in a smile. "We began to think of ourselves as the Guardians. We had great powers, never before dreamed. We could do things no man had ever done before. Move mountains with a thought, travel between worlds in an instant. Create whatever we wished, or even see the future. You see where I am going with this?" He did not exactly wait for her nod. "But one effect, a drawback, if you will, was immortality."

"Drawback?"

He nodded as if he understood where she was coming from. "You wouldn't think so, would you? For the first few hundred years, neither did we. But things do get tedious, after some time. We watched the ones we love wither and die. We saw the decline of our civilisation, into a backwards people who have no idea where they came from. The great heights from which they had plummeted. We saw oceans rise, and mountains sink, and our cities turn to dust." He glanced around him as if seeing things the way they had once been.

"I don't see where this is all going, old man." Weiz folded her arms on the table and leaned toward him.

"Background," he told her. "Details. The *reason* you are now what you are."

Weiz pressed her lips firmly together as she thought furiously. None of this made any sense. "Why now? Why us?"

Galsin looked about himself, obviously trying to order his thoughts. "It took us a very long time to work out *how*," he said. "*How* could we die? Wounds healed. Death... well death wasn't permanent. Same as you, sure as the sun comes up, we'd find ourselves in that spot, waking sometimes moments, sometimes days, later." He scratched at his beard, eyes looking into the distance.

"When we saw you descend from the sky…"

"Yes…" She rolled her hand in a gesture to continue.

He shrugged. "We thought to ourselves, here are some that would *know*. A people, very apparently human — a thing you'll have to explain to me, as I don't see how *that* could be — who knew the stars. Who travelled through space. People who could *understand* science. At the very least, you would be on par with our own understanding of the universe, at best, you'd know more."

"That knowledge was important to you?"

"To some extent." He cocked his head to the side as though acknowledging some flaw in the train of thought. "We would have tried with some of the natives, but we were afraid it would just breed into some kind of superstitious nonsense about Gods. Something we've well tried to stay away from."

"At least some of these natives knew who Greenway was supposed to be," Weiz told him flatly. "Dassun, they called him. And they were ready to worship him as a God, as he believes himself to be."

"Some perhaps, but not all. And not in the way he thinks."

"Cryptic."

"That one in itself is a longer story than the first. I thought you'd prefer I finished this one."

"Yes, do. Explain to me why your *compatriots* felt it necessary to decimate my airmen!" The rage threatened to engulf her again.

He shrugged. "I cannot say. I certainly do not agree with what they did. But some of them grew quite cold toward the end there. Whatever humanity was left in them…" He shook his head. "Some men lose their minds; I am afraid we are no less susceptible."

"And the shadow forms? Why were they dark Shadow Giants, but you're just a man?"

"Hmph!" He shook his head and muttered something inaudible, before saying, "We can all do that. You lot, too, obviously. You'll find there are many things we can *all* do, while very few things are ours alone."

"So, you're all just men inside?"

"More-or-less. And women, too."

Weiz found herself chuckling, deep in her throat and almost silent. She shook her head. "I'm stuck here because of a bunch of madmen who should have died thousands of years ago?" It was enough to beggar belief.

"Not just you," Galsin said sadly.

"Well, Greenway, I suppose. But he *wanted* to stay."

"The others will be here, soon enough."

Weiz shook her head. "No. No, they got out. They went home." *Home. Harvey.*

"They'll be back."

"How can you be so sure?" Weiz was trying hard not to let the anger grow inside her. It was difficult.

"They are, like yourself, and the others, attached to this world now. They cannot abide outside the six worlds for much longer than a few days. And if there is a way to alter that, I do not know it. Anselin, the Traveller, he only ever managed these six, no matter how he tried. And believe me, he *tried*."

Weiz thought that must have been the one to give his power to Harvey. *Harvey, my love.* "*Six* worlds?"

Galsin nodded. "Yes. Six. Though this is the only inhabited one, so far as I know. Though I am certain Anselin did take some extremely unruly types off to at least one of those worlds. He never did say what he'd done with them. We can't all Travel that way, you see. So, no one but he would know what's become of those other worlds."

Weiz leaned back, closed her eyes and breathed deep. This was all too much. It wasn't a gift. None of this had been a gift. They weren't God's, like Greenway thought. They weren't superhuman.

They were trapped. They were prisoners. *And the only way out is to die.*

That thought brought her up short, and she leaned forward once more. "If you can't die, as you say, and you awake where I awoke, then how is it I am here, and not they? We *killed* them. It was hard, it was disastrous, but we did it."

"Well.... You did and you didn't."

"Explain. A month after, one of our own was killed. The powers passed on, but she was definitely dead."

"The Bearer of Knowledge?"

"I suppose you'd have called her that."

"It would have been easy for her. She'd have known *how*. Though it took the original one a *very* long time to work it out, that knowledge would have been passed on directly."

The old man got up and moved to gaze out the window. He didn't look back at her as he spoke. Somehow, she knew, he was far away in his mind, in different days.

"It is the passing, you see. All that you have become, needs to be passed on. It cannot exist in a vacuum and will not allow itself to die. It requires a host. In some ways, you are now two beings, and the one will keep you alive as long as necessary to fulfil the function required. At the very moment of death, to the mortal body, you must consciously accede that the victor should inherit *It*."

"But the one who killed her didn't get the power."

He turned, then. Bright eyes round in surprise. "No?"

"Heinrich killed her. Deidra got the power."

Galsin shook his head. "And now I am the one.... Turn and turn about." There was a smile on his face.

"What are you so happy about?"

"You changed the rules." He clapped his hands and gave a small laugh. "I'll have to tell the others."

Weiz wasn't sure she liked the idea of that. "We won't be seeing any more Giants, will we?"

Galsin blinked at her. "What? No. No, no, I should think not." He paced all the way around the room as if searching. But his eyes were looking inward.

Sitting back in her chair, Weiz kept a cautious eye on him. She wasn't dead, she was grateful for that. But she was *here*. And that she could have done without.

The old man stopped in front of her. He chewed on his bottom lip a moment, and mumbled something she did not understand. Just as she was about to ask, he said, "I wasn't supposed to talk to you."

She raised her brows. "You weren't?"

He shook his head and looked away. "No."

"So why did you?"

"I couldn't just leave you there."

Galsin now seemed full of spring-loaded energy, and the way he moved showed the walking stick to be no more than a prop.

Weiz got up and moved outside. She'd had quite enough of the indoors when they'd been working in the mountain. She looked up at the sky, breathed in the fresh air, and sat down with her back against the uneven slats of the small hut.

Greenway was right. The thought was bitter, and she wanted to shake her head in denial. *That doesn't make him any less insane. It doesn't excuse what he did.*

Yesterday, she had died. Today, she learned she was trapped. And even so, it was still the most relaxing day she'd had since she left Earth ten months ago. There were no orders to give. No airmen in whose presence she would need to maintain an aloofness. She was no longer a Commander in the ATF AF. That was a new, and scary thought.

How long she sat there, at the front of the hut, she could not have said, but the sun was just a hazy smudge on the horizon when the old man came shuffling out.

"You and your friends are welcome to stay here," he said, looking up into the twilight sky.

"My friends." Why did that sound strange to her?

Galsin reached over and gave her shoulder a pat. "They won't be long in coming. You remember that field. Not far."

Weiz nodded. "I remember."

"There are more clothes in the back room, take some when you go."

"Why did you come to me?"

"I didn't want you floundering about, like we did. Lost for centuries. For eons!" He shook his head and leaned forward with both hands on the head of the walking stick. "I didn't want you to keep trying to leave. It would only hurt more people. And believe it or not, we do care."

"You're going now," she said, surprised at the sadness she felt about that.

"I must see the others," he told her. "In time, I shall return." He turned to leave.

"How can you be so sure, old man?" she asked. "How do you know they will come to that field?"

He looked back at her with pity in his eyes. "When they come, you'll understand."

Galsin left, walking slowly through the trees until he was out of sight. He gave her no farewell, and she asked no more questions. She just watched him go.

When the darkness came, she made a small ball of light and stared into it as she would have a fire. Searching inward for answers.

~

The next morning, and every morning after, Weiz went to the field and waited. Sometimes she walked around the perimeter, sometimes she paced. Occasionally, she sat.

A part of her wanted Harvey to show up. To take her in his arms and reassure her everything would be okay. Another part hoped he never would. That he had somehow found a way out. That the old man had been wrong, or that Harvey had somehow broken the rules.

On the fifth day, as she paced, she wondered if old man Galsin had just been an hallucination. A way to safeguard her mind against the realities of death. She argued with herself for most of the day, no longer certain that she wasn't dead.

It wasn't until the eighth day that a body appeared in the field. Dressed in navy blue cotton shirt, denim jeans and wearing hard soled velveteen slippers. Weiz ran over to it and looked down into the face of Kristin.

Shit, she thought.

The Comms Officer's eyes opened and blinked a few times. Then they settled on Weiz. She didn't get up, or even try to move. She just stared.

Before Weiz could tell her what was going on, Kristin said, "Yup. Must be hell."

CHAPTER NINE

Once the scene had changed around him, Greenway knew he'd lost. He didn't know where he was exactly, though he assumed somewhere close to the village given Harvey's parting words. But he wasn't ready to go there. Not yet.

How was he going to explain to them that he'd been defeated? That, hard as he had tried, he could not keep their Gods from leaving this world? Leaders didn't *explain*, but failures always diminished a leader in the eyes of his followers. He couldn't allow that.

He wandered through the woods.

"They tested us," he said to the air in front of him. "They tested us, and we were the ones who were worthy. We were meant to rule this world because we defeated them!" He imagined it was Harvey he was speaking to.

"We have to stay! We have to! Gods don't abandon their people!"

Gods don't kill their people. That small voice inside him was new. He stopped in his tracks, tried to listen for it, but it said no more. He moved on.

Greenway didn't know how long he'd been walking for when he came upon it. That jutting building top they'd spent the night in little more than a month ago. Had it truly only been that long?

"Fitting," he said.

It was almost night. He gathered firewood and crawled in through the entrance. He would stay here a while.

The fire lit, he sat with his back against the smooth wall and stared into the flames. He was alone now. Truly alone. He could have no peers among those who inhabited this world, for he was a God. And the other Gods had left. Abandoned them.

You handled this badly, the voice told him. He sat silently and waited for more. It didn't come.

"What was I supposed to do? Just let them go home? Just let them runaway?" He poked a stick at the fire.

The fire went out. The sun rose and cast dappled shadows a few feet inside the entrance. The light and shadows retreated, and darkness grew outside. And still, Greenway sat, occasionally poking at the ash and charcoal as if the fire were still lit.

He had loved life, once. He had believed in God almighty and Heaven above. He had believed in purgatory, and Hell. In Angels and Saints, in demons and Devils. Even as he'd lain here, that night with the others, before the fight with the Giants. He had believed.

There was nothing for him on Earth. He'd been searching for death long before they'd come here. But the others...

You were too harsh on them. That voice again.

"Be silent!" he yelled into the tunnel.

Wind funnelled into the small chamber and stirred the ashes, then left. Darkness outside. And still he sat.

He planned, and he plotted. He argued with himself, and he pleaded with himself. The voice didn't come again. It was all just him now.

Sometimes he stood and paced around the small space, and

sometimes he sat, staring at nothing. But he didn't leave. He didn't make another fire. He didn't go hunting for food. He was a God; he didn't need such things. Or sleep. Or any other human need.

Greenway didn't know how many days he'd stayed in there, only that it was close to midday when he finally emerged. He blinked up at the bright sky through the canopy of trees and sighed.

He would need to do this sooner or later. And sooner was better.

The path he chose was the one they'd followed on the Day of the Giants. When Kristin had led them back toward the camp, and then across to the village. He would be there by nightfall.

It was uneventful, and lonely. A resonance of his life before the change. The possibility that he was insane crossed his mind from time to time, but he always dismissed it.

When he came out of the woods onto the muddy field, farmers stopped in their work to look up at him. They didn't acknowledge his presence with more than that. They didn't put down their tools to come and greet him. They just looked at him for a moment, then went back to work.

He walked through the field to the other side and made his way down the dirt road to the village.

Women were kneading dough at communal tables. Some made salads, and yet others stood over boiling cauldrons of soup or stew. Children ran along the street, between huts and houses, and on the small grassy area just the other side of the village. They laughed, they played, and they fought, pulled apart by patient parents when they got too rough.

Eyes followed him, some from beneath drawn brows, others curious. None spoke to him.

He stopped when he was in front of the Temple, where he could see foundations, but nought more. No one was working on it, and only one man stood nearby at the village well. It was Fell, and the man was staring.

"Is Cardinal not back yet?" he asked the man.

"We heard," said the Garas, "what you did."

Greenway studied the man. He was not one of his followers, but he had allowed that. The man was usually courteous, if only by a hair.

"How?" was all he asked.

"Sometimes, the birds come." He motioned toward the other end of the village.

How long had he been gone? At least two weeks to get to the mountain, after a week in Djorik. Of that much, he was sure. Not sleeping did strange things to one's sense of time.

"And?"

The old man shook his head. "You are not Dassun."

"No. I am Greenway."

"They worship you no more." He brushed his hands against one another in the universal gesture of finality.

His rage boiled. How dare they defy him! How *dare* they! His mouth twisted in a snarl, and his jaws bunched, teeth clenched.

"My Temple is not finished," he breathed.

"And it will not be."

"You defy me?"

"I always have." The old man moved toward him, looking him directly in the eye. He stopped so close, Greenway could feel the man's breath on his neck. "Go back from whence you came."

Before he knew what he was doing, his hands moved to either side of the Garas' head, and with a savage twist, he snapped his neck.

He breathed heavily, looking down on the man who fell at his feet. *Ha, Fell fell. Ha ha.* But he didn't laugh. What humour he had was trapped inside his mind.

A mournful scream broke through his thoughts, and he looked back toward the village. A girl was running out to them, her eyes on the dead Garas. She fell to her knees beside him, and gently held his head in her hands. She spared not a glance for Greenway.

Other footsteps now. More villagers making their way over. Some intent on the woman who cried over the old man, others looking directly at him. He watched them and didn't move.

One young woman glared at him with golden-brown eyes, from the back of the gathering crowd. Her hand came up and shot forward. It wasn't until it hit him, bouncing harmlessly off his chest, that Greenway realised she'd thrown a knife. The woman had tried to kill him.

His calm snapped.

He brought his hands up, and with that gesture gouts of dirt and rock erupted. The land sang to him, a Gregorian chant complimented by the shouts and screams of the people who ran.

Spikes of brittle ore shot up from the ground to impale. Rocks and dirt grazed and scraped. The fleeing villagers took shelter where they could; some in huts, others in cellars and still yet some made for the woods. They were no longer men and women and children in his eyes. They were the enemy. And the enemy needed to die.

The one who had tried to kill him stared on, unmoving. Accepting. Greenway picked the knife off the ground, and with a lazy underhand, threw it at her. She moved slightly to the side and the blade overshot, grazing her neck as it passed. Greenway gestured to the ground beneath her feet, and a spear of hard earth shot up, impaling her.

Huts and houses collapsed. The foundations for his temple sank. The ground heaved and shook. Still the roar filled his ears.

"I will not be denied!" he shouted.

They do not deserve this, that voice again. That damned voice.

"Who are you?" he screamed at it. "What do you want from me?"

He spread his hands wide, and the ground began to open down the centre of the small village. He raised his arms above his head, and the land to either side tilted. The screams grew to crescendo, the chant of the land rising in pitch with them.

Even as he knew it wouldn't, the voice didn't come again.

Collapsed buildings slid into the chasm. Men and women, moaning and weeping went with them. And soon there was silence.

He let his arms fall to his sides, breathing deep. He cut one hand across the air, and the land levelled out, the chasm closed.

Where once the village stood, now only small remnants remained. A table here, a chair there. The broken remains of a cellar, and part of a sturdy house. Food and tools, trinkets and clothes, littered the space, and to Greenway it looked like nothing so much as the day after a fair.

His calm returned.

The only visible people were the woman on her spike, and the old man at his feet... and the woman holding his head. She had not moved.

She was silent as he looked down on her. Her tears fell in slow drops to the man's face, each a splash that broke apart and ran through the Garas' open eyes, then down his cheeks. Like she was crying for both of them.

Greenway backed away. The woman never looked up.

The image burned itself into his mind. Even as he walked away, he knew he would never forget it. It didn't touch him as it should. And a part of him knew that was wrong. But that was not on the surface of his thoughts. It was deep, deep down inside.

As he surveyed the area, the thought that he had gone too far crossed his mind. But he shrugged it off. *Done is done.*

Djorik would be next.

CHAPTER TEN

It wasn't where she'd found herself, or even the people who surrounded her, that got her attention at first. It was the *memories*. The sweet, heart wrenching, beautiful and haunting *memories*.

When Deidra opened her eyes on a clear sky, to the dim sounds of others talking, she knew who she was. She remembered. She could *feel*.

Deidra sat up, her heart pounding. She wondered how she'd gotten here, but as soon as she did, the answer was there in her mind. She shook her head. So that wasn't gone.

Harvey, Kristin and Lance stood with Weiz a few feet away, speaking softly. They turned to look at her when she coughed.

"Don't worry," she said, "I know I'm not dead."

There appeared to be a simultaneous letting go of breath, and Weiz smiled at her.

"I feel changed by that experience," she told them, levering herself to her feet. She was pleased to note she was still in her prison blues. It would take a while for them to become grimy and smelly, and all round uncomfortable. That hadn't bothered her before...

"I think we all do," said Harvey, holding out a hand to her. "I don't feel like I am bleeding to death any more. That's for sure." His smile lit up his hazel eyes.

She took his hand and squeezed it, then let it drop. "I know who I am," she said. She couldn't keep the giddy delight from her face. "I *remember*!"

It took a moment for the others to understand what she meant, but when they did, there were smiles all round. Weiz, usually quite reserved, threw her arms around the woman in an embrace.

"I am so happy for you," she whispered in her ear.

Deidra gave her an awkward pat on the back, and the woman stepped away. There were tears in her eyes, though they didn't fall.

She remembered everything. Remembered not being able to remember. She remembered her mother, and Dane, and the studio apartment she'd rented on Concord Avenue in Belmont when she'd attended Harvard. The taste of pizza, leftover lasagne, whiskey and beer! How she missed beer. She remembered picnics at Galveston Pier, and lectures at MIT. She remembered it all.

She remembered her sister's funeral. She'd died when Deidra was four, and she'd been two. She didn't know why. It was the one truth her parents had always kept from her. She remembered her first heartbreak, in high school, to a boy named Lester Rodrigez. And, more recently, the deaths of all those she knew from Io Research Station. *Alex.*

All of this flooded her in moments. Like a tidal wave of thought and emotion. Images and smells, and the complex minutiae that made any experience uniquely one's own.

"Are you alright?" Kristin asked.

Lance took a step forward. "We got you. You know that."

Deidra was staring at them all wide eyed, but not seeing them. Not really.

There was a certain elastic shock that came over her, as the memories crashed home. The elation of happy moments, the frustration of unattained goals, the devastating grief caused by the loss of people held dear. All the conflicts of her life, distilled and thrust into her at lightning speed.

Her ebon features turned grey and sweat beaded on her forehead. She fell onto her knees and put her hands on the ground.

Weiz and Lance were at her side in an instant.

"I'm alright," she said.

"You don't look alright," said Weiz.

"Just too much at once," she told them.

Deidra let them help her to her feet, and slowly the nausea and dizziness faded.

Before she could fully absorb it all, Harvey asked, "Did you have enough time?"

It took her a moment to understand what he was asking. Then she remembered the hangar. The ship, and the airmen getting on board.

She shook her head. "I'm not sure."

"We'll find out if they turn up," Lance said.

Kristin raised her head in confusion. "Why would they come here? They're home, even if it is the wrong time."

"They have to," said Deidra.

Weiz and Lance nodded as if they had expected no less, but Harvey and Kristin just looked sad.

"Come," Weiz said. "I didn't expect you all to turn up on the same day, hot on one another's heels. Come."

The Commander led them all to a small hut in the middle of a thicket. The inside was almost as bare of adornment as Io Station had been, but it had more charm. Weiz had them seated at a table and brought them all water in wooden cups, before she leaned up against the wall next to an open window.

"We're going to have to do something about Greenway," she said.

"He was right," Harvey said.

"He was right," Lance agreed.

Kristin sighed. "Just because we're stuck here doesn't make him right."

They all looked to her. She blinked at them in surprise. She might have been one of them in essence, but they'd never looked to her for an opinion regarding non-scientific matters before.

Deidra cleared her throat. "He doesn't know we're stuck," she said. "He may be right in the sense that we have to stay, but not for the reasons he has given. He isn't right. Probably isn't even sane. Power does strange things to some people."

Weiz nodded. "In that we're agreed."

"So, what do you propose?" Harvey asked.

When Weiz looked at him, her face softened. "I have no proposal — I'm making it all up as I go along. I told you all at the field about the old man."

Deidra shook her head. It was news to her.

The others nodded, thoughtful.

"So where is he?" Lance asked.

"I don't know," Weiz replied, "I've been waiting here for you lot to arrive."

"Who are we talking about?" From Kristin. "Greenway or the old man?"

"Greenway." The Pilot got up and began to pace the length of the table. "Not too fond of that guy."

"I don't imagine too many people are." Noting that Lance had given up his seat, Weiz took it and moved in close to Harvey. He placed a hand on her thigh, and she gripped that hand with her own.

Kristin didn't look at them. "What do you want to do about him, Commander?"

"The old man said there are six worlds," she told them all, "and it seems they're not inhabited. My suggestion is that Harvey should stick him on one of those and leave him there. He'll probably do a lot of damage, but he won't be able to hurt anyone but himself."

"The downside of that," Lance muttered, "is if he isn't already insane, he will be. Assuming we have any way to verify that wherever you dump him truly is uninhabited."

They all took silent pause at that observation. Did they have the right to condemn him so?

"Now that we're here, just how he wanted, do we even need to do anything?" Kristin asked.

Deidra felt out of her depth in this conversation. Tactics, fighting, military matters of any kind, were all out of her self-perceived purview. Science, and she was there. *Whatever is best for the most amount of people,* she thought, *is what you should do.* But she'd always found that to be a bit of a grey area. What if the split was fairly even, say fifty-one, forty-nine? Or if one group had a hundred, and the other had a thousand, only that group of one thousand was full of rapists and murderers? Can one life be more important than another?

Hypotheticals. One baby or ten adults?

"Six worlds," she whispered to herself. Now that it had been mentioned, and the curiosity had taken over, Deidra didn't need Weiz to explain. She knew.

"Harvey, take Kristin" — the woman stumbled over the name, but continued as if she hadn't — "and scout out where he might be. You were the last one to see him, so you should have a rough idea."

Harvey nodded and looked to Kristin. The Australian Comms Officer looked at him with undisguised annoyance but sighed and nodded. Weiz seemed to note the tension between them, and a thin smile graced her lips.

Harvey shot up. "Lance, give me your boots."

Lance stopped his pacing, "You had your chance to get your

own," he said.

The Captain shrugged. "They were too small." He made a "gimme" motion with his fingers, hand palm up. His face brooked no nonsense.

Lance muttered to himself in Italian, but he dropped himself to the floorboards and removed them.

Kristin looked down at her own feet. "I'll need to find some too," she said.

"I'll shift us back to the old camp site first, see if there's something there."

Lance threw the first boot at him and began on the other. "Couldn't have done that for yourself? These are comfortable."

Harvey sighed as he sat. "I'll give them back," he said as if placating a child.

Weiz shook her head. "Just get it done and report back."

It took only moments for Harvey to be ready. He and Kristin stepped out the front and disappeared. Lance watched after them and didn't turn his head back until Weiz cleared her throat.

"You got something for me to do, Commander?" he asked.

"Not yet."

He got up and returned to the table, sitting next Deidra. He glanced at her but didn't stare. She liked Viatri. He was a good man, if difficult at times.

The silence became awkward. Deidra drummed her nails on the table. Weiz went outside.

A small breeze filtered in through the open door.

"So..."

Deidra jumped. "Sorry," she said, "forgot you were here."

Lance smiled. "I can go." He made to get up, but she put a hand on his shoulder.

"Stay." He nodded and remained where he was. "You were going to say something?"

"Are you still...one of us?"

"It's still there," she said, "all jumbled and distorted. But I am me, too. More me than even that first day after Fields..." She left it there. He knew what had happened.

"So, you still know things?"

Deidra nodded. "I do. Is there something in particular?"

Lance got up then, looked down at his feet, grimaced, and started pacing. After a few moments, he stopped, looking down on her. There was struggle evident on his face.

She waited.

"Are we...? I mean, do we have to — stay, I guess. Do we have to stay? Is there no way around it? Anything we can do?"

His brown eyes stayed on her own. There was a plea in them. In his voice, in his stance. Like a child who'd discovered Santa wasn't real asking his mother to tell him there was some kind of mistake.

Deidra's heart went out to him. She hadn't gotten to that question herself. Hadn't wanted to think too hard on it. A part of her was afraid of losing herself again. It was that part that understood the question.

"I don't know," she told him.

Lance nodded slowly and his eyes dropped. "Right."

"I can try. I can't promise." She motioned to the chair. "Sit back down."

Lance shuffled over and sat. "There's not a lot for me to go back to," he said. "But home is home, you know?"

She did know. And for her, she had plenty to go back to. Dane would have been the first to know something had happened to her when the Docker got to Io. If Io was even there. It was likely they were presumed dead.

"If there's no way back, Viatri, it won't be for a lack of trying."

He nodded and kicked his heels up on the table, leaned the chair back and stared at the ceiling.

Deidra quirked a smile. The memories of 1957 were dim, a dark shadow on her mind, but she remembered him sitting that exact way, always.

Lance was a pilot without a ship. Weiz a Commander without a Fleet. Deidra a scientist without a lab. But Harvey had his crew. They had to hope it would be enough to pull them through.

~

They were at the foot of the new mountain.

"It's grown," Kristin said.

Harvey grunted. It was *still* growing. Very slowly but growing.

He let go of her arm and moved toward the piled ships. This was going to be a dangerous task. On extremely unstable ground, those ships could tip, or slide, or fall. They could be crushed. Even if he was stronger than the average man, and though death meant waking up in that field, he didn't relish the thought.

"We should probably leave it." Kristin was standing, fists on hips, looking over the debris.

Harvey turned to her. "You'll be right with your slippers, then?"

A fist lashed out to strike him in the arm, but he caught it, and shook his head. He let it go.

"You really are a violent bitch, you know."

"Yes," she agreed.

"Honestly, though. You want to hike through the woods in those?"

"We can't go up there," she said.

"No. But there is somewhere we can get boots."

Kristin eyed him a moment. "The graveyard?"

Harvey nodded. "It's the only place I can think of. Even if we knew this world, I don't think they have a convenient boot store."

"Ha," she breathed in a mock laugh. "Such a funny man you are."

For a moment he thought she'd try to hit him again, but she

made no move. He took her arm and shifted them to the other side of the mountain.

The base was almost at the outer edge of the graveyard, now. While the mountain grew tall it was still slim. They were at Fields's grave, still marked by the stone Greenway had made. Most of the others remained unmarked.

"It feels like years, and it feels like moments, since we were last here," he said.

"I know what you mean."

"Well, get it done. We don't want to be standing around here the rest of the day."

"Yes, sir!" She gave him a lazy salute and walked over to the foot of the mountain. When she came back, she was carrying two pieces of scrap metal. She tossed one at him.

"Really?" he asked.

"I don't really relish the idea of stealing boots off a corpse," she said. "And I definitely don't want to spend the better part of a day digging to get to them."

He shook his head. He was still being irrational with her. He knew it. She knew it. But he just couldn't help himself. Weiz was *alive*. *He* was alive. They had their chance to continue on, like a fairy-tale. All the difficulties, all the mistrust and frustration, didn't mean anything to him any more.

You know what you have to do, he told himself. *Just do it. Don't overanalyse. Just do it.*

They were almost finished. He could see the faded blue of Fields's coveralls through the dirt, and they were using their hands now.

Kristin located a boot and made quick work. He watched her pull them from the corpse and clean the insides with a torn piece of coverall.

"I'm sorry," he said. She looked up at him but continued with the boots. She was almost done. "I'm sorry."

She sighed and pulled herself up to the edge of the grave. "We're filling it back in," she said.

Harvey got out of the way. "Are you just going to ignore me?"

Kristin shook her head. She was already pushing the dirt back into the grave. He picked up his scrap metal piece and gave her a hand.

"Not ignoring you," she said. "How do I respond to that?" She heaved and the better part of the dirt pile fell into the hole. "You've been an arse. But I don't know what you're apologising for. Do I dismiss it? Say, you know, no worries, mate? All's good?"

"That —" He took a step toward her as she moved away.

"No!" She held up her hand. "I get to finish."

Harvey stopped and nodded. This was the reason he avoided apologising. To women, anyway.

"You've been an arse. But I get it. She died." She gave her head a tiny shake. "And now she's not dead. You get to start over. You get something nobody on Earth ever would. Congratulations. But you're not apologising for any of that."

"I'm not?" Harvey was now very confused.

"No, you're not. And if it is, it's the wrong thing."

"So, what should I be apologising for?"

"I won't answer that for you," she said with a sigh. "You'll need to work that out on your own, or it won't mean anything."

This woman was always chipping at him. Always confusing him. She both soothed and angered him. But this time, he didn't know what to think. Or feel.

"Come, then," he said, more roughly than he'd intended. "Let's go find Greenway."

She came forward, he took her by the arm, and they shifted.

CHAPTER ELEVEN

The air was thin and yet humid. The grass was thick and luscious, the sky blue and clear. There were trees off in the distance, scattered in thickets. It was not what Estard had expected an alien planet to look like. He could have been standing somewhere on Earth for all the difference he saw. Which was none.

He walked around the outside of the ship, feeling the hull with fingertips. He sucked at his teeth.

They'd landed a few hours back and Estard had been first through the hatch, eager to be out. He'd made it to the rear of the ship before he threw his guts up, but though some of the airmen had seen him, they didn't laugh as he'd expected.

Nothing was as he'd expected.

What did *you expect?* he asked himself. He didn't know. But it wasn't this.

Xavier said they were about a day's hike from the original camp. They'd have to pass through some woods, but it was an otherwise straight shot west. They'd stay here the night and start in the morning.

Estard felt at his coat pocket and pulled out his crushed pack of smokes. Only two left. He sucked at his teeth and put them back.

Despite his conviction earlier, he began to have doubts. It was his idea to come. He'd made it a condition. But why? Why did he want to be here? He couldn't help but feel he'd made a mistake. And it wasn't one he could fix.

Xavier rounded the nose of the ship and looked him up and down. Estard sat where he was and motioned for the man to join him. They stared at a pink and yellow horizon below the setting sun.

"Regrets?" said Xavier.

Estard choked back a laugh. "Some," he admitted.

"Why did you come?"

"I thought you were going to the future," he said.

"We did," Xavier said, "we have. Just not where we would have liked. But we'll fix that. When we find Deidra. Or she finds us."

"You're incredibly casual about it."

"There are three things I keep in my head, at all times," the Navigator told him, and held up a single finger for each as he listed them. "It is what it is, what it is. C'est la vie. And que sera sera."

Estard shot a laugh. "How sanguine."

Xavier shrugged. "I wouldn't go that far. But I suppose it's all a matter of perspective."

"What can I do for you, Xavier?"

"You can tell my why you came."

Estard shook his head. "I don't know," he said. "There were so many reasons in my head, when I decided to help you out. But now we're here.... I just don't know."

Xavier nodded as if he expected no less. "You'll work it out in your own time." He got up and brushed down his jeans. "Sleep when you can, we'll start early." He tipped an invisible hat and started back around the ship.

The now former Agent kept his eyes on the descending sun. He sucked at his teeth. He tapped his feet. He cracked his knuckles.

"Ahhhh, fuck it," he muttered to himself, and withdrew his smokes. He looked down on those last two, biting at his bottom lip. When they were gone, they were gone, and there was no getting more. He pulled one out and sparked it up.

Estard inhaled deeply and sighed it out. *I didn't think this through too well. Good work Julian. Good work.*

Before the sun set, he went back around to the others. They all spoke quietly among themselves in the dying light. Xavier was a little distance off, his arm around one of the other prisoners. *Not prisoners. Not any more. And Julian? You did that.* There was no fire, nor food. Nothing central to gravitate toward. He didn't want to interrupt them, or intrude, so he went inside the ship and sat down in the pilot's chair.

Everything was off, and it was just as well. He didn't want to make the thing fly by accident.

Estard leaned back and breathed deep. Sleep came quickly.

~

Estard was up before the sun, blinking into the darkness and wondering where he was. At first, he thought he'd fallen asleep in his comfy chair. When he remembered, he jerked upright. "Shit!"

He stumbled through the pitch dark to the hatch. It wasn't much better outside, though he could make out some outlines. He ran his fingertips along the hull, clipped the foot of a sleeping airmen and nearly face-planted. *Got to piss. Gotta piss, gotta piss,* ran through his head in operatic scales.

When he was safely on the other side, he whipped it out and got down to business. He looked around — and saw a set of gleaming ruby eyes staring right at him.

Estard reached for a pistol that wasn't there, his eyes locked on the apparition. He dribbled on his shoes, and his eyes snapped to his feet, which he couldn't see.

"Ah fuck!" he muttered as he put himself away. When he looked up again, the eyes were gone.

It wasn't long before first light. All of the airmen were up with it.

There would be no breakfast, and Estard's stomach growled angrily at him. It was going to be a long day.

They were moving before the sun was fully visible above the horizon. Estard spent most of this time debating with himself. The surreal feeling had passed, but he wasn't sure what he'd seen, if he'd seen anything. He thought about telling Xavier about it. Dismissed it as probable morning tiredness, then thought about it again. How could he know there wasn't something to it? It was an alien planet, after all.

The pace was steady, and they walked spread out. Xavier was in the lead with a woman, others had separated into smaller groups of three or four. Estard took up the rear, hands in his pockets and sucking at his teeth. No one tried to speak to him. They didn't even look back at him.

It was a little before noon when they saw the tree line up ahead. It moved along in jagged formation as far as they could see. They would have to go through.

Xavier turned and stopped them. "We'll take a break before we push on," he said. There was no argument.

Estard felt a tension among them, though he couldn't place it. It had something to do with going into those woods. The furtive glances, the shaky hands. The way they spoke to one another in hushed tones. They all wanted to put it off as long as possible, but none of them wanted to say anything about it.

By himself, Estard sat a few paces distant and took out his last smoke. He crumpled the empty packet and put it in his pocket.

For a while he sat staring at it, running his fingers along the white tube. It would be his last for a long, long time.

Xavier sat beside him, and Estard looked up.

"We never thanked you," Xavier said.

Estard shrugged, uncomfortable. "It's just something I had to do."

"Well, I thank you." The Navigator smiled. "I never gave much thought to how difficult this must have been for the Commander. Not the first time around. Now I can't get the thought out of my head."

Estard put the smoke in his mouth, thought about lighting it up, then took it out. He was supposed to say something, he was sure. He just didn't know what. "Yeah?" It seemed enough.

"She commands a bunch of airmen, from all over the world," he said. "When you're up in the air, that doesn't matter, because you're all flying for the ATF, you know your job and what the orders mean."

Estard nodded. *He's not really talking to me,* he thought. *He just needs a sounding board. I don't know what he's talking about.* "I know what you mean."

Xavier cast him a glance and a frown. "I doubt it," he said.

"True. But you're speaking to me, and not one of them, for a reason."

The Navigator nodded. "Got me there."

"So, finish your thought. It doesn't really matter if I understand."

"Alright," he said as he leaned back and looked up at the sky. "Weiz — the Commander — she's good. She knows what she's about. She fires off tactics, people listen, people stay alive. Up there, it's easy."

"But down here it's not," Estard finished for him.

Xavier shook his head. "We're not ground troops. We're airmen. Well, some of the comms officers are army. Most of us are air force, though." He scratched at his head. "And we're from all around the world. We all have different training."

Estard couldn't imagine an international army, or air force, or *space* troop. Or whatever they were. Not in his time. He tried to fit it into his view of the world, and it just wouldn't. He also didn't know who this Commander Weiz was, since she hadn't been one of the prisoners.

"That couldn't be easy," Estard said lamely.

"No." Xavier looked at him, then. Studied him.

"You want to ask me something," said Estard, "then go ahead and ask it."

"I'm not precise on dates, but I remember there were two world wars in your century."

Estard raised his brows. "You want to know if I was a soldier?"

"Were you?"

With a sigh, Estard put the smoke between his teeth and sparked it up. He might regret it later, but he was going to smoke it eventually, and now was as good a time as any.

He looked down on the other man and exhaled slowly from the side of his mouth. "For eight years," he said finally.

Xavier nodded and looked back to the sky. "I thought so."

"Why do you want to know?"

"Were you an officer?"

"No. Why do you want to know?"

Xavier sat up again and looked over at the others. There was sadness in his eyes. "Do you know how many of us there were the first time we landed here, Agent Estard?"

He shook his head. "Fifty?" he guessed. "None of you ever mentioned this place during our interviews."

The Navigator smiled, but the sadness stayed in his eyes. "More than two hundred," he said. "Thirty-four ships, and over two hundred airmen."

Estard looked over at the small group. He burnt his fingers on the butt of his smoke, and regretfully doused it in the grass. He was about to respond when he saw something move at the tree line. He squinted in that direction.

Just behind that first row of trees, Estard thought he could make out a dark figure that was much too tall. And had ruby red eyes. He blinked a few times, sure that he was seeing things. *You let this morning's fright get the better of you*, he told himself. *Now you're seeing things. It's all the talk of people dying.*

But Xavier had noticed his pause and followed his gaze. "Shit!" he breathed and was on his feet in an instant. "Oh, fuck me!" It was under his breath, almost a whisper.

"What -?" He didn't get a chance to ask.

The others hadn't noticed, not straight away, but now that thing was moving out of the tree line.

Airmen were on their feet in an instant, scrabbling up behind Xavier, who looked at the shadow form with near horror on his face.

"Fuck me," breathed the Navigator, and Estard could hear similar sentiments being muttered all round.

Estard was torn between keeping an eye on the shadow man and looking at Xavier for direction. He had no idea what was going on, but from their reactions, that thing was dangerous.

"What-?" he began again, but was cut off once more.

"We can kill it," Xavier said.

The woman he'd been walking with pulled him around to face her. "Don't you dare," she said.

"We just need some weapons made from these trees... or cover ourselves in mud... that's how the others did it. Wasn't it?"

She shook her head vehemently. "You don't want to end up like them and you know it."

He pulled himself loose from her grip, and she let her arm drop. "Do you want to run back to the ship? Or hide in one of these thickets?" He gestured around him at the mostly open ground. "Do you think it can't get to us if it wants to?"

"I thought the Giant Killers got them all," someone said from the middle of the group.

Estard kept his eyes on the shadow man, now, and let their voices fade into the background. It hadn't moved an inch since showing itself. It didn't even look real to him. If it was so deadly, so dangerous, as the conversation behind him implied, why didn't it come at them? Why didn't it move?

He took a step toward it.

Graininess slipped into his vision. His steps felt light, like there wasn't enough gravity.

A hand clamped down on his shoulder. He looked up at Xavier. "Don't," the man said.

"Do we just stand here, then?" he asked.

"For the moment. I don't know what else to do."

"Is it some kind of showdown? What?" Estard felt his temper rising. He tried to hold onto it. "If it's such a damned threat, why is it just standing there? What are you worried about?"

"It'll kill us all," Xavier said, and took his hand away.

The words, though he understood them, didn't fill Estard with a sense of danger. He was curious, and a little pissed off, but not frightened.

"It didn't do anything at the ship this morning, either," he told the man. "And if it wanted to kill me, it had me in prime position, then."

"It was at the ship?"

"I thought I was hallucinating or something."

"I don't know what to do," Xavier confessed, quietly enough the others wouldn't be able to hear.

Though he couldn't understand the terror that pervaded the group, he said, "We could just go around it. Walk a little further north or south before cutting into the woods."

Xavier shook his head slowly, his eyes drawn inward. "Those things...they track. They follow. And they're *fast*." His eyes refocused, and they were on the shadow man. "I don't want to go through that again. I barely got away last time. And like my girl said, I don't want to be like the Giant killers. Seems a curse to me."

"What are you afraid of?" He really wanted to understand.

"They don't come straight at you. They let you know they're there first. They want you to know they're watching. Like they're protecting something, maybe."

"So?"

"We don't know what makes them attack!" Xavier snapped. "Maybe I can walk straight up to it and all it would do is look at me. Or it could pull my head — right — off! And you won't know which till it happens."

"I could say that about most of humanity, Xavier." Estard ran a hand through his hair and sucked at his teeth. "But again, what is it you're afraid of? Why can't you kill it?"

"That one is a lot harder to explain," he sighed. But explain he did. About how they'd manifested powers. How it had changed them, in small and big ways. About a man named Greenway who had tried to stop them from leaving.

Estard took a deep breath, eyes on the Giant, still watching them. "This is your call. Everything is choice and consequence. But I'm willing to face it."

"Such is life."

"So, what are the choices?" Estard asked.

"I don't know."

"You do know. You're thinking of consequences. It makes you feel trapped. Start again."

Xavier breathed deep. "Back to the ship. Stay here. Move forward. Move south or north and then cut into the woods. I'm a Navigator, and mostly I use stars. This is beyond me."

"But the people here are looking to you. You can step aside, let someone else make the choice. Step up or step aside." Estard wasn't sure why he was trying to coach the man through this moment. All the airmen behind him could hear them, would understand what was happening. "What is the consequence of each choice?"

"If we go north or south, first, the Giant is likely to follow us. Even if we can't see it. Same if we move into the woods."

"That isn't a consequence. You're thinking of the wrong thing." Estard looked at the others. They were tough, but they were in a situation they couldn't see a way out of. They were waiting for Xavier to make a decision.

"You explain it to me," Xavier said.

"If we go into the woods, we will die. Not we *might* die. Death then is the consequence. We *might* die means there are other choices after the first that could keep us alive. You're coming up with the wrong answers, because the knowledge is too certain in your mind."

"You sound like my Academy teachers."

Estard shook his head slowly. "Look, I don't fancy standing here all day. And neither do your men. It's one enemy, but you're letting it block you from the path."

"You make it sound easy." Xavier chewed at his lip.

Estard looked at the others and addressed them. "Any of you get a gun on your way out yesterday?"

They all looked at each other, faces searching. One came forward. She pulled an M1911-A1 from the front of her jeans. It was Gordon.

Brows raised, he reached for it. She pulled it away behind her head and kept her eyes on him. "Why do you need it?"

"Why do you?"

They stared at each other for a while, then she handed him the gun. "Won't do you any good," she said.

Estard checked the clip, then the chamber. Satisfied, he moved forward. This time, Xavier didn't try to stop him.

He couldn't understand it. Even as he moved forward, his blood rushing in his ears, heart beating rhythmically in his chest. Everything was hazy and surreal. Like a dream.

As he got closer, the fear began to seep into him. The uncertainty. Was he doing something irrevocably stupid? like storming the beaches of Normandy.

At thirty yards, he stopped and brought the pistol up. It was doable at this range, if not ideal. He wasn't a master marksman, but he was a good shot, and he'd trained at this distance.

He breathed and sighted.

He pulled the trigger.

CHAPTER TWELVE

He wasn't lost any more. Not that he knew where he was. But he knew what he was doing.

Greenway had followed the northern road after he'd turned Djorik to dust and rubble. It had been just as easy as the village, and almost as quick. Some would have survived, but he was unconcerned with that. It wasn't about murder; it was about punishment. They had to understand his wrath.

Twice more the voice had come to him — on the road to Djorik, and again while he was destroying it. It wasn't his conscience, he was sure. His conscience pulled at him from time to time, and that was more feeling than words. He wasn't immune to it. But that voice... It was like someone else in his head.

Greenway stopped and looked to the sky. It was a little after noon, on his third day out of Djorik, and he had yet to see a village, much less a town. He feared, at times, that it was a road that went nowhere, much like the one to the ravine. But he was determined to press on to the end of it, wherever it went.

There had been many farms close to Djorik, but he'd left those alone. They'd disappeared behind him on the first night, and he hadn't seen human habitation since. Around him now were rolling hills, with sparse but large thickets amidst the grassy knolls. Ahead in the distance, forest loomed.

He pressed ahead.

The next village or town he found would be given the choice. Follow or die. If he was the only God left in this world, then he needed to take care of them. He didn't see this as a contradiction, but rather a contract. I'll do my part if you do yours.

He walked on.

~

When they'd come upon the village, Harvey knew. He couldn't believe that a man he'd so respected could do that. But he knew. He'd never truly known Aiden Greenway.

He'd taken Kristin to Djorik, after that. There'd been survivors there, but they hadn't known what happened. They thought it was some kind of natural disaster. The earth had heaved, buildings had collapsed, and whole sections of the town had been swallowed by the ground. But it had been three days done, and they didn't know who Greenway was, much less where he went.

They'd returned to the small hut and filled the others in. They'd spoken at length about their plans — or lack thereof. Then they had slept. They all knew it was unnecessary, but refused to let go of their humanity.

Harvey sat outside, his back pressed against the boards, and eyed the noon sky. Weiz was beside him, Kristin, Lance and Deidra, were inside.

"We'll find him," Weiz said, not for the first time.

"I still can't believe it," said Harvey. "The whole village. And that town. That's a lot of dead he's piling up behind him."

Weiz picked up his hand and squeezed it. "We'll find him," she repeated.

"What happened to him?" He wanted to know that, more than anything else.

"I can't answer that."

Harvey turned to look into her blue eyes. He could get lost in those. "I missed you," he said.

She leaned over and gave him a quick kiss. "I missed you, too." Weiz leaned into him, and he held her.

They stayed in silence for a while.

Harvey's mind was full of scenarios. Of all the different things he might do if he found Greenway. But short of killing him — which wouldn't work anyway — Harvey could think of no permanent solution.

"Do you think he's found other villages? Or towns?" Harvey asked.

Weiz shrugged against his chest. "Who knows? From what little we've seen it's hard to gauge what kind of society these people have."

"Might pay to find out."

"Where would you look?" She pulled away slightly so she could see his face. "If we had a working ship, I'd say do a fly over, take a good look at the land. But short of that, how could you find out? Even on Earth there are still places you could wander for days without finding a sign of civilisation."

"I don't have to walk," he reminded her. "I can shift around."

"That could be dangerous."

"Doing nothing could be dangerous."

"He won't come after us. He doesn't even know we're here." She leaned back into him. "Besides, he couldn't do away with us however hard he tried."

"All true." He planted a kiss on the top of her head. "But that doesn't mean we should let him just go around destroying every settlement he finds. We may not agree with him, but he was right about one thing — we have a responsibility."

Weiz barked a bitter laugh. "Do we really, though? He's not exactly making a good case for himself. We might be stuck here, but I don't exactly feel obliged to put my abilities to use."

"I don't mean to the people of this world. I'm not certain we should interfere with them at all." He sighed. "But he is one of us. And we just let him run loose. The responsibility is in keeping our house in order."

"I fail to see what we could have done about it."

Harvey looked down on her and stroked her hair. It was still so unreal to him that she was alive. "We were too caught up in getting home," he said. "We made the choice to just leave everything about this place behind. We didn't think of the consequences."

"It was our right," Weiz defended. "And it wasn't just about us. It was about everyone under my command!" She pushed away from him. "Was I supposed to tell them we weren't going home just because Greenway threatened to kill us?"

Harvey scrubbed his hands over his face and closed his eyes. When he opened them again, he kept them on her. "We left some of them behind," he said.

"We —" she began, but he cut her off.

"We left some of them behind. We knew he wouldn't just leave them." He breathed deep and tried to stay calm. They'd been his responsibility, too. "More than any of the others, Catherine, it was us who wanted to get out of here. To run away from what we've become. He wasn't wrong about that."

She looked like she might try to argue, but after a few tense moments, her shoulders slumped. She leaned back into him, and he held her tight. "You're right."

Harvey chuckled. "I usually am," he said.

Weiz hugged his arm. "Don't be a smart-arse," she said. "What do you plan to do, then?"

"You said there were six worlds."

"That is what the old man told me," she replied hesitantly.

"I think I should go scout them out. See what there is to be seen."

Her grip on his arm tightened uncomfortably. "You don't even know if you can breathe on those worlds. If they even exist."

"If they don't, I won't be able to get there." That was how he saw it, anyway. "It can't hurt. And worst case, I know where this hut is from the field."

She relaxed her grip and shot a laugh. "Yes, I suppose so. Death is not a worry for us, now. I have to remember that."

Harvey nodded. He had to remember that, too. "Doesn't mean we should be reckless." It was hard, looking down on Weiz and seeing again and again that moment life had left her eyes. He kissed the top of her head again. "I'll be as careful as it is possible to be," he told her.

"I don't like you leaving me again," she breathed. "But you should take Kristin."

He understood how much it cost her to say that. He was proud that she did it without stumbling over the name. "I'll try to make it quick," he assured her as he tried to get up. She didn't move.

"Stay here a little longer," she said. "There's no rush."

Harvey tried to stand again, and this time she moved. "Tell that to the people Greenway is slaughtering." He dusted off his jeans. "If I can't get him to stop, I'll have to take him somewhere else. It won't do us any good if we're just unleashing him on someone else."

Weiz smacked him lightly on the chest. "Why do you always have to make sense?"

He took her hand and kissed it. "Just built that way, I suppose."

Deidra poked her head out the door. "Kristin had a vision," she said, and withdrew.

Harvey sighed. "Like someone interrupting you in the last five minutes of a movie," he mumbled.

They went inside. Kristin was huddled over on a chair, gripping her head. Lance stroked her back, and Deidra stood to the side.

"I did not fucking miss that," Kristin groaned. "I did not fucking miss it."

Harvey waited patiently. He knew how it affected her, that it could take her a moment to work through the pain.

Kristin started to breathe easier and sat up. Lance looked ready to catch her. "The others are here," she said.

They all glanced at each other. There were mixed feelings about that. On the one hand, good to know they'd gotten out safe. On the other, they were stuck on this world.

"Not sure where they are. They're in danger, though I couldn't see from what." She cracked her neck. "Fucking useless vision."

"We know they made it," said Deidra. "That's worth something."

Kristin gave a twitch of a smile. "Glad someone thinks so. I'll take a hard pass on the delivery, though."

"You may not know where they are now," Harvey told her, "but it's possible you'll remember a helpful detail after you've chewed on it a while."

Kristin grunted and glared at him, then gave a grudging nod. "We'll see."

"For the moment," he continued, "you and I are going scouting."

"Looking for Greenway again?" Lance asked.

"To have a look at the other five worlds," he told them.

Deidra studied him. "Thinking of sending Greenway to one of them?"

Harvey nodded. "If I can't talk him down."

Lance looked like he might say something, but just shook his head. Kristin got slowly to her feet. "Let's get going then," she said.

She was pale and drawn, but Harvey had seen it often enough in those first months that he knew it would pass. He took a quick look at Weiz, and she gave him a tight nod.

Harvey took a step toward Kristin, took her by the arm, and shifted.

~

Deidra blinked at the place where Harvey and Kristin had been. Five other worlds to explore, and when she thought about them, nothing came to mind. There was a vague sense they were real, but it was a faint impression.

Weiz stared, too. Though Deidra suspected a different reason.

A warm breeze came in through the open window, and the smell of honeysuckle. It reminded her of days on Earth, before Io Station.

"Do we just wait for them?" Deidra asked.

Weiz snapped her head around. "I don't see what else we can do," she said.

"We could look for the others," Lance offered.

"Don't be stupid," Weiz said. "She didn't know where they were, so where would we start looking?"

Deidra sighed. She'd never done well with idle hands, and it had been weeks since she'd done anything useful. But she was also afraid to think too hard on solutions. What if the return of her memory was only temporary? What if she had to give it up all over again? It was a noble sacrifice when they had a goal, but if they were going to be stuck here, she saw no reason to give herself up again.

She took a chair and pressed her forehead against the table. She heard a chair being pulled up next to her and turned her head without lifting it.

"I understand," Weiz said. "It's never easy to wait."

"Less waiting, more thumb twiddling," Deidra mumbled.

The Commander shot a laugh. "Amounts to the same, really. But sometimes, you need information. Without it, you could spend the rest of your life spinning in circles, keeping busy doing nothing."

"Immortality," Lance said. "I don't know how I feel about that.

Pretty sure I died once already, don't fancy doing it more than a few times just for kicks."

Deidra raised her head to stare at him. "Your tangential powers remain intact," she told him.

"I don't know what that means." Lance threw his slippered feet up on the table. "Do you think the others will be alright? I feel badly for them, being stuck in all this."

"We're all stuck in this," Weiz said through gritted teeth.

"It's different for them, though."

"It's different for everyone," Deidra breathed. "We all have our reasons, a need to go home. I'll need to find a way for those who actually can."

"There then," Weiz smiled. "No thumb twiddling if you're busy with that. Judging from the last project, it should keep you busy for a good month, at least."

"Eager to be my assistant, again?"

Lance laughed and Weiz scowled at him, but she replied, "Getting everyone home was always the job. They're not there yet, so the mission is incomplete."

"I'm not military," Deidra reminded her.

"Moral obligation?" Lance put in.

"Oh, yes, guilt is what I need." Deidra let her head fall on the table. She thought about banging it a couple of times, but just let it rest.

"If you insist on feeling sorry for yourself," Weiz said as she got up, "I won't help you."

Deidra's head shot up. "Sorry for myself?"

"That's certainly what it looks like."

Lance looked out the window, clearly not wanting to get involved in this discussion.

"I have my memory," Deidra said.

"Yes, and I am happy for you," Weiz said.

"But you don't understand what that means."

"So, tell me."

Deidra breathed out slowly. "I might have to sacrifice it. Again."

Weiz's blue eyes widened in sudden understanding. "Do you think so?"

"I can't know for certain," she admitted. "But I think it likely. I am me, right now." Deidra shook her head and tried to find the right words.

"You already made the choice once," Lance said softly, though he didn't look at her. "But it is *your* choice."

Deidra nodded. "Yes. And it's not a choice I recommend anyone make even once. The first time I didn't understand what it meant, not until it was too late. And I remember being...that. I can't describe what it was like."

"If you don't," Weiz murmured, "they'll all be stuck here. For the rest of their lives."

"I know that!"

"But you don't feel compelled to help them."

"Of course I do! That's what makes it difficult."

Weiz was silent a moment before she said, "You do what you have to do. As we all do. Like Lance says, it's your choice." Then she backed away and walked outside.

Lance kept his eyes on the window. Deidra thought he was trying to give her some privacy with her thoughts.

Last time had been simple. It was something she was already working on, and her desire to get home fuelled her at first. Then when her own drive diminished, she thought of all the others counting on her. When the coldness seeped in, it was simply knowledge put to practical use, and whether it worked or not concerned her little.

Now there were thirteen airmen. Only thirteen. And Agent Estard. She couldn't help but think there weren't enough to warrant it.

Time was you'd have thought one person was enough to just do the right thing. Whatever the situation. But the last few months had changed her. Hardened her. Not with the coldness of what she'd become, or the knowledge she'd had at her fingertips. She couldn't pinpoint the change. She just knew it was there.

"I don't envy your choice," Lance said quietly. "But you need to make it, before it gets taken out of your hands."

"You think it can be?" she asked.

The Pilot shrugged. "We all pay a price," he said. "Yours is a little more obvious. Maybe you get to keep your memories this time around, maybe you don't. But eventually, you'll become this God or Guardian or whatever, because that's how it works. I don't think you can hold it off forever."

"What if I can?" She had a sinking feeling that he was right, but she needed to hold onto hope.

"Then you have to ask yourself, would you be any better off?" He let his feet fall from the table and looked to her with intense brown eyes. "Stop thinking about what you might lose, if you let it happen. Think about what you might gain. Maybe you'll remember yourself again once you've fully integrated the other *being*. Maybe there is some freedom in the choice."

"If there is, I can't see it," she told him.

"Give it a little time," he replied. "I think we have some."

CHAPTER THIRTEEN

The Giant collapsed to the ground. Estard shot again. He didn't have to get any closer to see that he'd tapped it twice in the head.

Everyone was waiting with bated breath behind him, but he wasn't paying attention. He had eyes only for the Giant on the ground. From the way the others had behaved, he was expecting the thing to get up and lunge for him.

A minute passed, and then two. He prepared to move toward it, make sure it was dead and safe for the others. Before he could take the first step, the shadow form broke apart, swirled into mist. Then it was gone.

Estard blinked at the spot where it had been.

"That shouldn't have happened."

Estard jumped at the sound of Gordon's voice so close to him. He stared at her, eyes round. "What do you mean?" he asked.

She looked him in the eyes with a frown. "I mean that should not have happened. Do you need me to say it slowly?"

"No need to be rude," he muttered, straightening his coat.

"Why? What was supposed to happen?"

The airman shrugged at him and looked back toward the others, who hadn't moved. "We unloaded most of what we had at those things, that first night. Bullets passed right through them. You shouldn't have been able to kill it."

He studied her face a moment. "There's more," he said. "Spit it out."

"If you did kill it," she said with a tilt of her head, "then it should have passed to you."

"What are you talking about?"

"They are... Gods." She raised her hands in the universal gesture of uncertainty. "When you kill them, you become them. At least, that is what we've been told."

Estard scoffed. "That doesn't even make sense."

Gordon shrugged and smiled at him. "Why should it? We're on an alien world."

"Then wouldn't it be more accurate to say they're aliens?"

"No."

Estard shook his head. "Doesn't much matter. I shot it, it's gone. Now we can move on." He handed her the gun back.

Gordon took it and replaced it in the front band of her jeans. "I don't think it will be that simple to convince the others."

Estard looked back at them again. They were huddled around each other, speaking in whispers. Xavier still had his eyes on the place where the Giant had been.

The former Agent sucked at his teeth. "What's the problem?" He wanted to know before he went back to them.

"Where there's one..." She let him intuit the rest.

"Can't spend the rest of our lives here," he mumbled, and brushed past her.

Xavier's eyes darted to him. "You killed it," he breathed, his face taking on a grey hue.

"Yes, yes," Estard said, nodding. "I killed it, it's gone, let's go." He motioned toward the woods.

Xavier looked at the woods, then looked to him a few times before he said, "There's probably more."

"You don't know that," Estard said firmly. He addressed them all. "Time to move! Let's go!" And he suited his own words.

At first, he was afraid they wouldn't follow. They all appeared fairly adamant that there would be something else down there in the woods. Estard wouldn't worry too much about ifs and mights. He wouldn't let fear freeze him.

Soon enough he could hear the soft padded footsteps behind him. The rustle of denim, the hushed voices. He smiled to himself as he took his first step into the tree line.

The light dimmed and danced with tiny spotlights as wind blew through the canopy. The smell of mulch and cedar was strong in the air. Estard breathed in deep and listened. There was nothing out of place. He could easily have been in any number of American forests. There was no discernible difference to him.

"You'll have to lead the way," he told Gordon as she stopped beside him.

"I thought Superman was leading our little rat pack," she returned with a shrug.

Estard glanced back at the Navigator. He was standing close to another woman, and they were speaking softly. "He froze up," Estard said.

"We all did," Gordon replied. "But we had the disadvantage of having seen those things before."

"You didn't."

Gordon barked a sharp laugh. "I nearly pissed myself," she said. "I didn't come to you till I was sure it was down."

Estard winked at her. "Good enough. Take the lead."

They moved further into the woods at a sedate pace. The airmen behind him had split into groups of two and spread out. Bodies were tense, and eyes searched. Xavier saw him looking and gave a nod.

"You'll have to tell me what happened last time," Estard said as he turned his attention to Gordon.

"Do I?"

"It'd give me a better grasp of the situation."

"Serves you right for jumping head first into it," she said.

"Dare say you're right. But, even so…"

Gordon related their previous encounters with the Giants. She didn't skimp on the details and, at times, Estard found himself chilled, despite the warmth of the sun. He didn't interrupt, or comment, until she was done.

"Now I understand your reluctance," he said.

"I never expected to land on an alien planet," Gordon told him. "But I had imagined what an alien planet might look like, from time to time. You wonder about these things when you're fighting them. This" — she turned in a tight circle, hands in the air, face up — "wasn't it."

Estard shook his head. It was like she'd dived into his head and pulled out his own opinion of the place. "And this is all that's left?" he asked.

Gordon kept moving forward, eyes ahead. She took a deep breath, and said, "There might be more of us, scattered out here somewhere."

They were at least an hour inside the tree line now. The woods became denser, and the canopy allowed in less light. The smell of cedar was so strong it was hard to pick anything else out. Animals rustled branches high up, and shrubs on the ground. The occasional bird would call in a short, warbled screech, and he'd hear the snap and flutter of the bird taking flight, but Estard never saw them.

Soft footfalls on twigs and leaves, the deep controlled breaths. That was all the sound the airmen made, now. No one wanted to talk.

Estard looked back every now and then and counted them all. In groups of two and spread out, sometimes a pair would drop from view and re-emerge, then he'd start the count again. Double check.

He hadn't been an officer in the Second World War. He'd been a grunt. A lucky grunt with a good Sergeant to follow. He was trying to emulate that Sergeant with this lot. Pilots and navigators, comms officers and gunners. He had to think of them as tank operators whose tank had gotten bogged down in a trench. They'd obviously been given the basic training, but they never expected to leave that tank alive, unless it was back at base.

Estard looked back again. Xavier wasn't far behind, his woman beside him. Stretched out to either side were airmen he couldn't remember the names of. He counted them out. He counted them again and took a better look. His eyes darted forward every now and then just to make sure he wasn't going to walk into a tree.

He counted three times. Then four. Then he stopped, dead still. Gordon took a few steps before noticing, and came back to stand by him. Xavier came to a halt in front of him. Others stopped where they were, and glanced at them, but didn't move from their path.

Estard's mouth moved silently as he counted them all out slowly, once more. "We're missing two," he breathed, almost a whisper.

Gordon and Xavier both looked around then, eyes travelling over their companions twice.

"Walt and Dames," Xavier said, his face taking on a sickly caste. "They might have fallen behind."

Estard shook his head slowly. "I've been counting every ten minutes by my watch. If they did, they'd have caught up. Something's happened."

They all looked around. Estard sucked at his teeth, his brain racing. If they split up and tried to look for them, the chances of others becoming lost were high. If they stayed, they could wait forever, and the missing pair might never turn up. Except for Estard, they all knew where they were supposed to be going. It was possible the pair had just swept too wide. He doubted it, but it was possible.

"We'll keep moving," he said.

Xavier looked at him as if slapped. "We need to find them," he insisted. "We can't leave anyone behind."

"It's a nice thought," Estard replied. "Not practical though. We keep moving."

"They're part of my crew!"

Gordon raised a hand. "We're all together, now," she said. "If we split up, we might lose others. Forward is the best way."

A roar sounded in the near distance. Estard looked around, trying to work out which direction it had come from. It had sounded like no animal he had ever heard before. The roar sounded again.

"What is that?" he asked.

The others were looking around just as furtively. "I don't know," Gordon said.

"Neither," said Xavier.

"Sounded like a mountain lion," the woman next to Xavier murmured.

"Bad timing, I know," Estard said. "But what is your name?"

The woman arched a brow at him, but answered, "Ellen Rich."

Estard gave a nod. "We should keep moving," he told them. "Whatever that thing is, I don't want to meet it. If the missing pair are still out here, they know where we're going."

Gordon turned on her heel and led the way. Xavier and Ellen waited a moment, then followed close behind.

The roar sounded again, closer. Estard's neck hair tried to run out of his skin. Gordon increased the pace slightly. No one said a word.

Estard tried to keep his heart rate steady and his mind clear. He concentrated on his breathing, while his eyes darted ahead and behind. His hand kept twitching toward a gun that wasn't there, and wished he hadn't given it back to Gordon.

He glanced at the woman. She wore a small frown on full lips, brows drawn down, and dark eyes making slow sweeps of the way ahead. Her right hand gripped the gun in her waistband, the shirt pulled out of the way.

A crash, a slap, and a wet thud made him turn quickly. His eyes searched out the members of the party and counted. Others were doing the same. Everyone was there, and he turned back — to face a Giant.

Estard took an involuntary jump backward, hand reaching for that gun. *Goddamn it!* he thought. He had no weapons. Not for that thing.

Gordon had the gun up, her hand steady.

The Giant was more than thirty paces away and not moving. It stared at Estard with ruby eyes. He felt as if the thing were smiling at him, but he couldn't see a mouth to tell.

Estard's heart tried to break through his rib cage. His mouth dried out.

There was a roar, closer than before, this time answered by two others. No one dared take eyes off the Giant before them, but some other danger was drawing nearer.

"We should scatter," Gordon said so softly he almost didn't hear her.

"You have the only weapon," Estard replied.

"It's only got one bullet." She barked a sharp laugh. "Well, why not? Seems to be a theme."

The roars came again. They seemed to be encircling them. Estard didn't know how they'd fight off any predators. His eyes refused to move from the Giant, who still hadn't moved.

"You need to take the shot before whatever is making that noise, gets here," Estard urged.

"If I miss, or hit but don't kill it, we're fucked," she told him.

"If you don't make a move, we're fucked," he breathed.

Gordon took a step forward, but it was too late.

Behind them, what looked like massive panthers with purple-black fur, elongated canines and sapphire blue eyes, burst from the surrounding woods to encircle them.

The airmen who'd spread out slowly backed into the centre, where Xavier and Ellen stood.

The catlike creatures circled. Their soft paws made little noise on the detritus. Snouts sniffed, and tails lashed.

Gordon still had her gun pointed at the Giant, but she'd chanced to look around. "We're fucked," she said.

Estard wasn't inclined to disagree.

The Giant was moving forward, now, its steps slow, steady, and making no imprint on the ground. It raised its head, and a keening wail rose, like nothing Estard had ever heard before. The sound made his eyes water, and his ears ring.

The cat creatures stopped in their tracks, ears pointing forward. The five he could see — he was sure there were more — slunk down on their bellies, tested the air with nose and tongue.

The airmen were so tightly clustered together they wouldn't be able to fight effectively if the cats charged. Not that they were likely to do much damage even if they weren't.

The Giant made the sound again, and Estard covered his ears. It still made his teeth vibrate, but the effect was diminished.

One cat stood, then roared, long and loud, before turning and disappearing into the woods. The others followed, and in moments, the only enemy they faced was the Giant.

Estard turned his attention back to that shadowman. It was studying the woods around them, but otherwise standing still. Appearing satisfied, the thing turned around — and Gordon shot it in the head.

It took a moment for the former Agent to understand what had happened, as he watched the Giant fall. The piercing cry had damaged his ears more than he thought, and the boom and crack of the gun firing had been dull and muted.

"What did you do?" Estard was stunned, and from the look on Gordon's face, so was she.

"I...ah...I —" She shook her head, blinking rapidly. "I —" But she couldn't communicate the thought.

They stood still and watched the Giant, prepared for it to get up and attack. Except for the rushing ocean sound in his head, the wait was eerily silent.

The shot had been true. The Giant collapsed into mist and disappeared.

Gordon clutched at her chest and fell to her knees. She dropped the gun and breathed, "Thank God."

Estard had mixed feelings. The Giants were enemies, but that one had helped them. True, it may have been marking its territory. Warning the other predators off its prey. But he suspected that wasn't it. It didn't feel right to him.

"Thank God," Gordon repeated, breathing deep.

"You didn't mean to kill it, did you?" Estard asked.

The woman shook her head fervently. "I fired on reflex," she said, eyes wide.

Estard sucked at his teeth and cracked his neck. He would have died for a smoke in that moment. *A smoke and a shot of whiskey. I could really use a shot of whiskey.* But all he said was, "We have to keep moving, those...cats could come back."

No one argued.

~

They had yet to reach the other side of the woods when they stopped for the night. It was well past sundown and visibility had become an issue. Much as they all wanted to press on.

Estard rested against the bole of a tree, Gordon close beside him. He couldn't see the others, but he was sure they were doing much the same. It wasn't a campsite. There was no food to pass around, no water to bath in or drink. Nowhere to build a central fire.

There had been no conversation as they travelled through the woods. No one wanted to draw the attention of those cats, or anything else that might be lurking. Xavier had mentioned that it was odd no one had come across them before, and Ellen suggested they may have migrated. But the discussion was short, and lasted only until they started moving again.

Out in the open without so much as a blanket roll, or a canteen of water, Estard was reminded of times best left forgotten.

He turned to Gordon. "You were relieved," he said softly, "when the Giant disappeared."

"Of course," she replied, just as softly. "So were you. So was everyone."

Estard wished he could make out her face. "It was different for you, though."

Gordon was silent for so long he thought she might have fallen asleep. He leaned his head back against the tree, prepared to do the same, when she finally answered. "I didn't want to be one of them," she said.

That was a concept he found hard to fathom. How could killing one, make you one? "Would it really be so bad?"

"I have people to get home to," she sighed. "I might get banged up some, and I could explain that. But mum comes home with supernatural powers?" Her laugh was as soft as her words. "My five-year-old might enjoy it, depending on what they were, but my eight-year-old would think me a demon."

"And your husband? Assuming you have one, of course."

"You assume right, but try not to assume too much," she warned.

There was a brief moment of silence before she continued. "He wouldn't like it. Alistair is a gentle, loving and patient man. But he might leave me in fear of what I might subject the children to. Couldn't say I'd blame him either."

Estard nodded to himself and let the matter drop. "How far do we have to go before we get to where we're going?"

"Hard to say," she said through a yawn. "I'd guess we're only halfway. We moved slowly. Get some sleep, Agent Estard. We'll start early."

"Call me Julian," he said.

She didn't respond.

~

Weiz could hear hurried movement in the thicket surrounding the hut. She stood and peered into the depths. She was not trained in these kinds of scenarios, so wasn't sure what to look for.

Harvey and Kristin have been gone less than an hour, she told herself. *And they would have shifted straight here. Deidra and Lance are inside. Greenway doesn't know where we are. So, who...?*

The answer came to her just as she caught a glimpse of faded red coming toward her.

Galsin strode from the brush kicking leaves. "Ungrateful bastards!" he yelled without stopping or looking at her. "Ungrateful bloody bastards!"

He strode to the door of the hut, stopped, looked back at Weiz and sighed. He inclined his head toward the door and went inside.

Weiz shook her head but followed.

The old man threw his walking stick at Lance before he got to the table. The Pilot caught it deftly and frowned at it, then the old man.

"Get your feet off my table, boy," Galsin said and gave him a clip across the ear as he strode past.

Lance's frown deepened, but he complied. Deidra sat silently, watching. Weiz took up the last chair and turned it to face the old man.

"Hmph." Galsin was still watching Lance. "Man shares his hut with strangers, I suppose he should expect them to behave like pigs unless he says otherwise. I say otherwise. Understand?"

Lance glanced at Weiz before saying, "Sorry."

Galsin gave a nod. He looked over the three of them with a frown. "Missing a couple, aren't you?"

"They're scouting," Weiz said.

"Right, well," he said, but seemed to lose his train of thought.

"Who are the ungrateful bastards?" Weiz asked.

The steely look Galsin gave her might have intimidated another, but Weiz kept her eyes on his. He growled, "Your men, that's who. Bunch of them up in the woods 'bout a day away. Headed for your old campsite, I think."

Lance smiled. "We should go meet them, Commander."

"Not Commander, Lance. Not any more."

"I know that," he shrugged. "Calling you anything else just sounds weird, though."

Weiz smiled. "We'll go meet them." She turned back to the old man. "What did they do, that makes them so ungrateful?"

"They killed me," the old man grumbled. "Shot me in the back of the head. Get a pack of *Dimineaux* off them, and what do they do? Kill me."

"A pack of what now?" Lance asked.

"Shot you?" Deidra said at the same time. "With a gun? I thought you could only be killed with something from this world."

"*Dimineaux*," Galsin repeated. "Large cats, big fangs. They migrate through here this time of year," he explained before turning to Deidra. "I can be killed by anything, same as you, unless I see it coming and phase."

Weiz shook her head. "You'll have to explain how that works

some time. For now, though, why would they kill you for that?"

"Because they're ungrateful bastards!" he roared.

Lance laughed. "If you didn't announce yourself, perhaps they mistook you for one of these dimi-things."

The old man glared blue daggers at him. "I was in shadow-form," he said through gritted teeth. "Habit, more than anything else, but the best way to claim territory against other predators. The *dimineaux* would make a meal of me, but they won't go near the shadow-form."

Deidra frowned at him. "If you were, as you say, in shadow-form, can you blame them? The last time they all saw the Giants more than half the men and women who landed here were brutally killed."

Galsin turned his glare to Deidra and muttered under his breath but didn't argue. "That's not why I came, anyway." He brushed the subject aside.

"Then why did you?" Weiz asked.

"I told you I would speak to the others," he replied. "I have. Almeron is keeping an eye on the one you call Greenway. Sending him in circles, though he doesn't know it."

"Sending him in circles?" Weiz raised a brow. "How are you managing that?"

"Almeron reads minds and transmits visions and words. We're keeping our distance from him, for now. But we decided it would be best to keep him away from populated areas."

"Thanks," Lance said.

"What for?" the old man asked.

"Keeping him occupied while we figure out what to do with him."

"Hmph. Well, we'll see how that goes." He scratched at his chin with a frown. "The man has a strong resistance to Almeron's power, and he refuses to sleep, so Almeron can't either. Whatever the man might think of our powers, I am not sure he realises he cannot keep going that way without consequence."

"What kind of consequence?" Deidra asked. "We can't die."

"No," Galsin agreed. "But you can be weakened. You can age. You can become so incapacitated that an enemy could kill you without thought, and even after you awoke in the field, that would not change. So incapacitated that you won't be able to move, but you'll live aeons beyond what might drive you insane." He huffed out a breath. "Consequences, my friends. You'll find them as you go along."

"What of the others?" From Weiz

"They're not all here yet, but Almeron alerted them, and they're on their way."

"And then what?"

"Then they'll choose."

Weiz frowned at him. "Choose? You have me asking a lot of questions, old man."

"Children ask many questions." He smiled for the first time since he'd walked in. "We'll choose to whom we give our power."

Deidra's head shot up. "You'll do what?"

"Choose the ones who will inherit our power."

"And if no one wants it?"

The old man shrugged.

They sat in silence a moment, and Weiz thought furiously. The remaining airmen were in the woods on the way to the old camp site. That was the easy part, she would take Lance and meet them there.

Greenway was being taken care of, for the time being, so she didn't have to worry about him finding out they were back or killing innocent people. But the other... guardians, were on the way. She wasn't sure how she felt about meeting them. Not after what the ones they'd killed had done to her camp. As amiable as the old man was, she wasn't willing to bet the others were the same. They'd need to take some precautions.

"Well," Galsin breathed, interrupting her thoughts. "I said what I needed to say, and since you lot are using my hut, I'll go elsewhere." He rose from his seat and snatched the walking stick from Lance. "I'll be back when the others arrive." He gave them all a last look and strode out.

"Lance," Weiz said, a few moments later, "Let's go get our men."

CHAPTER FOURTEEN

Harvey took them out to the plain, first. He wanted to be on open ground. He wasn't sure how this was going to work, but he hoped it came as naturally as the shifting from place to place. He couldn't imagine it would be too different.

"This might not work," he told Kristin.

The woman shrugged. "Makes no difference to me."

He grunted at her and closed his eyes. He tried to imagine six worlds lined up in a row. He imagined that a line ran through all of them, like thread. He adjusted them so the thread ran through a continent in sunlight.

Harvey took a deep breath and held out his hand for Kristin, who took it. "Take a deep breath," he said, "just in case."

"Just in case what?"

"In case we land in water."

"Ah —" But whatever she'd been going to say was lost when he took a step.

It wasn't quite the smooth transition he was used to. There was a roar around him, like gale winds in a tunnel. A blackness engulfed his vision and dissipated as stars loomed in the distance. They came at him so fast he had the impression of falling.

Then his foot hit the ground, and he was looking up at a long mountain range, its peaks snow-capped, and beneath a purple-grey sky. In the distance trees loomed, tall and proud. They were standing on an open grassland, three feet from a large lake.

Almost as soon as they arrived, Kristin let go of his hand and doubled over, dry heaving. He knew how difficult it had been the first time he'd taken her on a shift, but she was well past that. He could only assume that this was much worse.

The air was more than breathable. It was sweet and smelled of grass and static. Though, a hint of animal faeces did intrude on a whispery breeze.

"Fuck me," Kristin breathed as she stood. "Did it work? Are we on a different world?"

"Yes," he replied.

The ground began to hum, and he looked down. Soon after, he heard hoof beats in the distance. He turned to look out at the grassy plain. Kristin was looking in the same direction.

It wasn't long before they came into view. A wild herd of horses, running directly toward them.

Harvey glanced behind him at the lake. He took another look at the horses and grabbed Kristin by the arm, then shifted them a safe distance away.

Kristin wrenched her arm from his grip and turned on him. "A little warning before you do that," she said.

"Didn't fancy the thought of being trampled."

"We could have walked. They weren't that close."

Harvey shrugged and shot her a smile. He was sure things would get better between them, given time. He understood that he was to blame. He had tried to apologise, after all. *But I was apologising for the wrong thing*, he thought. *Apparently.*

They watched as the horses spread out along the lake shore. There were easily a hundred or more in the herd. While more than half moved forward until fore legs were submerged to the first joint, then dipped their heads to drink, others ran up and down the back of the line like cattle dogs rounding up sheep.

"They're gorgeous," Kristin whispered.

Harvey nodded. He was surprised to see them, though. Almost as surprised as he had been to see humans on that other world. He still hadn't worked that one out.

"Don't you think it's strange that we've seen so many Earth-like things?" he asked.

Kristin tilted her head and wrinkled her nose. "Sometimes I think perhaps Greenway had it right the first time. Maybe we're all dead and in some kind of purgatory." She shrugged. "I am not religious. But I do find it very strange that we keep coming upon things that belong on Earth."

"What's the connection, do you think?"

"If I knew that," Kristin said dryly, "then I really would be God. Not *a* god, but the penultimate, creator-of-all-things, worship-me-or-suffer-the-fiery-pits-of-hell, *God.*"

Harvey shook his head. He continued to watch the horses drink and take their turns. They didn't move until the horses were on their way again.

"If there is only one thing I can have an answer for," Harvey said, "it would be why there are humans on that world."

"Heinrich might have had the answers," Kristin suggested. "He did take us there on purpose, after all."

"I doubt he knew there would be humans there." He grabbed her by the arm. "Fair warning," he smiled, and took a step.

They followed the line of the grasslands, from forest to mountain to lake shore. Then he took them to the other side of the mountains, and everywhere he could get a clean line of sight. Kristin checked the ground for tracks, and any sign that could tell them what kind of world this was.

They travelled in this manner until they hit ocean.

"I see no sign of humans ever having been here," Kristin told him.

"Plenty of animal life, though."

"Is that a problem?"

"I don't know yet." Harvey frowned. "We'll go to the next one. This is probably going to take a few days."

"You know we could just be in a part of this world that has never been touched by human habitation," Kristin said. "Didn't take us too long to get to the sea, perhaps we're on an island."

He shook his head. "If it's an island, it would be at least the size of the UK."

"The UK isn't very big," she replied with a sideways glance. "And it doesn't mean there aren't people somewhere else in the world. They may simply be less advanced."

With a sigh, Harvey took her by the hand. "You might be right," he told her. "But we're still moving on. I have this place in my head, now. I can always come back."

"Your call," she said, and gestured for him to be about it.

He took a deep breath and imagined the worlds as he had before, in a row with a thread running through it. He walked that thread and landed in a meadow.

The sun was getting low in the sky, but it was still a few hours until dark. But they wouldn't need to search this world.

He looked around at the patchwork meadows. All fenced. Birds wheeled in the sky, and the sound of insects thrummed in his ears. Cows grazed in the next paddock over, and behind them stood a barn, and not far beyond that, a farmhouse, its chimney puffing smoke.

"Should we go say hello? Or just move on?" Kristin asked.

Harvey shrugged. "Best to move on, I think. This place looks more structured than Eridu. Might be worth coming back, but we know what we need to know for now."

Kristin sighed and held out her hand. "Then let's get it done. Moving around in this fashion is not as pleasant for me as it is for you."

He took the proffered hand, and in moments, they were on another world.

Heat that dried mouth and skin assaulted him. They were in a hardpan desert, the air still, heat shimmers rose from the cracked ground, and rock spires jutted into the air.

Harvey did a quick turn to find best direction, then grabbed Kristin's arm and walked. Every step took them miles away from where they'd come to this world. It took more than a dozen steps to find shade and water, beneath an overhang of rock, in a small hollow.

"Doesn't seem inviting, does it?" Kristin said as she knelt down before the small rocky pool to test the water. With a nod, she drank.

"We'd think the same of Earth if we landed in a desert there. We have plenty of them."

Kristin stepped back from the small pool and sank down against the rock. Harvey took her place, relishing the cool water as it slid down his throat.

"Are we going to search this world?" Kristin asked.

"We should. But, not today." He splashed water on his face and leaned back next to Kristin.

"You need to shave," she said.

"Of that, I am aware."

"We should scavenge the ships."

Harvey squinted at her. "I thought we decided that was a bad idea when we got your boots."

"Maybe," she replied. "But you need a razor, and I wouldn't

mind locating a few weapons."

"I'm fair certain all the weapons were used, or taken to the mountain."

"Did you search every ship?"

"No."

"Then how would you know?"

Harvey squinted at her with a half frown. "Is this really the best place to have this conversation?" he asked.

Kristin shrugged. "I say things as they come to mind."

Harvey grunted as he stood and held out his hand for Kristin. "Let's get back," he said.

She levered herself up and took it. "Three out of five isn't too bad."

They shifted.

When he let go of her hand, they were in front of the hut, and Harvey judged it to be three hours before sunset. He walked inside, expecting to see the others, but only Deidra sat at the table. Her head came up as he walked in.

"Where?" was all he asked.

"Out to get the others," she responded.

"Found them, then?" Kristin pushed past him and took a place at the table.

"The old man, Galsin — the one Weiz told us about? — he came to let us know where they were headed."

Harvey slowly moved to the table and drew out a chair for himself. "Sorry to have missed that."

Deidra shrugged. "Didn't miss much really," she told him, then related in short sentences what the old man had said.

"So, Greenway is taken care of." Harvey couldn't keep the smile from his face. "That will make things a lot easier."

"It's of limited value," Deidra warned. "He might break free of the trap, or the one holding it might fall. Galsin did outline the difficulties."

"But for right now, in this moment, we've little to worry about regarding Greenway?" Kristin wanted to know.

"For the moment," Deidra agreed.

~

The voice had yet to come again. He waited for it, hoped for it. He was curious from where it came.

Greenway walked slowly down the road that went nowhere, his eyes searching his surroundings. He had the sensation of being stuck on a treadmill, though the scenery moved, and he could see his boot prints in the dust of the road behind him.

He shook his head. *There is something not right,* he told himself. *Since I first heard that voice.*

Not for the first time, he tried to shout out with his mind. To get the attention of the one behind that voice. He wanted to know who could do such a thing. And why.

"Who are you?" he screamed into the wind that was picking up as the day drew to a close. "What do you want from me? Who are you?" And with each scream, he imagined his mind sending out those words in waves as broad as the sea.

Still, he had found no sign of life. Not so much as an abandoned village. His mind was beginning to pick apart the landscape.

"Harvey is gone," he muttered under his breath. "Harvey is gone, and he took the others with him. And none of them could be behind that voice."

I really could be going mad. "No," he denied aloud. "No, if I were going mad, I wouldn't question it. I wouldn't know it. Everything would seem perfectly reasonable."

And so, he walked on, in search of his new acolytes. If he was to rule the world alone, he was going to need help. A priesthood, those who could spread the word, and administer just punishment.

Perhaps he had let his temper get the better of him at the village.

And at Djorik. He was not perfect, and though his temper had not reared its head often in the many years since his wife's suicide, he'd always had it.

He was unaware of how much he was beginning to question his own motivations. Of how he was slowly talking himself into a more merciful approach to the citizenry of this world. But every now and then, that question loomed in his mind. *Am I going mad? Or is someone messing with my head?*

~

Harvey had shifted to the old camp site, leaving Kristin and Deidra behind. As the sun dropped, and twilight darkened the sky, he strode around the mountain that Greenway had made.

Lance and Weiz would be with him soon. If the others really were headed in this direction, they could arrive at any time. He was prepared for whoever got there first.

He still couldn't believe the entire situation. When he kept busy, when he thought of it in terms of life and death, he could forget for a small while how much he missed his son. He could forget that responsibility, in favour of the one before him.

Harvey sat down on the grass facing the woods.

It had been two-and-a-half months, now, since that first night on this world. A little over one month since they first went to the mountain. Nine days since they'd landed in Nevada. It felt like an age to him.

His son was with his grandparents. His mother-in-law. They were good people, just as his wife had been. They would take care of him. But that didn't relieve of him of his duty as a father. As the sole remaining parent. And yet, he could not go back to him. Not permanently.

You could at least go and say goodbye, he told himself. *Don't let them wonder what happened to you.* He grimaced at the thought. Truth was, the ATF had likely already contacted them and informed them that he had died in the engagement over Ganymede. They'd have had a memorial service, and his family would already be mourning his passing.

Jason was a smart kid. So much more like his mother. He was going to be an engineer, just like her. Harvey smiled thinking about it. He couldn't bring himself to speak of him with the others, not even Weiz. Somehow, speaking of him, made him feel as if he were giving up hope of ever getting home to him.

Haven't you? he asked himself. *You're stuck here. Connected to this world, and the five others. Do you really have any hope left that you'll see him again?*

Harvey was still arguing with himself when he heard movement in the woods.

There was still some light in the sky, but not much, and a few stars could already be seen. He rose from the ground and waited.

Gordon was the first to break the tree line, followed closely by Agent Estard. Then Xavier and Rich, Zim and Ellis, Hadley, Fyord, Constance, Bridges, Duntz, East. They all moved slowly toward him. His eyes remained on the woods, waiting. There were two missing.

Gordon and Estard reached him at the same time, and fell to the ground side by side, as if they were attached by rope.

"Walt and Dames?" They'd been his gunners. *His.*

Estard blinked up at him, wearily. "Don't suppose you have water? Or food?" He leaned back on his arms, and Gordon slumped forward.

All the others, seeing they were where they'd intended, let themselves fall to the ground to either sit or lay down. "A moment," he told the Agent, though his eyes wandered, distracted.

"They're out there somewhere," Gordon pointed to the woods. "We lost them yesterday, but we don't know what happened to them. They knew where we were headed, they could still make it here, if they didn't get lost."

Harvey gave a nod. It was possible, though he doubted it. "Wait here," he said, and took a step that shifted him to the edge of the river. He looked around for something to carry water with and saw Weiz and Lance on the other side.

He shifted to them. "Don't suppose you brought something to put water in," he asked.

Weiz shook her head then held up her palm. Bright colours flickered there a moment, before resolving into a bucket. "How quickly you forget," she chided.

Harvey let her fill the bucket from the river, then took her and Lance by an arm each, and shifted them directly to the waiting airmen.

They took turns and drank sparingly. Every face she saw brought joy to Weiz's eyes, and she moved among them like a mother tending her children. Most were startled to see her, and wide-eyed stares followed her as she moved from pair to pair. Harvey supposed they might feel the same about him and Lance, except they had *seen* Weiz's corpse. People did not come back from the dead.

"They won't all fit in the hut," Lance said softly beside him.

"No," he agreed. "But we'll find something for them. Somewhere. Until Deidra can work out how to send them all home."

Lance made a low whistling sound through his teeth and Harvey turned to face him. "What?"

"She might not," he said.

"Might not, what?"

"Find a way to send them home." The Pilot shrugged. "Don't shoot the messenger on this one. Give her a little time."

Harvey grunted and turned back to the others.

"Glad to see you're actually here," Estard said, looking up at him. "Xavier was sure, but I don't think anyone else was. And I had my doubts."

Harvey shook his head. He didn't know how to answer that. If it hadn't happened to him, he wasn't sure he would have believed, either.

"The price we pay," Lance told the Agent. "Good to see you, Agent Man."

Estard gave a tight smile. "Well, Xavier said it would only take a day. It took two. And we've had naught to eat or drink since we left Earth."

"We'll have to send Kristin to hunt something up," he replied. "We don't have anything ready to hand. Wait here." And again, he shifted, this time to the hut.

Kristin and Deidra were at the table, still, though both wrapped in their own thoughts. Both looked up on his entrance.

"Need you to go catch some food," he told Kristin as he took her by the arm. "The others have arrived."

She nodded but said nothing, and he shifted them to the collapsed village. He let go of her arm.

"Back here in an hour," he said. "Long enough?"

"This is why I need weapons," she said with a frown. "I can't catch rats with air."

"Perhaps not, but I figured you'd just sift through the village and come up with something."

She raised her brows at him. "High hopes, Captain. But I'll give it a shot."

"One hour," he said, and shifted back to the others.

Lance was down at the tree line gathering wood, and Weiz had made a globe of light to better see by.

Harvey frowned at the lot of them. Bruised eyes, sunken shoulders, rough breathing. From the look of them, he was surprised they hadn't all passed out. It was a feeling he could empathise with, and yet seeing it on them now, he also understood it was a feeling he'd not have to suffer again. And that separated them. Put an unpassable void between them. Despite everything they'd gone through in the past few months, this was the first time that it truly hit him.

He took a seat beside Estard. "We'll get you all fed, soon as we can."

The Agent gave a nod. "I never imagined all this," the man said, looking around.

Harvey shot him a sad smile. "Things are rarely ever what we imagine. You all need rest. We'll take care of you."

Gordon looked up at him. "Deidra?"

"She's here," he assured her.

"How did you get here, Captain?" Estard asked. "Xavier was so sure you'd all be here."

"I don't know, Agent. And, if you please, not a topic for tonight." Harvey took another look at everyone. "We'll see you fed, and you should all have a good sleep. We can discuss what's happening tomorrow."

Estard licked his teeth. "Yes, I suppose."

"And Agent?"

"Call me Julian, please. Agent no longer."

Harvey smiled. "Julian. Thank you, for getting them out." He stood and shifted back to the village.

It hadn't been an hour yet, but he couldn't make himself stay. It was an unexpected and uncomfortable feeling that enveloped him. He'd failed them. Agent Estard had helped them, but Harvey had failed. Perhaps no one else saw it, but it put knots in his stomach and a flutter in his heart.

He could hear Kristin moving things around in the village, but he couldn't see her. He walked slowly over to the remains, announcing himself loudly so she would not attack him. She was violent enough without mistaking him for someone — or something — else.

"Potatoes!" She called out, and it sounded like she was on the far side. "Flour! Salt." She appeared from underneath a collapsed hut near the centre, dragging a very large sack.

"This is why I don't do the hunting," he mumbled softly to himself. He turned to her. "Potatoes flour and salt. Just here, or in total?"

In that dim light between twilight and full dark, it was hard to make out her features as she looked to him. "Just here. Got some dried meat — can't tell you what it is — sack of what looks like dried peas, carrots and an onion."

Harvey gave a nod. "That's enough then. It should feed them all."

"Think we should steal some cooking utensils?"

"It's not stealing if the place is abandoned."

Kristin grunted. "Well, I picked out a couple of large pots and ladles, anyway. They did a lot of communal cooking in this place."

"I remember."

"Does it make you sad?"

Harvey blinked at her. He wasn't sure sad was the right word for it. But then, a lot of the time, he could not name his feelings. "I think guilt might be a closer guess," he said.

Kristin shook her head and led him to where she'd left her haul. "It's not your fault, Harvey."

"I could have taken him anywhere. I left him here." He picked up three sacks, shifted them to the camp and returned.

"You couldn't have known he would do it." She loaded his arms with three more sacks, and he made the trip again.

When Harvey popped back into the village, he gave Kristin a level look as she tried to balance two very large pots and a small sack. "That's everything?"

"Everything I found so far." She shrugged and had to rebalance her load to prevent a ladle from falling. "There's probably a lot more down there. I can tell you I wasn't expecting to find much of anything."

Harvey took her by the arm and shifted them back to the old camp site. He did a quick scan for Lance and moved to him. He was leaning over a small pile of wood, hand extended.

"What are you doing?" Harvey asked.

Lance didn't look up. "Trying to start a fire."

"With your hand?"

The tattooed eyes danced on the back of his head, and Harvey growled. "With lightning," Lance informed.

Kristin had arranged everything neatly, ready for the fire. Harvey picked up one of the cauldrons and walked to the river to fill it.

They were all together, and yet, they were apart. Their interactions, in the main, felt disconnected to him. Real, and yet unreal. For the two days that they'd been back, he had felt a void growing between himself and all but Weiz. Now, as he filled the pot, he wondered why that was.

When he returned to Lance, the fire had been lit and he was building another close by. Kristin had begun erecting a wooden tripod from which to hang the pots. Weiz was still out among the survivors, giving them water and speaking softly. He smiled at that.

There was a sense of community in all of this. Yet, though he helped, he didn't feel a part of it. He felt like an observer behind his own eyes, separate and alone. There was something not right about it.

The fires started, the pots in place, the food cooking, Harvey moved to the edge of the old camp site and looked down at everyone. They'd all moved to huddle together around the fires, and he felt content that they were safe.

Kristin came over to him, though he didn't see her until she was a few feet away. He said nothing, just waited.

"What's the problem?" she asked.

"I feel like an outsider," he said. "I don't know why. A week ago, I was one of them."

"And now you know you'll never go home again."

"I don't feel like one of *us* either."

"Whatever that means," Kristin mumbled in a whisper, then turned to face him. "We are changed. More than changed. Parts of us rebel, and parts of us embrace. You won't feel like you belong until you choose."

Harvey didn't take his eyes off the camp. "Choose what?"

"To rebel or embrace," she told him. "We were fine before, because we wanted the same things. Go home. Get to our families. See Earth again." She sighed. "Now we stay here. We have no choice in that. Not really. But if we rebel, we could keep trying to find a way to get back. And that makes us one of them. If we embrace, then it is this world we look to. The people here we need to look after."

"It seems so easy for the rest of you," Harvey confessed. "The way you all move among them. Like we were never separated. Like there is no choice."

"It's not easy," Kristin assured.

"Then how do you do it?" He really wanted to know.

A few times she took a deep breath as if to start, then sighed it out. When he looked at her, she smiled. "One on one, here," she said slowly, "and you're fine to talk to me. Weiz is the same, I am guessing." He gave her a nod. "Just connect with one at a time. Stop trying to make it a group thing."

"I don't see how that will help."

"Connect to the individuals, Harvey," she said. "Take a step back, speak to one at a time. That's how any sane person makes friends. Have you forgotten?"

He gave her a tight smile. "I think I had."

She hit him playfully. "Start to remember. You'll get there."

"And if I don't?"

Kristin shrugged. "Then perhaps you're speaking to the wrong people. Not everyone can get along."

He watched her move back toward the camp. Friends. He'd never thought of any of them as friends. His tribe, his people, his crew, his comrades and colleagues. But not friends. He'd need to work on that. *Not tonight*, he thought. *Tonight, they can rest.*

CHAPTER FIFTEEN

Deidra, left alone at the hut, contemplated her options, as she had all day. But now they were close by, all those airmen who wanted nothing more than to go home. And she dreaded the question they would ask when they arrived. How? Will you do it?

She was afraid for her sense of self. But she also knew that Lance was probably right, and the choice might be taken from her.

She sat with her head in her hands. She paced the floorboards. She went outside and stared up at the stars.

Dane came to mind, again and again. The day he'd taken her to the medieval fair, knelt down in the mud of the lists after the jousting was done, and asked for her hand. His brown eyes, soft and gentle. His crooked smile, genuine and humble. The way he laughed, a deep bass rumble, that travelled through her chest and swelled below the pit of her stomach.

She would have to forget him. Again. Though a part of her knew that she would not see him again, another piece fought that off. She could find a way. With all the knowledge that would be at her disposal, she could find some way of getting home again.

But would she want to? Would she care, then? That was the problem. If she forgot who she was, getting there would mean nothing. Not to her or Dane.

Tears leaked from her eyes at the near impossible choice. The frustration dug deep in her chest and took hold of her heart till she felt it was being squeezed by a giant hand. Her spine ached and the pit of her stomach felt leaden.

She didn't want to give it up.

She didn't want to stay like this.

Gazing up at the stars, she tried to calm her mind. "I won't have this again," she whispered. "I know it. This is the last chance I have to be me. But what does that even mean when everyone who knows me is on another world."

The stars winked at her. A quarter moon shone high in the sky to the west. There were no answers up there. But it was beautiful.

How would she look them in the eyes and tell them, "If I'm stuck, so are you"? It was not her desire, but she knew that's how it would sound.

Would it be so bad for them? She shook off the thought, knowing the truth of it. Of course it would.

She took a deep breath and spoke to the stars. "If it's got to be done, then let's get it over with." As she exhaled, she let the God take over.

~

He still didn't know what it was. That feeling of something not being right. But the suspicions in him grew, as he began to notice how alike the landscape was, day and night, for two days, now. The sensation of a treadmill just would not stop.

So, he stopped.

Greenway looked around. In the darkness it was harder to see details and distance, but he could see well enough to suit him.

Thickets and copses. Grasslands, and woods. No sign of anything resembling civilisation.

His attempt to make that voice speak to him again had proved futile. Though a small part in him tried to convince himself that it was his own voice, buried somewhere deep, there was an abiding rejection of that in his conscious mind. It just didn't *feel* right.

"I reject it," he whispered to the breeze. "I reject it!" he yelled into his mind. "I reject it!" he screamed into the wilderness.

There was a — *crack* he thought — and his mind tried to repair his vision. It swam and shifted and resolved again to what he had been seeing for the past two days.

Greenway twitched a smile. He knew now. It definitely wasn't him. Someone was playing with him. Someone strong. Not one of the others, even if they'd had such talent, they were gone. So, some remained.

"Come out!" he screamed. "Show yourself! Face me!"

Insects hummed and chirped. Leaves whispered in a slight breeze. Nothing changed.

As he had earlier, he sent out a mind wave — as he imagined it to be — along with a shout, "I reject you! I reject this! I reject it!"

There came a sense of warping. Like acid dreams, where things and people stretched and elongated, snapped back, and stretched again. The sensation made his stomach churn and his throat clench, even as he screamed out again.

The world around him shattered. The sensation of someone else in his head, disappeared.

He was standing in a clearing, and he could see his own boot prints had made a furrow in the dirt along the tree line. He'd been walking in circles here, for who knows how long.

Greenway chuckled. "Nice try," he whispered. "I look forward to meeting you."

He walked out of the clearing, and into the woods. He was going to find that road. He had a mission, and he did not intend to let this stop him.

"Ready or not," he said.

~

Estard had slept through to morning. It was unlike him, at any time, to sleep for more than a few hours without waking. Sometimes it was dreams he remembered. Often it was dreams he did not. He had the sense, though, that since landing here, he had not dreamed at all. And it was twice, now, he had slept through.

The small camp had a subdued hum. The fires had been lit, the stew reheated. A pot of water stood between, a ladle propped on top. The early morning sky was a faded blue-grey that made Estard think of clouds close to rain.

Gordon sat beside him, a small wooden bowl in her hands from which she slurped at the hot stew. He'd already had his fill, and his bowl sat in front of him on the dew-wet grass.

"They're all here," he said. Gordon made a sound of agreement without taking her lips from the bowl. "And they..." He didn't know how to finish the thought. Had powers? That was absurd. And yet, he had seen with his own eyes, the dead woman making lights from colours that sprang into her hand. The Captain, moving from one place to another in the blink of an eye. And that Pilot, Lance, starting fires with lightning from his hand.

Gordon put down her empty bowl and wiped her chin with a sleeve. "They're Gods," she said, as if that answered everything.

"You all keep saying that, but what does it even mean? I think maybe this is the dream," he mumbled. "And that's why I can't remember what happens between sleeping and waking, because that is the real world."

"Maybe," Gordon agreed as she put a fist to her mouth to stifle a burp. "But I doubt it."

"Oh?"

"Well, I'm not dreaming, and I'm fair certain I'm not a figment of your imagination." She shrugged. "When Deidra comes, she'll get us home. Took two months last time. But we have the ship now, so maybe it'll just mean a few adjustments and we can all be on our way."

Estard began to suck at his teeth but bit his lip instead. He found it difficult to believe that a woman who didn't even know who she was, would be able to get these people home.

"Excuse me," he said as he levered himself from the ground. "Think I'll stretch my legs."

Gordon gave him a small wave but said nothing.

He trod carefully through the short grass. The small mountain and what lay at its base called to him, but he ignored it. There was nothing there he'd be able to make sense of. So, he made his way to the edge of the stream.

It was perhaps fifty yards across, though it appeared shallow and clear. He leaned down and cupped his hands in the water, feeling the cold. The day had not yet warmed, but Estard removed his coat and shirt and began to wash. He pulled handfuls of grass and sniffed at them, decided it would do for soap and went to work.

"Good idea," Estard hadn't heard Harvey come up behind him, so jumped slightly, lost his footing and fell on his rear.

"I like to be clean," he replied dryly.

Harvey settled on his haunches beside him, but politely looked into the distance. "You got them out, and you got them through the woods," the Captain said. "I just spoke to Xavier."

Estard finished up and patted himself dry with the outside of his coat. "I'm not sure what you're expecting me to say."

Harvey shrugged and shot him a glance before looking away again. "I'm not sure either. Do you regret it?"

"Regret what? Coming?" He buttoned his shirt and thought about it. "I don't know yet. Figure it could swing either way. None of it feels real at all."

"Some things do take a while to sink in."

"They do," Estard agreed and turned to face Harvey full on. "Why are we talking, Captain? Meaning no disrespect, but you no longer need me to get you out, I am of limited value to you."

Harvey sighed and stood. Estard rose with him. "You interest me. You had no reason to help us, yet here you are. I don't think you could have fully comprehended what you were asking when you made coming a condition of your assistance, yet you do not regret it. I am a curious man."

Estard chuckled deep in his throat for a moment. "You want to know why I came." Harvey gave a sharp nod. "Everyone has asked the same thing. Well, those who'll actually speak to me. And truth, Captain, I don't know. I really don't."

"There had to be something," Harvey insisted. "No one just deserts his post on a *whim*."

The former Agent shook his head slowly and resisted the urge to suck on his teeth. "Plenty of people desert on a whim. Perhaps not in your time...."

Harvey grunted. "If you think it's a whim, you're not looking deep enough." He gave a small smile to take the sting from the words. "You'll need to start looking deeper, Agent, because you'll have another decision to make soon."

"I imagine there are many decisions to be made. To which are you referring?"

"Whether you'll stay here with us or go back to Earth with them."

"You're staying?"

"Unlike you, we don't have a choice."

Harvey walked off without another word, and Estard didn't try to stop him. He stood there blinking at the space where the Captain had been, pondering his words.

The sun was a little higher in the sky, and it became a clear blue.

Why? He'd asked himself the same question again and again and could not come up with a suitable answer. It hadn't been a whim. He'd thought long and hard about it before he helped them escape.

A beautiful girl? he thought. *A disappearing woman? The mystery of where they'd come from? One alone is not enough.*

Estard picked up a few pebbles from the edge of the water and began skimming them across the surface, one by one as he thought.

Perhaps all together, his reasons were still not enough. Not when it meant he could not go back. Was it simple curiosity? He shook his head.

It's the girl, he told himself. *It's the damned girl, and you know it. So why do you keep running from the thought?* He couldn't answer that any more than he could the other.

He'd never been married. But he'd had a woman, once, after the war. He'd loved her. He'd given her gifts and taken her to fine places for food and dancing. He'd introduced her to his parents and his friends. After a year, he'd proposed. She'd turned him down and admitted she held no affection for him. That she had been seeing other people, even while he courted her.

Estard's heart had been crushed. He'd known other women, but he'd never been taken by them.

He threw the last pebble into the river and watched it bounce four times before sinking into the water.

Go or stay? Here or there? It wasn't really a decision. Not for him. He knew who he was following. He just didn't want to admit it.

~

After his brief conversation with Agent Estard, Harvey shifted to the village. He had no reason to be there, nothing he needed to do. But he looked upon the devastation to remind himself of what Greenway had become. That he was still out there.

Kristin thought he'd forgotten how to make friends, and she was probably right. Before they'd been stuck on this planet, he'd been planning to retire. There'd been plenty of people in the ATF he'd respected, and comrades he was happy to see while on assignment, but all his *friends* were on Earth. And he'd had those friends so long, he could barely remember how he'd met most of them.

He took another step and shifted to Djorik. The townspeople were still clearing away the rubble.

Someone saw him shift onto the road and pointed in his direction, whispering softly to the person beside him. Harvey ignored them as he surveyed the damage.

The people were doing well. Carts and wagons full of stacked rock were coming out of the gates, led by what looked like oxen. For the most part, the outer wall still stood, though here and there small sections would need to be repaired.

Harvey didn't want to go inside. He felt like an intruder here. Though he had not moved, and no one approached him, several sets of eyes now watched him warily. With a sigh, he stepped and shifted back to the camp site.

His eyes searched for Weiz but could not see her. Nor Lance or Kristin. He frowned at the small group of airmen. Three months ago, there had been over two hundred. Now there were twelve. He had to believe that if Walt and Dames were going to come out of those woods, they'd have done so by now. He was saddened by their loss. They were the first from his own crew.

No, he told himself, *they weren't the first. Lance, Kristin and I were. We were lost as soon as we killed those Giants.*

The eyes of the airmen shifted to him, just as those of the townsfolk had, and he found himself becoming irritated by the attention. He tried not to let it show as he took a step and shifted back to the river.

Estard was gone, though he hadn't seen the Agent with the

others.

Harvey took a good look around. He wanted to know where the others had gone. Weiz, most of all. They needed to work out where they were going to take these airmen. They needed shelter, and food. Logistics. It wasn't his strong suit, but he did want to take care of them.

He was about to shift back to the hut, when he saw Kristin walking toward him from the side of the rising mountain. He waited without a word.

"How long do you think it will keep growing?" She indicated the mountain with a jerk of her head.

Harvey shrugged. "I'm not sure even Greenway knows, and he's the one who made it."

"You went to check out the town again?"

"You know me too well."

Kristin stopped beside him and kept her eyes on the far horizon. "I had a vision, while you were gone."

"Bad?"

"Another town. Greenway. Earth heaving and shaking." She shrugged but didn't look at him. "Doom and gloom, I guess. But I can't bring myself to feel any kind of urgency about it. Isn't that odd?"

"Perhaps it's not an immediate problem. Perhaps we have time to prepare." He didn't feel any urgency either. He did feel responsible, for Greenway, for the people he was terrorising. But no urgency.

"Maybe. Maybe not. I couldn't tell you." She looked to him. "I'll let you know if I have another." She made to walk away, but Harvey pulled her up short.

"Have you seen Weiz?"

"She went into the woods. Don't know why or how long she'll be." She started to walk off again, stuttered in her step and turned her head to face him. "Something isn't right," she said. "You feel that, don't you?"

Harvey nodded. "Since we got back from Earth," he replied. "Perhaps it will pass."

"Maybe." She sighed and looked around. "We still need to scout out those other two worlds."

"Not today, I think."

Kristin nodded and moved off without another word.

Harvey once again found himself staring at the far horizon. Kristin was right. Something was off and had been for days. All of the urgency had seeped out of everything, as if they had all the time in the world. Greenway might be wrecking another town or village even as he stood there, but Harvey felt no immediate need to find out.

He shook himself. He knew, intellectually, what the right thing to do was. He definitely did not want Greenway harming anyone else. He felt sadness and anger in equal measures at the thought. So, what stayed his hand? Why didn't he go out searching for the man, try to stop him?

What was he missing?

A great roar sounded in the woods, coming from more than one throat, and all thoughts fled. He knew that sound, and it sent shivers down his back.

The Giants had come.

Chapter Sixteen

Weiz froze where she was as soon as she heard it. Memories of that night flooding through her mind. Her breath came in ragged gasps, her hands trembled, and her heart felt as though it might come right out of her chest. Hard as she tried to calm herself, the visions of men being torn apart and tossed aside made it difficult.

She'd come into the woods to gather more firewood. A mundane task, but she'd felt the need to be doing something, and to be away from the staring eyes. Now she felt the need to be anywhere but where she was.

The roar came again.

Weiz closed her eyes and tried to remember Galsin, the old man, the old God. He was helping them. He was not trying to hurt them.

But he'd also said the others would choose. He'd also been deliberately tight lipped about what might happen if no one wanted to be chosen.

She didn't know how to become a shadow, the way the old ones did. Part of her thought that might be a mistake, in any case. She couldn't die. She needed to remind herself that she was in no danger.

Her feet moved stiffly for the first few steps, but loosened as she continued until she was running back to the camp. It wasn't far, and as soon as she broke from the trees, she saw them all, on their feet, staring into the woods with wary eyes.

There was yet another roar, and she tried to count how many there were to make such a noise. She thought three, perhaps four. She hoped Galsin was among them.

The silence stretched on, and the roars did not come again. Weiz saw Gordon and Estard up front and speaking softly to one another. Kristin was walking over from the mountain, and Harvey popped into view near Estard.

She made her way to them.

"— been calling to each other," Gordon was saying when Weiz got close enough to hear.

"But you don't believe that," Estard said. He glanced at her as she approached, but otherwise kept his eyes to the woods.

"The first time we saw them," Harvey told the Agent, "they didn't make a sound. Not a peep. Couldn't hear them walking through the woods, because their feet never touched the ground. If they're making that sound, it's because they want us to know they're here."

"But take one step in the wrong direction," Weiz said softly, "and they could tear us apart before we blink."

Harvey looked her in the eye. "Not us."

She shook her head to indicate that wasn't what she'd meant but said nothing more.

"Do we just wait for them?" Estard asked. "Shouldn't we... go somewhere else?"

"Galsin said they'd be coming. That he'd return with them," Weiz said. "It might be just that." She was sceptical, and it was obvious in her tone.

They all waited tensely, eyeing the tree line. Some of the airmen looked ready to fight, others to run. Weiz held up her hands and made a laser rifle. She didn't know how much good it would do if more than one attacked, but she wanted to be prepared. She might not be able to kill them, but it would take them time to return from the field.

Harvey looked at the weapon with a raise of the brow, and she knew he was asking if she thought it necessary. She gave him a twitch of a smile that said she was uncertain. He nodded and put his eyes back on the woods.

It felt like an age before the first man showed himself. It was probably closer to a minute.

"Put that away!" Galsin shouted at her, his walking stick thumping hard into the ground. "I don't know what it is, but it doesn't look inviting."

Weiz let the laser rifle disappear. "What was all that roaring about?"

The old man shook his head in disgust, but raised his walking stick and three others emerged from the woods as he stepped forward.

They were all dressed alike, in faded red robes that looked closer to rags. But there, any similarity ended. One was a woman who didn't look a day over eighteen, if that. She had long, black hair that fell to the small of her back. Dark eyes that stared out of a face so white it may never have seen the sun. She walked with back straight, and expressionless dignity.

Another was a man, who could have been anywhere between twenty-five and forty. Golden hair, shining blue eyes, tan skin and a ready smile. He strode like a warrior, graceful and alert.

The last was an old woman. She appeared ancient next to Galsin. She walked with a hunch, though she had no walking stick to aid her. Her grey-white hair was pulled back into a very tight bun, which pulled at the skin of her forehead. Wrinkles marred her face, and liver spots showed here and there. It was hard to imagine this old crone as a Giant.

Everyone was silent as they approached and stopped before Weiz and the others.

Galsin used his walking stick to point at his companions as he introduced them. "Merien," — the young one —, "Harlo," — the man —, "Gretta." — the crone.

Merien and Harlo nodded their greetings, but the crone looked beyond them to the others.

"They're here to choose," Galsin told them.

Harvey and Weiz looked to one another, then back to the old man.

"Are you not?" Weiz asked.

"I'll be the last," he said, looking her in the eye. "I feel there is much to be resolved before I make my choice."

Weiz craned her neck to see what the newcomers were doing. All three had sat down in a cross-legged position facing the airmen a few yards from the closest. Their eyes were closed, hands on knees. She looked back to Galsin.

"How will they communicate?" she asked.

Galsin waved his hand dismissively. "Not something to concern us today. It will take some time before they decide, and more urgent business is at hand."

"I do not like this choosing, business," Harvey said.

"Your likes and dislikes are immaterial to me," Galsin replied. "Greenway is out of the mind trap. Almeron is resting, he won't be able to help again."

Weiz cracked her knuckles and breathed deep. She'd hoped they'd have more time. "Where is he?"

"Two days north of Djorik, in the woods. Once he finds the road, I am afraid it won't be long until he comes upon people."

"What are we supposed to do about it?" Harvey snapped.

Galsin shook his head. "How you choose to deal with him is up to you." He looked behind them and pointed with his walking stick. "Can I have some of that?" He started moving toward the fires, without waiting for an answer.

Weiz and Harvey were forced to follow.

The airmen were watching the newcomers with wary eyes, and every movement spoke of a readiness to fight or flee. None were sure what was going on after all that roaring from the woods, and Weiz did not believe she'd be able to answer to anyone's satisfaction. How would they feel about being chosen? *I think they have about as much choice as the rest of us did. But at least they'll know it's coming.*

"How we choose, is the problem," Harvey told the old man.

"Explain the issue," Galsin sighed. He stopped in front of the fire, took a bowl and helped himself.

"Killing him would be pointless," Weiz said. The old man nodded around a mouthful. "He'd just end up back at the field, like the rest of us." Again, a nod.

"If I take him to another of the worlds," Harvey said, "and he died, he'd be back in the field."

Galsin licked his lips as he pulled the bowl away. "Probably. Haven't had an opportunity to test that."

"I died on another world, and ended up in the field," Harvey put forward. "As did Kristin."

"Faulty assumption," Galsin replied around half a mouthful. He swallowed before continuing. "I do not know why it took you all so long to get back here in the first place. You should not have been able to be away for more than two days. You would have arrived regardless."

Harvey and Weiz shared a moment of silent communication. His eyes said he didn't trust the man, and her raised brows indicated what he said was possible, either way.

"We travelled through time," Harvey muttered.

Galsin stopped still, eyes wide, brows climbing. He seemed to remember himself and put the empty bowl by the fire with some others. "Through time, you say?"

"Not on purpose," Weiz said. "And I was dead before we arrived."

The old man shook himself, neck sinking and back arching, one foot off the ground. He looked as if he felt something crawling on him. When he stood still once more, he said, "In all my many thousands of years, witnessing many things beyond your imagination, time travel was not something I ever thought possible."

"You have a strange reaction to it, old man," said Weiz.

"I had a twitch."

Harvey shook his head. "So, what do we do with Greenway?"

"Take him to one of the other worlds," the old man suggested. "Drop him off and leave him there, then see what happens. If he returns, think of something else. If he does not, job well done." He shrugged it off and pushed past them, moving toward the others he'd brought with him.

They were still seated cross legged, a respectable distance from the airmen, but now their eyes were open, and they were speaking softly among themselves.

Weiz glanced behind her as they followed, and spotted Kristin and Lance observing from the bottom of Greenway's mountain. She frowned at them, but let it go. They should have come over and joined them, but she'd have been lying to herself if she didn't admit she preferred the woman stay away.

Galsin stopped a few feet in front of Merien. "Were you able to gauge them?"

The younger woman looked up at him with a small smile. "They are weary, but fighters still. I could not pick out cowardice in any one of them."

"So, any could be suitable?"

"We must whittle the prospects."

"Will you wait for the others?"

"It is likely they'll arrive before we are done, father."

Galsin smiled and petted her cheek. "Good enough."

The crone looked to him. "I am not so picky, Galsin." Her voice was a dry rasp that suited her ancient appearance, but there was a strength behind them. "I would let whoever wishes to, come forward and trade lives. I was old before the turning."

"As you say, mother." Galsin bowed his head to her. "And you, Harlo?"

"I am in no hurry," the man shrugged. "Today, next year. It's all the same, really."

"Very good," said Galsin. "Continue your observations. Should be no more than two or three days before the others arrive." Then he left them and started toward the woods.

Weiz and Harvey followed once more. "Old man," Weiz said, "we're not done here."

"I brought who I needed to bring," he responded without turning around. "I said what I needed to say. What else is there?"

"What if none of them wants to be chosen?" Harvey asked. "Given the choice myself, and knowing the consequences, I'd have said no. How can I then ask it of the men and women here?"

Galsin did stop at that and turned to face them. "We are monsters to you." He looked each of them in the eyes. "The others, in their shadow-forms, tearing you lot to pieces, were perhaps more-so. They were to us, too. What had become of them... None of us would do that." He paused with a sigh. "But we are still monsters. We may not kill you, unless forced to do so, but monsters still. The choice is ours, and we must make it. We will not ask permission." He gave a nod when he saw they understood.

He turned on his heel once more and moved toward the woods.

Just as he hit the treeline, he held up his walking stick and shouted, "Do something about Greenway!" and then disappeared among the trees.

Harvey and Weiz were glued to the spot, watching as he left, each deep in thought.

Weiz knew that Harvey would be thinking about what to do with Greenway, but she was concerned for the remaining airmen. There weren't many of them left. And the old man said they'd have no choice in the matter. It made her feel as helpless as she had that first night on this world when she'd witnessed the massacre.

"Two days north of Djorik," Harvey muttered. "I don't know what I am supposed to do with him."

Weiz put a hand on his arm. "Do as the old man suggested," she said. "I doubt there is more we *can* do."

He looked into her eyes and nodded slowly. "You know, I can honestly say, I never once imagined my life might turn out like this."

Weiz smiled. "No. Me either."

"I'll take Kristin and scout out the remaining two worlds. See which one might be the best fit for our fallen Captain."

Weiz opened her mouth to reply, but the man had already shifted. Her smile turned sad, and she spun on her foot in time to see Harvey take Kristin by the arm and disappear.

She forced that out of her mind and concentrated on the task at hand. If Galsin and his lot were not going to give the airmen a choice, then Weiz needed to find a way to protect them. If it was two or three days until the others arrived, then that was how long they had to work something out.

The misty morning air was beginning to warm with the promise of a clear summer day. There was not even a hint of white wispy cloud in the sky, and what breezes came were short and sweet gusts, filled with the scent of the woods.

Weiz moved slowly toward her people. She wished for a fleet of ships and an enemy to face. *Even a squad of bombers*, she thought, *or a sky battle in the Earth-bound F1-86's.* At heart, she was a pilot. She understood flight tactics. She understood space battles. This kind of thing was beyond her. Space exploration was for astronauts, and they'd not yet gone beyond their own solar system. Fighting on the ground was for the Army, not the Air Force. She had rudimentary training in hand-to-hand combat, how to use a knife and guns, just in case her plane crashed, and she was forced to eject in enemy territory. But when they started fighting in space.... *It's all beyond me.*

It took her a moment to realise she had stopped and was staring at the men and women before her. Some of them stared back, probably wondering what she had in mind.

She spied Lance, still by the mountain by himself. She started toward him. He was a strange man, to her mind, but solid.

As she walked through the camp, eyes on the ground, the airmen followed her movements and spoke in hushed voices. She did not try to listen, though she knew she probably should have. She ignored the ones Galsin had brought, as best she could.

When Lance saw that she was moving toward him, he sat down to wait.

"We have a serious problem," she told him as she dropped to the ground beside him. She explained the situation as best she could.

"And you're asking me?" He seemed genuinely surprised.

"Your opinion is as valid as any," she said.

The Pilot looked out over the airmen with a frown. "We didn't have any choice in the matter," he said, "why did you imagine the others would be any different?"

"I suppose when you put a human face on these things, you make assumptions."

Lance shook his head. "All we can do is move them, and even that may not be enough. Best and only chance I can see is if Deidra finds a way to get them home before the others come." He looked to her, eyes searching. "But that's assuming the ones already here don't take liberties before they arrive."

"They said it unlikely."

"And you trust them?"

"Not even a little bit."

Lance sighed. "Then let's hope that Deidra has decided to help."

"It took her a month, last time," Weiz reminded him. "What makes you think she could do it in less, this time?"

"She had to do it from scratch, before. A few adjustments to the ship should be enough." He shrugged. "I'm not a tech, or a scientist, but I have to figure having the equipment already available will be a lot quicker."

Weiz grunted. "But she may not," she said. "She might need a whole new set of equipment."

"It's all moot, unless she's willing," Lance breathed. "No point in if's and but's and maybes. Have you spoken to any of them" — he nodded toward the airmen — "about what is happening?"

"Not yet."

"But you plan to?"

"I do."

Lance got up and brushed himself off. Weiz followed suit.

"I'll go back to Deidra," he said. "You go speak to Estard. For all that he is an outsider, they're all looking to him, now. He's trying to push it on Gordon, but he's the Captain. You get me?"

She gave a curt nod, and the Pilot moved off. She watched him until he got to the river, and heard him muttering to himself as he waded in.

They all had choices to make, but how much of it was actually in their hands? Was it fate? It was not something she'd considered, before. She'd never believed in a God, though she'd tried. She thought it would be nice to believe in something greater, but she could not bring herself to it.

Weiz gave a last heavy sigh, then made her way to Estard. The next few days were going to be long ones.

CHAPTER SEVENTEEN

When Harvey shifted into the new world, the last thing he'd expected was to be immediately surrounded by men with swords. They wore leather armour, much in the fashion of medieval England, as far as he could tell. Bows and arrows, maces, axes, spears and swords all pointed toward him and Kristin.

He kept one hand firmly around Kristin's upper arm. They were too close to these men, and even if he shifted on his first step, a spear or sword could easily get either one of them.

His eyes searched the area beyond the men. There were tents of hide, set up in semi-permanence, in rows that could pass for streets. He saw a few children poking curious eyes from tent flaps, and though some were pulled back from the entrances, others remained to watch. From what he could tell, at least twenty men surrounded them.

"I mean you no harm," he said, and hoped fervently that whatever allowed them to understand the people of Eridu would work here too.

None of the men answered.

The sound of boots squelching through the mud made two of the men turn. From behind a tent came a man in sky blue robes. He had a sword at his left hip, and a dagger at his right. A baldric of throwing knives slung across his chest, a quiver of arrows peaked above his right shoulder, and he held a long bow.

As the man approached, the men that surrounded them moved aside to create a path.

Harvey could feel the men still behind him, but he thought about taking the risk.

The new arrival stopped a few yards away and leaned on his bow. "Are you a sorcerer?" he asked.

Yes, this was the right time. He took a step forward, opening his mouth as if to answer, squeezed on Kristin's arm, and shifted.

They were on the great plain before the mountains, on the world where they'd seen the horses. As soon as he let go of Kristin, she rounded on him and struck him in the stomach. He doubled over and coughed, winded by the blow.

"Took your fucking time," she said.

He growled at her as his breathing steadied. "Bitch, if you don't stop hitting me, I swear I will leave you on this world!" He'd truly had enough of it.

She didn't look in the slightest bit sorry as she answered, "Then I'll kill myself and wake in the field."

He growled again as he straightened. "Whatever your damage, woman, you need to stop hitting people."

Kristin shrugged and looked around. "Fine. I won't hit you again. Can we go, now?"

He grabbed her by the arm, mumbling obscenities under his breath, and shifted them to the next world.

Stretched out before them was one of the most beautiful landscapes Harvey had ever seen. A waterfall gushed out of a mountain to his left, hitting rocks and breaking apart on its way down, so by the time it hit the river below, there were four separate flows.

What grass he could see was green and luscious, the trees full of colour and growing tall, a forest thickly canopied. The sun hung low in the sky, and the nearby clouds were edged with gold. He could see small animals near the calmer water of a lake, close to the waterfalls. The air was damp and warm, and smelled of sweet things he could not name. Crickets sang, and the hum filled his mind.

Harvey was about to take a step forward, but Kristin put an arm across him to hold him back.

"Don't know how you feel about plummeting off a cliff," she said through a forced smile, "but I'd like my ride to stay alive long enough to get me home."

He looked down and saw that they were mere inches from the edge of a sharp drop, which would have seen him fall at least eight hundred feet. He turned and saw behind them a grey-white stone cliff, rising higher. They were on a small ledge, not a path or plateau as he'd assumed.

"This place is gorgeous," Harvey said. "I could retire here."

"Yes, it's beautiful," Kristin agreed, "But it's a rainforest, and if our own on Earth are anything to go by, you'll find some of the most inhospitable creatures under its canopy."

"Such as?"

"Spiders, snakes, and scorpions would be my main concern. They're the ones you're least likely to see coming."

"But there are others?"

"I'd imagine there are some territorial beasts," she nodded. "Cats, mostly. Monkeys or Gorillas probable."

"Well, I won't bring Greenway here. I dislike the thought of what he might do to it."

"So, we move on," Kristin sighed.

"Yes," Harvey nodded. "Prepare yourself for that desert. We need to do a more thorough check of that world."

She held onto his arm, and he stepped in the desert. They were at the small rock pool they'd found the previous day, in the shade of overhanging rock.

Harvey walked out into the sunlight and shifted to the top of the overhang so he could get a good look at the dry, flat land.

"We should just leave him here," Kristin called up to him. "He can't shift around you like you, and deserts have a way of disorienting people. He could wander lost for a very long time."

"We'll get a better idea of how big it is first. There are people that live in deserts. I don't want to make a mistake." He shifted back down to her and held out his hand.

Kristin took it with a tight smile. "I have yet to see a single track of man or beast in this place. And if I found it anywhere, it would be near water."

Harvey shrugged, and they shifted.

The desert still surrounded them on all sides, the cracked hardpan, the rock spires, great and small, in the distance and close by. He shifted them again. Still the same. He shifted them four times, with the only sign of life being some plants Harvey didn't recognise, growing in the cracks of some of the rock spires.

"It will do," he said.

They shifted.

~

Estard lifted his face to the sun and closed his eyes. The dead woman — Weiz — had told him what was happening with the newcomers. Now he had to think on what that might mean. Whether he wanted to be chosen. How much did it mean to these people to get home.

I won't be going home, he thought. *Even if I go back to Earth, it won't be home.*

The way Weiz had explained it, they'd be immortal until they chose not to be. That didn't sound so bad to him. Fantastical, unreal, but not bad. And, even if he could get back to Earth in his own time, the only thing worth going back for was Bob. He knew Harris would look after the mutt, so he knew he'd be well cared for, but he'd been a very loyal dog and he missed him.

Estard opened his eyes and looked to the three cross-legged people at the very edge of the camp. He wondered what powers they had. He wondered why they were giving them away. How old they might be. Why did one look as though she might fall to dust in a strong wind, while another was a young woman? There was nothing particularly special about the man, except that he kept looking toward Estard, and it disturbed him.

"You're thinking about it, aren't you?" Gordon asked. She'd been privy to his conversation with the Commander.

"Yes," he admitted. "Yes, I am."

"Why?"

He shrugged and looked to her. "I'm curious," he told her. "Curse of my life, I think. Gets me into a lot of trouble."

Gordon shot a laugh. "Curiosity has gotten many people into a lot of trouble," she said. "Not a personal curse. I believe it is one that has infected our race since the dawn."

He chuckled with her. "You are probably right. But even so. It has been my main driving force for years."

"So, what power do you hope to get?" she asked him playfully.

Again, he shrugged. "I'm not sure I am that picky."

"There is not one power in the whole of the known universe that entices you more than another?"

"Truthfully, I am not very interested in power at all." He sighed. "Like many things, I am not sure why I want to do it. And probably won't know until its ten years done."

"You are a very strange man, Julian." Gordon patted him lightly on the shoulder and he smiled.

"No matter where I go," he said, "I am the odd man out. But that's alright with me."

"You already know how I feel about it," she said. "So, this is me hoping that the Commander and the others can come up with some way to get us out of it. Doesn't sound like we'll be given a choice. I'm reminded of the situation with Greenway all over again."

"You'll have to explain that."

"Greenway threatened us. Told everyone that we had to stay, couldn't leave." She pointed to the mountain that grew slowly behind them. "He made that. Probably the smallest testament to his power."

"Big bully. Got you." He indicated she should continue.

"For over a month, Deidra had been working on a way to get us home. When Greenway made his demands, the Commander and the others knew that we would not remain safe here, so they took the only ship that had enough fuel for an in-atmosphere flight, and a handful of airmen."

"I don't see the correlation," Estard admitted. "You all ran off and avoided him."

She shook her head. "No. We didn't. A good many of us were left behind." She glanced back at the Commander, who was speaking with a pair of airmen whose names he did not know.

"So, what happened then?"

"Greenway came back. Offered us a choice. Go with him or wander lost in this place alone. Deidra had given us all directions to where they'd flown the ship. Said they'd give us all a month to get there. Perhaps we could have started out immediately, but I doubt that would have stopped Greenway. Some did go off by themselves. We've not seen them since."

Estard remained quiet and let her continue in her own time. "We chose. Some flat out refused, and when we were asked to destroy the camp, they fought back. When they left, some may have been severely injured, and I'm not sure how many actually survived. Even if they all survived, I have no idea how we might find them."

"You think they're alive?"

"It's possible," she said softly. "I didn't want to follow Greenway. I had a plan, the ones back at camp knew, the ones that ran away." She shook her head and breathed deep.

"So, there are still some airmen wandering around out here," he said, more to himself then in response.

"I can't know for sure." She looked him in the eye then. "I was going to kill him. Wait for the best moment and kill him. But the longer we were with him, the more he began to make sense to me. When the right opportunity to do something about him never came, I felt relieved. Stupid, and relieved."

"Do the others know that you were with him? What you did?"

She shook her head slowly. "A few might have guessed. But no one has said anything. It is a shame I will carry with me for the rest of my life, Agent Estard. The only thing I wanted was to get home. So desperately, I want to go home to my children."

"I'll not say anything," he assured her. "But I think you should."

She gaped at him as if he'd gone mad. "Why would I want to do that?"

He looked around the camp at the others sitting in pairs or groups. There was barely any hope left in the lot of them, and it was obvious by the way they spoke, and the looks they gave each other. The way their shoulders slumped and smiles never touched their eyes. If she told any of them, it was likely they might lose that last piece of hope they held to.

"Not everyone," he said. "Just Harvey, or the Commander."

"And again, I ask why." She was becoming irritated.

"Why did you feel the need to confess to me, just now?" he asked in turn. "Because you needed to release your guilt? I understand what a mother will do for her children." In his mind flashed the child with his red truck, and he brushed it aside ruthlessly. He had no time for past mistakes. "I was not there, and do not judge. Why should your Commander? Don't you think they might like to know what happened? That there may be others out there?"

Gordon smiled at him. "Maybe. Probably. But, at the same time, what if it's a false hope? What if they're dead already?"

"What if they're not?"

There was a long pause before Gordon answered, "I do hope they're not. I really do."

He held up his hands in a placating gesture. "I suggest you tell one of the 'Giant Killers', as you call them. I don't think they'll hold it against you."

"I doubt that," she mumbled.

"Think on it," he said as he levered himself from the ground. "I'll not say anything, on that you have my word. But I still think you should."

She nodded thoughtfully. "I'll think about it. But I make no promises," she said.

"It's all that I ask." And he moved off toward the newcomers.

In his mind, the scene flashed again, and this time he let it play all the way through.

Stevenson was pulling the woman away from her son. The child was clutching at a red truck, crying, a hand held out toward his mother. The woman clawed at Stevenson's face, and Estard tried to pick the boy up. He wasn't just going to leave him in that farmhouse by himself, whatever their orders.

The woman screamed and lashed out, and Stevenson tried to pick her up around the waist, intending to haul her over his shoulder. But she'd somehow gotten hold of his revolver and was aiming it at Estard. Stevenson tried to take it away from her and she shot him in the head. From there, everything was in slow motion.

Estard put the boy down and drew his own gun at the same time.

The woman's finger was on the trigger, and he knew he was about to be shot. He dove to the side and lifted his gun at the same time, taking a blind shot from the hip. The bullet hit her in the chest, and she dropped the revolver. The child dropped the truck and fell on top of it. He'd shot him in the head, the bullet had gone clean through into his mother.

Tears had gathered in his eyes, but he pushed them back. It was not the time or place to relive such things. He had other business to be about.

He stopped in front of the old crone. Weiz had mentioned their names, but he could not recall them, and he wasn't sure how much it mattered, if they were all planning to die anyway.

They all looked up at him, the young one with a smile, the man with a curious frown. The old woman with grimace.

He wasn't sure how he would communicate with them, but the old woman touched his leg, just above his ankle, and he heard a voice in his head. *You wish to be chosen.* It wasn't a question, but he nodded anyway.

The old woman took her hand away, and they spoke among themselves for a moment, calm and quiet, and not a word of it did he understand. It wasn't long before the old woman looked back up at him, a tiny smile gracing her lips. She shooed him away with an arthritis riddled hand.

"I suppose that means no," he muttered to himself as he turned away.

As he made his way back over to Gordon, a black mist sprang up around him, and he fell to the ground with the sensation of choking. He put his hand to his throat, trying to breathe. It was over in moments, though it had felt like hours. And his thoughts travelled far and wide in that time.

When he got to his feet again, he turned swiftly to face the newcomers, and saw only the man and the old crone.

He heard people running towards them from the distance, but he did not look around to see who they were. He addressed the crone, though he knew she would not understand him.

"What did you do?" he asked, breathing hard.

He didn't understand the first words, when she spoke, but those after jumbled and rearranged, and sounded like English to his mind. "...chose you. You are one of us now. That was your desire."

Weiz was beside him, mouth agape. "What did you do?" Her indignation was a near mirror of his own.

"Go," the old woman shooed them away. "The first has been chosen."

Weiz ground her teeth and turned stiffly. Estard took a final look at the place where the young woman had been, then strode beside Weiz, back to the others.

"I thought you said it was the old woman would take a volunteer," he said.

"You should have stayed away from them," Weiz growled. "Not everyone is as stupid as you. Why would you do that?"

"I don't know," he answered.

Weiz shook her head and stopped to stare at him. "You can't go home now," she told him.

"I never could," he returned.

They continued through the camp, and the airmen followed their movements. He wasn't sure if it was awe or fear he saw in them. It may have been relief. Estard caught Xavier's look, and the frown, but the man said nothing as he passed.

Estard was going to sit back by Gordon, but Weiz grabbed him by his coat sleeve and shook her head. "We're not done. Come with me."

He gave a sigh and followed Weiz until they were on the other side of the mountain, and out of sight of the airmen.

"What is it?" He asked when she stopped.

Weiz was studying his face, lips pursed. "Do you have the slightest idea what you've done?"

"Not really, no." He sucked at his teeth, then made himself stop.

"For whatever reason they have, these airmen follow you," she said. "They look to you to be their example. They look for someone capable and strong. I don't know you, but you got my crew out of a tight spot, and I appreciate it. Problem is, the job wasn't done. Their eyes are still on you, following your lead."

"Not the smartest move," Estard breathed.

"Why did you do it? Why now, in front of everyone?"

"I didn't think about it," he said. "I am a man alone. I have always been a man alone. The things you say, they never occurred to me. Why? I was curious." He scratched at the back of his head and shot her a small smile. "Rarely do I know why I do something until much later."

Weiz gave the tiniest shake of her head. "You're not alone anymore. Now you're one of us, and that comes with a price. You may yet regret your...*curiosity*."

"Entirely possible."

"If you were under my command, I'd have striped your back and put you in the brig for a month."

"Glad I'm not under your command."

They studied each other for a moment before Weiz waved a dismissive hand. "Go. Just remember, whatever power she gave you could be dangerous, so try to work out what it is well away from people. We'll speak again later."

Estard gave her a mock bow and a wink, and as he moved off the only words running through his mind were, *What the fuck were you thinking?*

Chapter Eighteen

Deidra stood still and faced the woods as Lance approached. She was still herself, for the moment, but already she could feel the loss of some things. She just wasn't sure what they were. The sadness in her would pass, she knew, because there would be no room to mourn when the knowledge came.

The day was warm and bright, the smell of honeysuckle strong in the air. For all she knew, this might be the last time she would be able to appreciate such things.

She inclined her head to Lance as he stopped before her. "Welcome back," she said.

"You decided, then." There was sadness in his eyes even as he gave a tight smile. He reached out to her with both arms and wrapped her in a hug. "I am so sorry," he said softly in her ear.

A lump formed in her throat and tears welled in her eyes. She gave him a small squeeze and pushed him away. "I'm not gone yet. But it has begun. I do not know how long I have."

Lance stepped back to a respectable distance. "We need you to make a way home for these airmen."

"That was a given."

"The other... Gods, I guess." He shook his head. "That doesn't feel like the right word, you know. And to say 'other' — well that's neither here nor there is it?"

"You're the one talking." She gave him a smile.

"Well, they've come to choose. At least, three of them have, and there'll be four more in a day or so. They do not plan to give anyone a choice in the matter."

"So, you're in a rush."

"Looks that way."

"Where's Harvey?"

"Fuck knows. Scouting out the other worlds, maybe. Or confronting Greenway. Galsin gave us an update on that situation, as well."

Deidra nodded. "Guess we're walking then." She moved past him, and he fell in behind.

"So, you'll help?" he asked.

Deidra's heart came up to her throat and moved back down slowly. "I didn't give up everything I am just to sit and twiddle my thumbs," she said with an edge of irritation.

"Sorry," said Lance, and sounded as though he meant it.

The walk was longer than she'd expected, and uneventful. After an hour or so they were at the river, and Deidra could see Weiz looking over the small group of airmen from the side of the small mountain.

"That's new," she pointed to the mountain.

"Greenway made it after we left for the underground city," Lance said as he stopped beside her. "Might want to take off your slippers and roll up your jeans. It's not deep, but wet shoes are unpleasant."

She followed his advice and they crossed.

They went straight to Weiz who turned at their approach. "We have another problem," she told them.

"Straight to business," Deidra murmured.

Weiz gave her a sideways look and continued. "The first is already chosen. That Agent you lot brought back with you. Volunteered."

"If he volunteered, what's the problem?" Deidra asked.

"He is giving them what they want!"

Deidra shook her head slowly and breathed a sigh. Perhaps a part of her had already been lost to the God within, but she just couldn't understand why giving them what they wanted was such a bad thing. Especially if it meant those who did not want it were spared. At least he'd had a choice. She'd had none. She didn't blame Fields for passing it on to her, but with her memory returned, there was a bitterness in it.

"He's only one, and done is done," Lance said. "We'll take care of the rest as we can. What's the plan? We can't stay here."

Weiz looked Deidra up and down. "That you're here says much, and I thank you." She paused to glance back at the airmen seated around two small fires. "Is there a way for you to get these people home quickly?"

"Yes and no," Deidra said. She'd thought about it all night after she decided to let the knowledge take over. And as always since Fields's death, the answers were there as soon as she thought them.

"Please elaborate," the Commander said.

"It depends where they left the ship," she shrugged. "How long will it take us to get to it? Is there any damage to it? That sort of thing."

"If the ship were in front of you, and had no damage?"

"An hour."

"So, you can do it," Weiz smiled. "We have some hope. As soon as Harvey gets back, I'll have him take you to it."

Deidra looked down on the camp. "These are all that is left?"

Lance gave a sad smile. "Better than nothing."

"What about the ones we left behind last time?"

"Greenway got at them," Weiz said.

The thought saddened her, but she wondered, *how long before it wouldn't have? How long before I don't care? What will I become, then?* She knew it only mattered as long as she remembered. When the transformation was complete, she'd simply become a vessel of knowledge and curiosity.

The only part of her she would retain was all the knowledge she'd gained over her forty years of life. But she wouldn't remember how she'd acquired it. The moments, the epiphanies that led her to it. She'd be a library without imagination. She accepted that and fought it in equal measure.

Lance and Weiz were both studying her with hope and sadness. They'd all have to give something up, but none as much as she.

She was about to ask about Harvey when he popped into sight a few feet away, holding Kristin's hand.

They both moved straight toward them. Kristin gave Deidra a smile, then seemed to realise what it meant and frowned. She came straight toward her and gave her a brief hug. "Maybe one day, you'll know how to bring yourself back, as you'll know all else," the woman whispered to her.

Deidra squeezed her hand in a gesture of thanks. It was not something she'd considered before, and it gave her some hope for the future.

"What did you find?" Weiz asked.

Harvey outlined the lay of the other worlds they'd come across, and Deidra found herself fascinated by what he described. And the fact that at least two of them were populated by people, was even more surprising.

Perhaps, one day, I'll know how people ended up on four separate planets, she thought. *That's a mystery I would very much like to solve.*

"The desert planet, then," Weiz breathed. "It's your best option,

I agree. And as far as I know, he doesn't know that he cannot be killed. So, even if he does eventually wake up in that field, it won't be any time soon, and we can work out something a little more permanent before then."

Weiz put a hand on his shoulder. "Do what you have to do. We'll worry about the rest later." He gave her a sharp nod, and she continued. "For now, I need you to take Deidra to the ship. And if you can manage it, start ferrying the airmen over, too. We want them to get home before the Giants start choosing." Harvey gave another nod.

Before Deidra had a chance to say a word, Harvey had her by the arm and they'd shifted. They were on a grassy plain of rolling hills, populated sparsely by small thickets.

"I'll be back with the others soon," he told her, and disappeared.

She turned to the ship behind her and gazed up at the hull. It was different in daylight. A dull bronze, smooth and shaped somewhere between a bullet and a saucer. The landing struts were spindly and didn't look as though they should be able to hold the weight of the ship.

Deidra sighed at it. Even to look upon it, she felt memories disappear in favour of the knowledge behind its making. Of the people who had made it. Knowledge of all the vast experiments that had led to its creation.

With a deep breath, she entered through the open hatch, and paid no attention to those arriving behind her. It was time to get to work.

~

Harvey ferried them in groups of four and made short work of it. Some of them were nervous about the trip, and Xavier muttered something about a useless walk, though Harvey didn't know what he was talking about.

Within five trips, everyone but the young man and the crone

were at the base of the ship.

He took Weiz by the hand and led her a little away from the others. He smiled looking into her eyes, then gave her a long kiss. His heart soared, and as he pulled away, he leaned his forehead against hers.

"I'm off to be a hero," he said.

She chuckled at him. "Just get it done, and it'll be one less thing we need to worry about."

He pulled away from her. "For the time being, at least." He let go of her hand and gave a salute.

"Just go, you idiot."

He took a step and found himself north of Djorik.

Two days, the old man had said. He wasn't sure how far north he was yet, but it was at least a day. He kept his eyes north and moved in stages, as he had when he'd searched the other worlds.

When he started to come upon planted fields in a variety of colours, he knew he was getting close to a town. From the sheer amount of them, he supposed a town possibly twice the size of Djorik.

He felt concern at the thought. And an urgency reached him that had not been there before. His heart quickened, and his thoughts raced, imagining the things that Greenway might be doing to the people. He felt his anger rising.

When he reached the gates of the city, he saw Greenway standing outside, looking up at the guards on the walkways. There were four just outside the open gate. It didn't look as though Greenway had begun his demands, as yet. A small mercy.

Harvey came up behind him, and Greenway swung around, taking a quick step back. It took a moment, but when Greenway recognised him, he relaxed, and began laughing.

Harvey sighed. He'd known Greenway was likely to gloat, but laughter was not quite the reaction he expected. He moved forward, intending to shift them to the desert world, but Greenway moved away from his grasp, quicker than a snake.

He raised a finger and shook it side to side. "Ah, ah, ah," he said. "What are you doing here? Thought you'd taken off with your pets."

Harvey grunted at him. "What happened to you? You used to be a good man." *And I respected you. One of the very few.*

"And now I am a good God." He spread his hands wide. "I have come to educate the people."

"We're not Gods," Harvey told him. He watched for an opening, a moment when Greenway wasn't paying enough attention. He'd spring at him, then.

Greenway took another step back as if he'd read Harvey's thoughts. "Semantics," he said.

"You can't go on hurting these people, Aiden." He took a step forward. Greenway took another step back.

"Close enough, Harvey."

Harvey looked around and noticed that they were drawing a crowd. He wondered if any of them understood what they were saying. He took it for granted that they were speaking in plain English, but he was never too sure.

"Why are you hurting them, Aiden?" he asked. "Why are you trying to dominate them? If you believe that you are their God, why would you do this?" If Harvey truly believed he was a God of this world, he would not be killing its people. That was the part that he could not understand about the man in front of him.

"They must learn," Greenway said.

"Learn what?"

"Who rules them."

"But *why*? Why do you have to *rule* them? There is such a thing as a benevolent God. You know that." Harvey wanted to understand.

Greenway studied him a moment, and for the first time since the

Night of the Giants, Harvey saw a piece of the old Greenway. The Captain who had been his friend on long missions. The man who had shared stories and drank wine with him.

He took another step back before he answered, his eyes never leaving Harvey. An iciness came over him, and Harvey's old friend was gone. "Cities require mayors," he said quietly. "Kingdoms require kings. Empires require emperors. And worlds require Gods."

"Earth has done well without the interference of Gods," Harvey said. "Why should this world be any different?"

Greenway smiled at him. "You'll understand when I am done." He gave a wink, bent his knees.

Harvey dove at him. But he was too late. Greenway leapt into the air, moving to the south, and Harvey hit the dirt. He smacked the ground with his fist and rose to his feet.

The crowd that had gathered watched wide eyed as Greenway grew smaller and disappeared into the distance. Moving like that, Greenway would be able to go short distances almost as quickly as Harvey. This was going to be a problem.

He took a last look at the crowd, then shifted back to the ship, all too aware of the gasps that arose around him.

He could have gone after Greenway, tried to follow his flight path. He knew he should have stayed on his trail. But that strange feeling was on him, even as he had faced the man. The sense that nothing was urgent, though he knew it should be.

Harvey tried to shake it off as he moved toward the ship. None of the airmen were hanging around outside, as he'd expected. Only Estard and Kristin could be seen in the near distance. He stopped at the hatch to eye them curiously for a moment, and a smile twitched on his lips. He ascended the ramp.

Inside, the airmen were in the passenger section, Deidra, Weiz and Lance were at the bridge.

"Greenway got away," he said, leaning against the cabin wall.

Weiz turned to face him with a flat stare. "He got away?"

He made a flying gesture with his hand. "I didn't have a chance to get my hands on him. He's wary."

"No offence, Captain," Lance put in, his eyes watching Deidra work on the front panel. "But that's a load of shit."

Harvey straightened his back and glared at the Pilot. "Excuse me?"

Lance looked at him. "Load – of – shit, Captain."

Harvey took a step toward him, and Lance held his ground. They were staring, eye to eye, and both held about them a sense of violence.

Weiz stepped between them, facing Harvey. She put her hands lightly on his chest and looked up into his eyes. Whatever she said was drowned out by a loud bang on the hull.

~

Estard looked at the ship, and the airmen. He watched Harvey pop in with another lot and leave again. It was all over with quickly, then the man went off.

He was intending to have a few last words with Gordon, before they all left. He'd grown fond of her. But when he put his first foot forward, Annabelle Kristin sidestepped in front of him and punched him hard in the face.

Dazed and blinking, he looked down at her with surprise. "What the fu—" She punched him in the gut, and he cut off, breath whooshing from his lungs as he took a step back to brace himself.

"Idiot," she hissed. She brought her fist up, and he knew she was going to hit him again, but this time he grabbed her hand as she struck, pivoted, and flipped her to the ground. He knelt down, still holding her hand, and twisted her arm, a knee on her chest.

He opened his mouth, and she twisted beneath him, heaving him off, and snatching her hand away.

On his feet, he faced her in a ready stance. Despite his confusion, he felt a smile grow. The situation was ludicrous. He had no idea why she was hitting him. He kept his eyes on her, waiting for the next blow.

She looked him up and down, muttered something under her breath, then turned and walked away.

Estard glanced behind and saw the airmen were entering the ship. He thought of joining them, but instead followed Kristin at an unhurried pace.

This was the woman who had made him curious. The one whose eyes and smile kept popping into his mind at the strangest times. And this was the first time he would have an opportunity to speak to her since they'd left Earth.

Kristin stopped a short distance away but didn't turn to look at him as he approached.

"What was that about?" he asked.

"You're a fucking moron," she replied, still not looking at him.

"Often, and in many ways," he agreed. "But for what particular thing did I deserve a beating?"

She spun and gave him a clenched teeth smile. "You gave it up."

Estard rubbed his jaw and searched her eyes. "Gave what up?"

"Your freedom." She turned away again. "You just threw it away."

Gently, he took her hand until she faced him again. He kept his eyes on hers, and let the silence grow a moment, until he was sure she wouldn't look away. "I gave up nothing," he said softly. "I have gained much."

Her brows lowered, her arm tensed, and he braced himself for another blow, but she didn't move.

I don't honestly know how I really feel about you, he thought. *We barely know one another. Not much more than names, and yet I am drawn to you.* He wanted to say it out loud, but he was afraid she'd bolt like a rabbit. He had to be careful, take it slow.

She looked away and pulled her hand from his, but she didn't move. To his mind that was a good sign.

"Why did you do it?" she asked.

Estard let out a long sigh. "Why does everyone keep asking me that?" He scratched at the back of his head, consciously trying not to suck on his teeth. He badly wanted a smoke and damned himself for his lack of foresight before the escape.

"Because people want to give you the benefit of the doubt," she told him. "You ask questions when you better wish to understand the motivations and thoughts of others."

"Or require instruction," he said.

Kristin glanced sideways at him and gave a shrug. "That too. And many other reasons. But it's not the point."

"Then what is?"

"Why did you do it?" she asked again.

"Why does it matter?"

She turned to face him. "You really don't know, do you?"

Estard shook his head. He wanted to take her hand again but refrained. *Careful with the rabbit.* "I really don't. It just felt like the thing to do at the time."

She shook her head, and he saw the small smile reaching her lips, but it faded quickly, her gaze drawn behind him.

Estard turned to see what had caught her attention and saw a Giant. Dark mist and red eyes, staring from no more than ten paces away.

He sidestepped so he was beside Kristin. "What do we do?"

"We can't kill it," she said. "That's what it wants. If we do, then someone inside that ship won't be going home."

Another shadow form appeared close to the first, shimmering into existence. Then another.

Estard wanted to reach out and hold Kristin's hand, but put his hand to his hip, where his holster should have been. A few well aimed shots could disable, but he had no gun. No one did. The few they'd had, were out of ammo.

He licked his lips and glanced at the ship, then returned his attention to the shadow forms. There were four, now, and they advanced slowly. The one in the lead shimmered, and shrank, in a few moments, it was the old crone. Bent backed, and holding a knife, she appeared determined. She did not say a word.

They stopped a few paces away, and the crone turned to one of her companions, and stabbed it in the chest.

Estard and Kristin watched wide eyed, as comprehension dawned. They didn't look to each other, but Estard knew that she was beside him as he launched himself at the old woman. The shadow form she'd stabbed was falling to the ground and erupting in mist that travelled toward the open hatch of the ship.

"No!" Kristin screamed as she shouldered into the crone.

The bent backed woman was much harder than she appeared, as she moved smoothly with the impact, then reversed and threw Kristin against the hull of the ship.

Estard collided with one of the Giants, and they toppled together to the ground. He straddled the monster, and began smacking it in the face, his thoughts singing in round to a nameless tune, *pass out, pass out, pass the fuck out*. As his fist came down on the bridge of its nose again and again.

He was vaguely aware of others attempting to restrain the crone, and the other Giants. He couldn't have said who was helping him, as his focus was on the one beneath him.

Even as he continued to beat at the face, the form shimmered and shrank to become the young man from the camp. His face was bloody and welted, his eyes swelling.

Breathing hard, Estard levered himself up, sure that the man had passed out. He hoped it was enough. They'd been informed it would not take Deidra long to make the required adjustments to the ship, but in his experience, enemies rarely stayed down as long as one would wish.

He looked around and saw that the other three had been engaged by Lance, Harvey and Kristin. Gordon was standing in the hatch door, a hand to her throat, face pale and shocked, but he barely glanced at her.

Estard threw himself at the crone, landing a heavy blow on the back of her head. She stumbled sideways and rounded on him, giving Harvey time to land another blow. She stabbed out with the knife, and Estard smacked her wrist, causing her fist to fly open and the knife to drop.

Who'd have thought an old woman like this could cause so much trouble? He'd learned many years ago never to underestimate a woman, but this was absurd. Her fists dealt blows as hard as any man, and she shrugged off their attacks as if shooing flies from around her head.

"Stop!" he yelled.

And all went still.

Estard blinked, unsure of what he was seeing. Everyone had stopped stock still. It was like looking at a photo. Kristin had one hand around a Giant's neck, the other halfway toward a crushing blow. Lance had the other by an arm, his knee in its chest, its feet part way from the ground. The old crone was slapping away a blow from Harvey, and he had a foot off the ground as if he were about to kick.

He took a step back. Then another. There was no breeze. No sound. Nothing moved. Nothing at all.

Is this my power? he wondered. To make time stand still? How far could he take it? What would break it? He could obviously move within this stillness, but could he make others?

Estard forced himself to concentrate on the problem at hand. There would be plenty of time to work it out after all was said and done. He was immortal now, after all. And that was the first time he'd actually considered that, though he pushed it aside quickly.

He moved to the crone first and pulled her to the ground. She was as stiff as she looked, and did not move from the pose she was frozen in. As soon as his fist hammered into her face with all the force he could muster, the scene around him came to life once more.

Estard didn't have time to ponder what was happening. Even as he hit her, she shot a hand out and grabbed at his neck. She squeezed with the grip of a vice, and he felt the blood flow to his brain cut off. Spots danced in his vision, as he hammered at her again. He saw a booted foot clip her above the ear, and suddenly the hand released him and fell to the ground.

Falling off the old woman, Estard touched his neck tenderly, and gasped in breath. He looked up, prepared to jump back into the fray, but both Kristin and Lance had the other giants beneath them, and they were shimmering and shrinking.

"I don't know what you did," Harvey said beside him. "But it made a difference."

Estard gave a grateful nod. "Nice kick," he rasped. It hurt to speak.

Harvey gave him a hand up, and they looked down at the Giants, now in their human forms. The two Lance and Kristin straddled did not look at all familiar. Neither one was the old man.

"We stopped the fuckers," Kristin breathed.

Gordon stumbled through the hatch, wide eyed and shaking her head. A few moments later, Galsin strode out. He was holding a knife, red with blood.

Harvey lunged, but appeared to hit an invisible barrier, and was held, struggling to move.

Galsin strolled unconcernedly from the ship. He looked down on the others of his people and shook his head. "You fought much better than I was expecting," he said.

Kristin eyed Harvey, then the old man. That Galsin had

somehow bound him, was obvious. She waited until the old man had his back turned and jumped at him from behind. Galsin didn't even turn, just held up a hand, and Kristin was stopped in mid-flight, held by invisible bonds.

Estard yelled, "Stop!" and looked around. Everything was still moving. He yelled again. Still, nothing changed.

Galsin looked at him. "It will take you some time to work that one out," the old man said. "But don't worry, you have plenty of it."

Estard growled in frustration and tried to move, only to find that he, too, was bound.

Without haste, Galsin leaned over each of the unconscious forms and slit their throats, starting with the crone. "We would have taken our time," he said. "We were prepared to take volunteers."

"What are you doing?" Estard asked as the man moved to the next body.

"What they came for, boy," he slit the next one's throat. "We aren't like the others. The ones these people faced before." The crone began to collapse into mist, and the old man smiled as he moved to the next of his comrades. "We would have waited, until someone decided, much as you did. But you tried to run, and you gave us no choice."

One after the other, the bodies turned to mist and moved away into the ship. Estard struggled against his bonds, trying to make the power work. Concentrating all his thoughts on making time stop. But no matter how he tried, nothing happened.

The old man came to stand before him. "Though we had no blood relatives among us, I looked upon the one who gave you her power as a daughter," he said. "I believe she chose well, with you. I am not disappointed." He whirled suddenly to face Harvey.

Harvey looked as if he were trying to speak, and Galsin made a gesture with his hand. Harvey gasped and spat. "What did you do?"

"I wouldn't worry too much. Those who we had to kill will

awake in the field. We didn't take more than was necessary, we're not like our brethren were." He gave a shrug. "Really I don't understand all this fuss."

"They just wanted to go home!" Harvey screamed.

Galsin waved away the comment. "They're home. It's done." He glanced at Kristin and Lance, then turned back toward the ship. "We'd have done it out of site, and not bothered you, but we'd tested it earlier and found that proximity was an issue."

Estard felt laughter build inside him. This was ridiculous. Absurd. Un-fucking real. None of it made any sense.

"How did you even get here?" Harvey asked.

"Shadow forms move swiftly," the old man said.

A chuckle escaped Estard's lips, and he couldn't hold it in. His chest heaved against the invisible bonds with his effort to choke it down, keep it inside. But it burst forth, and everyone turned to stare.

"This amuses you?" Galsin asked with a raise of a brow.

Estard shook his head, and a tear leaked from the side of his eye. "This is insane," he said. "Truly, insane." He struggled with the laughter. He knew it was hysteria caused by frustration. It was a fault he saw in himself, time and again.

"I am the last," Galsin said. "When I am gone, it is finished. You'll have no more Shadow forms to fight. No more *Gods* to concern you. The rest can leave. Let it be enough."

He raised the blade to his throat, and Estard saw that he wasn't alone in struggling against his bonds, even as the old man slit his own throat.

They looked on helplessly. The bonds didn't disappear until the body did.

They were too late.

Chapter Nineteen

Deidra gasped as she sat up. She hadn't seen it happen, who had done it. She just remembered the feel of cold steel against her throat, and then the blood flowing. She'd been surprised.

She turned at the sound of muttering and saw Weiz getting to her feet. She seemed to be swearing emphatically in German, and for a moment she was reminded of Heinrich. The man who had somehow gotten them all into this mess.

With a shake of her head, Deidra got up and dusted herself off.

How had Heinrich known where'd they'd end up? That was a question that had bothered her a lot before she'd lost her memories. Now she had them back, even temporarily, it bothered her again. How had he known? That he had, was not in question.

"Do you know what happened?" she asked the Commander.

Weiz whipped her head around, eyes glaring blue fire as she said, "Galsin."

"Shadow forms," she muttered to herself, before she could ask how. "They'll all be at the ship, I think."

"What are you talking about?"

"When you first landed here, when we were stuck in tachyon frequency. They could see us."

"You'll pardon me if I don't follow your line of thought," Weiz grated out. "I just had my throat slit."

Deidra raised a hand to her own throat at the memory. It was unpleasant, but she felt no anger. Already some things were starting to go missing. If it kept up at this rate, it wouldn't be long before it was all gone. But she'd made her choice.

"The Shadow forms use tachyon frequency particles," Deidra continued. "I was wondering how they managed to follow us so quickly when Harvey had Travelled us all there."

"Hmph," Weiz breathed. "Galsin told me only Harvey can Travel. The rest of us were stuck to more mundane means."

"For the most part we are. We certainly cannot travel to other worlds the way he does, and even short distances take a little time. It's not instantaneous, the way it is for Harvey."

"Just fast."

"Yes."

They stared at one another for a moment, and Weiz whirled away, hands clenched. "So do we wait for Harvey to come get us, or do we use this newfound power?"

"We wait," Deidra said. "I don't imagine it will be long."

The Commander turned back to her, tears gathering in her eyes, though they'd yet to fall. "I don't know if I can cope," she whispered. "If they've done it again. If the night of the Giants came again, I don't know... I just... I don't know..." She trailed off, jaw clenched and eyes wide.

Deidra remembered when she'd first met this woman in person, not long after she'd become a 'god'. She'd been ruined by the deaths of so many of her people, and hard as she tried not to let it affect her job, she'd often disappeared, leaving Harvey and Kristin to take over.

Deidra shook her head, wondering how someone so sensitive had been given the position of Commander. That she was a valued member of the ATF AF, was unquestionable. Her leadership, on the other hand. *If people didn't respect her so much because of past deeds, she'd not be able to hold them together at all.* But she would say none of that. For all her faults, she was a good woman and she cared.

Before she could say anything, Harvey arrived.

He moved straight to Weiz and put his arms around her. He spared Deidra a glance and a small frown. He sighed heavily and stepped back from the Commander's embrace.

"No one's dead," he said. Deidra nodded, and Weiz breathed a relieved sigh. "But they got what they came for. We tried... we fought." He shook his head. "We have six new companions, and none of them wanted it."

Weiz's face hardened. "So, it's done? No more running from it."

"It's done," Harvey said, and put a gentle hand on her shoulder. "No more running."

"I still have work to do," Deidra said. "Before something else gets in the way, I should finish it and let these others get home." She paused for a brief moment. "The ones who still can."

Harvey put a hand on her shoulder and shifted them back to the ship.

All of the airmen were outside now, separated into two groups. Five were by the hatch, glancing around furtively. Six were a little distance off, some were weeping, others just looked dazed. Kristin and Estard were not far from them, just watching.

A part of her was concerned for them, but another part of her was all business. She had to do what she could for the ones who needed it. There was no one else. No other scientists from the Station.

Even as she thought it, she wondered what had happened to Ulrich. He'd been at the mountain; she'd made sure of it. He was a solitary and nervous man, but he was a genius. She recalled asking someone to check on him, thinking that he'd committed suicide, but wasn't sure anyone had. When Greenway had attacked, Ulrich wasn't at the ship. He could be alive, somewhere out there.

Deidra ascended the ramp and went back to the bridge. The eyes that followed her showed relief, but none said a word.

When she sat down to begin work on the console, Weiz came in and sat beside her, providing her with the tools she needed as she asked for them.

"We should go back to that mountain," she told the Commander. She had to say this before she forgot that she cared.

The other woman looked at her with a small frown. "Why?"

"I want to know what happened to Ulrich," she said, without looking up. "Before I forget."

~

Harvey was halfway between the two groups, Lance at his side. He wasn't sure which ones needed the reassurances more. Those who were staying, or those who were going. If he had a choice in the matter, he'd be in the group leaving. Most of them would. Except that Agent guy. He chose it. He was the only one to choose it.

Harvey snorted. *Idiot*, he thought.

"Captain?" Lance looked to him.

"What?" He looked to Lance. The man's head turned, and his tattooed eyes danced.

Harvey closed his eyes for a moment and just breathed deep. "Sometimes," he said, as he opened his eyes. "I completely understand Kristin's violent urges."

Lance faced him again and shrugged. "Done is done is done," the Pilot said. "But I've been thinking."

Harvey looked to the sky, hand shielding his eyes. He moved his head side to side, searching.

"What are you looking for?" Lance asked.

"Flying pigs," he said, as he took his hand away and looked down.

"Oh, ha ha."

"What were you thinking?"

"Maybe we don't *have* to be here."

"If we're going to disappear right back here every time we leave, I don't really see a way around it."

Lance ran a hand over his head, it was starting to grow stubble. "It took us a week, last time. And the event didn't seem to trigger until one of us died." He shuddered a little at that, as if remembering something he'd rather not. "Maybe if we all stay alive, we can stay longer."

Harvey shook his head. "A day, a week — a month! — it's not long enough."

"So, you're giving up?"

He hadn't thought of it as giving up before. "I don't know," he mumbled. "Do you get the sense that something isn't right?"

Lance shrugged. "All the time."

"Since we got back here, I mean."

"You thinking of something specific?"

Harvey shook his head and looked at all the airmen. Xavier was in the small cluster by the hatch, holding tight to Ellen. He was thankful that at least one in his crew would manage to get back.

"I have no sense of urgency," Harvey said. "Until the Giants came here, to this ship, everything has felt stretched out. Like it doesn't matter. Like it can *wait*." He bit at his lip, trying to find the words to continue. "I keep telling myself, 'do it now, get it done', but the feeling that drives..." he waved a hand, shaking his head.

The Pilot was nodding. "Yeah," he said. "I get it."

"You do?"

Lance rolled his shoulders and looked away, clearly uncomfortable. "It's depression, sir."

Harvey snorted at that. It was ridiculous. "I don't feel

depressed."

"A little disconnected? A sense of dissociation? Like maybe this is happening to someone else, and you're just along for the ride?"

"What are you talking about?"

"Never mind, sir," Lance said softly.

"I'm not depressed. And it's not just me," Harvey said, looking toward Kristin and Estard.

"Didn't think it was."

"I went to face Greenway, maybe five minutes before everything went down here. I felt the urgency in that moment, but he got away, and I let him. As soon as he was in the air... I just left."

Lance squinted up at the sky. "Are you going to try again?"

Harvey gave a nod. "Yes. As soon as we've seen this lot safely off, and we've sorted out what to do with the new ones."

"New ones. I feel for them, but no more than I feel for myself. I don't want to give up on home, Captain."

"We're immortal. We have plenty of time to work these things out."

"Maybe that's the problem."

"How do you mean?"

"You say you have no sense of urgency," Lance shrugged. "Maybe it's because you feel you have all the time in the world to get things done."

"Maybe," Harvey agreed. He gave a sigh. "Come, let's go speak to the new gods."

Lance shook his head. "Gods. Leave them be. They're still in shock. They'll come to us when they're ready."

Harvey raised a brow, but let it be. "I still need to find Greenway and do something about him." He sat himself down.

Lance joined him on the ground. "I thought you'd already worked that out."

"I just have to find him again," he said with a small smile.

~

Greenway walked in a tight circle inside a small clearing. It wasn't the same one that the other mind had trapped him in, it was much smaller. But he liked the irony of it. At first, he'd just been pacing, back and forth, as he considered what Harvey's arrival at the town gates meant. Then, he circled.

Harvey had left, he was sure of it. He would not have missed that ride at the mountain if it meant leaving this world in dust. His only concern from the very beginning was to get home. It was the only concern for almost every airman left alive after the night of the Giants.

Greenway would go back to the town. He would educate them, as he had told Harvey he would. But now, Harvey was likely to get in his way. He would try to stop him.

"What does he think I'll do?" he wondered out loud. But he knew the answer. "He'll have seen the village, and Dojrik."

He had some small regret over what he'd done, letting his temper get the better of him that way. But he was a God, and the people needed to understand what that meant. He hadn't been lying to Harvey when he said worlds needed Gods.

Greenway placed one foot in front of the other, inside the prints he'd already made in the soft earth. The trees whispered in a slight breeze, and he could hear cicada's sing in fits and starts.

Town first? Or Harvey first?

If Harvey could lay a hand on him, he'd try to put him somewhere he'd not be able to get to anyone. He wondered what would happen if he killed Harvey. He was sure, though he couldn't say why, that Harvey's power would not transfer to him. But what *would* happen?

There were things he needed to learn. Powers that he needed to hone. He needed some way to find out what all his abilities were, and in order to do that, he needed a sanctuary. A place he could be without having to worry that someone might come up behind him and slit his throat. Where someone would not try to take it all away from him.

Another thought came to the front of his mind, and he stopped in his tracks. "If Harvey is here, then the others are, too." He didn't know how, or why, but he knew it to be true. They'd all gotten on that ship. They'd all gotten away. And yet they were here.

Town first? Or Harvey first?

This was the decision he needed to make before he left the clearing. He needed to know which direction to go in. He needed to have some kind of plan in place.

At the gates of the town, he had planned to tell them who he was, give them a little show, and make his demands, as he had done in Djorik the first time. He'd have them build him a temple. A sanctuary. He'd recruit acolytes and priests. And he would do the same in every town he came across, so he would always have a place to go.

Gods did not walk among men, that was true. But he needed a base to start from. He would prepare them for greater civilisation. For technological marvels. He may not need it now, but he missed the convenience of a car, the thrill of piloting a plane. He missed the noise of a big city, and the convenience of being able to get whatever he wanted, whenever he wanted, while Earthside. And he intended to bring some of that here, to this world.

Do I miss Earth? Is that all this is? It wasn't.

A small red-winged bird landed on the ground in front of him, and he tilted his head at it. It was in the soft depression of a boot print, and it pecked down at a worm writhing to the surface. Catch firmly in beak, it flew off.

Greenway watched it with a small smile. That was something he had never seen on Earth, though he knew it happened.

"If I go for the town, Harvey may or may not show up," he

sighed. "If I go for Harvey, it's even odds he shoves me in some out of the way place to die."

He looked up to the sky and saw a small flock of the red-winged birds flying north, toward the town.

"I have to do it," he told himself as much as the clearing around him. "It's the right thing to do. It is my duty. Harvey is the one who is trying to run from it. But I know."

He needed to bring them forward. Make them capable of protecting themselves. Give them faith in something greater than themselves.

All his life he had gone to church. He had said the prayers and made the offerings. He'd confessed his sins and made penance. But the whole time, he searched for a sign that God was real. That he was actually out there, watching over them. He wanted to believe, to have faith, and he'd tried so hard, especially after his wife had committed suicide. He understood the importance of *knowing* that your god was there. Not just an idea.

Greenway shook his head and breathed another sigh.

He gathered his legs under him and launched into the air.

He'd made his decision.

CHAPTER TWENTY

Estard kept a respectful distance as the ship took off. He watched it ascend into the atmosphere, until it became no more than a pinprick in his vision and disappeared. Even then, he kept his eyes on the clear sky, sending up a prayer that they'd all make it home safe.

Deidra didn't go with them. They were on their own. If they didn't make it back to Earth in the right time, no one would know. But they were all ready to take the risk, and if they weren't in the time period they were meant to be in, then so be it. There were only five of them. Out of all those who'd escaped with him, only five were leaving.

After a few moments, he felt a presence beside him, and turned to see Gordon. Her eyes were red, her face tear streaked, and she bit at her bottom lip as if trying to stifle another sob. He put an arm around her and held her without a word. She buried her face in his chest, and her body shook.

He looked over her head and saw Kristin staring at him. He gave her a nod, but stayed as he was. She moved away.

After Deidra had finished her adjustments, she'd had Lance shoot lightning at it. She hadn't stuck around to watch the take-off. She'd whispered something to Harvey, and they'd disappeared, along with Weiz.

The others who'd been chosen, still gazed silently at the sky. He wasn't sure if they were in shock, or just wishing they'd been on the ship. It was hard to tell from some of their expressions. Not all of them had been crying, but wide eyes stared into the distance, jaws slack.

A heart wrenching sob was directed at his chest, and he thought he heard Gordon say something, but he didn't understand it. He stroked a hand through her hair soothingly and made a soft hushing sound.

He was wondering what they were supposed to do next, and he knew he wasn't the only one. Even Kristin and Lance were looking forlorn. There was nowhere they needed to be. Nothing they *had* to do. So, what were they supposed to do? They had no homes to go to. They had no people needed tending. For the first time since this all began, Estard actually felt lost.

Once again, Gordon seemed to say something. "What was that?" he asked.

She raised her head to look into his eyes. "My sons," she said through gulps of air. "I'll...never —" She buried her head back in his chest. Even with her hands covering her eyes, he could feel a wet patch through his coat.

Estard let Gordon continue until she was ready to push herself away. He couldn't imagine the loss, as he'd never had children, but he had some notion of what it was like to be the child.

Gordon turned her back on him and scrubbed at her face. Her breathing steadied. He let her take her time, and didn't move, though his eyes searched for Kristin.

"Do you think there'll be a way to change this?" Gordon asked without turning to him. Her voice was so strained, it took him a moment to understand her.

"Where there's a will there's a way," he said. "If we don't carry hope with us, whatever the situation, we might as well lay down and die."

She made a sound halfway between a cough and a laugh. "It might have been better if I had." She turned to face him again, but visibly steeled herself against further outburst. "If I had died, they could mourn and move on."

"From what you've told me of what happened before you came, it's possible they already have." He didn't know what else to say. He'd never been a great people person, though he liked them well enough.

"Think I'll take a walk," she said, and put a gentle hand on his arm. "Shake this off."

Estard gave her a small nod and she moved away. He watched her for a moment, frowning. When Weiz had explained how the whole thing worked, Gordon had been doubly thankful the Giant she'd shot in the woods hadn't given her its power. He felt for her. For all of them, but for her most of all, because he had gotten to know her.

A hand smacked him lightly on a shoulder, and he turned to Kristin. She was watching Gordon, too.

"What now?" he asked.

"Think she'll be alright?"

"I think they'll all be fine, once they've adjusted," he shrugged. "But how long that takes.... Well, everyone is different."

"Hell, I'm not sure I am used to it yet," Kristin said. "It's been months, and still, I think about going home. 1957 was a bit of a disappointment. No offence."

Estard smiled. "None taken."

"I really thought we'd get them away." Her eyes were drifting over the scattered airmen who sat, or stood, or walked. "Deidra didn't have much to get done. Who'd have guessed they'd come up like that?"

"We did what we could," he said softly.

"But who would think an entire group of people could be *suicidal*." She shook her head. "You'd think at least one or two of them would have held back. Even if they thought they wanted to die, there's a basic survival instinct, isn't there?"

"There's always been those who would rather die. Our own history is littered with mass suicides. Gordon told me what time you're all from, and I imagine there've been a few added to the list."

Kristin nodded. "True enough. Doesn't mean I get it."

"Think I'd be a little worried if you did," Estard mumbled.

They stood in silence a while, watching the airmen. Lance was by himself, sitting and plucking at the grass. Gordon had stopped, her back to everyone, back straight and staring into the distance.

"So, what comes next?" Estard asked after a while.

Kristin held up her hands and shook her head. "All I can tell you is, if I am stuck here, I want my own damned place. I've had more privacy bunking on a Docker. I wouldn't mind a shower and a change of clothes, either."

Estard quirked a smile. "I think it's likely to take a while before we get any of those things."

"A woman can dream."

~

Harvey stood on the ledge of the mountain, taking in the damage around him. "Didn't think about how bad it would be," he said.

Weiz had her fingers entwined with his, and he felt a slight squeeze. "How long has it been? Nine days? Ten? If anyone survived the collapse, they're likely far from here. Or dead from starvation."

Deidra was assessing the closed entrance to the mountain city, and didn't turn as she said, "Takes a lot longer than that to starve. It's certainly not comfortable or remotely healthy, but a person can survive more than forty days without food, provided they have a sufficient amount of water." She ran her fingers along the crack and pushed. A small section of the rock face opened up before them. "Given the rain on the day," she continued, looking back at them, "I'd say it's entirely possible anyone left here when we took off, could have easily survived." She moved into the wall.

Harvey and Weiz shared a look. Weiz disengaged her hand, and Harvey felt a pang, but he understood why. She raised it to create a small globe of light and moved forward. Harvey took up the rear.

Once inside the first empty room, Harvey heard cracks. The kind that indicated rock movement, and instability.

"Are we sure it's safe to be in here?" he asked.

Deidra waved away his concern. "Some of the buildings may have toppled, but the worst has passed. Most of the damage was to the mountain. That may have destabilised some of the structures, but as long as we tread carefully, we should be fine."

Harvey let out a soft grunt and shook his head, but he followed as she moved forward.

"Are we really expecting to find anyone?" Weiz wanted to know. Her light brightened and grew, and she sent it into the air like a flare. As it rose, the broken city danced in shadows, but once high enough, it was almost like daylight.

"Do I actually expect to find any *survivors*, you mean?" Deidra said. "No. I don't expect anyone will be alive down here. But I need to know."

"And you don't think we should have done this before the others took off with the only means of getting home?"

"There are others we've left behind that could turn up at any time," the Scientist sighed. "I doubt I could have held them back any longer. If it comes to it, we'll find them another way. But my focus is here, and now, Commander. I *need* to know."

Harvey understood that, more than he'd care to. Needing to

know one way or another. He remembered when his wife had died, he'd needed to see the body before he could believe it. She'd been sick, an incurable illness they didn't yet have a name for. They hadn't known it was coming. It had been relatively quick, and the symptoms no more than a flu over a few days. They'd found her dead in a train carriage on her way home from work. It was hard to believe. Sometimes seeing the body was the only way to let go. He was thankful he'd been home at the time.

They moved slowly and carefully through the city streets, staying to the centre. Cracks resounded around the cavernous city, and the occasional thud of falling rock or masonry. Each time, Harvey's eyes searched, trying to find where it came from, but the echoes made it difficult.

The dust they'd experienced the first time around, was gone. The air less dry, though hardly humid. The most prominent smell he kept catching whiffs of, was wood smoke. *Green* wood. Distinctive, and not particularly pleasant.

They began their search two streets away from the place they'd found the ship. The outer limits of where'd they'd set up. Ulrich had been assigned further in, but it was agreed he could be anywhere. The last Deidra remembered seeing of him was three days before they'd left.

They called out softly as they moved through the ruins, not wanting their voices to echo through the vast open space. They kept their feet light, and their movements slow. Weiz maintained the light above them, but also provided torches for them to check the darkened innards of the small buildings.

Harvey found no sign, except for old, scuffled boot prints, that anyone had ever been here. It felt as much the ghost city as it looked. He'd never wanted to be in this place. It reminded him of old crypts.

They found the bodies of a few dead airmen, and more than a few townspeople, all already beginning to rot. Oddly, to Harvey's mind, they didn't smell that way. He'd been around decomposing flesh — he knew the foulness of it. It was enough to make most people vomit. But all he could smell was the green wood, burning.

Their last stop was the place where they'd found the ship. Weiz took the lead and moved to the side of the entrance wall as Deidra input the code. The door whirred open, but the trap was gone.

"I don't remember closing it," Harvey said.

"We didn't," said Weiz.

Deidra moved ahead to the limit of the light provided by Weiz, and the Commander increased its intensity.

"Anyone here?" Deidra called softly. "Ulrich? Anyone?"

Something moved. They all stopped.

"Someone there?" Deidra asked, a little louder this time.

There was no response. When no further sound came, they continued forward.

When they hit the end of the ramp, Weiz created a small ball of light and let the torches vanish. Harvey disliked the sensation of a solid object turning to mist in his hand, but he refrained from saying anything.

In the centre of the room, where the ship had stood, was a pile of charred wood. A small distance off, was another pile, unburnt. As they moved forward, he could see a body, curled into a foetal position, opposite the charred pile.

Deidra moved swiftly to it and examined the face. She felt for a pulse and checked the eyes.

"Well, I'll be fucked," Weiz breathed.

"He's alive," Deidra said. "Barely. But he is."

"Who is it?" Harvey asked.

"It's Ulrich," Deidra nodded, a small smile on her face, a tear sliding down a cheek. "He's the last one." She held a shaking hand to her mouth and swallowed. "The last person I knew, before everything."

Harvey couldn't believe it. That weedy little scientist had actually survived being trapped in the mountain. Surrounded by dead bodies and fallen masonry, this little fucker had made it. Even if barely.

"Why wasn't he on the ship with us?" he asked.

Weiz shook her head. "We can ask him when he wakes."

"Do we keep looking for others?"

"You can," Deidra said, "if you like. But I don't know who else is missing."

"No one else would be in the mountain," Weiz told him. "The only ones unaccounted for are the ones we left at the camp, who didn't choose to go with Greenway. I'm sorry to say, I don't know who went where, and who got away."

"Is there anyone who might?"

"Gordon," she said. "I saw her with the ones who came out of the woods. But she wasn't here with us, when we were fixing up the ship."

Harvey blinked a moment. How had he missed that? They'd been trapped in 1957 together, and he hadn't even noticed. He just assumed that everyone who'd been on the ship had been in the mountain start to finish. He shrugged it off.

"We can't stay here," Deidra said before he could open his mouth. "We need to get him warm and fed. He may die on us, yet." She straightened and looked directly at Harvey. "If you don't mind. Take him out first."

Harvey gave a sharp nod and moved to the small man. His face was grey, his hair plastered to his head. As Harvey bent to pick him up, he could hear a hollow rattle in his chest. He scooped the man up as gently as he could and shifted.

He immediately lay the man back down and gestured to the closest airmen — Zim. The man came over. He had a stunned look on his face, and his gait was slightly unsteady. Harvey wasn't sure he was up to the task, but he needed someone to be.

"Gather some firewood and set it by this man. Have someone come and stay by him." He didn't check to see if the man understood, before he shifted back to Weiz and Deidra.

"Let's go," he said. When they were close enough, he took each by the shoulder and shifted them to where he'd left Ulrich. "I'll be back." And he shifted to the first camp.

He looked up at the small mountain, still growing, still shifting. It was like having Greenway taunt him. It had probably been his intention when he'd created it.

Harvey shook his head and got to work. He still couldn't believe the scrawny little scientist was actually alive, but he would do what he could to keep him that way.

He grabbed up the pots, still part filled with stew. He dumped the remains into a single pot and shifted to the river. There he cleaned out the empty one as best he could, then filled it with water.

Once back with the others, he set them down in front of Deidra. "Best I could do on short notice."

"Thank you," she said.

Zim had found some firewood and laid it down, Weiz was arranging it to start a fire. She was shaking her head and muttering to herself under her breath.

If it wasn't all so completely ridiculous, I'd think I was dreaming. He frowned at the people around him. His imagination just wasn't this good, though, so he knew it was real.

None of them were doctors, or medics. They weren't trained to heal people. His gaze was drawn to the pale face of Ulrich, and he thought to himself, *I don't think you'll make it, boy. I'm sorry. But I really don't think you will.*

"Miracles happen," Kristin said behind him, and he spun into a defensive position before he could stop himself. She smiled at him, as he relaxed.

"I honestly just cannot believe he's alive," Harvey said. "I think it over and over in my head. I can't fucking believe it."

Kristin shrugged and arched her neck to look past him. "But he is, and now he's here, he might just stay that way. Were there others?"

"Not in the mountain," he told her. "I need to speak with Gordon, though. There may be others around, we should gather them up. It's been a hostile land, and we don't know what else is out there."

"Will Deidra get them all home, too?"

"Can't speak to that," he said, looking back at the woman, fussing over the near dead man. He returned his attention to Kristin. "Where's Gordon?"

Kristin screwed her face up. "Might want to leave that be for the moment," she said softly. "She's taking it hard. She's got kids."

Harvey gave a nod and inhaled deeply. He understood completely. "Where is she?"

Kristin motioned toward the woman with her head, and Harvey walked slowly toward her.

The thought of gathering up the stragglers, the ones who'd gone missing, or who just hadn't been there, gave Harvey a sense of purpose. Something he'd felt he was losing. Another day and Ulrich would not have been alive when they found him. Others may yet be dead, but they deserved to be found. To be buried and remembered. And unlike them, their lives were finite. It could not wait.

When he came up beside Gordon, he made sure he was slightly in front so she could see him clearly without moving, but he also kept his back to her, so any tears could be private.

"I have a son," he told her. It was harder than he thought, to say those simple words out loud. His chest tightened, and a rock formed in his throat. "His mother died last year, and I am all he has."

He felt a hand on his shoulder and resisted the urge to shrug it off. "I say this, so you understand," he continued. "You are not alone here. Most, if not all of us, still want to go back. Still have people we need to get back to." He turned to her then and looked into her eyes. "But for right now, it's one foot in front of the other. Stay alive, keep going. And hope."

Fresh tears spilled down her cheeks, and she wiped them away with the sleeve of her shirt. She looked to the sky and swallowed a few times before she spoke.

"I have two boys," she said. "They're with their father, but they're young. Five and eight."

"Jason is twelve, almost thirteen, now."

"Do you think we'll get back to them?" She studied his eyes, clearly looking for hope.

"I have to believe it," he told her truthfully. "It won't be today. But Deidra will find a way, if it can be done, she will find it." He let out a long breath. "She wants to get back, too. So, she won't give up easy, either."

Gordon sighed. "That's good to know," she said. "Probably exactly what I needed to hear." She gave a small laugh.

"This next..." he hesitated and bit at his cheek. "You were with Greenway."

Her face darkened, and her eyes hit the ground. He couldn't tell if it was embarrassment or anger. "Estard told you," she breathed.

"Estard?" He raised a brow. "No. Weiz did."

"Guess it was too much to hope for that no one would notice," she muttered. "What will you do?"

"What do you mean?"

"What will you do with me? I assume there will be some kind of punishment. Exile, maybe." She shuddered, as if that was something she truly feared.

Harvey shook his head and waved away the comment with a frown. "Nothing like that. Nothing at all like that."

"What then?"

"I just wanted to know who else is out there." He pointed back toward the others. "Found Deidra's scientist friend inside the mountain. Alive. Barely, and he still may not make it, but even so, we found him."

"You know what happened?" she asked him quietly.

"Not for certain, but I have an idea. I came back that night. I was intending to ferry you all to the mountain, after I knew where it was and where we were all headed. But, well…" He shrugged. "You were all either gone, or dead."

"Greenway didn't wait." Gordon licked her lips and looked as if she might start crying again.

"Did anyone get away?"

"Yeah, as far as I know, they all did."

"All of them? You're sure?"

Gordon gave a sharp nod. Harvey rested a hand on her shoulder and looked away. He wished there was some kind of comfort he could offer, but it was the best he could manage.

Harvey gave her a sad smile, patted her shoulder and left her to be. There was nothing more to be said on the matter.

A few people to look out for. Walt, Dames and whoever had survived Greenway's attack. He had no clue where to start looking for any of them, but if there was a chance, he had to find them.

~

Greenway faced the gates, his eyes on the soldiers above. He didn't want to turn the place to rubble, like he had Djorik. He wanted to address this place specifically, but he didn't know its name. People were already paying attention, though. As he'd walked up the road, people had pointed and spoken to each other in hushed tones.

Greenway waited for a crowd to gather. He made the ground rise beneath him like a stage, so he could look down on them. The way they gazed up at him with awe made him twitch a smile.

When there was a sufficient crowd, he began his oration. He'd never had a way with words. He wasn't eloquent, or persuasive. He'd have made a terrible politician. But he was honest, his words raw.

"I don't know why you're all here, now," he said. "But I will give you purpose. Your Gods have returned to this world and require your aid!" He looked around for signs of fear and awe, but the crowd just stared at him with mild curiosity.

Greenway raised two pillars of earth to either side of the road. Each was twice the height of a tall man and made within seconds. "I demand your aid!" he screamed at them.

No. No eloquent speeches for him.

The people looked at the pillars. At him. At each other. Some began turning away, walking back inside the gates. The guards had not moved from their posts and didn't appear to be interested in the display.

Greenway made more pillars rise, in rows to either side of the gate. Some people cursed and spat as they quickly dodged away from the erupting earth. But that was all the reaction it caused. No screams, no huddling. No bowing or gibbering. No one was going to fall on their knees for him here.

With a roar, he made fist sized clumps of earth rise from beneath their feet. The muttering of the crowd grew as the ground shook. Someone shouted when a gout of dirt and rocks showered down on them. But still, no indication of fear. Only irritation, mixed with a touch of surprise. Why did they not fear him?

Some in the crowd spat at his feet as they turned to re-enter the town. One man threw a piece of fruit at him, which landed at his feet and rolled back into the crowd.

He snapped.

A spike of earth drove up from the ground and impaled the man. The walls of the town shook as he made the ground roll. "I will not be denied! You will stand and listen!"

He made spikes drive up from the ground to block the gate. He made the ground rumble, and stones burst from the earth. He made spikes that impaled, and pillars that blocked. They needed to listen! He demanded it. It was his right.

The mutters of the crowd grew louder, but not in fear. In *anger*.

A guard at the gate braced himself against the walls, removed a cudgel from his belt, and struck at the spikes blocking the gate. They shattered as each blow landed, and some of the citizens got through before Greenway raised them again. But the guard continued, his fellows following suit.

Greenway stared at the scene, for the time forgetting the people surrounding him, as he made the spikes rise to the top of the barbican. But the guards weren't dissuaded, they simply continued smashing away at the larger obstacle.

Atop the wall, one guard now had an arrow aimed at him.

He couldn't believe the complete indifference these people showed him. His power meant nothing to them.

The arrow came at him, and he battered it aside with a fist, but something else punctured his side. He roared. An arrow jutted from his ribs. It had gone deep and would be difficult to extract. For the first time, since the night of the Giants, he felt very mortal.

He stepped back off the stage he'd made and raised it as a shield, while he looked at the wound. It took him a moment to realise he wasn't alone.

There was a man, dressed in dirt stained white and grey. He leant against the mound of earth and watched curiously as he bit into a piece of fruit. Black eyes and hair, a tanned, clean-shaven face.

"Might want to get that seen to," the man told him, taking another unconcerned mouthful.

Greenway blinked at him, so stunned by the reactions of these people, he didn't know what to say. They'd shot him with an arrow! A fucking arrow! He could feel it brush against his lung when he breathed. It hadn't punctured, but left in there much longer, and it would tear through.

Gritting his teeth against the pain that would come, Greenway gripped the shaft and pulled. The wound tore, blood poured out, and he felt a moment of dizziness. After a few deep breaths, he turned his attention to the man.

"Have you come to serve?" he asked. Maybe at least one person in this forsaken town had some sense. The rest he would kill on principle.

The man took another bite of his fruit, examined the core in his hand, and threw it to the side of the road. Mouth still half full, he replied, "No one serves Gods in this place. And you, are not a God."

Maybe if he'd not been wounded, he'd have seen it sooner. Could have reacted quicker. But the man's arm was up in a flash, and he shot Greenway with what looked like a laser gun.

His vision blurred, turned purple, and then nothing.

~

He was in pitch darkness, and he could hear nothing except the sound of his own breathing.

"What the fuck was that?" he whispered to himself. "What the fuck?"

He turned his head from side to side, straining to see something in the dark. What had the bastard done?

He bellowed at the top of his lungs, "What did you do?"

The sound echoed around him. That didn't make any sense. He yelled again. Again, the echo.

One hand to the wound in his side, the other arm outstretched, he shuffled sideways across what felt like stone. After only a few steps, he hit a wall of rough stones. He tried to keep his breathing even as he followed the wall.

What the fuck happened? It didn't make any sense. Had Harvey got to him? Brought him here somehow? Done something to his eyes? But, then, who had that man been? No, it wasn't Harvey, he was sure of that much.

"Where am I?" he yelled. There was no answer.

He trailed the walls twice. Every corner was at a right angle to touch, and he passed them eight times. When he stopped, he was sure of two things. The first was that he was in a cell, no larger than nine square meters, and it was completely empty. The second, was that there were no doors or windows.

He couldn't have said what changed, exactly, but he could suddenly feel a presence in the room with him. "Who's there?" he asked.

"You are perceptive, I'll give you that." It was the voice of the man from the town.

Greenway lunged toward the sound but collided with a wall.

"That won't do you much good," the man said conversationally.

"Where am I?"

"Some place you won't be bothering anyone, for a very, very, very, long time."

Greenway strained to see something in the darkness. Anything at all. "Who are you?"

"Me personally?" There was a pause. "I am no one important. My people, though... well, that's something else altogether, isn't it?"

Greenway heard no shuffle of feet, no sound of breathing. Hard as he tried, he couldn't pierce the gloom. He didn't ask any more questions, he just listened.

"We were content for the past thousand years or so to leave things as they were," the man continued. "They did nothing that demanded our attention, and we left them to their own devices. They knew better. But you don't, do you? You're new here."

"What are you talking about?" Greenway spat.

There was a loud sigh that popped, and it was then he realised he was being spoken to through a speaker! A god-damned speaker! In *this* world!

"You'll learn." The sound cut out, and the presence he'd felt faded. He breathed deep and long, trying to make his brain work.

Pain shot through him, crawled on his skin. It burrowed into his mind and sliced at his innards.

What the fuck was going on?

Chapter Twenty-One

Estard watched Harvey pace back and forth behind the women. Occasionally he'd stop and look down at the unconscious scientist, mutter something, then resume. Weiz held to the scientist's head, while Deidra attempted to get food and water into him.

Deidra was in her element, here. He could see that. She was nothing like the lost little lamb that he'd interviewed on Earth little more than a week ago.

Things here were beginning to settle. The shocked airmen who'd been looking forward to getting home a few hours ago, were now sitting around a fire Lance had prepared for them. They didn't speak to each other, barely even looked at one another, but they were together. Except Gordon. She stood off in the distance, staring out at the plain.

The woman would come back to them when she was ready. He wasn't sure what Harvey had said to her, but he'd seen her reaction, and he knew it might take a while before she was ready.

Estard glanced at Kristin, who stood beside him. Images of her in the interview room popped into his mind, and he let them play out. He didn't know how much of a chance he had to make something happen, but he took her presence near him as a good sign.

"Do I assume we're just camping here the night?" he asked no one in particular.

Harvey stopped and looked at him. "We won't all fit in the hut," he said.

Weiz snorted, and Ulrich stirred. There was a moment when all eyes were on the man, but when it was clear he wasn't going to wake, the Commander looked to Estard.

"We stay, for the moment," she said. "Until we find a better place to be."

Estard sighed. Sleeping out in the open, on the ground, was not his idea of comfortable. He doubted it was anyone's.

He felt a light touch on his arm and looked to Kristin. She nodded her head away from the others, and he followed her as she moved away. When they were a respectable distance from them, Kristin stopped.

"What is it?" he asked.

"We need to do something," she said.

"Yes. But what?"

"That's just it. I don't know. I don't think anyone knows." She bit at her bottom lip and frowned at the sky. It was a little after midday, so far as Estard could tell.

"You all still want to go home, don't you?"

She gave him a small smile. "Caught that feeling, did you?"

"Do you believe you can?"

Kristin shook her head slowly, then shrugged. "Maybe. Maybe not. Deidra might work something out. But even if she does, it's going to take a long time."

Estard reached out tentatively to take her hand, but she pulled away. He let his hand drop. "What is it you need me to say to you?"

"I need you to tell me why you chose this," she said. "When everyone else would probably be willing to cut off a limb if it meant going home. You *chose* this. You stood before those things and *asked* for it. Tell me why."

"I told you. I don't know."

She punched him and he staggered a step. "That's bullshit."

"I don't —"

Again, she hit him. He grunted and clenched a fist, ready to fight back. "Tell me why," she said again.

He looked at her. Her brown eyes, her dark hair. The image of her waving a hand in front of her face to dispel his smoke. The crinkled nose.

She moved to hit him again, and he yelled, "You." He was prepared to block the blow but didn't have to. "It was you."

Kristin stopped and took a step back. "Me?"

Estard swallowed. He hadn't wanted to say it. Hadn't wanted to admit that, not to her. Not until much later, if ever, after he gauged how receptive she might be to his advances. His heart wrenched in his chest at the thought the admission might ruin any chance he'd had.

"Yes," he said. "You."

She took a deep breath and sighed it out. "You're an odd man, Estard."

"Julian, please."

Kristin stared at him. She looked him up and down and seemed to measure his every achievement, count his every mistake. Those eyes sifted through his memories and weighed his heart. He wished he knew what she'd found.

"Maybe," she said softly after a while. "But not today. There's still one thing left to do."

She didn't wait for him to respond. She turned on her heel and walked back to the others. He watched her go and didn't move.

He hung onto that one word. Maybe. It wasn't yes, but it wasn't no, either. He had some hope. Something it was possible to work toward. Maybe.

Estard rubbed a hand across his chin and tried not to suck on his teeth. He'd have to find something to shave with, soon. He looked down on himself. And a change of clothes.

He couldn't keep the small smile from creeping across his face. Maybe. It wasn't all he'd hoped for, but it was enough.

~

Harvey kept an eye on them as they walked away. He didn't know why it bothered him. But it did. Something was going on there, but he couldn't work out what it was.

The Scientist stirred again, and Deidra said, "He's coming back to us. It will still be a while before he wakes, but he's getting stronger."

Harvey grunted. He didn't know what to say.

He saw Kristin punch Estard and smiled. He didn't know why that made him feel better — he hated it when she hit him — but it did. She hit him again. She looked like she was going for a third, but she stopped. *Careful with that one, Estard. She bites.* He had to consciously restrain himself from laughing. He should not have been watching. They may not have had a great amount of privacy out in the open like this, but it was rude of him to stare. Almost like eavesdropping.

When Kristin began stalking toward him, he turned his face away, tried to pretend he'd been paying no attention. But he felt a guilty flush in his cheeks, and knew he'd been caught out even before Kristin stopped in front of him.

Harvey thought the woman had meant to hit him, and was prepared for it, but she glanced down at Weiz, and apparently decided against it. He was very glad for whatever minor shield Weiz could afford him.

"We still have to deal with Greenway," Kristin said.

The statement struck him a blow. How could he have forgotten? The Giants coming, the missing people to think of. The airmen that had to stay. They should not have kept him from remembering the danger Greenway posed to the people of this world. He growled deep in his throat.

This time Kristin did give him an open-handed whack. "Don't growl at me," she said.

Weiz frowned up at the both of them. Deidra studiously ignored them all.

"Woman has a point, John," Weiz said.

Kristin gave the Commander a nod. "So, what are we going to do about it? You know where he is."

He swallowed a second growl. He *didn't* know where he was. He suspected the man would remain close to the town he'd found him at, but he didn't *know*.

Harvey moved his eyes to Weiz, then Kristin and back again a few times, before he yelled, "Viatri!" He wasn't taking Kristin on this one, she'd have no defence against the man.

Lance trotted up beside Deidra, looked at the two women, and stuck his hands in his pockets. "Sir?"

Harvey didn't ask, he just grabbed the man by an elbow and shifted them to the town.

"Shit," Lance moaned, as he wrenched his arm free of Harvey's grip.

It was immediately apparent that Greenway had already been there. Pillars of earth stood in random places, to the side of the road, and in front of the gates. Dirt and gravel coated the wide road, and its surrounds from the furthest pillar all the way to the walls.

The gates were closed. Eight guards stood looking down on them, four of them with bows in hand, arrows knocked.

Harvey bit at his cheek. "What do you think, Viatri? Is he

inside?"

"Greenway?"

"No. The fucking Easter bunny. Who else?"

Lance shook his head. "Hard to tell. Why don't we just ask?"

Harvey took a deep breath and a step toward the gate.

The guardsman raised their bows in his direction. Another step, and they drew. This was going to have to be close enough. Harvey put his hands in the air and hoped they understood the significance of the gesture.

"The man who did this," he called up to them, "is he inside the walls?"

The ones not holding bows conferred briefly with each other. "No," the one furthest to the right shouted down.

"Do you know where he is?" He couldn't be far, not if he had people with him.

Again, the guards spoke among themselves, then the one on the right shrugged and faced him again, "The man from Bahana took him."

This time it was Harvey exchanging looks with Lance. The Pilot shrugged at him, and Harvey shook his head with a frown.

"What does that mean?" Harvey asked.

The guard pointed behind them, and though Harvey's first thought was that they'd shoot him in the back if he turned, he had the sensation that someone was coming up behind him. The little hairs on the back of his neck rose, and he clenched a fist as he whirled on his heel.

Lance kept an eye on the guards.

From behind the first pillar on the road, a man emerged. Dressed in dirt stained white and grey, he smiled at them.

"You got me," he said.

Harvey frowned at him. "You took Greenway?"

The man shrugged. "Might have done."

"He's gone?"

A slow nod, eyes moving between Harvey and Lance. "He is."

"Where?"

Another shrug. "Can't say."

Harvey fought the desire to take the man back to the others and interrogate him. How much did it really matter, as long as Greenway had been stopped? If he'd been taken somewhere he couldn't hurt anyone, wasn't that best for everyone? Shouldn't he just let it lie?

But his hackles were up, intuition whispering in the back of his mind. *Threat.* If the man could do something about Greenway, he could do something with them. The question was: what? He couldn't kill them.

"Where?" he asked the man again.

The man's smile broadened as he said, "I'll show you," and brought up his hand. It held what appeared to be a laser gun, and Harvey moved with instinct, shifting behind the man before he could pull the trigger.

Harvey's arm wrapped around the man's throat in a choke hold, and he kept it that way until he was sure he'd passed out. Then he breathed a sigh and turned to Lance. He looked around, confused. Lance wasn't there.

"Viatri," he called. But there was no answer. "Lance Viatri!" he yelled. Still no answer. "Shit."

Harvey pulled at the unconscious man's arm and shifted them back to the others. "Tie him up!" he told Kristin.

She shook her head, "With what?" she asked.

"Sit on him then! Disarm him and keep him in one spot. I'll be back."

His heart was racing. He didn't know why. Didn't understand what he was worried about. Lance wasn't dead. He'd be fine.

Harvey stepped to the field and waited.

One minute. Two.

Ten minutes passed, and still no sign of Viatri.

He ground his teeth and paced. Whatever the man had done, Harvey hadn't seen it. He'd been pretty intent on the back of the man's head as soon as he'd moved.

"Fuck," he muttered. "Fuck, fuck, fuck."

Twenty minutes passed.

Lance wasn't going to wake up in this field. That meant only one thing, to Harvey's mind. That man knew how to kill them, and make sure they stayed that way.

"Shit!" He kicked at the grass and shifted back to the others.

Kristin had relieved the man of his outer shirt, and torn strips from it to tie the man up. His wrists and ankles were bound, and then pulled together behind him. He was lying sideways on the ground, and still appeared unconscious.

Harvey moved straight to him and kicked him hard in the guts. Kristin took a step toward him, arm outstretched, and he glared at her, as the man coughed and rolled.

The stranger seemed to test his bonds, and realising he was tied, stopped struggling. He closed his eyes and breathed slow.

Harvey kicked him in the face. There was a satisfying crack, and the man groaned. Blood dribbled from the corner of his mouth and coated his chin.

"What are you doing? Where's Lance?" Kristin asked.

Harvey took a deep breath. He wanted to kick the man, truly hurt him, but it seemed his blow to the face had rendered him unconscious again.

"He killed him," Harvey whispered. He didn't know why it was so hard to say. So difficult to bring volume to the words. He cleared his throat.

"What do you mean? He'll be at the field, if that's the case." Weiz said as she came up beside Kristin, whose mouth hung open.

The others gathered around, curious about the stranger.

Harvey shook his head. "He's not at the field," his voice came out a little stronger. "Did you see the weapon he was holding?" Kristin gave a sharp nod. "That's what he shot Viatri with."

Weiz frowned at him. "That doesn't make sense. If he's dead, he'll turn up at the field." She reiterated, whether for herself or them, Harvey couldn't tell.

Harvey looked to the sky and closed his eyes. No, it didn't make sense. He *should* have been at the field. He *wasn't*. What else could it be?

"Deidra," he said, so softly he doubted anyone else heard. She would know, if anyone did. "Deidra," he called, looking back to the women.

The Scientist left her friend's side and came toward him slowly. "Captain?" she asked.

"Do you know anything about this man?"

She frowned and shook her head. "Why would I? I've never met him before."

"But you *know* things."

Everyone was looking to her now, but she kept her eyes on Harvey. "I don't know everything. I'm not omniscient."

Harvey clenched his fists and cracked his knuckles as he struggled for calm. It was like they didn't understand what he was telling them. "Lance is *gone*," he grated. "You have to know *some*thing."

Estard knelt over the stranger on the ground, and ungently moved him about, checking him over.

"What are you doing?" Harvey asked.

The Agent didn't look up at him or stop what he was doing as he responded, "Checking for any kind of identifying marks."

"What good would that do us?" Kristin wanted to know.

Estard stopped then. "I don't know," he said. "But any investigation starts with understanding the person you deal with. What have they done? What do they do? What is important to them? Is it just one person or a group?" He breathed a sigh and began to suck at his teeth before he continued. "Sometimes, a tattoo can tell you much about a person, if they have them. What it is, where it's placed."

"So, what do you know about this man?" Harvey asked.

Estard shrugged. "He has no visible markings. He hasn't said a word since you brought him here. Where are the things you took off him?"

Kristin moved a little distance off, then came back with a handful of small objects and the laser gun.

Harvey watched as Estard moved a few steps away and laid the objects down on the ground, then examined each carefully. Deidra joined him, and though he glanced at her, he said nothing.

All eyes were on them.

The man at his feet mumbled, and Harvey looked down on him. Was he talking in his sleep? The man shifted, and Harvey looked down into his open eyes. He mumbled again.

Harvey leaned down and pulled him up to his knees. "What are you saying?"

The man spat to the side. "He's not dead," he wheezed out.

Harvey pushed him back down to the ground, and the man let out a groan. Weiz was eyeing him sideways but faced toward Estard and Deidra. Kristin, for all her outward calm, had her fists clenched so tightly at her sides the knuckles had gone white. She, at least, had understood what he was saying.

Deidra was frowning at some small object in her hand. She didn't examine it, merely stared. Estard had stopped and was watching her.

In a blink, Deidra was gone.

In a blink, Deidra returned.

"What the...?" Kristin breathed.

Everyone else was silent. They waited for Deidra to say something as she turned the small object in her hands.

She looked up at Harvey, "I feel like I should know something," she said. "But it's more a feeling, than knowledge. Which is very strange." She shook her head.

Weiz looked as if she were about to move toward her, but instead, sidestepped to Harvey and held out her hand. Harvey took it and gave a small squeeze.

"He did something with Greenway," Harvey whispered to Weiz. "After Lance, I almost forgot. But the guards at the gate of the town, they said 'the man from Bahana took him.'"

Deidra's head snapped up, and dark eyes bored into him. "Did I hear that right?" she asked. "'The man from Bahana took him.'"

Harvey gave a slow nod. He was surprised she'd heard him. "Does that mean something?"

"Yes, Captain, it does."

"What?" Kristin demanded. "What does it mean?"

The Scientist looked over to her friend beside the fire, then back at the people surrounding her, but it was Harvey she addressed. "It means, if there are more men like this one, we are in a great deal of trouble."

Chapter Twenty-Two

Deidra still held to the device in her hand, running it over her fingers. She understood what it was, and how it was used. But not where it went. She just knew that they couldn't let the man on the ground anywhere near this equipment.

Everyone had their eyes on her, and she was all too conscious of it. She felt like rolling her shoulders, hiding her face, but she just stared at the Captain.

Her memories had already begun to fade, and she didn't know what she'd lost. But her feelings were still intact, and what rolled through her now was fear. Deep, primal, fear. Like prey that knew the predator was nearby. Only, she didn't know why. On an intellectual level, there was no reason for it.

"Do you know," Harvey asked, "what happened to Viatri? To Greenway? Are they dead?"

Deidra shook her head. "Not dead," she said. She felt again the object in her hand. She picked up the gun. Small, light, apparently made from tin or aluminium. She'd have to take it apart to know how it worked, exactly, but she knew it was a transport device, like the one in her hand. Though the destination would be different.

Harvey picked the man up by his shirt front until he was on his knees again. Their faces were so close their noses almost touched.

"Where?" Harvey grated through clenched teeth.

The stranger smiled at him, his teeth coated red with blood. "You'll see," he said.

Harvey leaned back and punched him in the face, a blow that cut open the skin of his brow. "Where?" he asked again. The man just spit blood on the ground and continued smiling. Harvey hit him again.

Deidra stopped paying attention. She was not one for torture.

She dug down deep inside of her, cutting out everything else that happened around her, and searched for the knowledge. She knew it would mean losing more of herself, perhaps faster than before. But she knew she had to do it. What was this man, that he inspired in her the instinct to flee and hide? What could he do to threaten an immortal? Did he have the means? Did he know *how* to kill them permanently? But if that were the case, why would the Giants have come after them in their desperation to die?

Deidra searched her mind for the memories of the being that had formerly housed her power. It should have been simple enough, but all she was getting was a static buzz. She pushed hard at it, trying to get through, but it was like pushing up against a steel door. Firm and unyielding.

Time and awareness disappeared for her. She could no longer feel her body, so deep in her mind was she.

Snatches of conversation she couldn't quite hear or understand. Darkness. A feeling of deep fear. Stone, hard and cold.

She floated through the void of her mind.

Why am I afraid? she asked herself. *Who is this man? Where is he from?*

"*Stop!*" Galsin's voice echoed through her mind. She hesitated momentarily, waiting for him to say more. But nothing came, and she continued on.

Why would the memories be closed to her? Why would she not know? There had to be a way through. A way past that barrier.

The part of her that was still Deidra Ward suspected it was not a natural barrier. That it had somehow been caused by something that had been done to her. Or the person who had held her powers before. Before Fields. The original Giant.

Deidra moved backwards in time. Back to 1957. Back to the strange planet. Back into Fields. She was a different person, with different thoughts, helping as best she could.

Back again, to the morning when Fields had killed the Giant. Back into the being who had lived for thousands of years.

She pulled it back, again and again, through years of mundane existence. Years of solitude, years of friendship. Years of unfeeling knowledge. She felt herself merging with the being, until what was happening to that person, was happening to her, as sure as she was sitting on the ground next to Estard.

She hit the barrier.

She fought, she clawed, and she chewed at it. She smashed at it with invisible fists and battered it with invisible elbows. Then, like a soap bubble, it popped, and she sunk into that moment. She became Tatiana, Guardian of Knowledge on the planet Urago.

It was an unfamiliar sensation, the way the hairs on her neck stood up. The way her heart pounded, and her breathing intensified. Her guts churned and her bowels felt loose, though she managed to hold on. It had been so long, it took her a while to identify what was happening.

Fear, *she told herself.*

She was in a dark place. Absolute pitch. It was a cell, though she had trouble remembering how she'd gotten there. She remembered what had come before.

Tatiana had seen others, too. When she'd been in the other room. She'd watched with interest, at first, before they'd started on her.

They'd hooked them up to machines. She couldn't remember the last time she'd seen machines. Five thousand years? Six? More?

Four others had been in there, and different parts of their bodies were being experimented on, the doctors very careful to keep them all alive. To keep them all awake, and aware of what was happening to them.

Tatiana did not understand what they were looking for, or why. She felt the bandage on her own head. They'd cut it open, stuck probes in her brain. She hadn't felt that, but the others had screamed. Strapped down as they all had been, none could help the other, and she knew Entis and Callinda well enough to know they'd try to, even if it was obvious, they could not.

So many of them had disappeared, over the last few years. Enough that the remaining twenty or so had finally congregated and agreed to battle the common threat. They had no fear of death, they'd simply arise in the field, as they had so many times before. But whoever the enemy were, they were doing something else. Those taken, never came to the field.

The cell had no door, and no window. There was no way to gauge the thickness of the walls, not that knowing would help. Her more mundane powers had been nullified. Even her knowledge was hazed and stunted. But without that, she was no one.

Am I someone now? *She wondered. She hadn't thought of such things before. She'd always had a sense of individual, but she'd not considered what that meant.*

She needed to get out of this place. The easiest way out, since she did not know where she was, was death. If she could find some way to kill herself, she'd wake in the field, and it would be over.

A light surrounded her cell, so bright she couldn't see anything.

She was strapped down again.

No more!

Deidra reeled back. Her mind soaring until it reached the present and slammed into her body. She gasped in the shock of it.

The being, Tatiana, had known someone else was watching from her mind. Or perhaps it was the thing that inhabited both of them? It was difficult to know. But she'd been flung away as easily as a soft toy.

Estard had his arm across her back, holding her up, and his face wore concern. Harvey had stepped away from the man and was reaching out to her.

Kristin fell to her knees, head clutched between her hands, and both men instinctively wanted to go to her, but only Harvey did. Estard kept his eyes on them, even as everyone else had eyes on her.

Weiz glanced once at Kristin with a frown, but when she spoke, it was to Deidra.

"What happened, there?"

Deidra shook herself off and leaned forward, freeing Estard to move. He just gave her a tight, worried smile. "I couldn't find the memory," she breathed. "So, I forced my way through." Her voice was cold, detached. She got to her feet and shook herself again.

Everyone looked at her expectantly. They wanted to know. Wanted *her* to know. That was her purpose.

Deidra breathed deep. She was herself. She knew who she was. She could still *feel*, which to her mind, was more important. The fear that had infected Tatiana had worked its way into her, and as she'd been flung back across the void, the knowledge of things had been given. Not all things, even concerning this situation, but enough.

"They didn't come at us because they wanted to die," Deidra said, and couldn't quite keep the shock out of her voice. "That first night, after the landing, they thought we were them." She pointed at the man on the ground.

"Why would Galsin not have said so?" Weiz asked.

"He didn't know, I don't think," Deidra told her.

Harvey helped a swearing and muttering Kristin to her feet. Deidra spared the woman a sympathetic glance.

Weiz clicked her fingers to bring Deidra's attention back to her. "Explain, please. What is going on?"

"Whatever it is these men do, it's worse than death." She gave a sigh. "I could not see those memories. She pushed me out. Torture, experiments, I don't know what they do, exactly. But of more than thirty captured, only two got away. The others never came back. Not even through death.

"Galsin and the others knew they would come again. They spent a lot of time hiding."

Estard was on his feet, eyes drifting between herself and Kristin. "How did they get away?" he asked.

Deidra frowned at him. "I don't know. I just know that Tatiana did, else I would not be here. And Greta, the old crone. She hadn't looked that way before they'd gotten to her."

"Explains her fervour," Weiz muttered.

After a short, hushed exchange, Kristin and Harvey took a step forward.

Deidra turned to them. "What did you see?" she asked.

"Oh, I'm fine, thank you," Kristin said. "How are you? Good. Alright then."

Weiz opened her mouth to respond, but Harvey shook his head wide eyed, and the woman backed down. Estard took a step toward Kristin, but a look stopped him.

"Are you alright?" Deidra asked dutifully.

Kristin shook her head and closed her eyes. When she opened them, she spoke. "Meteors," she said. "I don't know anything about this lot of current arse-turds, but we are going to have a meteor shower, sometime in the near future. A very dangerous one."

Weiz and Harvey shared a look, but it was Weiz who replied. "I don't recall any asteroid fields on approach to this world."

Kristin shook her head and shrugged, raising her hands. "I don't make things happen, Commander, I just see them."

"Rough timeline?" Estard wanted to know.

"Soon," she said softly. "Assuming this world is as much like Earth as it looks, then, before the summer is out. Which I'd estimate at two months, at the outside. But the feeling I get is much sooner."

"How much sooner?"

"A day or two, maybe."

Weiz turned her attention back to Deidra. "Could these men cause it, somehow, do you think?"

Deidra shook her head. "Wouldn't if they could. They're not interested in doing that sort of thing. They're perfectly courteous to the human inhabitants of this world. It's only us that they hunt."

"Well, that's just fucking perfect!" One of the airmen in the small gathering threw up his arms and walked away. Others drifted off with him.

Deidra blinked at them a moment with a frown. So hard to believe it had only been a couple of hours since Galsin and his friends had done what they'd done. Her sense of time after that dive into the past was skewed. But for these men and women, it would seem that in a matter of hours, one enemy had been replaced with another, and to top it off a dangerous meteor shower was going to take place.

They needed some time to breathe. Get their feet under them. Time to understand what was happening to them as people, before something else came along. As difficult as those months had been on them, Weiz, Harvey, Kristin, Lance, Greenway and herself, had all had that much. Time to adapt. Time to accept, to a certain degree, what had happened, and what that meant.

"What do we do?" Harvey asked.

"About what?" Weiz wanted to know.

"Any of it. All of it." He stepped away from Kristin and moved toward the Commander.

"None of this seems real," Estard breathed. "Not since I helped you all out of the bunker."

"It's real," Kristin assured him.

"I know it is. But it's also...unreal." He shrugged. "I don't know how else to put it."

Kristin gave him a small smile. Deidra looked away. So, something was happening between those two.

A cough and moan brought her attention back to Ulrich.

Still by the fire, he had one hand on the ground, and was attempting to lift himself to a seated position. His head dropped, and his arm shook.

Everything else flew out of Deidra's mind as she pushed passed Harvey and Weiz to drop down beside the young scientist.

"You're alright," she told him. "I thought you were dead, when we went back for you, but you proved me wrong." She smiled, and let out a small chuckle, but tears threatened in the side of her eye. She picked up the small bowl of water and offered it to him.

When he finally had himself in a seated position, he took the bowl gratefully, and consumed it in slow sips. He stared into the distance. His movements shaky and slow, he stretched his legs.

Deidra didn't know what to say. How to explain. She opened her mouth several times to tell him what had been happening, only to find that she didn't know where to start. But he didn't look at her. She wasn't sure he was even aware of her presence.

"How are you feeling?" she asked, instead.

"You left me behind," he said, his voice so weak and dry she barely heard it. Still, he stared at the distance. "You left me behind."

A tear fell. "I hadn't seen you in days." Deidra tried to put a comforting hand on him, but he pulled away, still not looking at her. "I thought you'd killed yourself," she told him. "When we had to go, it was in such a rush, none of us thought about who was there."

He was silent for a long time, and she let him be. If he wanted her to feel guilty, he didn't need to try. But, the truth of it was, had she not regained herself when she'd awoken in that field, she would not have felt it. And he'd spent enough time with her after the God had taken hold to know that.

Ulrich looked to her now, sad eyes trying hard to focus without his glasses. "I was working on the calculations," he said. "You never saw the whole picture. You didn't know what he'd done."

Deidra sat very still. The whole picture. What Heinrich had done. She'd contemplated it, fussed over it, obsessed on the subject. But she hadn't *known*. Had never found the man's notes or seen all the readings. She'd been too focused on how to reverse it from her own part of the project.

She waited patiently for the young scientist to continue. He took a few sips of water and looked at the pot of stew by the fire.

Deidra filled a bowl and gave it to him. He took it without a word, and like the water, started with small sips. After a few mouthfuls, he wiped at his lips, put the bowl down, and lay back on the ground.

"I'm tired," he said, and closed his eyes.

Deidra got up and left him be. He would be weak for a while, yet. But he was alive, and from the look of things, would remain so.

And he had something to tell her. Something important. Though whether he understood that, she did not know.

Everyone had split off again. In pairs or by themselves. Speaking in hushed whispers or sitting in companionable silence. Staring into the distance or eyes turned inward. They were a camp of lost souls, to her mind. And she wondered how long she would care. A few more days? Would it be enough?

She wished Dane were there, and at the same time was glad he wasn't. It was difficult for her while she understood what she was losing. But he would always look at her and know what he had lost. He loved her, and she knew it. She felt it. She missed that. She could have used a hug. But as she looked around at the others, she realised, that as much as they were all stuck there together, she was on her own.

It's why you wanted to find Ulrich, she told herself. *It may not have been in the front of your mind, but you knew it.*

How long? Too long, and not long enough.

Deidra knelt down in front of the unconscious man from Bahana and studied his plain face. Bruised, bleeding, but relaxed.

She clamped fingers over his nose and covered his mouth. A short time later he spasmed, struggled, tried to strike out. His eyes shot open, and he looked at her, shaking his head furiously, attempting to dislodge her hand. But she was stronger than she looked, now, and forced enough pressure on him he couldn't move.

Deidra made sure he was dead before she moved away. Then she stepped over to the objects on the ground and picked up the gun. She shot it at him, and he disappeared.

Harvey was at her side and grabbing at her arm. He spun her around before she'd even realised he was there.

"You could start a war," he said, his tone firm, his eyes wide.

Deidra shook her head. "We were already at war," she told him. "We have been since the day we got here. We just didn't know it." She let the laser drop and walked away.

How long?

CHAPTER TWENTY-THREE

Harvey stood outside the hut and looked to the morning sky. He knew he should have stayed with the others, but after what Deidra had done, he couldn't bring himself to be around them.

There'd been a simplicity to his life that he would never get again. He knew that now. He mourned it.

He hadn't brought anyone back with him, not even Weiz. He needed time to himself, with his own thoughts.

Every time he thought they'd hit the end of it, something else turned up. Something else got in their way. Through it all, the only thought that came to him was *get home*. Even now, knowing that he was somehow connected to this world, that he wouldn't be able to leave, he kept thinking he just needed to get back. Back to Jason.

He slumped against the wood slats and closed his eyes. He hadn't slept. He didn't need to, but he should have. He didn't want to be like Greenway. Didn't want to give up what was human in him. He still *felt* human.

What *had* happened to Greenway? To Lance? Where had the

man from Bahana sent them? Deidra hadn't told them that. Hadn't really told them anything about these people. What they wanted, why they were here. She'd as much as announced they were at war already, but not the reason behind it.

"If the Giants were afraid of them," Harvey told the air in front of his face, "we should probably all be pissing ourselves."

Deidra had been so cold, when she'd sent that man away. He'd seen the difference in her the first time around, as day by day she'd lost herself to the monster. This had been different. This had been a coldness born of fear, of hate, of anger. Which to his mind, was much scarier. Especially coming from that woman, though he couldn't say why.

Harvey knew he should return to the others. They had basics to attend to, and an enemy to watch for. He breathed deep and let out a long sigh. They needed to know who that enemy was, and Deidra had sent the man away. He thumped his thigh with a fist.

His head had to be clear before he took the step. He couldn't be upset or angry with Deidra. She had her reasons, and for the most part he was inclined to trust her. Which was more than he could say for most scientists. They were a breed unto themselves, in his mind, and Heinrich had been more what he expected.

Harvey pushed himself off the wall and took another deep breath. He let it out slowly, and repeated that a few times. He gave himself a nod, then shifted.

Kristin was the first person he saw, off by herself, back to him, she was gutting something. He cringed a little inside and turned away. Not a lot of things made him queasy, but the thought of sticking his hand into the warm body cavity of a fresh kill and pulling out its guts — bile rose.

Behind him, Weiz, Deidra, Ulrich and Estard sat near the ashes of yesterday's fire. The others weren't far off, and were all huddled together, shooting the occasional glance at Deidra or Kristin.

When Weiz saw him, she came to him. He held his arms open, and once she'd stepped into them, he shifted them a little further away. Having so many people in close proximity was always a little awkward.

"Done sulking?" Weiz asked, looking up into his face.

"Thinking, not sulking," he replied as calmly as he could manage. "It's the question of what now and what's next that I've thought on all night."

Weiz gave his waist a tight squeeze and took a step back.

"And?"

"And what?"

"What's now and what's next?"

Harvey held out his hand and she took it. "Let's walk," he said. "It's a beautiful morning."

She gave him a tight smile and fell in beside him. She didn't say anything and waited for him to be ready. Weiz had always understood his moods. Knew when to pester and when to let him come around in his own time.

He didn't make her wait too long. He took a few deep breaths, a few short steps.

"If we are planning to stay on this world, there are few decisions to be made," he said. "And even if we don't, there are yet other decisions." He saw a small flower growing up from the grass and considered plucking it as he walked past but left it. Weiz was not the type to find such things romantic, as his wife had.

"Yes, decisions always," Weiz agreed. "It's a general part of life."

"If we stay here, we need to make arrangements. Where will we settle? What part will we play in this world? If any? We require the necessities, food, water, shelter. I dare say more than a few of us would like a shower and a change of clothes." He gave her faded red rags a meaningful glance.

"Unlike the rest of you, I haven't had a good wash since the morning we left the Docker."

Harvey gave a small nod. Until they'd returned to Earth in 1957, they'd all been in the same boat. He was very glad for his change of clothing, and the clean shave with a real razor. He scratched at the stubble, wishing they could have brought some of those small conveniences with them. Some soap would have been great.

Weiz gave his arm a pinch. "Don't drift off on me. Tell me the rest."

"If we choose another world to settle on, we have to ask ourselves whether we plan to go back, or if we're giving in."

"You want to keep trying?"

"You don't?"

Weiz stopped and Harvey took half a step before he faced her. "Where you go, I go," she told him.

"My son is on Earth. For as long as is practical, I will try to get back to him." He gazed into her blue eyes.

"Then that is what we'll do." She gave his hand a squeeze and they resumed walking.

"We have to find Lance and Greenway," Harvey continued. "Whatever the situation is with these people, it can't be good if the Giants would choose death over being captured by them."

"Deidra doesn't know where they are," Weiz breathed. "We spent half the night talking about it."

"So, tell me about it."

Weiz gave a shrug. "She needs to try and break through some barriers, or something. It wasn't clear to me what that particular issue is. But I do know that she's attempting to access the memories of the Giant."

"Can she really do that?" Knowledge and memory were closely linked, but they weren't the same thing.

"It's how she knew even as much as she did."

They walked in silence for a short time, wrapped in their own thoughts.

"Do you think we could do that?" Harvey asked after some time.

"Do what?"

"Access the memories."

Weiz blinked and frowned. "I don't know. I'd say probably not. The way Deidra described things, she has access to the knowledge of this world. And that had to come from somewhere. Everything the Giant knew, she knows. But she has to search for it. It's not just there all the time."

Harvey gave a nod. He didn't think things would be that simple. "So, we have to wait for her, then."

"When aren't we waiting on her?" Weiz chuckled. "Right from the beginning she worked to get us all home. Even yesterday, that was what she was doing. Without her, the rest of us would have no hope."

Without her we probably wouldn't be here in the first place, he thought, but pushed it aside. "What did she tell you?"

"Last night?"

"No. Last year."

"Don't be a smart arse," she told him.

"But you like that about me," he grinned.

"Don't push it though."

"So, what did she say?"

"More of the same, really," Weiz sighed. "The Giants knew. They wanted to get away from them. No mention of where Bahana is, or who these people are. But she's afraid. Very afraid."

"That's the part I'm not grasping," Harvey admitted. "What could an immortal possibly fear?"

"Torture. Pain without end. Awareness without the ability to move..." Weiz looked him in the eye, and they came to a halt. "Going insane. Losing limbs. Being killed over and over again, in new and fascinating ways."

Harvey held up his hands in surrender. "Alright. Alright. I get it. You've thought about this long and hard."

"Even before last night," she informed.

"So, what do we do about it?"

"I thought that was what you were thinking on all night. I hadn't got that far yet."

Harvey looked to the sky and sighed. "Deidra killed the man. Sent him back to his own people. I'd wanted to question him. I want to know where Lance is. And Greenway. How do you prepare to fight an enemy you know next to nothing about?"

"We know their tech is significantly advanced," Weiz offered. "At least as far as our own, perhaps more so."

"That gives me more reason to fear them but doesn't help me fight them."

"I doubt they're from this world."

"So, we can't simply come down on their city, or town, or hidey-hole."

"We're more blind with this than we were with the Giants," Weiz said softly. "And we lost to them. There are fewer of us now. Yes, fewer for them to take or kill, or whatever it is they do. But also, fewer to fight. We don't know their numbers, or how close they are."

Harvey cracked his knuckles. The more she said the worse the odds got in his head. What were they supposed to do? How had the Giants gotten away from these people the first time? Had they hidden? Had they fought? Had the people just decided they'd had enough and gone away? There was no way to know.

Unless Deidra could tell them. Unless Deidra remembered, somehow.

"So, we fortify," Harvey said. "We build our own place. We'd need to do it anyway. I doubt we'd be much welcome in any of the towns and villages around here."

"Or you could move us all to another world. We can hide until the threat disappears."

Harvey nodded. "If I do that, Deidra won't be able to find a way to get us home." To him that was more important than anything else, except survival. And this situation might mean just that.

"We can always come back," Weiz soothed.

"But how long will that take? A year? Ten? A thousand?" He shook his head. "I'm not throwing the idea off the table altogether. If it comes down to it, we should. But it's a big decision."

"They're all big decisions, John." She moved in and held him around the waist. He pulled her close and rested his chin on her head.

"Why am I the one making them?" He wanted to know.

"We could put it to a vote," Weiz suggested.

Harvey chuckled. "You got me picturing electoral posters and polling booths."

Weiz laughed with him. "John Harvey for president."

They held each other for a short time, then Harvey pulled back. He took Weiz by the shoulders and stared into her face. Her blue eyes and worry lines, her blonde hair and pale features. The quirk of her lips, the flip of her nose. He wanted to soak it all in. He let his hands drift down her arms, slow and soft.

A smile grew on her face when his hands got to the small of her back and he leaned in to kiss her, deep and long.

Weiz pulled away a little. "Any chance we'll be disturbed?" she asked thickly.

Harvey bit his bottom lip and pulled her hips into him, so she could feel his excitement. "Not a chance." He kissed her again.

She melted into him, and for a while, nothing else mattered.

~

Lance screamed.

There was a blinding white light in his eyes, and he couldn't see anything. But he could hear people speaking, in hushed tones he didn't understand. He could feel their hands on him. Their knives cutting, slow and deep.

The skin on the back of his head was pulled back and he heard a drill. He struggled, but his body wouldn't obey him. Not so much as the twitch of a finger.

The sound as the drill hit the back of his skull induced nausea, but his body wouldn't even let him vomit. His stomach churned, but he couldn't heave, or cough. His muscles wouldn't even tense.

Lance was screaming. But it was all in his head. His mouth hung slack, and he could feel drool dripping from the corner, but no voice emerged.

He didn't know how he'd gotten here. Didn't understand what had happened. The man had shot him with something, and he'd been in a dark space. He'd thought he was dead and in moments would wake up in the field. He wasn't sure how much time had passed, but he knew he wasn't dead. He believed in hell, and it might even look like this, but he was immortal now, so he knew it couldn't be. He was face down on an exam table, and there were people cutting into his head, and his back. That was all he knew.

Harvey would come for him. Kristin and Weiz would come for him. He held to that thought. He had to hold to it. They would come for him and get him out of here.

He could hear beeping and tapping. He could feel knives on his back, and skin being pulled away. But he couldn't feel the back of his head any more. The drill had stopped, and his stomach settled.

Come get me, Harvey, he thought. *Come fucking get me.*

~

Greenway had spied the tattooed eyes when they'd brought the man in. His first conflicting thoughts upon seeing Viatri had been: *suck shit, arsehole,* and *may God have mercy*. On the one hand, they'd openly opposed each other, and on the other, they now faced an enemy that could cripple their power.

When they'd first brought him into this room, he'd fought tooth and nail, and found he had all the strength of a mewling babe. And roughly the same vocabulary. He couldn't speak or move. He had a light directed into his eyes, but he could see his periphery.

They were experimenting on them. What they were trying to find, Greenway could not even speculate, but he'd been in enough R and D facilities to understand what was happening. They cut into his chest and stomach and were playing with his insides. The pain had faded into the background, after a time, and his mind descended into the depths to protect itself.

Greenway was going to find a way out of this place. If Viatri was here, that meant he could have help. Despite their differences, he doubted the man would object to the proposal. Who would want to stay in this place?

The problem was, he didn't think they'd be sharing a cell. So far as he could tell, they were impenetrable. He'd tried using his Earth shaping powers after the short conversation with that man over the speakers, and nothing had happened. He'd tried using his strength, punching at the walls, only to end up with bruised and bloody knuckles. He'd traced his hands along every piece of space he could reach and hadn't found so much as a crack or seam.

But he was a God. And Gods could not be caged.

He would find a way.

Even as they cut into him, and studied his insides, he wanted to smile. They might have had him now, but when he got free, he would rain such vengeance down on them they'd wish they'd never laid eyes on Aiden Greenway.

And now Viatri was there. His power was formidable. Together they would be able to escape. They had to.

He could feel warm breath on his ear, and he heard a woman's voice say softly, "You do well." A gentle hand caressed his cheek. He wanted to pull away, but he still couldn't move. "When we're done here, we might let you see your friends." Breath and hand left him.

Greenway blinked into the light. That automatic response was the only movement he could manage.

Friends. They had more than Viatri. Harvey would be best. If Harvey were there, he'd be able to shift them out.

If they nullified your powers, they would nullify his, he told himself. *We need to work out how to do this without our God power. We have to do this as we would have before all of this.*

Hands moved inside his abdomen, and he felt wetness around his groin. Either he'd pissed himself, or he was bleeding out.

I will not die here, he thought. *I will not let that happen.*

He'd die fighting. He'd die attempting escape. He'd allow himself to die in any other way, but he wouldn't die here, like this. He just wouldn't let it happen.

Viatri, we'll help each other. We'll get out of here, somehow. We'll find the others and work it out. Greenway held to those thoughts like a life raft in deep ocean waters.

Greenway wanted to laugh and cry. He'd been walking the precipice for so many years, now, he wasn't sure he hadn't just tipped over the edge. He'd struggled with it. With every decision. But how could he know?

It was a simple thing that let him know he was still in his right mind. In a million years, Greenway would never have imagined Lance Viatri as his saviour.

CHAPTER TWENTY-FOUR

Estard put all of his will power into sitting still. He would *not* go and fiddle with the strange man's gadgets again. He would *not* drum his finger on his now filthy and damaged dress shoes. He would sit still, he would breathe, and he would *not* suck on his teeth!

A small groan escaped his lips, and his legs shook. He was all too conscious of looking like some kind of heroin addict. He had never tried to quit smoking before, and was not prepared for these withdrawals, so until the wave passed, he was determined to stay away from the others.

Gordon had gone off by herself even before dawn twilight settled in. Deidra was absorbed in fussing over Ulrich. Kristin was off somewhere butchering her catch. Harvey and Weiz had taken off god-knows-where, and the others he didn't know well enough to remember names.

With a breath somewhere between a sigh and a growl, he leant over and picked up one of the small gadgets. It was a white cylinder, about an inch thick, and three inches long. It had several small grey buttons along the length of it, and Estard hit them gently, one at a time. Nothing happened until he got to the last, and then one end lit up like a torch, only more focused. A single red dot showed on his opposite hand and didn't contract or expand as he moved it closer or further away.

"It's a multi-tool," Kristin said behind him. He jumped as his head snapped around, and he dropped the object.

"Give a man a heart attack," he breathed.

She smiled as she took a seat beside him and grabbed up the small cylinder. She pushed at a few buttons, and the little red light became a hot knife she demonstrated on the grass. She switched it off, looked at him with amusement, and tossed it back to him.

Estard caught it but kept his eyes on her. "How'd you know?" he asked.

"We have similar ones, on Earth," she shrugged. "Not as small, but very similar basic design. You just have to know the sequences for each tool."

"Oh. So, it does more than cut grass, then?"

Kristin leaned over and smacked his shoulder, but it lacked force. "I'm worried about them," she said. "What might be happening to Viatri."

Estard breathed deep and tried to keep still. "Are you and he…?"

"No."

"But you're close?"

"He flirts, I give him shit. It's our thing."

"I see."

Kristin smiled broadly and let out a chuckle. "Jealous? Don't be. Sinatra and I are barely friends and will never be more."

"But you care about him." Estard's insides were dancing.

"He's part of my crew. The rest are gone. Just me, Harvey and Lance, now."

Like a squad, then. He could deal with that kind of closeness.

Understood it. It didn't matter how much an individual member might grate on your nerves, if they were in your squad, you had each other's backs.

"I can respect that," he said.

"Good."

Estard gave a tight smile and changed the subject. "Deidra's planning to do something after she's sure Ulrich can look after himself."

"I don't know if her 'gift' is a blessing or a curse," Kristin sighed. "Any more than mine, really."

"How do you mean?"

"Could be today. Could be tomorrow or next week." She paused and pursed her lips. "But that woman is going to lose every bit of who she is. Every memory, every feeling. And she's doing it for us."

Estard rolled his shoulders and tilted his head to the side. "Why?" he asked.

"Because it's the only thing she can do."

"No," Estard shook his head. "I mean, why is she going to lose it?"

"Because that's her price," Kristin said sadly. "We all have one, but hers is the most obvious."

"What's yours?"

"Blinding headaches and nightmares. Knowing that there are things that are going to happen, but not how or when, or how to stop it." She shrugged. "What's the point in seeing the future if you can't do anything about it?"

Estard grunted. He had no answer to that. But he began wondering what his price might be. He hadn't considered there might be one. *Because I never think things through*, he told himself. *I just jump in with both feet and wait till I hit the bottom.* But his gut instincts rarely steered him wrong.

He stared out at the rolling plain and fiddled absently with the multi-tool. He still wasn't sure how he felt about any of what was happening. But his gut told him he was in the right place, that he'd done the right thing. Condemn him though the others might, for choosing something they ran from, he knew that it was best for him, this way.

His mind turned to Harris. He hadn't thought of the man since he left. He knew, somehow, that he'd take care of himself and Bob. He'd be given a new partner, and one day he would be good at the job. Unlike Estard. Harris was in it because he believed it was the right thing to do. Estard had just been curious. Still was.

He gave himself a small smile. Maybe he'd only joined so he could be here, now. With these people in this place. Like somehow, he'd known all along where he'd end up. It was doubtful, but it was a nice thought.

Estard looked to Kristin. There was a part of him that still couldn't figure her out. What it was that he wanted from her, exactly. Sometimes he wanted to hold her, and sometimes he wanted to hit her. Not that he would ever do the latter. But both feelings were as intense as each other.

"You're staring," she said, breaking him from his thoughts.

"Sorry."

"We need to get Viatri back." A pause. "And Greenway, too, I suppose."

"How?" he asked. "We don't even know who these people are. Or where. So far as we can tell, it was just this one man. No one has come looking for him."

"That we know of."

Estard gave a nod. "That we know of."

"I guess that's why Deidra's going to do what she has to do. There is no other way to know." Kristin breathed deep and sighed slow. "I haven't had any visions about them. I've had only two since we got back here, and neither of them has given me a clue."

"The meteors," Estard offered. "Could be about them. There's no way to know."

Kristin shook her head with a frown, her eyes turned inward. "No. There's a familiar feeling about that one, though I can't pick it. It's like I should understand how they'll be there. Meteors."

"Hmmm." Estard looked to the gadget in his hand and put it in his pocket. Once he'd figured out how to use it, it would come in handy.

"It'll —" Her eyes went wide, and she grabbed at her head, squeezing at the temples with her palms. "Fuck," she breathed.

Without thought, he went to her and placed his arms around her shoulders. She was sitting, so it wasn't likely she'd hurt herself, but he figured just having that support might help.

She shuddered and swore and let out a long groan. When it passed, she swore and squeezed her eyes shut. Then she fell back against him and panted like she'd sprinted a mile.

He didn't ask. He let her take her time, and just sat there holding her. Waiting. Not daring to move in case she decided he was being too familiar. It felt nice, and he didn't want it to stop.

"They took his eyes," Kristin breathed softly after a while. A tear slid down her cheek.

"Who?" He meant it for both.

"Lance." She clenched her jaw and spoke through her teeth in a hiss. "They cut them right off the back of his head."

Estard let out a breath he hadn't realised he was holding. The tattoos. Better than blinding the man, but still not good. Why would they do something like that?

He remained silent and waited.

"I think I was seeing through Greenway's eyes," she said. "Nothing else makes sense."

"So you saw where they are?" He felt hope well in his chest.

Kristin shook her head. She was still leaning into him, and her cheek brushed his shoulder. "There was light everywhere, so blinding I could barely see anything. But it was the feel of a morgue table. The sense of many people gathered and observing."

"Then how do you know they took Lance's eyes?"

"I could see them stitching up the back of his head. Just in the periphery."

He wanted to fold his arms around her. He didn't want to scare her off. Estard gave her shoulders a brief squeeze instead. "Is this something that has happened or will happen?"

"Is happening. Right now I think."

"Is there anything we can do?"

"No."

His heart sank with the sadness in those words.

~

Deidra walked far enough away from everyone that a casual glance would not pick her out against the horizon. She wasn't sure what was going to happen, but she didn't want to be interrupted. The first time, getting through had been difficult, and she didn't think it would be any easier now. If anything, she was prepared for it to be harder.

She took a deep breath and lay down. She was going to have to go deep, and she would need to fight the monster inside her every step of the way. But she had to know. If Tatiana had been captured by them, she'd obviously gotten free. Deidra needed to know how.

Clearing her thoughts of everything except that static, Deidra dove. She hit the barrier and pushed, just as she had last time. This had to be done, and she would do it, no matter the cost. They had Lance. And while she was still herself, she felt that soft spot she had for the man.

She didn't know how long she was at the barrier, wearing away at it with her mind, when something yanked her backwards.

There was nothing there to see, but she heard a voice in her mind. "You can't," it whispered.

Deidra firmed her will and ignored the voice. She dived back at the barrier with all the strength she could muster. She hit it, once. Twice. And was yanked back again.

Inside her mind, a vision formed. Swirling black smoke that coalesced into a woman wearing archaic armour. Her long dark hair fell down her back in waves, her slanted brown eyes stared intensely from an oval shaped face. Mocha skin gleamed as though covered in oil.

"You can't," the apparition warned.

"I can," Deidra replied.

"There's nothing there."

"I saw it."

"You saw a memory of a memory I pushed you to." A spear appeared in her hand, and she thumped it on the invisible ground.

The air around them shimmered, both the static and the darkness swirled. They brightened, took on shape and colour. They blurred and stretched, and then with a pop, firmed into a memory image of Tatiana in the woods, eyes alert and searching. Then, a flash of bright light, and darkness. The sound of breathing.

The air turned to static again, and Deidra returned her attention to the apparition in her mind. "How are you doing this?"

"We are one," the other woman said. "When the bond completes, there will be no separation between us. No difference. You already know this."

Deidra found that she did but was no less disturbed by it. "Why can't I see what is behind the barrier?"

"Because there is nothing beyond the barrier, except a darkness that will pull you in."

"I don't understand."

"It is the point where the mind breaks," the woman gestured around her. "This is the dividing line. I showed you what came before the barrier. And you saw some of what came between." She threw the spear at the barrier, and it shattered. "But there, it is death walking."

"If I cannot see it, then tell me," Deidra pleaded. "We need to know what we are facing."

The woman smiled at her. "I do not know. I did not make the barrier. Skynar made it to protect me."

"How did you escape?"

"I didn't."

"You make no sense."

"Anselin rescued me. I know not how. Only that he did. The healing Skynar gave me extended both ways across the damage that broke me."

"They broke you?" Deidra could not imagine it. But it gave her a sense of the fear she'd felt, the reason behind it.

Tatiana's smile turned sad. "Harvey must follow the men from Bahana. He's the only one who can get them out."

The apparition stepped toward her, and Deidra mind pulled back slightly. "Why?"

"I cannot say, only that they know how to strip us of power. But they can't take his." The woman stepped forward again, and this time Deidra remained still. Tatiana placed a hand on her chest. "You don't have to forget," she whispered, as she faded into smoke.

"What does that mean?" she yelled, even as she sat bolt upright on the grass. She punched a fist down into the soft earth in frustration.

She'd learned nothing about what the enemy were.

"But you know Harvey can help them," she breathed. "She told you that much."

With a grunt, Deidra levered herself off the ground and surveyed her surrounds. For all intents and purposes, it was a day like any other. Hot and humid, the sky relatively clear. The grass stretching out in rolling hills that disrupted sight lines without being obvious. The occasional thicket, dips and hollows.

If the men from Bahana were capable of stripping them of their powers, were they also capable of killing them permanently? It was a sour thought that made little sense. She had vague and detached memories of being Tatiana, discussing the possibilities with the other Guardians.

They had known the men from Bahana would come. Meira had seen it in a vision, and they were determined to fight and die, as many times as it took, no matter the cost. They would not allow themselves to be captured. Those who were captured did not return. Except Tatiana and Greta, none knew what it was like to be held, and neither could speak of it after Skynar's healing.

They didn't believe the descendants of the beings they had once been could endure the powers. But when they discovered the Earthlings were not from Bahana, they had a way out.

Deidra sighed and began on her way back to the others at a slow trot.

Galsin had lied. Not about what they were, but about why they were giving away their powers. At least partially. She sensed, deep down, that they had been tired of their lengthy existence. Some had gone mad. But their rush to have the Earthlings take over was more about fear. About shifting the responsibility and focus to someone else.

Once she returned, she sat down between the ashes and Ulrich, facing the man. He was awake and alert, eyeing her curiously. She looked him up and down, wondering what to do with him for the time being.

"Deidra?" he asked.

"Hmm?"

"What's wrong?"

"I want you to be in a safe place," she told him. "But I don't know if there are any."

He gave her a small smile. "If it's all the same, I'd rather keep some company. I may not be socially adept, and people tend to make me nervous, but I'd rather know you're all here. I'm not sure how long I was alone, but, it was long enough."

Deidra took one of his hands and squeezed. "I just don't want you to get hurt."

"When the station was damaged, I pissed myself." He shot a laugh. "It was the scariest moment of my life. I thought I would die, and I hadn't yet made my mark on the world. I am an orphan, and I've yet to start my own family. I'd yet to make a ground breaking discovery." He eyed her seriously. "No mark, you see? And I thought I'd die."

Deidra wasn't sure whether to smile or nod. "But you didn't."

"I didn't," he agreed. "But then we were stranded here." He looked around and gestured to everything and nothing. "Which was fine, because you were working on getting us home. But then Greenway happened, and I damned near pissed myself again when Harvey explained what was happening."

"But you didn't," Deidra said again.

Ulrich continued as if she hadn't spoken. "Then the mountain. It was an interesting place, and if it were on Earth I'd have liked to study some of what was inside." He shook his head. "Then Greenway again, and all the fighting. I hid. I'd been doing calculations, trying to find the whole picture, because Heinrich would not tell us. And I hid and waited for someone to come and get me.

"But you all left." He shook his head and shot another laugh. "You all left me behind. But it was my fault. I should have run to the ship." He was silent a moment. "Deidra. I don't want to be left behind again."

Deidra squeezed his hand again. "You won't be," she assured. "I won't let it happen again."

~

Harvey scrubbed a hand through his hair. "Are you sure?"

"Sure as it's possible to be," Deidra replied.

Weiz squeezed his hand. "We just need to find them."

Harvey had finally been relaxed when they'd returned to the others. That had lasted all of a few minutes before Deidra told them about her delving.

"It can be done if I do it alone, is not the most encouraging thing to tell a person," Harvey sighed. "Do we move everyone else? Get you all to another world?"

Deidra shook her head. "I think if it were that simple, Anselin would have done it."

"The mountain is unstable, the hut too small." Weiz glanced at the people a small way behind them. "They have to go somewhere. They can't stay here, out in the open like this."

"We can take a few to the hut." Harvey shrugged. "Maybe all of them. We'll need to start building shelter anyway, it'll give them a place to start. It's also closer to water. And the field, if anything should happen."

Deidra gave a sharp nod. "We'll start there, then."

Harvey didn't wait, he just strode toward the others and said, "You lot, on your feet, I'm relocating you."

Some jumped up, and others rose slowly, but no one argued. In the first group he took four and shifted back as soon as they let go of him. The second group was Estard, Gordon, Deidra and Ulrich, and the last, Zim, Weiz and Kristin.

Every one of them had taken the shift with him before, but even so, some hunched over looking sick.

Inside, the airmen sat against walls, and left the table and chairs. There weren't very many of them, and if they didn't all plan to lie down, they'd all fit inside fine. The place was bigger than he'd thought. He supposed shelter of any kind would be welcome to them after four days without it.

"Can I have your attention please," he asked as he strode in. Kristin slapped him on the back, as she moved past him, and Weiz stopped at his side. There were only ten people here, and he didn't recognize all of them. He should have, they'd traversed time together.

"What you all choose to do next," he said after a few moments, "is up to you. We have a new enemy, which you all already know about. A new situation. They have Greenway and Viatri."

"Greenway deserves whatever he gets," said a woman close to the door.

"Let him finish, Hadley," Zim whispered. Harvey made a mental note of the name, he didn't want anyone to feel left out. Not now. Not when the group was so small.

Harvey gave Zim a small nod and continued. "There could be a few of us alive out there. I did not expect to find Ulrich in the mountain, but here he is." The Scientist was at the table, and he smiled shyly. "I am told others never came to the mountain, either with us or with Greenway, and I want to find them."

He looked to everyone in turn. He wanted them to understand that he wasn't giving up on them. That if they were out there alone, he would do the same for them. The look in their eyes told him they got it.

"It is going to take some time. Time we may not have with this new enemy on our back. You all know about them by now." There were nods all round. "But we don't leave men behind. We're all stuck here for the time being, and we're all in this together. So I encourage those of you who had the misfortune to be chosen yesterday, to find your power. See what it is you can do, and if it might be helpful."

The new airmen among them looked to each other, then back to him and each gave a nod. They would be hesitant, but they understood.

"Deidra may be able to help some of you," Harvey nodded toward the woman, though they all knew who she was. "So if you find yourself floundering, ask her. For now, I'll leave you all to rest."

Without waiting for discussion or response, Harvey turned on his heel and marched out the door. He didn't hear Weiz come out behind him, but as he took a step she put a hand on his shoulder.

"So that's it?" she asked softly. "We look for the missing men and practically ignore this new threat?"

He turned to face her. "We had such a good morning," he sighed as he stroked her face. "Why couldn't it have stayed that way?"

She gave him a tight smile. "It's the burden of leadership."

"How did I end up in charge?"

"You just did."

"You don't want it back?" He arched a brow.

Weiz pursed her lips and shook her head slowly. "Not on your life. I'm not cut out for it. Not down here. Put us all back in the skies, or back into space, and I'd wrest it from you in a heartbeat. But not down here."

"Pity," he said and turned back around.

"You never answered my question," Weiz said.

"Didn't I?"

"What are we doing, John? What the fuck are we doing?"

Harvey sighed, took her by the arm and shifted to the river. "We shouldn't have that kind of discussion where they can hear us."

Weiz grunted and pulled her arm away, but otherwise didn't move. "Will you answer?"

"I don't know, Catherine." He shook his head. "I don't know what we're doing. Without a clear picture of who or where, we have no means to get at this enemy."

"But we have to do something."

"We are," he said. "We're doing all we can to prepare. We're trying to make sure no one else gets taken that way."

"What if it was just that one man?" Weiz asked. "What if he was the only one they sent, and they don't plan to send more?"

"Then I'll never find Lance. And Greenway." He sat down and stared at the water. "But I doubt he's the only one. And if he had been, he wouldn't be any more. Deidra saw to that."

Weiz sat beside him. "You're right."

"Say that again."

She gave a small laugh. "It's ridiculous," she told him. "You know, this place may as well be a graveyard with all our dead. But, so long as I have you, I feel I am home."

He reached for her hand. "We had such a good morning," he said with a smile. "How about a good afternoon?"

Weiz laughed, and he laughed with her. But he couldn't escape the feeling it might be the last time, for a good long while.

CHAPTER TWENTY-FIVE

They'd put him back together, and where he should have stitches, were raised red scars. His hands played along them, curious and wondering. It was not a level of technology they had on Earth, and he knew the ATF RD would die to get their hands on something that could do that.

As Greenway lay in the pitch darkness of his cell, he pondered. There had to be some soft spot, some weakness. He just needed to find it. Knowing there were more of them here, he had to figure they'd be able to find a way out.

"There has to be a way out," he whispered.

Viatri. If he could just get to Viatri, they had a chance.

His mind bubbled with frustration. They were being held in separate cells, which was smart. He'd have done the same thing. But beyond even that, they had no way to speak to each other. No common area. If they'd not brought the man in at just the right angle, he'd never even have seen him in the exam room.

Greenway stretched out his mind, trying to find that place that allowed him to move the Earth. Metal and clay, rocks and sand, they all made up parts of the earth. So getting these walls to move should not be difficult.

But he couldn't find it.

"Are you ready?" A woman's voice came through the speakers, and he started.

"Ready for what?" he groaned.

"To see your friends."

Greenway shook his head. Were they about to make a mistake? Could it be that easy?

"I'm ready," he told the voice.

He was enveloped in light.

~

Darkness. Blinding light. Darkness. Blinding light. And now darkness again.

Lance felt at the back of his head and though it felt tight about his temples and the back of his neck, the area he was sure they'd cut into was smooth. They'd actually shaved his head for him, which was something. But he wondered what they'd done.

Was it all in his head? There was no way to know. He wasn't even sure how long he'd been in this strange place. He hadn't slept, but he didn't need to, so it was no gauge. They'd taken him to the exam room twice and performed procedures he'd rather not think on. He thought he'd spied Greenway there, with his belly open on the table, but had no way to confirm it.

He sat up straight, his back to a corner and breathed. He wasn't entirely sure that Greenway hadn't been right about purgatory. Only now it seemed they'd moved from that place to hell.

"Are you ready?" He heard a woman's voice, and he jumped to his feet, on guard.

"Who are you?" he asked.

"Are you ready?"

Lance shook his head. "Ready for what?"

"To see your friends?"

Lance squinted into the darkness and tried to work out where the voice was coming from. There was a strange quality to it he felt he should recognize but couldn't quite put his finger on.

"What friends?"

There was the distinct impression of a pause before the woman's voice came again.

"You're not ready." There was a click.

Lance carefully planted himself back in the corner and scrubbed a hand across the back of his head.

"Bitch," he whispered. "You ain't got my friends." At least, he fervently hoped not. But he decided he wasn't going to believe her unless she started giving names and addresses.

They hadn't asked him any questions. There'd been no interrogation. He'd had no chance to speak to a single soul here. Wherever here was. It was all just darkness, or blinding light.

~

Greenway blinked into the haze. His vision was blurry, and he couldn't quite make anything out except the grey floor tiles. There were things lining the walls, looked like tanks, but he wasn't sure.

"Stand up," the woman's voice ordered.

Greenway gritted his teeth and complied. He spun in a small circle, and his vision slowly began to clear.

A glass cylinder rose up from the floor to surround him. He had barely a hands width of space to either side of him, and when he spun, he bumped into it. His heartbeat quickened and there was a hitch in his throat that made it hard to breathe.

Greenway slapped hard at the glass in front of him. It didn't so much as shake. It was as steady as a steel wall.

He tried to take a few deep, calming breaths. "What are you doing?" he asked. "You said you were taking me to see my friends."

"And I have," the voice replied. "They're all around you."

Now he really looked.

As he spun slowly, he counted thirty seven glass tanks, and each one held a human. They were submerged in blue water, naked, and hooked up to several tubes. Worse, they were aware. Eyes followed. Hands touched glass.

Who were these people?

"These are not my friends," Greenway said. And it was true, he didn't recognize a single one of those faces. Not remotely.

"They are now," the woman told him.

Tubing whipped up from the floor and sank into him.

He screamed. Tried to wrench them out even as the extremely viscous blue water began to fill the tube starting at his feet. In moments, he could not move. Could not speak. One of the first tubes must have had that sedative they'd used on him in the exam room.

Greenway stopped struggling. There was no point. All he managed to do was frustrate himself.

But even as he closed his eyes, ready to give in, he heard a disturbing chorus in his mind. *Welcome,* they said.

Never since the day he'd found his wife dead, had Greenway wanted to curl into a ball and cry. Until now.

~

Estard rested his shoulder against a tree and watched Gordon as she spread her hands and closed her eyes. He wasn't sure what she was trying to do, but she'd gotten the mannerisms down. If he was watching Macbeth, he could definitely picture her as one of the witches.

Her eyes flared open. "What?"

He arched a brow. "What?"

"You said something."

"No I didn't."

"Yes you did."

"No," he said firmly. "I didn't."

Gordon shook her head. "Could have sworn I heard you say something about witches."

Estard blinked but had a thought. "Close your eyes and try again," he told her.

With a sigh, Gordon resumed her position, gestures and all. If she could read minds as he now suspected, which was creepy and a little invasive, then he wouldn't need to say a damned thing. But he'd also have to be careful not to think anything she might take offence to.

Can you hear me? Gordon?

He repeated the thought a few times before she finally said, "It's hard to concentrate when you keep asking stupid questions," she snapped.

Estard laughed and clapped his hands together. They'd been at this for the better part of the day, and it was now well past sundown. The light of the moon was plenty to see by, so they hadn't let that stop them.

"Finally," he breathed.

Gordon opened her eyes and frowned at him, hands on hips. "Finally, what?"

"You can read minds."

She squinted at him. "Are you fucking kidding me?"

Estard shook his head and took a step toward her. "It took you a few tries to pick it up, but I didn't say a word."

Gordon snorted. "You're fucking with me."

"Look at me. Watch my mouth. Listen." Estard tapped his temple. "Concentrate, but don't take your eyes off me."

With a sigh, Gordon said, "Fine."

Let's go back to the others. He didn't need to repeat the thought that time.

Gordon gasped and put a hand to her mouth. "Fuck me," she said and gave herself a shake.

"We can be glad of this much," Estard muttered. "At least you have to concentrate to hear it."

Her face paled. "What if I didn't need to?" she asked.

"Then you'd hear everybody's thoughts all the time," Estard shrugged. "I guess, anyway. Also, you'd have known from the moment you got the power, if that were the case." He looked to the sky. "Since we've worked on this for the last ten hours, I'd say we're pretty safe on the assumption you have to concentrate."

Gordon smiled and looked relieved. "Good. Not too comfortable with the thought of knowing what everyone is thinking."

Estard held out a hand palm up, a gentlemen's offer to lead her back to the hut. She placed her hand in his, and they walked.

"Can't tell you how glad I am you're the kind of person who would rather let private thoughts stay private," Estard said. "I've known too many people in my life that would have taken this opportunity to ransack everyone's brain."

Gordon shook her head. "Not me. I'd rather not know. If it ain't my business —" She slashed a hand through the air to demonstrate what she thought of it. "Only drama."

When they stepped out of the trees, Estard saw Kristin star gazing, her back pressed against the hut. Gordon removed her hand and gave him a small smile.

"I'll be inside," she said, and moved quickly.

Estard glanced after her and put his hands in his pockets.

"Success?" Kristin asked.

"Yes," he replied, and moved to sit beside her.

"And what amazing feat can this one perform?" There was amusement in her words.

"You make it sound like we're circus performers."

"I'm not entirely sure we're not."

"We'd make a lot of money, back home."

Kristin gave him a lazy slap on the leg. "Wouldn't mean much, *Julian*. So what can she do?"

Estard shrugged. "Read minds. If she's concentrating, anyway."

Kristin gave a grunt. "That would suck."

"Must be a woman thing."

"What?"

"Gordon doesn't much like it either."

"Just makes her smart," Kristin said.

Estard rubbed a hand across his stubble. "What about the others? They all work out what they can do?"

Kristin pressed her lips and wrinkled her nose in a way that reminded him of their first meeting. "Bridges is a Firestarter, and Ellis can move things with her mind. For the rest.... Deidra says without being told what they are, they might not find it."

"Does she know?"

"Don't know. I'd think so. She's in there talking to them about it now."

Estard wanted to reach out and take a hand, but reminded himself she was a rabbit. He couldn't make any sudden movements.

Deidra poked her head out the door. "We've got them all," she said, and disappeared again.

Estard blinked at the empty space, then at Kristin. "What?"

Kristin shook her head. "They all know what they can do, now," she translated for him.

"Oh." He moved his mouth, looking for words. He wasn't sure what to say, he just knew he didn't want to leave her side. But he had no wish to sit in awkward silence either.

"Did you see that?" Kristin asked suddenly.

Estard looked up and around, head moving quickly side to side. "See what?"

Kristin pointed. "In the sky." She looked to him and let her hand drop. "There was a flash. Made me think of a Docker."

"I don't know what that is," he said.

"Why would you," Kristin sighed. "It's a very, very large space ship. It carries all other craft, since most are not designed for extended flight."

Estard was interested now. This was the kind of thing that would have got his blood flowing as an Agent, and he found he still felt that way. "Tell me more," he said.

Kristin glanced at him. "Dockers take on twenty carrier ships for ground troops," she told him. "And two-hundred MM class ships — those are our fighters. Carriers are designed for planetary take-off and landing. They hold three hundred personnel a piece and hold as many weapons as an armoury."

"And the fighters?" He felt like a small boy at the fair grounds, watching acrobats and tumblers.

"Designed for space battle. Armoured hulls, gun stations. But small. They manoeuvre well, but use up a lot of fuel, particularly when the shields are hit, or we dip into gravity."

"They have shields?"

Kristin laughed at him. "Seems I've found your point of interest, Agent man."

Estard shrugged boyishly. "You got me. You going to answer?"

"As long as you know, this ain't foreplay," she told him seriously.

He felt his face going all different shades of red, and he stifled a gasp. She was forward, he'd say that. But from what he could tell, most of these people held to loose morals about such things. "Noted," he choked out.

Her eyes twinkled with amusement in the moonlight, but she didn't laugh at him again. "Shields are relatively new," she said. "I don't know the science behind it — perhaps Deidra does, and you can ask her — but in essence, they stop heavy fire from hitting the hull and doing direct damage."

Kristin's eyes returned to the sky, and she sighed. Estard wanted to ask more questions but didn't want to push. He raised his eyes to scan the sky with her and remained silent.

After some time had passed, he saw a fireball high in the sky, with pieces shooting off it like a massive explosion. He turned his attention to Kristin. She was looking at him. He nodded and looked back up. Red streaks were trailing away at great speed toward the horizon.

He was on his feet before he knew what he was doing, dragging Kristin up with him. "Your meteors," he breathed. He was no astronomer to know what effects such things would have, but he had the distinct impression they should probably be moving.

"Shit," Kristin whispered, her eyes still on the exploding fireball. "Whatever that was, it was huge." She clutched at his hand, eyes wide.

"You don't know what it was?"

She shook her head. "I can tell you that it would have been a few days away by ship. So we've probably got a couple of hours before the debris starts raining down on us." She licked at her lips. "And you'd better hope we get no large chunks, or we're about to go the way of the dinosaur."

"So this is it?" he asked. "This is the meteor shower from your vision." She nodded. "What do we do?"

Kristin squeezed his hand so hard he thought his fingers might fall off. "I don't know."

~

The place shook. A small rumble at first, and then the room tilted.

Lance sprawled across the floor. He had nothing to hold on to, no way to stay steady.

He crawled his way back to the corner and tried to brace himself, even as the room seemed to want to turn upside down. He could faintly hear the sound of klaxons. The air around him flickered.

Lance tried to breathe normally. If something was going on out there, it could provide an opportunity for him. They just had to let him out.

The room rumbled and tilted again. The air flickered. Again. Then again.

Lance squinted at the bursts of light. He wasn't sure what he was seeing. It was almost like a room beyond the room.

The wall behind him began to feel soft, as though his hands were sinking into it, even as he tried to hold himself still.

There was another shake and rumble, then a whining noise. The room didn't tilt this time, but the flickering continued, and he had the unpleasant sensation of falling backwards through jelly.

For a few tense moments he was surrounded by a blinding light. But all the flickering must have helped him adjust a little, as he began to make out the walls. It was a very well-lit white walled room.

"What the fuck is going on?" he wondered aloud. There was no one there. Not anywhere he looked. No hands grabbing at him while he was blinded, to pull him along.

He moved his head first. Then his arms. He wasn't drugged, he could move.

Lance sat up and tried to orient himself. The shaking continued, but it was less than the first shocks. The klaxons were no longer a distant sound.

"This is it, you idiot," he berated himself. "Get up and get moving, before someone comes to check on you."

With a heave and grunt he was on his feet. He felt a little unsteady at first, but each step made him feel a little stronger.

He had no idea where he was going. But his eyes searched the white walls for a way out. It wasn't obvious. No clear doorway. But there was a small grey panel that looked like a keypad. He moved straight toward it.

It had no buttons. There was a faint backlight, but no words written on the screen. He waved his hand over it, and nothing happened. He pressed his palm to it, though it seemed a little small for that. To his relief, a small beep sounded, and a door appeared directly in front of him.

He stepped out into a blue and grey hall. On the opposite side were windows, looking out onto a dark night. Lance looked up and down the hall, and sure that no one was close, he moved straight to the window to try and get a bearing of where he might be.

When he took in the full view, he gasped. "Shit," he whispered. "Shit, shit, and fuck me sideways."

He was in space.

~

The tank was half full when he felt the first rumble.

He was still trying with every ounce of his strength to move a muscle and couldn't.

Greenway could still hear the voices echoing in his mind, *welcome*. They were glad to see him. Were happy to have him there. But he didn't know where they were coming from.

The fluid continued to rise, even as the room tipped.

Danger, the voices said. He wanted to scream at them to shut up.

There was no good reason for a room to tip.

The shaking continued, and klaxons sounded. It was almost deafening. A loud *whoop-whoop* followed by a buzz, repeated again and again at a grating tempo. It almost made his eyes water, and he'd have held his hands to his ears if he'd been able to move them.

Greenway wanted to growl. To do *something*. This sense of helplessness was not something he was accustomed to.

The room shook and tilted again.

Greenway's shoulder fell against the glass and a spark flared in one of the lines attached to his abdomen. The shock hit him, and he shuddered.

When the room righted itself, there was a hissing sound, and the lines suddenly removed themselves from him, even as the viscous fluid began to retreat.

Greenway was still shuddering from the shock when the tank emptied.

CHAPTER TWENTY-SIX

Harvey lay on his back staring at the stars, while Weiz had a quick cold wash in the river. It was a warm night, and if the grass wasn't irritating his back, he'd probably have enjoyed being naked. As it was, he was just waiting to dry off.

He saw a flash in the sky and leant up on his elbows. "You see that?" he called.

Harvey heard a splash and heavy feet moving toward him. "I saw." Weiz shook her head over him, spraying him with a fresh mist.

"What do you think it was?" He took in her naked form in the moonlight. But she wasn't planning to stay that way. Already, she was donning the faded red rag pants.

"Couldn't say," her voice was muffled as she dragged the shirt over her head.

Harvey was about to say something funny, he was sure, but got distracted by the explosion in the sky. "Fuck me," he breathed. "What was that?"

It was a giant red fireball in the night sky, spewing chunks out that streaked across the horizon. For something to be that visible, it would have to be huge. And close.

"Kristin's meteor shower?" Weiz ventured as she sat beside him.

Harvey grunted. "Yeah, but what was it?"

"I know as much as you do."

"Think we should get back to the others?" He smiled. "Think they noticed we've been gone all day?"

"I'm sure they're occupied with other things," Weiz squeezed his thigh, and he pulled away instinctively.

"If we're going back, you can't be doing that," he said.

"If we're going back, you better get dressed," she told him.

Harvey sighed and stood, picking up the clothes he'd had under his legs. He kept his eyes on the sky as he dressed and occasionally saw a fire filled rock hurtling past.

"They're not in the atmosphere," Harvey noted.

"Not yet," Weiz agreed. "But whatever that was, it was big, and we'll be rained on soon enough."

"But they're burning." He dropped to the ground and tugged on his shoes. "Without hitting the atmosphere, they're burning. In space."

Weiz was staring at him, her brow drawn. "Huh." She shook herself. "Well, wish as we might to have the equipment that would allow us to see what is happening up there, we're just going to have to guess."

Once he had the boots firmly tied, he stood and held out a hand for Weiz. "I stole Viatri's boots," he said sadly as he pulled her to her feet.

"Better give them back," she returned.

Harvey took a step, and they were in front of the hut.

Only Kristin and Estard were outside watching the sky. No one else was in sight.

"Everyone else inside?" Harvey asked.

A mute nod from Kristin and an, "uh-huh," from Estard, and neither looked down.

"Any idea what that explosion was?"

"Not a clue Captain," Kristin glanced briefly at him. "But it was big. Really big."

"You told Deidra?" Weiz wanted to know.

Estard looked directly at the commander when he said, "No, actually," then turned his head slightly and yelled, "Deidra. Come outside please."

It took a few moments, and Harvey could hear shuffles and murmuring coming from inside, but Deidra came out, trailed by Ulrich.

The Scientist raised her brows at Weiz and Harvey but didn't say anything. She turned her attention to Estard. "Something you needed?"

Estard explained what had happened, and the woman's face went from a healthy dark brown to grey. She looked as if she wanted to sick up.

"You know what it is," Weiz accused.

Deidra grimaced and looked at Ulrich, who also looked a little green.

"One of you does," Harvey agreed.

"A guess, and no more than that," Deidra said. "But from the approximate location, and the size.... We can't be a hundred percent sure."

"But the guess," Weiz encouraged.

"Io," Ulrich answered.

Everyone stood there blinking at each other for a moment, but it was Estard who looked most confused.

"Io?" Kristin asked.

Deidra gave a slow nod. "Io."

"How?" Harvey wanted to know. "You sent it back where it

belonged on the second day."

Deidra raised her hands. "Maybe I didn't."

"But you saw it disappear."

"Maybe it came back." She shrugged. "The place was hardly stable. There would be nothing else out there that would account for that explosion. Not that we know this system, but I feel pretty confident from your descriptions that that's where Io was when we arrived."

"The equipment was burning out," Ulrich added, "the station was close to melt down. It could have malfunctioned. It could have come back."

"You're an astrophysicist?" Weiz asked the man.

Ulrich gave a sharp nod. "Among other things."

"Can you give us a rough estimation of what we should expect?"

"From a description and not an observation, it would be very rough indeed."

"Whatever you can give us is better than the nothing we have," Kristin said.

The little man shrugged uncomfortably. "An hour, maybe two, and we'll start seeing smaller debris entering the atmosphere. Nothing harmful, most of it will likely burn up on entry. A short time after that, the larger rocks, and some might hit the ground. But they won't cause much damage." He looked at Deidra who gave him an encouraging nod. "The biggest ones will come, a little slower, might give us a day or so. But if they hit..." He raised his hands, but it was well understood what he was not saying.

"How likely do you think that is?" Harvey asked.

"Hard to say. I'd give it an even fifty-fifty. It really depends on the force of the blast, and the location of it. If it was directional from the surface of the moon, and it pushed most of the debris in the opposite direction, we have little to worry about."

"But if the explosion came from the core of the moon," Deidra said, "the vast majority of the pieces will be smaller, but the chances of being hit by a large one grow exponentially."

"And if it was directional and headed toward us?" Kristin wanted to know.

"Then we're fucked." Ulrich stood red faced for a moment before saying, "Excuse my language."

Any other situation and Harvey might have laughed. Instead he ground his teeth and closed his eyes. He didn't want to have to do this. He didn't want to be forced into this kind of choice. But like most things, he felt it was being taken out of his hands.

"I might have to move you all," he sighed.

"Moving us won't achieve anything," Deidra said. "Even if a large one hit the other side of the planet, the damage would be too extensive."

Harvey shook his head. "I meant move you all to another world."

"Would we still be immortal, if this planet disappeared?" Estard asked.

All eyes turned to the man. "This planet won't be destroyed," Deidra said slowly, "however many meteors hit it, it will still be here."

"Yes," Estard agreed. "I know. But what if it was destroyed?"

Harvey shook his head. What possible relevance could this question have? "Do you have any idea how hard it would be to destroy a planet?" he asked. "And I don't mean make the surface uninhabitable, but actually disappear."

Estard sighed. "Never mind." He waved it away. "It was just a thought."

"We'll sit on this tonight," Weiz said. "Maybe watch the meteor shower. And decide tomorrow whether or not we actually have to move."

Harvey could deal with that. "Objections?"

"Shouldn't we be including the others in this discussion?" Estard asked.

"Not yet," Harvey said. "We'll get there though. Everyone is entitled to make their own decisions about these things."

Estard looked disapproving, but he kept his opinion to himself and gave a nod. Harvey still wasn't sure how he felt about the Agent joining them. If he was honest with himself, he hadn't given it much thought. But the way the man looked at Kristin gave him the urge to play interrogator.

I am old enough to be her father, he thought. But he didn't see her as a daughter. *Brother maybe*. He refused to look at her any other way. *Not jealous*. No, never that.

Harvey looked to Weiz out of the corner of his eye and noticed her frown. He cocked his head, and she squinted at him. It was a look that said he should know what he'd just done wrong, and they would talk about it later. Probably at length.

He let out a sigh. "Let's get some rest," he said, and went inside.

~

Something must have been heavily damaged, because the ship was still shaking. He didn't know how long it had actually been since he'd found his way out of that cell, but Lance thought it was a good five minutes, at least.

He was wandering the halls, slowly. Careful of running into anyone. A few times he saw people running past in adjacent corridors, but as yet, no one had spied him.

The klaxons were still ringing out loudly — *whoop, whoop, bzzzzz* — and it was not helping the headache stemming from the back of his head. But he pushed on, despite the nausea growing from chest to guts.

Lance trailed his hand along the walls. He'd passed out of the section with the windows and deeper into the ship. He didn't know where he was going, but he knew what he was looking for. Smaller ships. Something he could escape in. He had every confidence in his skill as a pilot. There was nothing he could not fly, in atmosphere or out.

He heard booted feet coming from behind at great speed. He looked around, but couldn't yet see who they belonged to, or where they were coming from. He was in the middle of a long corridor, doors to either side. He didn't want to risk being caught out in the open, so he took the first door to his right and pushed in, praying there'd be no one on the other side.

Heart pounding, Lance pressed his back to the closed door, and while his eyes searched the room, he listened intently for the sound of boots to pass.

He was in a lab. That much was clear. A table, large enough to fit two men, with a tray of instruments nearby. Machines that looked like monitors from a hospital on Earth, took up most of the space on the right side of the room. To the left, shelving units filled with boxes, disposable gowns, sheets and clothes. In the far left corner was a fridge, and a cabinet, both filled with what he assumed were medications.

"Could be the infirmary," he mumbled. But there was a part of him that doubted that.

The sound of boots faded in one direction, but he could hear more coming, and stayed where he was.

Lance looked to the shelves and scratched at his chin. Maybe if he got changed into some doctor's garments, he wouldn't be so easy to notice, wandering around.

You could just kill yourself, Viatri, it would be a quick trip back. But he shuddered at the thought. Trying to blast his way out of the cell had been one of the very first things he'd tried to do after he worked out what was happening. His powers didn't work, so he wasn't sure enough dying would take him back to the planet, and he wasn't prepared to test the theory.

"You're powers didn't work on Earth, either," he told himself as he pulled on an oversized light blue shirt. "And we all got back from that one." The image of Kristin being shot in the forehead was not one he wanted repeated again in his mind.

Lance took a good look around as he pulled a pair of elastic waistband pants over his jeans. He was hoping to find a pair of shoes, as he no longer had his slippers.

With a grimace, he backed up against the door and listened intently as he tied a surgical cap over his head. He really didn't like having anything on his head except a flight helmet.

When he heard nothing but silence for at least a minute, he poked his head out the door to look each way up the corridor. Satisfied that no one was there, he stepped out.

Lance continued on in the same direction he'd been moving, trying to walk naturally in case someone did see him.

Just as he got to near the end of the corridor, someone turned in, coming his way.

Heart beating wildly, Lance shoved into the only door left before the hall ended and shut it behind him. He waited for the sound of boots to pass, but they didn't. He didn't hear footsteps at all.

"Hey," he heard from outside. "Hey!" A fist pounded on the door.

Sweat formed on his brow. His eyes took in nothing about the room he'd forced himself in.

"Hey!" The voice came again. "You shouldn't be in there." The fist didn't pound again, instead there was a hiss, and Lance felt the door slide behind him.

Desperate not to be caught, he swung around, guessed roughly where the man's head would be from the short glimpse he'd got of him, and swung his fist as hard as he could. It collected the man on the jaw, and he grunted.

The man staggered back a step but stayed upright. Viatri shook his hand. The guy had a very hard jaw.

"What-?" The man asked, clearly stunned.

Lance stepped in and smacked him right on the bridge of the nose before he had a chance to say anything else. Blood poured out, and red eyes blinked. Lance hit him again. And again. Until his eyes closed, and Lance was sure he'd passed out.

"I'd be sorry," Lance whispered to the man as he dragged him into the room, "if you hadn't kidnapped me."

Now he wasn't trying to dodge someone, Lance took a good look at where he was. The room was almost completely empty except for a shelf next to a door at the other end, and even the shelf had nothing on it.

With a sigh, Lance dragged the heavy man to the second door, and opened it. Well, *tried* to open it. There was a beeping when he put his palm on the pad. It was fucking locked. He chuckled to himself. He supposed that some doors would be locked, but why hadn't his cell been?

He raised the other man's hand to the pad, and the door clicked open. With a nod, Lance continued dragging him until his feet were inside.

Lance looked down at those feet for a moment. They had some nice boots, though they looked a little small. "Better than nothing," he said and sat himself down.

He wasn't looking at the room he'd dragged the man into. The only thing he was intent on, was getting the boots off the man and onto his own feet. But the sound of rubbing on wet glass brought his head up, and he paused in tying the boots, as he berated himself for not checking the room was clear.

All around him were tubes filled with blue fluid, and in the centre of the room, a man, half naked, was inside an empty tube. Lance squinted at him. "Greenway?" he asked.

The man didn't move or say anything. Lance wasn't sure if he hadn't heard or couldn't answer. Given the things these people were capable of, either was possible. He looked to the door, and back to the man in the tube.

Lance could just leave him here. Solve that pesky little problem that was Greenway's God complex.

"Greenway?" Still no answer. Lance finished tying the boots and wiggled his toes. They were extremely tight, but he decided for the time being, they'd be better than going barefoot.

He looked at the door again. He got up and took a step toward it, then hesitated. Greenway might have threatened them all, caused the destruction of a village and town, and from the look of it, had been on his way to knocking another down. But even a murderer deserved better than this. Lance Viatri did not believe in torture. And, more importantly, to his mind, Greenway was one of them. A man from Earth.

Lance moved to the glass cage. Greenway was looking at him, alert and aware, but he didn't move.

"Ah, shit, man," Lance scrubbed a hand across the back of his head where they'd cut into him. "Blink if you can hear me." Greenway blinked. "I didn't expect to run into you. I'll see if I can get you out. Can you move?" Greenway didn't move. Lance nodded.

The rumbles in the ship had slowed, but the klaxons still sounded. Whatever was going on was still in effect.

Lance looked around the room, trying to find something that stood out. A clue as to what button he might need to push, or lever he'd have to pull. There was nothing but the glass cages. Those people didn't move any more than Greenway did, but their eyes seemed to settle on him, and place an itch between his shoulder blades.

I might get this mother fucker out, he thought, *but you creepy arse people can stay right the fuck here.*

Lance put a hand on the glass and motioned toward the door. He didn't know where to find the controls for this place. There certainly weren't any obvious ones.

Greenway's eyes blinked, and Lance moved away.

"I could just leave him here," Lance mumbled to himself as the door slid open. "The man has caused us a lot of headaches. He *is* a mass murderer." But he knew he wouldn't. Knew he couldn't. He was just that kind of guy.

With a sigh, he placed his hand on the outer console, while keeping his body in the doorway, in case it tried to close. It beeped at him a few times, but otherwise it made no sound as he hit random symbols. He looked back to see what kind of effect it had, and grimaced when he noticed the fluid draining out of two of the tanks.

It didn't take long before he managed to hit the right random button, and Greenway sprawled on the floor where the glass cage had been.

Lance took a deep breath and prepared himself for the heavy load. There was no way he'd be able to blend in now.

~

Almost everyone else had managed to fall asleep for a while, but Harvey stood outside watching small red streaks in the sky. Occasionally a large one would hit the atmosphere and skim for a short time, yellow and red tail drawing out behind it, but still would be gone before it came close to the ground.

Harvey found it odd sometimes, how the most destructive things could be so beautiful. He wasn't afraid of this, not yet. But he thought of the amount of books and movies written about comets and meteors coming for the Earth, and all the creative ways people had tried to make sure the damned things never hit.

A few times, face toward the sky, he thought he saw a flash, just like that first he'd seen at the river. But what that could be, he didn't know. It made him think of a Docker, or maybe Persius station, glinting and blinking in the reflected moonlight. But there was nothing up there. That much had been obvious when they'd decided to come down to the planet what felt like an age ago.

Harvey shook his head. Even if there *was* a ship up there, they'd have moved after that explosion. Staying in orbit around a planet about to be bombarded by debris would be extremely idiotic. Unless they couldn't.

Lips pursed and scratching at stubble on his cheeks, Harvey kept his eyes on the section of sky where that flash came from. There was a thought forming in his mind.

The people of this world would not have something in orbit. But that man from Bahana, wherever Bahana was, might.

~

Lance had hauled Greenway over his shoulders and taken him directly to the lab to dry him off and put some clothes on him. By the time Lance was ready to get back to the ships innards and start searching for a docking bay, Greenway could move his fingers and toes. Even managed to croak out a few words, even if Lance couldn't understand them.

In the hall now, Lance had one arm draped behind his neck and an arm around Greenway's back and chest, half supporting and half dragging the man.

Greenway was mumbling something unintelligible in his ear, but he tried not to pay attention. He didn't want to run into someone else from this place. With his extra burden, it was going to be harder to dodge them, and he wasn't much of a fighter.

"How the fuck I get into these situations, I don't know." He spoke as if to Greenway, but it was really more for himself. He'd already made his decision to help, but every step he took, he questioned the wisdom of it. Harvey was probably going to have a fit. Or Weiz.

They were in a cross section of corridor when he heard boots. He looked around but wasn't sure which direction they were coming from. Greenway was breathing in his ear again. *"hmph, hmph."*

Lance shook his head. He couldn't understand a word. His eyes darted. He'd go for a door, and hope, if seen, he'd be mistaken for a doctor transporting an injured colleague. Hopefully. There'd certainly been enough shaking and tilting, even if it had calmed down now.

The closest door was to his left, and he moved toward it with haste. By the time he had the door open, he could see three people coming up the corridor from the opposite direction, boots making loud echoes in the hall.

He dragged Greenway through the door.

Unburdened for the moment, with Greenway propped against the door, Lance leaned back against the wall and looked around. He felt more tired than he had in months. Even when he'd not had his powers on Earth, he'd not felt this way.

His muscles ached. Partly from whatever surgery these people had performed on him, and partly from the strain of carrying Greenway. They felt tight and stiff, and he wondered how much longer he'd be able to support the man before he collapsed.

Lance eyed the man leaning up against the door and thought about leaving him there while he searched. It would definitely be a lot quicker, and the chances of someone trying to stop him slimmer. But he shook his head. If he left him here, there was every chance he would lose track of where he was. This ship was big. Or he'd been walking in circles. An unpleasant thought.

"I don't know how to get out," Lance said.

Greenway's head turned to him, but his words were still muffled. Still incomprehensible.

"I'm of half a mind to leave you behind," he told the man honestly. "It's lucky for you I don't believe in torture, 'cause you certainly deserve to be locked up. I hope you know that."

Lance was glad the man couldn't argue. He had a feeling, had the situation been reversed, Greenway wouldn't have thought twice about leaving him behind.

The sound of boots faded, and almost disappeared.

"We could rest here a little while," he said, "but the longer we wait, the greater the chances they'll find us."

Greenway closed his eyes and let his head drop, then raised it again and repeated the gesture. Lance shook his head.

"I have no idea what you're trying to tell me. Body language is not my strong suit."

Greenway let out a growl, and finally, a word he understood. "Wait."

"You want to stay here?"

A nod.

"Why?"

"Hurrrrwy," the man said and let his head droop. "Horrrrvy. Hervy. Harvey."

Oh. Lance squatted in front of the man and looked him the eye. "Harvey isn't here. It's just you and me. And *between* you and me, if you don't start moving on your own two feet soon, we're fucked. So work on that, will you."

The glare Greenway shot him could have seared a rock, but Lance just moved to sit next to the man. If he wanted to wait, Lance would wait a little. He wasn't entirely sure he could keep carrying the Captain, anyway. But he was anxious to be out of this place.

"We'll wait," Lance breathed. "But not too long."

~

Harvey kept his eyes on his feet as he walked through the small hut, trying to discern which strewn body was Deidra. It was difficult in the darkness, and he was just glad he had managed not to step on anyone. A faint light through the window picked out the ebon skinned woman with arms stretched and head bowed over the table.

"Deidra," he whispered loudly.

Her head shot up.

"Come outside." He turned and carefully threaded his way back out, not waiting to see if she followed.

It took a few moments, but the Scientist joined him. He pointed to the sky where the flash kept recurring. "Keep your eyes there."

The woman didn't respond but did as bid. It took a little longer than Harvey was expecting, but eventually the flash came. "You see it?" he asked.

"Hmmm. The flash?"

"Yes." He pulled her around to look at him. "Do you think it might be a ship?"

Deidra seemed to consider for a moment. "It'd have to be a fairly large one," she said slowly. "You wouldn't get that kind of reflective flash off anything smaller than a Docker."

"But it's probably a ship?"

The woman shrugged. "Seems a likely culprit. What are you getting at?"

"Who would have ship here?" he asked. "We don't have any up there. We didn't bring a Docker with us. These people are far too primitive, here. So whose ship is it?"

"The men from Bahana," she said, as comprehension dawned. "I hadn't thought of that. It didn't occur to me that they'd stay in orbit. The last time they were here, their technology was... much less refined."

"But they still managed to capture quite a few Giants, as I understand it."

"Yes," Deidra agreed. "But, they didn't have the beaming tech they apparently have now. That's definitely new, and makes them a whole lot more dangerous."

"Can I get up there, with my power? Will that work?" If he had a chance to go get Lance, he was taking it. Greenway too. He couldn't leave the man in the hands of monsters, whatever he might have done.

"You could. But what if there isn't a ship up there?"

"Then I'll end up in the field."

"And if you get on the ship? How will you find Lance?"

"One step at a time," he sighed. "It'll be my first experience on an alien ship, if there is one up there." He quirked a smile. "Could be interesting. Want to come?"

Deidra shook her head. "Hard pass, Captain."

Harvey almost smacked himself. Having yet to experience it himself, he couldn't understand the extreme fear of these people that Deidra had. He was more afraid of what might happen when the meteors started putting craters in this planet. He couldn't move the planet out of the way.

"Do you think I should go?" He wasn't sure if he wanted her permission, or reassurance.

"I think you're Lance's best shot of getting away from them. I told you." She looked him in the eye. "They can't take your power. I don't know why. But you are different from the rest of us in some ways."

Harvey bit his lip. Different from the rest of them? She hadn't said that before, and it made him uncomfortable. "Well, then," he breathed, "either I'll be back with Lance, or I'll wake up in the field. Either, or, I'll be back. Wish me luck."

Deidra gave him a nod. "Good luck, Captain."

He gave her a salute and smiled, as he took a step and shifted.

~

Lance watched Greenway struggling to move. His hands were slow, and weak, but he was rubbing them over his legs. They'd not been in the room for more than ten minutes at the outside, Lance was sure, but already Greenway was showing vast improvement.

"Think you'll be able to keep up?" Lance asked.

Greenway grunted. "Not yet," he said. At least he was forming whole words. "But soon."

"Good. My feet are itching."

The former captain didn't even look at him. "We need Harvey."

Lance rolled his eyes. "Well he ain't here," he said. "At least, not that I've seen."

"How do you know?"

"Have you seen him?"

"No."

"That's how."

"We need him," Greenway insisted.

"Well, I need a wax and manicure, but I doubt I'll get that anytime soon, either." Lance got to his feet. "Work with what you got, man. Not with what you wish for." How much he had hated it when his mother had said that to him. It was true, though.

The boots were pinching at his heels, and he thought he might get blisters on his toes from the rubbing. If he had the chance, he would steal a larger pair.

Greenway rolled over so he was on hands and knees and tried to stand. He fell on his face twice, and Lance let him. Not that he was amused by it, he just felt the need to make the man suffer a little.

"Why do we need Harvey?" he asked, eventually.

Greenway rolled his head to look up at him, his face inches from the floor. "He's the only way out of here."

Lance felt at the back of his head. "He didn't bring us here, and that means there is another way out. Harvey might be easy, but he ain't here."

Greenway heaved and growled as he pushed himself to his feet, mumbling obscenities through clenched teeth. When he finally stood, one hand against the wall, he glared at Lance.

"Do you know *how* we got here?" the man asked.

Lance shook his head. "I just remember blinding light, then a dark cell."

"We were shifted, the way Harvey shifts."

"Look, even if he *were* here, they took our powers. So how could Harvey help?"

Greenway had both hands up against the wall, now, and was exercising his legs. "I don't know. I just know he can."

Lance walked a circle around the edge of the empty room. It was exactly like the room before he'd found Greenway. Just a shelf by the inner door, with nothing on it. He didn't plan to open this door. He didn't want to know what was on the other side. *Probably some sick lab or trophy room. Maybe some actual alien looking aliens.*

He couldn't fathom what made Greenway so insistent about Harvey. What made him believe the man would be any more capable than they were?

Lance stopped in the middle of the small room. "One last question, then. If Harvey *were* here, and could somehow miraculously use his abilities when we can't, what makes you think he'd be able to find us in here?"

"I don't," Greenway grated, still moving his legs. "I just didn't want you to carry me anymore."

Lance threw up his hands with a sigh. "What made me think it was a great idea to let you out of that tube?"

"You couldn't leave without me," Greenway said.

"I'm of a mind to just leave you here to find your own way."

"You wouldn't."

"How do you know?"

"Because you would have done it by now." Greenway pushed himself off the wall and took a few staggering steps before propping his shoulder against another wall.

Lance was about to just walk out the door, show the man he wasn't afraid to leave him behind, when Greenway signalled stop and silence. He put a finger to his ear, then pointed at the corridor. Lance swiftly moved to the left side of the door, placed his back against the wall, and listened.

Boots. Lots of boots. It was more than he'd seen or heard in this place since he'd fallen out of his cage. There had to be at least a dozen sets, probably more, and coming closer.

Lance eyed Greenway up and down. He looked like the kind of guy who could handle himself in a tussle. But he'd never seen him fight.

"Can you fight?" Lance asked in a whisper.

Greenway made a 'maybe but doubt it' gesture. He'd stopped stretching, and now just leaned up against the wall, eyes on the door.

The boots weren't slamming on tiles. No one was running. Somehow that made it all the more frightening to Lance. The steps were at the pace of men about their jobs.

Suddenly, the klaxons stopped and everything else became louder to his mind. They'd left a whining in his ear, like static in the background of an open channel.

Despite the relative coolness, Lance felt sweat break out on his head when the boots stopped nearby.

Maybe I can get some shoes that fit, he told himself. With that many people out there, if they were caught, they were done for. But all he could think about was how uncomfortable the boots were.

Sets of feet resumed their walk at intervals. Lance imagined that they'd stopped in a corridor cross section, and the group had divided. If the ship were damaged, as Lance suspected it must be, they could just be maintenance crews sent out to fix things. But Lance had a gut feeling, the people out there were looking for them.

Lance eyed the inner door. He really did not want to go in that room. Not if it was anything remotely like the one he'd found Greenway in. They probably wouldn't be able to get that door open, anyway. But he wanted to be elsewhere if the door to the hall opened.

Before he had a chance to do or say anything, both doors opened.

~

Harvey's boot clapped down on grill metal. The hollow reverberation made him stop. He was in a hold, by the look of it. Surrounded by bags and boxes, a soft orange glow coming from bulbs at either end of the room. The path before him was clear, the dulled metal grill running through the centre to a door.

He scratched at his stubble. He had not expected the place he landed to look so familiar.

"Little creepy," he whispered to himself.

The choice here was fairly simple — keep moving and get through this place as fast as he could manage, combing for Lance, or stay in here for a while and search through the bags and boxes, see what kind of useful things might be inside. It didn't take him long to choose the former. He knew he might be running on limited time.

Harvey didn't walk to the door, didn't bother to open it, he simply listened for a moment to judge whether someone was out there, then took a step and shifted.

"Holy fuck!" Someone breathed behind him, and Harvey spun, arm lashing out to take the man in the side of the head.

It was pure reflex. But as he made to follow through with a second blow, Harvey stopped dead in his tracks.

Chapter Twenty-Seven

After Harvey left, Deidra watched the sky. She hadn't been asleep, anyway, just thinking. She was losing more, now. Faster. Her emotions were intact. She could feel. But she couldn't remember much about herself as a person. Ulrich was kind of a last dim light in her real life, and she had to admit, at least to herself, it was a big reason she'd wanted to look for him.

The meteors were starting in earnest, now. Rocks that hit the atmosphere and burned up. A very few making it past that first stage of entry. But those that did were, in this moment, too far away and too small to be of much concern. Wherever they hit, they'd make very little impact, probably the equivalent of a small ground eruption from Greenway.

Deidra wasn't sure how to feel about what was happening. Wasn't sure she completely *understood* what was happening. It was just one thing after another. A meteor shower was just a meteor shower, and this one would be nothing special if they hadn't seen the explosion that precipitated it.

The men from Bahana, though.... She wished she knew more about them. Wanted to understand the gut wrenching fear that travelled through her bones at the very thought of them, after she'd delved into the mind of Tatiana.

Deidra's eyes were in the sky, keeping watch on that uneven flash. Harvey had been right — it was probably a ship. But if it wasn't, he was in for a rude awakening. One step into that void, he'd freeze to death before he could succumb to asphyxiation.

She was vaguely aware of someone walking out of the hut behind her but didn't turn or say anything.

"Any danger, yet?" It was Kristin.

Deidra shook her head. "Won't be for a while. Most of the meteors will hit the other side of the world for now. Planetary rotation, relative pull, original trajectory..."

"Can't sleep?"

"No."

"Me either."

Deidra breathed a sigh and forced a smile. She hadn't wanted to share this time with someone else, but it was clear Kristin didn't want to be alone.

"Harvey has gone up there," she told the younger woman.

Kristin gave her a quizzical look. "How?"

"We think the flash is probably a ship. He went to check it out."

There came a roaring whistle, and the sudden smell of sulphur, even as Kristin said, "Fair enough." Deidra wasn't sure where it came from, but as she looked around, it shot from behind to the front above them, a red-gold tail streaking. No more than a second later, it hit the ground hard enough that the dirt from the impact could be seen above the trees in the pale moonlight.

Kristin looked at her, wide eyed. "That was too fucking close," the woman breathed. "Way too fucking close. You just said..."

More roaring whistles. More red-gold streaks flashing by

overhead. Most landed so far away, Deidra wasn't in the least bit worried. But that first one had given her pause.

People were stirring inside, and one by one, they were drifting out to join Deidra and Kristin watching the night sky. It was difficult for Deidra to keep her mind or her eyes on the flash, now.

Kristin pressed up uncomfortably close beside her and whispered in her ear. "If Harvey is busy elsewhere, how the fuck are we getting away from this?"

Deidra blinked at the night sky and bit her lip. She really hadn't thought of that. Not that anything could kill any of them, except for Ulrich, but it would not be a pleasant way to go. And what if that field they woke up in was gouged out by meteor strikes? A repeated death until the meteors stopped? She cringed.

Kristin tapped her on the shoulder. A gentle reminder that she'd asked a serious question.

"I didn't think they'd come this close," Deidra said. "Nor did Ulrich. A miscalculation in trajectory."

"Fine," Kristin nodded, "but how do we get a safe distance from it?"

"By foot? We can't."

~

Lance held his breath as the first man walked through. The man didn't even glance to either side of him, and passed by as if he and Greenway weren't there. Then another, and another, until six were inside the room.

That was when they turned.

Wide-eyed, Lance lunged for the outer door, and was vaguely aware of Greenway doing the same.

Lance prepared to sprint down the corridor, in any direction, but was pulled up short by the dozen men standing in his path. One took a single step forward and looked him up and down.

"You are not familiar to me," the man said. "What are you doing here?"

Lance glanced at Greenway. Greenway shrugged. It was a chance. Perhaps the surgical clothes were enough to fool these men.

"What am *I* doing here?" Lance asked in as arrogant a tone as he could muster. "What are *you* doing here? This area is for research, and that's what I'm here for."

The man frowned. Lance's heart tried to beat right out of his chest. Had he overplayed his hand?

"This is the armoury," the man said slowly, taking another step forward. He motioned for men to come forward, and Lance prepared to run. But the man's words stopped him. "Did you get turned around? Never did like the design of these ships, everything looks like everything else. Easy to get lost, especially if you're new." He shook his head. "Search them," he told the others.

"Very easy," Lance said, as he spread his arms and planted his feet wide in a gesture of cooperation. The fucking armoury. They could have had weapons! Too late now.

"Please do excuse me, sir, ordinarily I would not do this, but I do not know your face, and we have hostiles aboard."

Lance felt his guts churn and wasn't sure if it wanted to go up or down. "Oh, I understand." And was silently thankful they *didn't* have any weapons on them. Though from the look Greenway was giving the man searching him, he wished they had some.

"Good, good." The man looked bored, now, sensing no threat from the men in front of him. They were clean, no weapons, nothing dangerous. He nodded at the men who had been searching them.

"I'll have Merich and Tye here escort you to the transition chambers. We've been evacuating the research staff since the first hit."

"What happened?" Greenway asked. "The rumbling, the klaxons, the tilting... we just started running until we felt we were safe."

Nice play, Greenway. Nice play.

The men from inside the armoury were bringing out weapons that looked an awful lot like shotguns and rifles. Their escorts got the first.

"There was some kind of anomaly," the man shrugged. "Don't rightly know what, I'm just security. But, we took a good few hits from meteors, and the long-haul engines got the brunt of it. Now, we've been boarded."

Lance and Greenway glanced at each other. "These people don't have tech," Lance said without having to feign his surprise.

"Don't know who they are, sir. But we're digging them out. You should be off now, can't have you getting in the way." He motioned to the escorts, and each of them were taken by an arm, and led away.

An additional two men followed behind, their rifles raised.

Lance suddenly wished he knew when he was speaking English and when he was speaking some alien language. It was odd that he couldn't tell, as it all sounded and felt the same to him. There should have been some difference. He wanted to be able to speak to Greenway without the men with them knowing what he was saying.

From the way Greenway was staring at him as they were marched along the corridor, he was thinking the same thing. They needed to communicate.

Lance had a feeling their little gambit pretending to be researchers here hadn't worked as well as it appeared. Mostly because their escorts felt more like guards. But he wanted to be sure Greenway felt the same way before they made a move.

He racked his brain for some way to ask that wouldn't be too obvious. "Why are we being evacuated?" he asked the man who held his arm.

The man didn't look at him when he answered. "Because the ship is damaged."

"Can't be that bad," Lance pushed. "We're not shaking any more, and the klaxons stopped."

The hand squeezed his upper arm, but it seemed an unconscious gesture. "I just work here," the man said.

Lance turned to Greenway and gave the man a nod, quick and sharp, his eyes darting to the men behind them.

Greenway didn't even bother to respond, he just turned and leapt onto the ones behind them before they could even take aim. Lance twisted his arm free of the one who held him and delivered a cracking blow to the jaw. The man dropped in one, for which Lance was thankful.

Lance rounded on the other man, who had his gun trained on Greenway, but seemed hesitant to fire. Lance tackled the man to the ground, pushed the gun away, grabbed him by the hair and slammed his head into the ground. It was over in moments.

Greenway was panting when he turned his attention back to Lance. "Don't think they bought it?" he asked.

"Nope," he replied.

"What tipped them off, you think?"

Lance shrugged, as he checked the unconscious men for their boot sizes. "No idea." He pulled the boots off the first man he'd hit. The man stirred and mumbled, and Greenway smacked him so hard his head bounced.

"What are you doing?" Greenway wanted to know.

"I don't know about you, but I like having comfortable shoes." Lance gave Greenway's bare feet a meaningful glance. "Maybe it was your shoelessness that tipped them off."

Greenway grunted and squatted down next to one of the men. It didn't take either of them long, and even as Lance stood his feet were thanking him for finding a pair that didn't pinch and rub.

"You don't think they would have taken us to this transition room?" Greenway pulled his laces tight and stood.

"They might have," Lance said. "But what *is* the transition room? For all we know it's a killing chamber of some kind. I got the distinct impression of a slaughter house in my head."

"Your mind goes to strange places, Viatri."

"I am aware."

"Where to now?"

"Away from these guys."

Greenway grunted and mumbled something unintelligible under his breath. "How does Harvey work with you?"

Lance took off down the hall at a fast trot, no longer so concerned about what lay ahead so much as what might leap on them from behind.

~

The meteors were getting closer. Less than half a mile and getting larger.

Deidra watched with a mixture of horror and fascination. On the one hand it was incredibly beautiful, on the other, they would kill whoever they hit.

Kristin was not wrong. They needed to move somewhere, and fast. But Deidra could think of no place to ride it out. She was sure she knew this world better than the rest of them, but on foot from here, there was no kind of natural shelter. Without Harvey, finding a safe place was impossible.

Weiz was the only one paying no attention to the light show. She was searching around her as if she'd lost something.

"What do we do?" Kristin was still beside her, still asking her for answers.

"We could run," Deidra said. "But it wouldn't do us much good. There's no telling where any will land. We could get lucky, dodge the bulk of them, but if there's even one particularly large one, we could be on the other side of the world, and it wouldn't matter. You know all this. Why do you keep asking me?"

"I suppose I'm hoping that your much smarter brain can figure something out."

"Look, if there were some kind of deep cavern or cave we could get to, I'd suggest it. Given the direction of the meteors, having our backs to a mountain wouldn't be so bad, either. But we can't get to any from here."

"We need Harvey," Kristin said.

"Yes we do," Deidra agreed.

"Where is he?" Weiz asked suddenly.

Deidra and Kristin looked at each other. Neither one of them wanted to be the one to say it. When it came to Harvey, Weiz was entirely too volatile. True, she'd much improved since their return to this world, but Deidra suspected it was surface level only.

"He went to check something out," she said. "He'll be back."

~

From the window of the strange ship, Harvey could see the meteors raining down on the world. There were so many and moving so fast. Some of them looked like dust, to his eyes, but he knew them to be fist sized chunks. As far as he could tell, there were no incoming ones of a significant enough size to do unavoidable damage, for which he was thankful.

They'd be hitting the surface, by now. He knew that. But the where, he could not tell.

They'll be fine, he told himself, *the odds of them coming down near the hut are slim. I'm sure of that.* Only he wasn't. His gut was telling him to worry. He knew that if even one the size of a penny hit, it could kill a person. Even if that happened, he knew they'd just revive in the field, so what was he so worried about?

Harvey knew he should get down there and move them. As quickly as he could. Take no chances. Kristin would not have had the vision if they were not somehow directly involved.

Lance and Greenway could not wait, though. These people had a means of making sure they did not end up back in the field with the rest of them. Harvey could already be too late to save them. From what little he could get out of Deidra, he doubted they'd been killed, but they probably would wish they had been.

Harvey took a deep breath and turned from the window. The decision was a maybe versus a certainty, and he had to go with the certainty, no matter what his gut told him.

He continued his search.

~

"Do you think they've really been boarded?" Lance asked after they took the first right hand turn. "Or do you think it's just another deception?"

Greenway shrugged. "Can't see a reason they'd lie about it."

"But who would it be?"

"Who cares," Greenway growled at him. "I am more interested in where we go from here. How the fuck do we get out? I don't plan on spending the rest of my days wondering around this god forsaken ship."

"Why did I let you out?" Lance asked himself in a mumble. To Greenway, he said, "Maybe, if they really have been boarded, we can hitch a ride with whoever is attacking them."

"They might be worse than these guys."

"Do you have a better suggestion?"

"They have that instant travel tech. Whatever it was they hit you and I with."

Lance snorted and shook his head. "Wouldn't know where it would send us."

"It would be better than here."

"Not if we get dumped in the void."

They took another turn down an empty corridor and Lance had the feeling he was close to where he'd started this run for his life. Windows lined up against the left hand wall, giving a partial view of the world below them. The doors along the other wall, widely spaced and closed.

"Look at that," Greenway breathed as he moved to a window.

"We don't have time to stand around and gawk," Lance replied.

"Just look!" Greenway didn't turn his attention away from the window.

Lance sighed and clenched his fists but moved to the window beside the man. He saw small flares in the atmosphere, and a whole lot of dust.

"Maybe they got hit by some of this," Lance said.

"If they've got a brain between them, they'd have seen it coming and adjusted position."

"Perhaps they were preoccupied."

Greenway shrugged and turned away from the window. "Someone down there is about to have a real bad day."

"Surprised you care."

"They're my people. That's my world. Of course I care."

Lance followed, letting Greenway take the lead as they moved. "You feel that way when you were destroying that village? That town? Sacrificing our people?"

"They needed to learn!" Greenway screamed and rounded on him, a fist raised.

Lance held up his hands. "You got problems. And I don't like you. But we got to keep moving."

Greenway grunted and turned stiffly. "I don't know what we're looking for."

"Some place where they'd keep a smaller ship. An escape pod. Something." Lance responded. "They got to have something like that."

"Maybe that transition room they were talking about."

"Maybe," Lance agreed hesitantly. "But I'd much prefer a ship. We don't know where any transport tech might take us."

They rounded a corner and bumped into a man, crouched and holding a gun. Behind him were five more.

~

They had to move.

Deidra looked at the people around her, all held enthralled by the meteors. Ulrich was the only one who looked terrified. Then, it was likely he was the only one who understood the significance of what was happening.

As the planet rotated, the impact zone shifted with it. And very soon, those meteors would hit where they stood.

Deidra wasn't a leader in crisis. At this time, she had only the vaguest memory of Io station after the partial collapse. How she'd run, following Alex. She shook her head to clear the thought.

"We have to move," Deidra croaked out. Faces turned toward her in question, and she said, a little louder, "We have to move *now*."

She suited her own words, dodging behind the hut and starting off at a steady run. She heard the rest of them coming up behind her, and even saw some taking off ahead of her. It was going to be a free for all.

Ulrich came up beside her, and Kristin kept pace.

"Thought you said it wouldn't make a difference," Kristin said.

Deidra was not a particularly fit woman, and unaccustomed to speaking when undergoing such heavy exertion. "We're all faster and stronger," she shrugged. "Maybe it will make a difference."

Kristin nodded toward Ulrich. "Not him," she breathed. "Should we get someone to carry him?"

In Deidra's mind, she could hear Ulrich say, *don't leave me behind again*, though he said nothing now. Without asking the man how he might feel about it, she gave Kristin a sharp nod. It was the only way they'd be able to run fast enough to give them a chance.

Kristin cupped her hands around her mouth and shouted, "Zim! Come here!"

A few moments later Zim was in front of them, and Kristin told him what she needed. The man grumbled for a moment, then said, "Won't know 'til I try, yes?" He moved to Ulrich, requested his permission, then lifted the man onto his back, and took off at a run.

Kristin's attention returned to Deidra. "Think you can run a bit faster now?"

As if to emphasise the question, a meteor hit so close it sprayed them with dirt.

Deidra didn't bother to answer, she just increased her pace as much as she could. Kristin kept a steady stride beside her, though Deidra didn't understand why. The woman was clearly capable of running much faster.

More small meteors hit the ground around them, and it was like bullets being sprayed into the grass. Deidra knew they would feel like bullets, too, if they hit a person. Even the shock of a non-fatal wound might be enough to send the body into shut-down mode.

Deidra's eyes dodged all around, and it was like watching hailstones. One hit someone running in front of them, and they were lifted clear off their feet to land on their back. Deidra couldn't tell who it was in the darkness, until they reached them. It was Hadley.

Kristin bent down to check her pulse.

"No time," Deidra said. "She's one of us, now. No need to worry."

Kristin didn't look pleased, but they took off once more.

They were in the middle of it. There was no getting around it. No safe place to hide. No matter which direction they chose, those meteors were coming in hot and fast. The airmen had spread out in all different directions, and to Deidra it was almost like watching some kind of shadow ballet.

"It makes no difference," Deidra panted. She was trying to convince herself that moving sooner would have changed nothing.

Kristin turned toward her, eyes wide and mouth open, just as large one hit, and they were engulfed in darkness.

~

"We got 'em." The voice came through loud and clear on his earpiece. "Section eight zone two. Clear of hostiles, ready for extraction."

Harvey breathed a sigh of relief. "This is Harvey, section one, zone five. Coming in for pick up."

"Copy that."

Harvey took a step and shifted into a corridor much like the one he had been in, only much further down the ship. They'd be somewhere in this block.

His men had been instructed to stealth, so the sound of running boots and shouts were not coming from them. Harvey hurried his pace, even as the first guns fired an ear piercing tattoo down an adjacent corridor.

He lifted his own machine gun as he rounded the corner and almost collected Greenway.

The hall reached at least fifty yards, and at the far end were several men, dressed in the same manner as the man from Bahana in white and grey. Harvey surmised it must have been a uniform. These were the first he'd seen.

He shouldered Greenway aside and didn't spare a word for anyone as he dropped the gun, and dived, shifting as he did so. It was probably an idiotic move, as the Earthmen were shooting directly at them, but Harvey wanted to even the playing field.

In mid dive, arms spread wide, he tackled at least three of the Bahana men, and shifted as he touched them. They hit the ground in zone one, and Harvey pushed away, shifting as soon as he was sure he touched none of them.

Back behind the six Earthman, with Greenway and Lance, Harvey expected to continue the fight, but though they all crouched, no shots were being fired.

"Let's go!" he shouted.

"I knew you'd come," Greenway said as he reached toward Harvey. But his touch never came, as a blinding light hit him from behind.

Before thought, Harvey shifted with every hand that touched him, back to the Carrier where he'd first landed. He turned to count out the men with him. Five of the Earthmen, and Lance.

"Shit!" He wanted to break something. "Let go!" he told them. "I have to go back."

All but one let him go. This one held tightly to his arm. "No point, sir," the man told him. "Whatever they were hit with, they're not there now."

Harvey wrenched himself from the grip and turned on the man who held him. "Get them out!" he demanded. "Get them all out now."

The man put the call through, and each team responded. No losses, no confrontations. They were all on their way.

"What the fuck is going on?" Lance asked.

Harvey shook his head at the man and gestured to the others. "You lot get back to the main hold. I'll join you soon."

A few smart salutes, and the men were gone.

Harvey took a seat on a large ammo box and motioned for Lance to do the same. He let out a breath and swallowed as he tried to make words come out.

Lance looked around, really seeing where he was for the first time. "Not that I don't appreciate the rescue," he said, "I really do. But what the fuck? Where'd these guys come from? If they've been here the whole time, they must be going stir crazy. Why didn't they land?"

Harvey couldn't answer all of it, and the one thing that kept hammering on his mind was Greenway disappearing before he could get a hand on Harvey.

"Greenway is gone," he breathed. "And another soldier is gone." He closed his eyes. "We won't know how many have been taken until the rest get back."

Lance shifted on his seat. "I don't know what to say, Captain."

"There's nothing you can say." He clapped his hands and opened his eyes.

"So what's happened?"

"A mission of spectacular idiocy." Harvey sighed. "Seems the brass on Earth wanted to know exactly what had happened. They had a rotation of scientists due on Io station three days after the event, so they were available to recreate the experiment."

"Didn't Deidra say the station was destroyed when she tried to get us all back the first time?"

Harvey gave a nod. "Yeah. But she was wrong. Not habitable, for certain, but not completely gone. The idiot scientists fucking fixed it." He shook his head and muttered some obscenities under his breath before he continued. "We have thirty carriers, six hundred soldiers, fifty scientists, and a handful of techs. Plus, the other half of our fleet. All of them are stuck here with us, now."

"Why?" Lance wanted to know. "If they got here, they could get us back. Maybe if we do it right, this time, we won't end up back here."

Although Harvey completely understood where the Pilot was coming from, he didn't share the confidence of his supposition. "Even if that were the case," he told him softly, "Io is gone. It fucking exploded. The whole damned moon. The debris is flying everywhere."

"What do you mean?"

"I mean I thought I was either going to land in space, or on that ship you were on. I certainly didn't expect to land on this ship. Or have any kind of help finding you."

Harvey rubbed a hand over his stubbled chin. He was sore about losing Greenway only seconds before he had him safely away. He realised he had to do something about the man but leaving him with the Bahana men seemed a cruel and unusual punishment. He couldn't do it.

"Do you think they're still on the ship?" he asked Lance.

The Pilot looked at him with confusion. "What do you mean?"

"Greenway. The other soldier — I haven't learnt their names yet. Do you think they're still on that ship?"

Lance shrugged. "I don't know. We were told they were evacuating. Could be real. Maybe not. They said they'd been boarded."

Harvey gave a soft grunt. "That would be us," he said. "What kind of evacuation procedure?"

"How would I know?"

"I don't know."

"They said something about a transition chamber."

"I have to go collect the others from their drop points. I'll be back and we can work it out then." He shifted before Lance could protest.

~

Greenway sucked in a deep breath just before his head was covered in viscous fluid. The leads were attached to his body, but he could move this time. There was no welcoming array of voices this time, just a muffled silence.

He could see others, in similar glass prisons, all in various stages of undress. They appeared awake and aware, yet calm. There was someone he assumed to be a tech, dressed in dark grey and blue walking around the room checking every chamber.

Greenway's chamber was last, and as the man glanced at him with curiosity, he put a hand to his heart and Greenway could hear him, as though speakers had clicked on in his ears.

"This is never an easy ride," the man said, "but it will be much smoother for you if you can relax. Would you like a sedative?"

Greenway shook his head. He couldn't speak even if he wanted to, but it seemed such an odd question. They'd not given him any kind of courtesy as a prisoner before. It made him wonder what was about to happen. And, as his eyes roamed across the many glass prisons around, who the others might be.

The man gave him a gentle nod and moved outside the chamber.

A few moments later, he heard a different voice. Female and almost robotic. "Evacuation procedure seven, nine, seven is about to commence. All non-essential personnel to divert."

Greenway tried to make himself relax. If that would make it easier, then that was what he needed to do. But even as he saw the others close eyes and sink a little, his heart pounded. He wasn't supposed to be here. He'd gotten out. He'd gotten away, and Harvey had found them. He'd had such faith that Harvey would find them.

The robotic voice repeated inside his chamber, and a light whirled in the room beyond. There came an odd pulling sensation, as if he was being sucked down a drain with the fluid around him, though he did not move.

Every bone and muscle in his body felt as if it were trying to tear itself loose of the rest, and Greenway tried to scream, though the fluid prevented it. He wasn't sure how he even breathed.

Moments later, he was surrounded by white blinding light.

~

Estard pulled up short when he noticed Kristin go down. He hadn't been able to take his eyes off her the entire time. So afraid that something might happen, too cautious to get close. She'd been running close to Deidra and Estard had been sure to stay a few paces behind.

Larger meteors were raining down all around, now, leaving short furrows of earth in their wake. Smaller ones still struck like violent hail, raising gouts of dirt as they pierced the skin of the world.

Everything had happened so quickly, he hadn't had a chance to digest what it might mean. He came to a halt beside the mound of dirt the meteor had created and dug at it with his hands until he found Kristin. Dimly, he was aware of Gordon beside him, doing the same for Deidra.

Fear of the meteors and what would happen if he were hit, moved so far back in his mind, that despite the fact they fell close all around him, it was like they didn't exist.

Estard pulled Kristin clear and brushed dirt from her face. Her eyes were closed, and she was very still, but she was breathing.

"Julian!" he heard someone say as he drooped his head over Kristin, so relieved that she lived. "Julian!"

A hand came down on his shoulder and pulled him around. It was Gordon, hauling Deidra over her shoulder.

"Julian, we have to move. We can't stay here. The meteor rain is getting worse."

The sounds around him hit like a wave, at once slapping him awake, and stunning him in place. The roar and whistle of approaching meteors, the small explosions as they hit the ground or popped in the air. The smell of dirt and sulphur, of grass and sweat. The dimmer sound of feet thudding down on the grassy plain as the others ran.

Gordon's hand came down on his shoulder again. "We have to —" She got no further as a meteor the size of a penny shot through her head and exploded out through Deidra's back.

Estard watched mute as they fell to the ground in an undignified heap. He knew, somewhere inside, that something was supposed to happen. That they should disappear and wake elsewhere. That they would be fine. And Kristin would be fine. Nothing should be able to hurt them. Not permanently.

He couldn't move. Couldn't make himself move. It was as if

every muscle in his body worked against him. He knew it was the shock. It would only take one of those meteors striking him, and he was finished. He didn't know why he felt that, when the rules of their existence had been made clear to him even before he'd chosen to become one of them. But he did. He felt it deep inside of him.

Perhaps it was because those who had fallen had remained as they were. One of them, a little too far off to tell who it was in the darkness, lay half covered in dirt, an arm and a leg completely separated from the body in gory chunks.

He felt at Kristin. The only movement he could manage. He searched for a pulse, some reassurance that she, at least, would be fine. That somehow they could get through this.

But he couldn't find the heartbeat. A hand held an inch from her mouth couldn't feel breath.

Estard shook his head. No. He wasn't going to let this happen. He couldn't. She was the reason. The whole reason.

None of them were disappearing the way they were supposed to. None of them were waking in the field.

Estard bent over Kristin and breathed into her mouth. "Live," he whispered between each breath. "Live." He leaned back a little and began compressions.

He was completely unaware now. Despite the fact the meteors had caused this, he forgot about them. They still roared and whistled, still caused small explosions on impact. They still smelled of sulphur and burnt grass. But to him, they no longer existed. The only thing in his mind, the only thing he had any room for, was Kristin.

"No," he said, unaware that he was speaking aloud. "No. No, no, no." He shook his head in denial with every breath, and every compression on her chest. When he breathed into her mouth, he willed life. But it wasn't enough.

Anger and frustration welled inside him, and his face turned toward Gordon. He liked her. She was a good companion. But she was dead. As Deidra appeared to be. And none of them were disappearing.

"Why aren't they coming back?" he asked the air. "Why aren't they going where they're supposed to go? This shouldn't be happening." He shook his head vigorously. "This should not be happening."

A meteor struck so close he felt the heat of it singe the side of his head. It was like being doused in cold water.

Every muscle inside him tensed. His anger, frustration, desperation and despair condensed into a small ball in his chest. It seemed to release as a stream from his mouth as he shouted, long and loud, "Stooooooooooooooooooooop!"

And it did.

~

Harvey took Lance up to see the Colonel.

Lance had been inside a Carrier before, though only on the way up. They were designed for ground troops. For short flights from a Docker, to the ground, and back up. Just like MM ships, they weren't designed for long hauls, and didn't have bathrooms or galleys. So he wasn't surprised when Harvey led him out onto a Docker.

The Colonel was in the Hangar with a hundred troops, all dressed in battle ready gear, as if they expected to move at any moment.

"Colonel Sumner, this is Pilot Lance Viatri. Lieutenant." Harvey handed him off and gave him a pat on the back with a whispered assurance that he'd return soon.

Sumner looked him up and down as if deciding what manner of shit had been dragged in on his boot.

Lance rubbed at the back of his head. The cap still covered it. A part of him wanted to make the eyes dance for this ground walker, but even if the stinking piles of turd on the other ship hadn't cut into his head, he felt it was probably a bad idea.

"Pilot?" The Colonel asked as if Harvey hadn't just introduced them.

Lance gave a nod. "Sir."

"Can't say I have much use for a pilot, but you never know." He looked at the men standing at attention in their designated positions. "I understand from Harvey that Commander Weiz is still in commission planet side, so you're still under her command. I'll not be giving you orders, son."

"Uhm, thanks, I guess." Lance wasn't sure what to make of that.

"Grab a change of clothes, get kitted up if you like. We brought plenty to spare." The man looked him up and down again. "We'll get everything sorted out once we've landed — which won't be until the meteors pass. I tell you this — I never expected to find anyone alive out here, and Harvey showing up the way he did... well. Well, we'll need to have a clear debriefing."

"Sir," Lance replied.

"Off you go, son." The Colonel nodded back in the direction from which he'd come. "I just needed to see your face, so you'd not be confused for an enemy."

Lance shot off a lazy salute as he spun on his heel. Not one of the soldiers so much as glanced at him as he strode past. They might as well have been statues for all the movement they made. It was slightly unnerving.

Once he was back in the small hold with Harvey, he sat down on a crate of supplies. "What the fuck was that about, sir?" he asked.

Harvey sighed. "He wanted to see your face."

"He said that. But it seemed like more."

"Maybe it was. Maybe it wasn't." Harvey shrugged. "I like the man. Don't know him well, but we've shared a Docker more than once and he's generally pleasant and has a good reputation for keeping his men alive."

Lance frowned at the Captain. "There's something you're not saying."

Harvey twitched a sad smile. "I'm usually better at hiding those things."

"Not this time. Spill it, Captain."

"He's good friends with Greenway."

"Ohhhhh."

"Yeah." Harvey swiped a hand over his stubble and bit at his bottom lip for a moment. "I don't think a report on what's happened here is going to be given a whole lot of credence."

"Well, positions reversed..." Lance held up his hands.

Harvey shot a laugh. "I know. Same, same and same. But having lived it all, it'd be nice to be believed."

"They know they're stuck, right?"

"I told them Deidra would fix it up so they could get back using the ship."

Lance supposed that was true. He hadn't really thought of it, since they'd used alien tech for their little time trip.

"The Colonel mentioned something about meteors."

Harvey looked to the hull as if there were a window there. "The Io debris," he said. "I had to make a choice, when I left. Come get you and Greenway or stay with the others get them away from the danger zone if required."

"Thankful you chose me," Lance breathed. Although he'd managed to get out of the cell himself, he was fairly certain he would have ended up back in it if Harvey hadn't have come along. It was probably where Greenway was now. Oddly, despite everything the man had done, Lance felt pity for him.

"You and Greenway had been stripped of your powers," Harvey shrugged. "No telling what was being done to you or what effect it might have. Even if the rest..." He swallowed. "Even if those I left behind are trapped in that storm... There's the field."

Lance gave a slow nod. He remembered what it was like to wake in that field. The disorienting sensation of transition. It wasn't pleasant. But it was definitely better than the alternative.

But there was something in the way Harvey had said it. "You don't sound convinced of that," Lance ventured.

"Something Kristin said, when she had the vision," Harvey breathed.

"What? What did she say?"

"That it was dangerous."

Lance put both hands on the back of his head and sat still for a moment. "That could mean anything."

"Yes."

"But?"

"But I think she meant it to say, if we were caught in it, we may not survive it."

"Why would you think that?"

"Just the way she said it."

Lance shook his head and wished he had something to kick his legs up on. "I think you're reading too much into it."

"You're probably right."

"Another but?"

Harvey stood and took a deep breath before he answered. "I had a talk with a navigator and one of the scientists on this ship. It's kind of a good news, bad news type of situation."

"Since I'm not a mind reader, you'll have to explain."

"Good news is, there are no chunks of debris large enough to cause an extinction event on a trajectory with this planet."

"Bad news?"

"The debris field coming at it is going to last for hours. And it's going to be like rain. Where it hits, no one will avoid it. It's going to cause mass devastation, and anyone caught in it will die. It will strike across roughly two thirds of world."

"Shit," Lance responded slowly. "I've never heard of anything like it."

"There's never been anything close to remotely like it on Earth. At least, not in recorded history."

"They have a target area where they think it will hit?"

Harvey nodded. "And the hut is right in the middle of it. Whatever direction they might choose to run in, there is no getting away from it. Not for them."

Lance shot up. "Then what are you doing here? Go! Get them!" If he had the Captain's power there was nothing that would stop him from bringing the ones he cared about to safety. And it was clear to anyone paying attention how the Captain felt about the women of his group.

"I can't," Harvey said with a shake of his head as he dropped back onto the box.

Lance pushed at him. "What do you mean you can't? You're in one piece, your powers clearly work. What the fuck are you waiting for?" It took Lance a moment to realise he was yelling and standing over the Captain ready to beat the shit out of him. He backed down and breathed in some calm but didn't apologise. He was right about this.

"I can't," Harvey said again. When he looked up Lance saw a tear falling from the corner of an eye. "I tried. After I had you. As soon as you all let go of me, I wasn't even going to say anything, I was just going to get them. We're as safe as it gets, up here. Under the shelter of the Bahana ship."

"Try again," Lance demanded.

"I have been!" Harvey yelled back in his face, spittle flying. His fist came down so hard on the box he was sitting on, it dented and popped.

For the first time since it all began, Lance felt he was getting a real look into what the Captain thought and felt. He'd been holding them all together for months, except for that brief stint in 1957. Even then, he'd tried.

Lance remained silent and let Harvey continue through clenched teeth. "I don't know what's causing it. Whether it's the meteors themselves, or something the Bahana men have done. I'd say maybe the hut just isn't there, but I know I don't need a perfect image of a place to go there, just a basic understanding of where it is in relation to myself."

Lance backed up another step and sat back down. "Or could be a mixture of things," he said.

Harvey nodded sadly. "Or it could be a mixture of things," he agreed.

"Have you tried going to one of the other planets you and Kristin were checking out?"

Harvey's head came up, a glint in his eye. "Not yet." He rose so fast Lance almost tipped backward, startled. The Captain took a step and disappeared, within a few heartbeats, he'd returned.

"So that works," Lance said under his breath.

"But I can't get down there. Something is keeping me from getting down there."

~

Estard didn't know what he was doing. Had no idea what to expect, if anything. These fledgling powers of his had limited use, to his own mind. But, he also knew he had yet to explore everything he was capable of.

With closed eyes, he fed all his frustration and sorrow, his hopes and memories into the surface of his mind and pushed against himself. Let the pressure build. He wasn't sure what he wanted to happen here. What he thought he could do. He was working on a deep instinct, as he always had.

The only thing he knew, as he felt power building, was that he wanted some kind of miracle. Something that would bring these people back to life. Have them smiling and breathing again. All of them.

When the pressure in his mind turned painful, he opened his eyes and his mouth, and let it all rush out in a wordless scream. He knew all that power had to do something and go somewhere.

The meteors began moving again, slowly at first, and then with great speed.

Backwards.

He moved backwards, like a puppet. He was no more than a character in a movie being rewound. Each painful step that had brought him to this moment played out in reverse. Each word spoken, sucked back into his mouth, in sounds that made no sense to his ear.

His brain moved forward. So, he understood the chronology, and what was happening.

He felt himself suck breath from Kristin. He watched the meteor lift from the ground, and Gordon with Deidra draped across her shoulders. Had a morbid moment of fascination as it passed through the wound, and it closed up behind it as the meteor trailed back into the sky.

Estard's hands were on Kristin, pushing her back into the dirt rubble of the larger meteor, even as Gordon did the same with Deidra.

Backwards.

A part of him marvelled at what was happening. At what he was capable of doing. Another part of him hoped against hope that it would be enough to save them. Somehow.

The speed of reverse began to slow as he backed away from the meteor crater. His mind protested. Screamed that if it stopped now, it would not be enough. Could not be enough. It had to go further.

His backward step almost became a forward step, and Estard

pushed against his power, as hard as he could. He was not trained, didn't understand how it worked, or what kind of miracle he was making. He just knew it wasn't enough. Not yet.

Estard strained. Pushed. Fed into the pressure.

He got a few more backward steps.

Then the world stopped.

Meteors froze in the sky. Airmen froze in their flight. Everything was muted, except for the sound of his own heavy breathing as he rushed toward the dirt pile.

Every moment would count, he was sure of that. They weren't deep, and he pulled both Kristin and Deidra out. He supposed they'd have stopped along with everything else, and maybe, just maybe, it would be enough to give them a chance.

He didn't know how long he had. But he knew he couldn't breathe life into Kristin when time did not exist for her. He knew he could not take care of Deidra as well, so while the meteors stood frozen in the air around him, he moved Gordon into position beside the Scientist. It would seem odd to her, but if she mentioned it, he could explain later.

As when everything went into reverse, when time started again, it was slow, but not for long.

Estard checked that Kristin was breathing, and satisfied, hauled her over a shoulder and yelled at a confused Gordon to take up Deidra.

He felt drained. Like a part of his very life force had been sucked right out of him. But he was determined to go on.

Estard thought about trying to build enough of the power in him to make it go further back. Back to the hut. Back to before Harvey had left them and give him a warning that he needed to be here. But he didn't have the strength for it. Didn't even know exactly how he'd done it in the first place.

As he ran with a bouncing Kristin over his shoulder, he

wondered how much good it had actually done. He didn't know whether she'd live. Whether she still lived. But after seeing what had happened to Gordon and Deidra the first time around, he didn't want to stop and take the chance.

How long would this go on? Could he pause time again? Get ahead of it? Keep moving through the stillness of meteors trapped in the air?

He tried. Even knowing that the others would be left behind in the storm, he tried. But nothing happened. He didn't know if it was a lack of concentration, or if his power had limitations he couldn't begin to guess at. All he knew, was that he was running, with the rest of them, Kristin over his shoulder, and Gordon likewise hauling Deidra through the deadly rain, praying they could dodge all the bullets being hurled at them.

His feet kicked at something, and he lost his balance. Kristin fell awkwardly from his shoulder. Gordon kept on with no more than a harried glance. He didn't blame her. If she'd stopped, he'd have only told her to hurry on.

Estard stooped to retrieve the fallen woman, and as he pulled her around, he noticed that her eyes were open and staring. He dropped to his knees and felt for a pulse. He placed an ear on her chest and tried to hear for a heartbeat, the sound of lungs working. But there was nothing. No sign of life in the limp figure.

As before, he couldn't just let her go. He ignored the danger around him, trying to make her breath. He performed CPR, and as tears trickled down his face unnoticed, he deliberately tried to let the pressure of power build again. He would not let this happen. *Could not* let this happen. He had to save her. If there was one reason for him to be here, it was that.

When the pain threatened on the thread of the pressure, he didn't let it go, as he had last time. He pushed at it, until it became so searing and blinding that he felt he might burn to ashes if he didn't let it go.

And once again, time moved backwards.

~

Greenway was vaguely aware of people pulling at him. Of restraints being attached to wrists and ankles. Of an angry voice berating underlings in a firm tone. But he could not see, though he was sure his eyes were open.

"What is he doing here?" It was the voice of a woman used to being answered quickly and surely. A commander of some kind. Research or military? Greenway was too foggy to think hard on the subject, and though he could feel, he certainly couldn't move. He felt sure they'd dosed him. Again.

"The transition —" someone tried to answer, but the woman cut it off.

"It doesn't matter. He's here." Greenway tried to move his head to see the face of the voice, but his head would not obey. "We were preparing for it before all this, but he should have gone directly to the others. Not here. We'll have to take him overland, and given reports of what he can do, that could prove dangerous."

"He's been suppressed," another voice interjected. "He won't be able to do anything."

"We won't know until we know." There was the sense of a dismissive gesture, and Greenway felt himself being moved.

It wasn't like being in the cell. Or like being open on a table, but the sense was of somewhere in between. He didn't believe he was on a ship any longer. For some reason he had a firm sense of being grounded, though he couldn't have told why.

His vision wasn't coming right, though he could feel himself blinking. Perhaps they'd put something over his eyes? They usually just shone a light in them, but it was possible they couldn't easily do that in this place.

Greenway wanted to know where he was. That was his main

concern for the time being. Not get free. Not revenge. Just working out where he was, and who had him now. That he wasn't expected in this place in particular, meant it was probably vulnerable. That if he could wrest himself free, he could do a good amount of damage in his escape. But he also needed his bearings.

Harvey had come. Had been less than a hand span away. All his faith that the man would come find them had paid off. He knew Harvey. Better than anyone but Weiz. He knew the man was incapable of leaving men behind no matter the situation, and no matter how much he hated them. Greenway had seen him do it, time and again.

Greenway would have laughed if his body would obey him. Would have shaken his head and laughed in the faces of his captors. Yes, they had him, for now. Yes, they were likely to torture him, possibly even break him. But they had started a war with a man who would not give in. A man they could not capture or keep penned up like some kind of animal.

Dimly, Greenway was curious what these people were looking for with all their fine experiments. Why wouldn't they just ask? But he knew Research guys were all of a feather.

His sense of movement stopped. He became aware of hushed voices for a moment, then he was being moved again, but he sensed new people. At least three, walking close. He wondered if they were an additional escort, or if they simply happened to be walking in the same direction.

"What happened to Grayson?" one of them asked.

"Sent back beaten to death," another offered.

Greenway wanted to smile.

"A pity. He was a promising hunter. Have the others been dispatched?"

"Full complement on the ground and searching. They're on their own until we can get another ship out there."

"They'll lay low for a while, then."

"Seems the likely course."

"We cannot abide their existence." Another man joined. The voice was older, more mature and refined.

"And yet we cannot kill them," the first replied.

"That is why we have this place, Eodin," said the older man. "Our forefathers foresaw our difficulties. They suspected there would be others, though only those three ever got away, there was always the possibility of others."

"As you say, Greatfather."

"And you, Olid? You seem less than pleased by our new resident."

There was a pause before the last voice spoke. It was a young woman, from the sound. "I simply wonder at the need for such restraint," she said. "If they're suppressed, can they not live among us?"

The old man cackled delightedly. "Oh, sweet child, you know nothing of these people. Of the reason we hunt them." He chuckled deep in his throat. "You will learn. You will learn."

"So we go to war, Greatfather."

"So we go to war, Eodin."

Greenway found himself suddenly very curious as to what the ancient Gods had done to these people. He could understand why they might confuse him for one of them, after all, he did have their power. But he had done nothing to them. Certainly nothing that would deserve this kind of treatment.

He felt a brief touch on his wrist, gentle and warm. Somehow, he knew it was the girl. Perhaps, once they had him where they wished him to be, she could be a pawn he could use. If she truly protested the treatment he was undergoing, perhaps she could even be persuaded to set him free.

Without knowing where he was, it was going to be a difficult road back to where he belonged. If he couldn't get there himself, he felt sure Harvey would find him somehow. But until he could be sure of that, he needed to make his own plans.

They stopped and he had the sense of being lifted and set down again on a higher platform.

Greenway still couldn't see. Didn't know what was happening, and his frustration of the situation was deepening even as he tried to remain stoic.

"Welcome to Bahana," he heard the young woman say so quietly it was less than a whisper. He almost thought he'd imagined it, except for one thing — he didn't know what Bahana was.

~

The time rewind took him only as far back as it had the first time, and Estard found himself swearing at whatever God or Gods might be listening. Why have such a power if you could not make it do as you wished?

But despite his frustration, he rushed to the dirt and pulled Kristin and Deidra clear before time started again. Moved Gordon to take place in front of Deidra. And when time started up, he demanded that Gordon take the Scientist and start running while he performed CPR on Kristin. He wasn't moving anywhere until the woman opened her eyes.

Gordon was confused but obeyed without question. She already had some inkling of what Estard's power was, and if she'd really wanted to know she was capable of rummaging through his thoughts to find the answers. But none of them had a lot of time.

For the third time, Estard felt for pulse and breath, and found it. But this time he didn't just wait for her to wake on her own. He breathed into her, performed compressions. Did everything he knew how to do, trying to force her to wretch, or cough. Something that would indicate to him that she was going to survive.

As before, after a few moments, she stopped breathing. Her heart stopped beating. And nothing he did could restart the flow.

A vast cavern opened in his chest, forced a lump into his throat and made his eyes water. Tears spilled even as he tried to hold them back. He didn't have time for this. He needed to see.

There was no reason he could determine that Kristin should just die like that. He wasn't medically trained, and he had no one around who was, who could tell him. There was no blood, nothing stuck in her throat or mouth to stop her from breathing. No wheezing he could hear after he first pulled her free that would indicate any kind of internal damage, or blockage.

Estard was so consumed with his efforts the meteor storm might as well have been on another planet for all he noticed.

He pulled open her shirt and checked her ribs and chest for signs of bruising or internal bleeding. Without sufficient light, it was difficult to tell.

A meteor shot through her leg, half severing the limb, and Estard growled.

He was determined.

He needed to get back *before* she was buried, however shallowly. He needed it, and he demanded it. Of his power, of himself. Even if it meant he'd have to take her place.

Estard put the world on pause. He gathered everything inside him. Every thought, every emotion, and pushed it into that place where he felt pressure build. Every piece of who he was, every memory he'd ever made.

The pressure built quickly, and the sharp pains came on its heels. They blinded him, and pushed at him, and struggled for release, but he held on. He condensed every conceivable thing into this ball of pressure and pain, until the only thought he had left was "stay alive."

And then he let it go.

Time did not resume and speed backwards this time. His footsteps did not retreat in reverse. The meteors didn't flash back up into the sky.

He was beside Kristin, and then he was inside a house.

In an instant, he'd gone back in time. But he wasn't where he was supposed to be.

Beside him, Stevenson had hold of a woman's arm, and in front of him, a young boy holding a red truck.

Estard's mouth felt dry. His head swam, and he felt giddy.

This one. Again. He couldn't do this one again.

But it was just a memory. It had to be. There was no way he could actually be here.

Estard pulled his gun even as the woman shot his partner. This time, instead of diving, he pushed the child aside, and raised his weapon. *Just a dream*, he thought, even as he pulled the trigger.

The woman went down in a spray of blood, a bullet through her chest. The child dropped the truck and fell over the woman, screaming and crying. Estard stood mute and confused over the scene, his partner's dead body still leaking blood onto the floorboards.

This was too long ago. It was too late. There was no changing this. He didn't understand what was happening, even as he felt a tug that dragged his mind forward. That pushed him past memories that had never happened. Through a timeline that didn't exist. Couldn't exist.

Until he was in the moment, a few minutes before the meteor struck and covered Kristin and Deidra in dirt.

Time was still, and silent, and he forced his will to keep it that way as he approached Kristin at a run. He pulled her off course, at least thirty yards to her left. Then he ran back and did the same for Deidra hoping they wouldn't notice the difference. He didn't want them to know what he was doing.

Estard moved back a few paces behind them and allowed time to resume.

Kristin and Deidra ran as if they hadn't noticed. He caught them up, determined to be nearby should anything else befall them. If at any moment it looked as though they were in danger of being struck down, he would stop time, and reverse it just enough to move them out of harm's way.

Estard kept his eyes on Kristin, and Kristin looked back to him with the shadow of a smile.

He wanted to reassure her, let her know that he was here and looking out for her. That he would —

~

Deidra gasped. The meteor had struck like a shotgun, and the way Agent Estard's head blew apart from his shoulders, spattered Kristin and herself with blood and brain matter. They looked to each other with wide, horrified eyes.

But they did not stop. They kept moving, not saying a word. They would not be safe until the meteors stopped falling.

EPILOGUE

Harvey's eyes searched the devastation that was the field. The field, where they would arise, should anything kill them. Lance was beside him, mouth open and eyes wide.

There wasn't much grass left after six hours of being rained on by cosmic debris. It was worse than he'd ever imagined it could be. Harvey had never seen anything remotely like it on Earth.

"Well, they're not here," Lance said. "That could be a good sign, you know."

Harvey took a deep breath. It could be. There was no way to tell. They'd already been to the hut, and didn't know where everyone had gone, because none were there. The hut itself was a mess of timbers broken and scored, shot through with flame and dirt. It would not be rebuilt.

Through the small copse of trees, almost half had been uprooted or broken. And in every direction around the grassy plain, could be seen the furrowed tracks and craters of small meteors. But there was no sign of which direction anyone had gone in.

"I could shift around aimlessly for hours," Harvey sighed. "But I'm not really sure what I am looking for."

"Weiz," Lance offered. "Dare say she's first on your list."

Harvey nodded. He'd not argue with that. "Should we head back to the carriers?"

Lance shrugged. "The others will find us. Those ships are not difficult to spot."

"You don't feel like we should be doing something?"

"I do want to know what happened to everyone," Lance admitted. "But I also know we're best off letting them come to us. Even if only one of them, it will help us find the rest."

"We still have those men from Bahana to worry about."

"Among other things, Harvey." Lance looked him up and down. "One thing at a time, Captain. Let's just get back to the carriers and get this Colonel up to speed."

"You're right. They might be idiots, but they're idiots with fortuitous timing." Harvey expected at least a smile from the Pilot, but all he got was a shrug.

The man's brief captivity had already changed him. Harvey wondered how much, and for how long. And if the same could be said of Greenway. He still needed to find the man.

Once the others had been found, and everyone was on the same page, the war with Bahana would begin.

"Let's go," he said. And he shifted.

ABOUT THE AUTHOR

Lee was born and raised in Sydney Australia. Prefers cats over dogs, coffee over tea, and cars over bikes. She also thinks the biography section of the book is a little strange.